MW00643407

CELTIC
WEIRD

CELTIC WEIRD

Tales of Wicked Folklore and Dark Mythology

Edited by

JOHNNY MAINS

THE BRITISH LIBRARY

This collection first published in 2022 by
The British Library
96 Euston Road
London NW1 2DB

Cataloguing in Publication Data
A catalogue record for this publication is available from the British Library

ISBN 978 0 7123 5432 5

Frontispiece illustration and illustration on page 324 from John Romilly Allen, *Celtic Art in Pagan and Christian Times*, London: Methuen and Co., 1904. Frontispiece: sepulchral cross-slab from Pen-Arthur, Pembrokeshire by John Romilly Allen. Page 324: slab with spiral ornament outside the entrance to a passage of tumulus at Newgrange, Co. Meath by George Coffey.

Cover design by Mauricio Villamayor with illustration by Mag Ruhig. Original interior ornaments by Mag Ruhig.
Text design and typesetting by Tetragon, London
Printed in the Czech Republic by Finidr

CONTENTS

ISLE OF MAN

WALES

CORNWALL

GAELIC

INTRODUCTION

Celtic myths and folklore have always been extremely weird. In Ireland there is Balor, the Demon King, tyrant leader of the Fomorians. He had one eye, which could kill you if he opened it and always had to keep that one eye closed to stop him tripping over all of the dead bodies in his wake. There's also the tale of Angelystor, the Welsh spectre who lives under a 3,000-year-old yew tree and announces the names of those who will soon meet their doom. The Welsh also have, alongside the Cornish and Bretons, Ankou, the servant of death and the first child of Adam and Eve who is doomed to collect the souls of others before he himself can go to the afterlife. The Scots have the Mester Stoor Worm, a sea serpent who can destroy humans and animals with its stinking breath. And finally, in the Isle of Man, there is the Buggane, a massive ogre who couldn't cross water but sported a large red mouth and huge tusks.

Many of those myths, told in the oral tradition, were the ancient ancestors of the Celtic Revival tradition, where they were rescued and studied and debated and the concept of Celtic identity became a pulsing, living concept and the legends, folklore and poetry became forever locked in Celtic DNA.

From there, one would have thought that the languages of the ancient tribes would have been brought back from the brink and would have flourished and have been a part of everyday culture. Alas, while people may like to buy stickers and fridge magnets of Celtic crosses, native languages are on the brink. In 2020 a study concluded that only 10,000 of 50,000 Gaels spoke Gaelic as an everyday language,* less than 1,000 people speak Cornish,† and

* *Gaelic Crisis in the Vernacular Community*, University of the Highlands and Islands.

† <https://www.bbc.com/culture/article/20180412-the-rebirth-of-britains-lost-languages>, accessed August 2022

French government policies have given little support to preserving the Breton tongue—even though there are currently half a million speakers, most of them are over sixty years of age. In Ireland and Wales the numbers are better, but it can simply take a few generations of neglect on the behalf of authorities for those numbers to plummet.

While the languages that form the Celtic traditions may be dying, there is still a keen interest in the historical study of traditions and folklore. This volume is a tribute to the many works that have come before it. In 1905, the Celtic Revival was in full swing, with a magazine called the *Celtic Review* leading the charge, aiming to present a journal which was 'for the social, religious and literary history not only of the Celtic races themselves, but also of the many people with whom they came into contact during the long centuries in which the Celts have influenced so strongly the Western world', but it came with the sad understanding that 'the study of Celtic literature of the past opens a wide yield of investigation as yet comparatively untouched'.

But nine years after 1905, there was of course the Great War which culled many Celtic voices and historians. Traditions that had been given and were to be passed down to future generations, instantly snuffed out by the cruel machineries of man, in turn creating their own awful lore. Then the Second World War compounded an already decimated landscape.

We recover. The stories come back; they always do. Folk tales, myths and legends are interpreted by different generations in different ways. Sometimes you can see their influence, other times, maybe only a whisper. And that's where research has flourished in the last few decades—with the digitization of manuscripts and newspapers and magazines—it has never been a better time to be a researcher and a book like this is easier to put together than it was, say, twenty years ago. And there is also the duty to honour the many 'locality legends' books that you can still find in tourist shops and newsagents to this day. While *Celtic Weird* is not that kind of book, I read many of the micro-published Cornish and Scottish legends books, just to get right in my head what kind of anthology I wanted to do and how I wanted to go about doing it. The resulting book is a weird hybrid;

stories that are hardwired as they can be into folklore and others that are distant cousins, but are no less powerful, no less important because they may have been written by a jobbing author in the 1960s for a popular horror anthology of the day.

There are also some outsiders hidden within the pages from this book, stories by non-Celtic authors who were entranced by folklore and myth and perhaps wanted to make sense of those traditional tales by putting their own spin on it. The Breton section is the most obvious to point out here, but all three stories absolutely nail the sense of place and lives lived. The Scots section also has a very welcome interloper; Robert Aickman, with his spin on ancient folklore with his masterpiece 'The Fetch'. It is a conventional and old-fashioned story, but Aickman's writing turns 'The Fetch' into a work that's deeply uncanny and is one of my personal highlights of this book. Other tales that have been an honour to include are Katharine Tynan's 'The Death Spancel', a 'lost' work I first came across in 2017 and is a tale that I really want to see reach a larger audience. It's also thrilling to include stories by Nigel Kneale, Edith Wharton and Dorothy K. Haynes, all authors I read during my teenage horror years and to include them is also my way of thanking them for the many hours of enjoyment I took from their words.

It would be remiss of me not to talk about Gaelic and Manx sections where the writers are all male. With regards to Gaelic literature, women also transmitted oral stories, but they have yet to come to the fore for a variety of reasons. Hopefully there will be funding to translate and transcribe stories in the near future and that anthologies edited by others down the line will remedy this imbalance. With the Manx tales (apart from the Kneale story the two others could have been written by females under a pseudonym, but there is no evidence to suggest it), try as I might I couldn't find any older supernatural tales written by women. I hope to address this in any future work I do, and if there are any Manx researchers out there who know of some, please get in touch.

ACKNOWLEDGEMENTS

Thanks must go to Jonny Davidson for offering me the gig of a lifetime; it has been a pleasure to work with him. This book, that you hold in your hands, would not have been possible without his care, time and amazing ideas and thoughtful interventions. It's always lovely when someone steps into your life, and Jonny is one of the great ones. Thanks also to Mike Ashley, Andrew Screen, Mairi Kidd, Mary Ann Kennedy and the kind staff at Sabhal Mòr Ostaig on the Isle of Skye in Sleat, only a few miles away from where I used to live in Saasaig, Teangue. I spent many an afternoon amongst the ruins of Knock Castle, staring out to sea and dreaming. This book is for all fellow dreamers.

A NOTE FROM THE PUBLISHER

The original short stories reprinted in the British Library classic fiction series were written and published in a period ranging across the nineteenth and twentieth centuries. There are many elements of these stories which continue to entertain modern readers; however, in some cases there are also uses of language, instances of stereotyping and some attitudes expressed by narrators or characters which may not be endorsed by the publishing standards of today. We acknowledge therefore that some elements in the stories selected for reprinting may continue to make uncomfortable reading for some of our audience. With this series British Library Publishing aims to offer a new readership a chance to read some of the rare material of the British Library's collections in an affordable format, to enjoy their merits and to look back into the worlds of the past two centuries as portrayed by their writers. It is not possible to separate these stories from the history of their writing and as such the following stories are presented as they were originally published with minor edits only, made for consistency of style and sense. We welcome feedback from our readers, which can be sent to the following address:

British Library Publishing
The British Library
96 Euston Road
London, NW1 2DB
United Kingdom

Scotland

1910

THE MILK-WHITE DOO

Elizabeth W. Grierson

Elizabeth W. Grierson was born in Hawick in 1869, the second daughter of farmer Andrew Grierson. Predominantly a children's writer, her books included *The Children's Book of Edinburgh*, *Children's Tales from Scottish Ballads*, *The Children's Book of Celtic Stories*, *Vivian's Lesson* and *The Scottish Fairy Book*, published in 1910 and from which the following story, 'The Milk-White Doo' is sourced. She acknowledged that her work owed much to the four-volume collection *Popular Tales of the Western Highlands* by John Francis Campbell (1862), but here she did herself a disservice. Grierson imbued her folklore tales with a true sense of wonder, tapping into the Lowlands of Scotland in particular, teasing out the many of its hidden supernatural inhabitants. She was dedicated to two churches for the last forty years of her life, Old St Pauls in Edinburgh and St Cuthbert's, Hawick and undertook many trips abroad as a missionary. Working and writing till the end of her life, she died in 1943. 'The Milk-White Doo' *is* certainly a tale for younger readers, but it would be wrong to dismiss it. 'Doo' is a gateway weird tale for kids and includes the right ingredients for a nasty story: child murder and cannibalism.

THERE was once a man who got his living by working in the fields. He had one little son, called Curly-Locks, and one little daughter, called Golden-Tresses; but his wife was dead, and, as he had to be out all day, these children were often left alone. So, as he was afraid that some evil might befall them when there was no one to look after them, he, in an ill day, married again.

I say, 'in an ill day,' for his second wife was a most deceitful woman, who really hated children, although she pretended, before her marriage, to love them. And she was so unkind to them, and made the house so uncomfortable with her bad temper, that her poor husband often sighed to himself, and wished that he had let well alone, and remained a widower.

But it was no use crying over spilt milk; the deed was done, and he had just to try to make the best of it. So things went on for several years, until the children were beginning to run about the doors and play by themselves.

Then one day the Goodman chanced to catch a hare, and he brought it home and gave it to his wife to cook for the dinner.

Now his wife was a very good cook, and she made the hare into a pot of delicious soup; but she was also very greedy, and while the soup was boiling she tasted it, and tasted it, till at last she discovered that it was almost gone. Then she was in a fine state of mind, for she knew that her husband would soon be coming home for his dinner, and that she would have nothing to set before him.

So what do you think the wicked woman did? She went out to the door, where her little step-son, Curly-Locks, was playing in the sun, and told him to come in and get his face washed. And while she was washing his face, she struck him on the head with a hammer and stunned him, and popped him into the pot to make soup for his father's dinner.

By and by the Goodman came in from his work, and the soup was dished up; and he, and his wife, and his little daughter, Golden-Tresses, sat down to sup it.

'Where's Curly-Locks?' asked the Goodman. 'It's a pity he is not here as long as the soup is hot.'

'How should I ken?' answered his wife crossly. 'I have other work to do than to run about after a mischievous laddie all the morning.'

The Goodman went on supping his soup in silence for some minutes; then he lifted up a little foot in his spoon.

'This is Curly-Locks' foot,' he cried in horror. 'There hath been ill work here.'

'Hoots, havers,' answered his wife, laughing, pretending to be very much amused. 'What should Curly-Locks' foot be doing in the soup? 'Tis the hare's forefoot, which is very like that of a bairn.'

But presently the Goodman took something else up in his spoon.

'This is Curly-Locks' hand,' he said shrilly. 'I ken it by the crook in its little finger.'

'The man's demented,' retorted his wife, 'not to ken the hind foot of a hare when he sees it!'

So the poor father did not say any more, but went away out to his work, sorely perplexed in his mind; while his little daughter, Golden-Tresses, who had a shrewd suspicion of what had happened, gathered all the bones from the empty plates, and, carrying them away in her apron, buried them beneath a flat stone, close by a white rose tree that grew by the cottage door.

And, lo and behold! those poor bones, which she buried with such care:

> 'grew and grew
> To a milk-white Doo,
> And I took to my wings and away I flew.'

And at last it lighted on a tuft of grass by a burnside, where two women were washing clothes. It sat there cooing to itself for some time; then it sang this song softly to them:

'Pew, pew,
My mimmie me slew,
My daddy me chew,
My sister gathered my banes,
And put them between two milk-white stanes.
And I grew and grew
To a milk-white Doo,
And I took to my wings and away I flew.'

The women stopped washing and looked at one another in astonishment. It was not every day that they came across a bird that could sing a song like that, and they felt that there was something not canny about it.

'Sing that song again, my bonnie bird,' said one of them at last, 'and we'll give thee all these clothes!'

So the bird sang its song over again, and the washerwomen gave it all the clothes, and it tucked them under its right wing, and flew on.

Presently it came to a house where all the windows were open, and it perched on one of the window-sills, and inside it saw a man counting out a great heap of silver.

And, sitting on the window-sill, it sang its song to him:

'Pew, pew,
My mimmie me slew,
My daddy me chew,
My sister gathered my banes,
And put them between two milk-white stanes.
And I grew and grew
To a milk-white Doo,
And I took to my wings and away I flew.'

The man stopped counting his silver, and listened. He felt, like the washer-women, that there was something not canny about this Doo. When it had finished its song, he said:

'Sing that song again, my bonnie bird, and I'll give thee a' this siller in a bag.'

So the Doo sang its song over again, and got the bag of silver, which it tucked under its left wing. Then it flew on.

It had not flown very far, however, before it came to a mill where two millers were grinding corn. And it settled down on a sack of meal and sang its song to them.

> 'Pew, pew,
> My mimmie me slew,
> My daddy me chew,
> My sister gathered my banes,
> And put them between two milk-white stanes.
> And I grew and grew
> To a milk-white Doo,
> And I took to my wings and away I flew.'

The millers stopped their work, and looked at one another, scratching their heads in amazement.

'Sing that song over again, my bonnie bird!' exclaimed both of them together when the Doo had finished, 'and we will give thee this millstone.'

So the Doo repeated its song, and got the millstone, which it asked one of the millers to lift on its back; then it flew out of the mill, and up the valley, leaving the two men staring after it dumb with astonishment.

As you may think, the Milk-White Doo had a heavy load to carry, but it went bravely on till it came within sight of its father's cottage, and lighted down at last on the thatched roof.

Then it laid its burdens on the thatch, and, flying down to the courtyard, picked up a number of little chuckie stones. With them in its beak it flew back to the roof, and began to throw them down the chimney.

By this time it was evening, and the Goodman and his wife, and his little daughter, Golden-Tresses, were sitting round the table eating their supper. And you may be sure that they were all very much startled when the stones came rattling down the chimney, bringing such a cloud of soot with them that they were like to be smothered. They all jumped up from their chairs, and ran outside to see what the matter was.

And Golden-Tresses, being the littlest, ran the fastest, and when she came out at the door the Milk-White Doo flung the bundle of clothes down at her feet.

And the father came out next, and the Milk-White Doo flung the bag of silver down at his feet.

But the wicked stepmother, being somewhat stout came out last, and the Milk-White Doo threw the millstone right down on her head and killed her.

Then it spread its wings and flew away, and has never been seen again; but it had made the Goodman and his daughter rich for life, and it had rid them of the cruel stepmother, so that they lived in peace and plenty for the remainder of their days.

1969

THE CURE

Dorothy K. Haynes

Dorothy K. Haynes (Dorothy Gray) was a Scottish horror author, born in 1918. Her mother died in 1929 and her father, then unable to take care of her and her twin brother, sent them to the Episcopal Orphanage at Aberdour to be educated. Her first published work was at age eleven in a local magazine, and her first novel, *Winter's Traces* was published when she was 27. She won the Tom-Gallon Trust Award in 1947 for her short story 'The Head' (although it was never published until 1972). Her first collection, *Thou Shalt Not Suffer a Witch*, was published by Methuen in 1949 alongside her novel *Robin Ritchie*—a weird 'small town' book. Haynes really hit her stride in the seventies writing stories and selling reprints for the paperback horror anthologies that were doing the rounds, which included the *Fontana Book of Great Horror Stories* and the *Pan Book of Horror Stories*, amongst others. Dorothy was diagnosed with breast cancer and died in 1987. A reprint of *Thou Shalt Not Suffer a Witch* came out in 1996 from B&W Publishing and included additional later tales. Scotland's answer to Shirley Jackson, 'The Cure' sees Dorothy writing one of her saddest, bleakest stories.

THE women came early, calling and crowding at the door. 'Are you ready, Missis? We thought we'd go with you for the company, like. Just one or two of us...'

'You might want some help with the boy.'

She had not bargained for that. All night she had lain awake and worried, and now she had made up her mind. She would do as the neighbours said; but if David was to go, he must go with her alone, so that he could change his mind and run back if he wanted to. After all, he might be twelve years old, but he was little more than a baby.

She told them, but they would not listen. 'You're too soft with him, Mrs Weir. I wouldn't put up with his capers.'

'It's time he started acting like a man. With his father gone, you could do with a man in the house.'

Her lips were white, but she kept her temper, seeing their food on the table, and so many other things, the very coat the boy was wearing. 'I told you I'd bring him. You can come if you want to; but I'll need time. It's not a thing you can do in a minute.'

They withdrew, not very willingly, and she stood crumpling her apron, looking down at her son. The clock whirred, but did not strike, and the lid of the kettle lifted on a slow puff of steam. 'Come on, David,' she said, trying to force a sprightliness into her voice. 'Wash your face, now. I've warmed the water for you.'

The boy did not answer. He hardly ever answered, and sometimes she wondered if he heard properly. Unless, of course, it was too much bother to him to speak. Everything was a bother to him nowadays.

'Do you hear me, son? You can't go up dirty.'

The child began to blubber, his face turned to the fire. 'I don't want to go,' he mumbled. 'I don't *want* to!'

A finger tapped at the window and a face peered through the pane, and suddenly, her anger at the neighbours was transferred to her son, so that, for the moment, the fear of failure was less than the fear of his being a coward. She went over to the fire and shook the snivelling boy by the shoulder. 'Get up now, David. Wash your face and get outside. Do you think your father made this fuss when *he* went?'

It was cruel, but the snivelling stopped. Wiping his eyes, David got up and laved his eyes at the basin. His legs trembled, thin as sticks, but he said nothing as his mother brushed the hair out of his eyes and straightened his clothes. 'Now,' she said. 'It's for your own good, son. Don't look, don't think. Just walk straight on, and keep your eyes shut at the end…'

Holding his hand, her own hand trembling, she led him outside, and his weak eyes screwed against the sun. The clouds were incredibly white, puffed up and sailing, the trees and grass too green to be true. He had not been out for so long… the brightness puckered her own forehead, so that she looked at the ground; and then she forced herself to face the neighbours.

They stared at her, impatient, their faces half hidden in their great hoods, and she could see that they were itching to get away up the hill. She did not want to see them gabbing and whispering in front of her. Her lips quivering, she held her son's hand tighter, and went to the head of the procession.

They went slowly, because the road was bad, full of spring puddles and ruts and potholes. There were great splashes of dung where cattle had passed, and all the gutters were swimming. The houses leaned over the street, one side in sun, the other in shadow, and everywhere windows opened, and heads poked out to ask questions. 'Davie Weir,' the women who were following told them. 'Going to be *touched*. Him whose father was hanged,' and the word was passed back, eagerly, impatiently, to the old folk by the fire. 'Dick Weir's wife. Taking her son to the gallows. Up to the *gallows*!'

'Oh!' They had heard of it, this dreadful thing, the old superstition that the touch of a hanged corpse could heal, but few of them had seen it carried out. There weren't so many hangings nowadays. There had been no excitement in the town since Dick Weir had been hoisted a month ago, and there were some people who said that the law had been too hard on him. Weir had always been a sober, steady man, but his son was a weakling, never without coughs or fevers or aches in his bones, and the only way for a poor man to get medicine and dainties was by stealing.

Well, now that he was dead, it looked as if he might be more use to the boy than when he was alive. It was worth going to find out. The weavers came from their narrow houses, fluff in their hair, their looms silent. The baker left his shop, and a smell of new bread came with him, warm and delicious. He stuck his floury hands in his apron and ambled after the crowd, and the blacksmith left his forge to the apprentice and the horses stamping and jingling in the gloom. 'Going to be *touched*,' they mouthed, and nodded to each other. 'Dick Weir's son,' and they shook their heads with the pity of it; but there was a brightness and stir about the morning, just as there had been a month ago, and more of the people followed on, Old Andra, the bellringer, the two idiots who were propped all day against the church railings, and a squatter of children whose mothers were glad to be rid of them for a while.

The woman walked on, leading her son, seeing and acknowledging no one. She had not been out since the hanging, and it was like the first walk after illness, light-headed and unreal. She could not fix her mind on what would happen at the top of the hill; and maybe Dick had been the same. It should have been a comfort to her; but surely he must have realized, as the chains were put on him, and he faced away over the wide view... He had always been an outdoor man. He must have screamed and fought, if he were human. She herself, sitting with the boy, had stuffed her hands into her mouth till she choked. Outside, the noise had increased, and then quietened again, except for one awful sound, like a groan or a sigh, that she heard, and yet did not hear; then the people had come back to the streets again, in twos and threes, but they did not tell her what it had been like. 'He carried himself well,' was all they said.

They had been more than good to her. She had looked for work, cleaning or washing at the big houses, but nobody would employ a woman whose husband had been hanged. It was the neighbours who kept her going with small gifts, oil for the lamp, loaves and logs, and their company in case she felt lonely.

Sometimes she almost longed for loneliness. They were kind, but they never left her, talking, talking from dawn till dark. They sat about the kitchen, loth to forget about the hanging and let the excitement die. She did not want to speak about her husband. What she wanted was quite to remember him—or to forget. They asked about David, and tried to rally him, and laugh him out of his turns, and she could not explain that David did not like to be teased. Everything was out of order. There was spilt milk on the table, and the fire smouldered bitterly; but without the neighbours there would have been no milk and no fire.

And then, out of kindness, they made their suggestion, a word, a nudge, a hint behind the hands.

'They say it's a great cure, Missis. Rachael, the orphan, they took her...'

'You owe it to your son, Missis. What's a wee unpleasantness? He's not too far gone...'

'No!' she screamed at them. 'I couldn't! It's not right...'

'It's his own father,' they argued. 'If you thought anything of the boy...'

She was angry at that, but they kept their patience, talk, talk, talk, till at last, out of weariness and dutiful gratitude, she gave in.

Up past the school, where the houses began to thin out, the path mounted the hill. Lambs leaped, wobbly-legged, and the turf smelled sweet. They climbed like pilgrims, stopping sometimes because the boy was tired, and soon the ones behind began to press forward to see what was happening. They looked ahead, pointing to the top of the hill, but Mrs Weir and her son never looked up. She kept her head down, and led the boy by the arm, like a blind man.

The ground was levelling now, and a wind blew against their faces. The woman felt rather than saw what was about her; behind, the babble of voices, and in front, nothing but a faint swish, like cloth rubbing on wood, and a sickly smell...

The boy looked sideways at her, for guidance. His face was sick, green-looking, but she could not help him. She could not lift her hands to cover her eyes, although what was above seemed to be drawing her. She stood there, as if in prayer, and there was nothing she could do. Nothing.

Suddenly, one of the women pushed forward, grabbed the boy by the waist, and half lifted him. 'Go on, son. Up. Let him touch you...'

Something creaked, and chains clinked a little. Other hands lifted him up from behind, thrusting roughly, hurting him. 'That's it. His hand...'

He was light in their arms, for all his struggles. His eyes were tight shut, but his fists threshed pettishly, landing weak blows on arms and faces. Higher they pushed him, and there was something on his shoulder, cold, listless, something that slid off again uncaringly. The boy began to scream, shrilly, thinly, and at the sound his mother looked up, in spite of herself.

She made no sound, but her breath gagged back in her mouth, and her face was grey. This limp thing, bumping about like a sack, this was not her husband. If it had been recognizable, it would have broken her heart. Now, she felt only fear of it, the thin hair fluttering, the faint whiff of decay as it swung. Even the clamorous women were retreating, their handkerchiefs spread to their faces. The body turned again, grinning and suddenly she felt herself swinging with it, round and round and down in a cold dampness and roaring...

And then, her son was beside her, no longer screaming. His thin arms circled her, his slight body leaned in to support her. There were tears on his cheeks, and his mouth puckered childishly with crying, but there was the first hint of maturity in his face. 'Get away!' he shouted to the crowds pressing in to stare at him. 'Get away from her. Can't you leave us alone?'

'Davie!' His mother shivered, and pulled at his sleeve to quieten him. 'Mind yourself now, Davie. They wanted to help—'

'Look at them,' he said.

Her hands at her mouth, her mouth nibbling, she looked, and the hooded women stared back at her, callous, curious, licking their lips over the drama. For a moment, it seemed to her that the judge and the hangman were innocent, and that these were the real people who had strung her husband on the gibbet.

But now it no longer mattered. She stood in a daze, her hands still at her mouth, and her son seemed to tower above her, older, wiser, with infinite power to protect. As he pushed forward, they fell away on each side of him, the weavers, the blacksmith, and the mob who had followed for the fun of it. He passed through them without a glance. They stood for all the things he had learned and spurned at the foot of the gallows—the poverty that forced a man to steal, the cruelty of those who hanged him; and the ignorance of those who, even now, were rejoicing that the touch of a hanged corpse could really heal.

1980

THE FETCH

Robert Aickman

Robert Fordyce Aickman (1914–1981) has been recognized as the modern master of the 'strange tale'. Born in 1914, his grandfather was Richard Marsh, author of *The Beetle*, a work that was as popular in its day as Bram Stoker's *Dracula*. As well as being a member of both the Society for Psychical Research and The Ghost Club, Aickman was the co-founder of the Inlands Waterway Association which helped to restore and preserve England's canal network. He contributed three stories to *We Are For the Dark* (the other three were written by Elizabeth Jane Howard) in 1951 and edited the eight volumes of *The Fontana Book of Great Ghost Stories*. His other work includes the collections *Dark Entries*, *Powers of Darkness* and *Cold Hand In Mine*, the latter book containing the World Fantasy Award-winning tale 'Pages From A Young Girl's Journal'. Aickman was diagnosed with cancer in 1979 and refused conventional treatment, preferring alternative and complementary medicine instead. He died in February 1981. With 'The Fetch', from Aickman's 1980 collection *Intrusions*, he buries deep into Scottish folklore with his tale of the Cailleach or 'carlin' (storm hag). It's a story that once read, is never forgotten.

I

IN all that matters, I was an only child. There was a brother once, but I never saw him, even though he lived several years. My father, a Scottish solicitor or law agent, and very much a Scot, applied himself early to becoming an English barrister, and, as happens to Scots, was made a Judge of the High Court, when barely in middle age.

In Court, he was stupendous. From the first, I was taken once every ten days by Cuddy, my nurse, to the public gallery in order to behold him and hearken to him for forty minutes or so. If I made the slightest stir or whimper, it was subtly but effectively repaid me; on those and all other occasions. Judges today are neither better nor worse than my father, but they are different.

At home, my father, only briefly visible, was as a wraith with a will and power that no one available could resist. The will and power lingered undiminished when my father was not in the house, which, in the nature of things, was for most of the time. As well as the Court, and the chambers, there were the club and the dining club, the livery company and the military historical society, all of which my father attended with dedication and sacrifice. With equal regularity, he pursued the cult of self-defence, in several different branches, and with little heed for the years. He was an elder of a Scottish church in a London suburb, at some distance from where we lived. He presided over several successive Royal Commissions, until one day he threw up his current presidency in a rage of principle and was never invited again. After his death I realized that a further centre of his interest had been a club of a different kind, a very expensive and sophisticated one. I need not say how untrue it is that Scots are penny-scraping in all things.

I was terrified of my father. I feared almost everything, but there was nothing I feared more than to encounter my father or to pick up threads from his intermittent murmurings in the corridors and closets. We lived in a huge house at the centre of Belgravia. No Judge could afford such an establishment now. In addition, there was the family home of Pollaporra, modest, comfortless, and very remote. Our ancestry was merely legal and commercial, though those words have vastly more power in Scotland than in England. In Scotland, accomplishments are preferred to graces. As a child, I was never taken to Pollaporra. I never went there at all until much later, on two occasions, as I shall unfold.

I was frightened also of Cuddy, properly Miss Hester MacFerrier; and not least when she rambled on, as Scottish women do, of the immense bags and catches ingathered at Pollaporra by our ancestors and their like-minded acquaintances. She often emphasized how cold the house was at all times and how far from a 'made road'. Only the elect could abide there, one gathered; but there were some who could never bear to leave, and who actually shed tears upon being compelled by the advancing winter to do so. When the snow was on the ground, the house could not be visited at all; not even by the factor to the estate, who lived down by the sea loch, and whose name was Mason. Cuddy had her own methods for compelling the attention of any child to every detail she cared to impart. I cannot recall when I did not know about Mason. He was precisely the man for a Scottish nursemaid to uphold as an example.

My father was understood to dislike criminal cases, which, as an advanced legal theorist and technician, he regarded with contempt. He varied the taking of notes at these times by himself sketching in lightning caricature the figures in the dock to his left. The caricatures were ultimately framed, thirty or forty at a time; whereafter Haverstone, the odd-job man, spent upwards of a week hanging them at different places in our house, according to precise directions written out by my father, well in advance. Anybody who could read at all could at any time read every word my father wrote, despite the millions of words he had to set down as a duty. Most of the other pictures in our house were engravings after Landseer and Millais and Paton. Generations of Scottish aunts and uncles had also contributed art works of their own, painstaking and gloomy.

I was afraid of Haverstone, because of his disfigurements and his huge size. I used to tiptoe away whenever I heard his breathing. I never cared or dared to ask how he had come to be so marked. Perhaps my idea of his bulk was a familiar illusion of childhood. We shall scarcely know; in that Haverstone, one day after my seventh birthday, fell from a railway bridge into the main road beneath and was destroyed by a lorry. Cuddy regarded Haverstone with contempt and never failed to claim that my father employed him only out of pity. I never knew what he was doing on the railway bridge, but later I became aware of a huge mental hospital near by and drew obvious conclusions.

My mother I adored and revered. For better or for worse, one knows the words of Stendhal: 'My mother was a charming woman, and I was in love with my mother... I wanted to cover my mother with kisses and wished there weren't any clothes... She too loved me passionately. She kissed me, and I returned those kisses sometimes with such passion that she had to leave me.' Thus it was with me; and, as with Stendhal, so was the sequel.

My mother was very dark, darker than me, and very exotic. I must suppose that only the frenzy of Scottish lust brought my father to marrying her. At such times, some Scots lose hold on all other considerations; in a way never noticed by me among Englishmen. By now, my father's fit was long over. At least he did not intrude upon us, as Stendhal's father did. I am sure that jealousy was very prominent in my father, but perhaps he scorned to show it. He simply kept away from his wife entirely. At least as far as I could see. And I saw most things, though facing far from all of them, and acknowledging none of them.

Day after day, night after night, I lay for hours at a time in my mother's big bed, with my head between her breasts, and my tongue gently extended, as in infancy. The room was perfumed, the bed was perfumed, her nightdress was perfumed, she was perfumed. To a child, it set the idea of Heaven. Who wants any other? My mother's body, as well as being so dark, was softer all over than anyone else's, and sweeter than anything merely physical and fleeting, different and higher altogether. Her rich dark hair, perfumed of itself, fell all about me, as in the East.

There was no social life in our home, no visiting acquaintances, no family connections, no chatter. My father had detached himself from his own folk by his marriage. My mother loved no one but me. I am sure of that. I was in a position to know. The only callers were her hairdresser, her dressmaker, her maker of shoes and boots, her parfumier, her fabricator of lingerie, and perhaps one or two others of the kind. While she was shorn, scented, and fitted, I sat silently in the corner on a little grey hassock. None of the callers seemed to object. They knew the world and what it was like: and would soon enough be like for me. They contained themselves.

I was there whatever my mother did; without exception.

Cuddy dragged me off at intervals for fresh air, but not for very long. I could see for myself that Cuddy, almost familiar with my father, was afraid of my mother. I never knew why, and am far from certain now, but was glad of the fact. It was the key circumstance that transformed the potential of utter wretchedness for me into utter temporary bliss.

My mother taught me all I know that matters; smiling and laughing and holding me and rewarding me, so that always I was precocity incarnate; alike in concepts, dignity, and languages. Unfortunately, my mother was often ill, commonly for days, sometimes for weeks; and who was there to care, apart from me, who could do nothing—even if there was something that others could have done? My lessons ceased for a spell, but as soon as possible, or sooner, were bravely resumed.

Later, I strayed through other places of education, defending myself as best I could, and not unsuccessfully either; and, of what I needed, learning what I could. It was not my father who dispatched me. He regarded me without interest or expectation. To him I was the enduring reminder of a season's weakness. The ultimate care of me lay with Trustees, as often in Scotland; though only once did I see them as individuals, and hardly even then, because the afternoon was overcast, and all the lights were weak, for some reason that I forget.

Before all that formal education, I had encountered the woman on the stairs. This brief and almost illusory episode was the first of the two turning points in my life and I suspect the more important.

I had been playing on the landing outside the door of my mother's room. I do not know how long she had been ill that time. I feared to count the days, and never did so. I am sure that it was longer than on various previous occasions. I was alarmed, as always; but not especially alarmed.

My mother had been instrumental in my being given a railway, a conjuring outfit, and a chemical set: those being the things that small boys were supposed to like. My father should have given me soldiers, forts, and guns; possibly a miniature, but accurate, cricket bat; but he never once gave me anything, or spoke at all in our house if he could avoid it—except, on unpredictable occasions, to himself, memorably, as I have hinted.

I mastered the simple illusions, and liked the outfit, but had no one to awe. Even my mother preferred to hug me than for me to draw the ace of spades or a tiny white rabbit from her soft mouth. The chemical effects, chlorine gas and liquid air, I never mastered at that time, nor wished to. The railway I loved (no other word), though it was very miniature: neither 1 gauge (in those days) nor 0 gauge, but something smaller than 00. The single train, in the Royal Bavarian livery of before the First World War, clinked round a true circle; but en route it traversed a tunnel with two cows painted on top and one painted sheep, and passed through two separate stations, where both passengers and staff were painted on the tin walls, and all the signs were in Gothic.

That day, I had stopped playing, owing to the beating of my heart; but I had managed to pack everything into the boxes. I needed no bidding to do that, and never had done. I was about to lug the heap upstairs, which by then I could perfectly well do. I heard the huge clock in the hall strike half past three. The clock had come from Pollaporra, and reached the ceiling. I looked at my watch, as I heard it. I was always doing that. It was very late autumn, just before Christmas, but not yet officially winter. There is nothing in this world I know better than exactly what day of the year it was. It is for ever written in the air before me.

My ears were made keen by always listening. Often, wherever I was, even at the top of the house, I waited motionless for the enormous clock to strike, lest the boom take me by surprise. But the ascending woman was upon me before I had heard a footfall. I admit that all the carpets were thickest Brussels and Wilton. I often heard footfalls, none the less, especially my father's strangely uneven tread. I do not think I heard the woman make a sound from first to last. But last was very close to first.

She had come up the stairs, beyond doubt, even though I had neither heard nor seen anything; because by the time I did observe her, she was still two or three steps from the top of the flight. It was a wide staircase, but she was ascending in a very curious way, far further from the rail than was necessary and far nearer to the wall, and with her head and face actually turned to the wall.

At that point, I did hear something. I heard someone shut the front door below; which could not be seen from where I stood. I was surprised that I had not heard the door being opened, and the words of enquiry and caution. I remember my surprise. All these sounds were unusual in our house at that time.

I felt the cold air that the woman had brought in with her from the December streets and squares, and a certain cold smell; but she never once turned towards me. She could easily have been quite unaware of me; but I was watching her every motion. She had black hair, thin and lank. She was dressed in a dirty red and blue plaid of some kind, tightly wound. I was of course used to pictures of people in plaids. The woman's shoes were cracked and very unsuited to the slush outside. She moved with short steps, and across the carpet she left a thin trail of damp, though I knew that it was not raining. It was one of the things I always knew. Everything about the woman was of a kind that children particularly fear and dislike. Women, when frightening, are to children enormously more frightening than any man or men.

I think I was too frightened even to shrink back. As the woman tottered past, I stood there with my boxes beside me. My idea of her motion was that she had some difficulty with it, but was sustained by extreme need. Perhaps that is a fancy that only came to me later.

I never had any doubt about where the woman was going but, even so, I was unable to move or to speak or to do anything at all.

As she traversed the few yards of the landing, she extended her right arm and grimy hand from out of her plaid, the hand and arm nearer to me, still without in any degree turning her head. In no time at all, and apparently without looking, she had opened the door of my sweet mother's room, had passed within, and had shut the door behind her.

I suppose it is unnecessary for me to say that when my mother was ill, her door was never locked; but perhaps it is not unnecessary. I myself never entered at such times. My mother could not bear me to see her when she was ill.

There was no one sympathetic to whom I could run crying and screaming. In such matters, children are much influenced by the facilities available. For me, there was only my mother, and, in fact, I think I might actually have gone in after the woman, though not boldly. However, before I was able to move at all, I heard Cuddy's familiar clump ascending the stair behind me as I gazed at the shut door.

'What are you doing now?' asked Cuddy.

'Who was that?' I asked.

'Who was who?' Cuddy asked me back. 'Or what?'

'The woman who's gone in there.'

'Whist! It's time *you* were in bed with Christmas so near.'

'It *wasn't* Father Christmas,' I cried.

'I daresay not,' said Cuddy. 'Because it wasn't anybody.'

'It was, Cuddy. It *was*. Go in and look.'

It seems to me that Cuddy paused at that for a moment, though it may only have been my own heart that paused.

It made no difference.

'It's bed for you, man,' said Cuddy. 'You're overexcited and we all know where that ends.'

Needless to say, it was impossible for me to sleep, either in the dark or in the light: the choice being always left to me, which was perhaps unusual in those days. I heard the hours and the half hours all through the night, and at one or two o'clock my father's irregular step, always as if he were dodging something or someone imperfectly seen, and his periodical mutterings and jabberings as he plodded.

All was deeply upsetting to a child, but I must acknowledge that by then I was reasonably accustomed to most of it. One explanation was that I had no comparisons available. As far as I knew, all people behaved as did those in my home. It is my adult opinion that many more, in fact, do so behave than is commonly supposed, or at least acknowledged.

Still, that night must have proved exceptional for me; because when Cuddy came to call me in the morning, she found that I was ill too. Children, like adults, have diseases that it is absurd to categorize. Most diseases, perhaps all, are mainly a collapse or part-collapse of the personality. I daresay a name for that particular malady of mine might in those days have been brain fever. I am not sure that brain fever is any longer permitted to be possible. I am sure that my particular malady went on for weeks, and that when I was once more deemed able to make sense out of things, I learned that my mother was dead, and, indeed, long buried. No one would tell me where. I further gathered that there was no memorial.

About four weeks after that, or so it now seems to me, but perhaps it was longer, I was told that my father was proposing to remarry, though he required the consent of the Trustees. A Judge was but a man as far as the Trustees were concerned, a man within the scope of their own settlement and appointment. Thus it was that I acquired my stepmother; *née* Miss Agnes Emily Fraser, but at the moment a widow, Mrs Johnny Robertson of Baulk. To her the Trustees had no objection, it seemed.

I still have no idea of why my father married Agnes Robertson, or why he remarried at all. I do not think it can have been the motive that prompted his earlier marriage. From all that, since his death, I have learned of his ways, the notion would seem absurd. It was true that the lady had wealth. In the end, the Trustees admitted as much; and that much of it was in Burmah Oil. I doubt whether this was the answer either. I do not think that more money could have helped my father very much. I am not sure that by then anything could have helped him. This is confirmed by what happened to him, conventional in some ways though it was.

Moreover, the marriage seemed to me to make no difference to his daily way of life: the bench, the chambers, the club, the dining club, the livery company, the military historical society, the self-defence classes, the kirk; or, I am sure, to those other indulgences. On most nights, he continued to ponder and by fits and starts to cry out. I still tiptoed swiftly away and, if possible, hid myself when I heard his step. I seldom set eyes upon my stepmother, though of course I am not saying that I never did. I took it for granted that her attitude to me was at least one thing that she shared with my father. That seemed natural. I found it hard to see what else she had any opportunity of sharing. It had, of course, always been Cuddy to whom I was mainly obliged for information about my father's habits and movements, in so far as she knew them. Cuddy was much less informative about my stepmother.

One new aspect of my own life was that my lessons had stopped. I believe that for more than a year I had nothing to do but keep out of the way and play, as far as was possible. Now, there seemed to be no callers at all, and assuredly not parfumiers and designers of lingerie. No doubt my stepmother's circle was entirely in Scotland, and probably to the north of the Forth and Clyde Canal. She would not have found it easy to create an entirely new circle in Belgravia. I suppose there were two reasons why I suffered less than I might have done from the unsatisfactory aspects of my situation. The first was that I could hardly suffer more than I was suffering from my sweet mother's death. The second reason was my suspicion that any other life I might be embarked upon would be even more unsatisfactory.

In the end, the Trustees intervened, as I have said; but, before that, Cuddy had something to impart, at long last, about my stepmother. She told me that my stepmother was drinking.

It debarred her, Cuddy informed me in a burst of gossip, from appearing in public very often. That was exactly how Cuddy expressed it; with a twinkle or a glint or whatever may be the Scottish word for such extra intimations. I gathered that my stepmother seldom even dressed herself, or permitted herself to be dressed by Cuddy. One thing I was not told and do not positively know is whether or not the poor lady was drinking as hard as this before her second marriage. It is fair to her to say that the late Johnny Robertson was usually described as a scamp or rogue. Certainly my stepmother's current condition was something that would have had to be concealed by everyone as far as possible at that time in Belgravia, and with her husband a High Court Judge.

In any case, after the Trustees had taken me away and sent me to an eminent school, I began to hear tales. At first, I knocked about those who hurled and spat them at me. I discovered a new strength in the process; just as the grounding (to use the favoured word) provided by my mother enabled me to do better than most in class, not so much by knowing more as by using greater imagination and ingenuity, qualities that tell even in rivalry among schoolboys. The jibes and jeers ceased, and then I began cautiously to enquire after the facts. The school was of the kind attended by many who really know such things. I learned that my father too had long been drinking; and was a byword for it in the counties and the clubs. No doubt in the gaols also, despite my father's dislike of criminal jurisdiction.

One morning, Jesperson, who was the son of a Labour ex-minister and quite a friend of mine, brought me *The Times* so that I could see the news before others did. I read that my father had had to be removed from his Court and sent for treatment. *The Times* seemed to think that if the treatment were not successful, he might feel it proper to retire. There was a summary of the cases over which he had presided from such an unusually early age (some of them had been attended by me, however fleetingly); and a reference to his almost universal popularity in mainly male society.

I was by then in a position at school to take out any chagrin I might feel upon as many other boys as I wished, but I was too introspective for any such easy release, and instead began for the first time to read *The Divine Comedy*.

There was nothing particularly unusual in what had happened to my father so far, but the treatment seems, as far as one can tell, to have been the conclusive ordeal, so that he died a year later in a mental hospital, like poor Haverstone, though not in the same one. My father returned in spirit to his sodden, picturesque wilderness, and is buried in the kirkyard four or five miles by a very rough road from Pollaporra. It was the first instruction in his will, and the Trustees heeded it, as a matter of urgency, to the last detail.

I could not myself attend the funeral, as I was laid low by a school epidemic, though by then in my last term, and older than any of my confrères. My stepmother also missed the funeral, though she had returned to Scotland as soon as she could. She had resolved to remain there, and, for all I know, she is there still, with health and sobriety renewed. Several times I have looked her up in directories and failed to find her, despite reference to all three of her known surnames; but I reflect that she may well have married yet again.

My father had left her a moiety of his free estate, in equal part with the various organizations he wished to benefit, and which I have already listed. She possessed, as I have said, means of her own. My father left me nothing at all, but he lacked power, Judge though he was, and a Scots solicitor also, to modify the family settlement. Therefore, I, as only surviving child, inherited a life interest in Pollaporra, though not in the house in Belgravia, and a moderate, though not remarkable, income for life. Had my brother survived, he would have inherited equally. Thinking about him, I wondered whether the demon drink, albeit so mighty among Scotsmen, had not rather been a symptom of my father's malady than the cause of it. Thinking of that, I naturally then thought about my own inwardness and prospects. Eugene O'Neill says that we become like our parents of the same sex, even when we consciously resolve not to. I wept for my mother, so beloved, so incomparable.

II

Immediately, the question arose of my going to a university. The idea had of course been discussed before with the Trustees, but I had myself rejected it. While my father had been alive, my plan had been simply to leave the country as soon as I could. Thanks to my mother, I had made a good start with two European languages, and I had since advanced a little by reading literature written in them: *Die Räuber* and *Gerusalemme liberata*. The other boys no longer attacked or bullied me when they found me doing such things; and the school library contained a few basic texts, mostly unopened, both in the trade sense and the literal sense.

Now I changed my mind. The Trustees were clamant for Edinburgh, as could be expected; but I scored an important victory in actually going to Oxford. Boys from that school did not proceed to Edinburgh University, or did not then. It had never been practicable to send me to Fettes or Loretto. My friend, Jesperson, was at Oxford already. Oxford was still regarded by many as a dream, even though mainly in secret and in silence.

I read Modern Languages and Modern History, and I graduated reasonably, though not excitingly. I surprised myself by making a number of friends. This brought important benefits, in the short term and the long.

I now had no home other than Pollaporra, which, as will be recalled, could not always be visited during the winter, in any case. I spent most of the vacations with new friends; staying in their homes for astonishingly generous periods of time, or travelling with them, or reading with them. With the Second World War so plainly imminent and so probably apocalyptic, everyone travelled as much as he could. I met girls, and was continually amazed by myself. My closest involvement was with a pretty girl who lived in the town; who wrote poetry that was published; and who was almost a cripple. That surprised me most of all. I had learned something about myself, though I was unsure what it was. The girl lived, regardless, at the top of the house, which taught me something further. Her name was Celia. I fear that I brought little happiness to her or to any of the others, do what I would. I soon realized that I was a haunted man.

As for the main longer-term benefit, it was simple enough, and a matter of seemingly pure chance. My friend, Jack Oliver, spoke to his uncle, and as soon as I went down, modestly though not gloriously endorsed, I found myself en route to becoming a merchant banker. I owe Jack a debt that nothing can repay. That too is somehow a property of life. Nothing interlocks or properly relates. Life gives, quite casually, with one hand, and takes away rather more with the other hand, equally unforeseeably. There is little anyone can do about either transaction. Jack Oliver was and is the kindest man I have known, and a splendid offhand tennis player. He has a subtle wit, based on meiosis. From time to time, he has needed it. I have never climbed or otherwise risen to the top of the banking tree, but the tree is tall, and I lived as a child in a house with many stairs.

It was Perry Jesperson who came with me on my first visit to Pollaporra. He had borrowed one of his father's cars.

Even on the one-inch map, the topography was odd. It had struck me as odd many years before. I had always thought myself good with maps, as solitary children so often are; but now that I had been able to travel frequently, I had come to see that one cannot in every case divine from a map a feature of some kind that seems central when one actually arrives and inspects. In that way, I had made a fool of myself on several occasions, though sometimes to my own knowledge only. When it comes to Scotland, I need hardly say that many one-inch maps are sometimes needed for a journey from one place to another, and that some of the maps depict little but heaving contours and huge hydroelectric installations.

Pollaporra stood isolated amid wild altitudes for miles around. Its loneliness was confirmed by its being marked at all. I knew very well that it was no Inveraray or even Balmoral. It stood about three and a half miles from the sea loch, where Mason lived. That of course was as the crow flies, if crows there were. I had miled out the distance inaccurately with thumb and forefinger when I had still been a child. I had done it on many occasions. The topographical oddity was that the nearest depicted community was eight miles away in the opposite direction, whereas in such an area one would expect it to be on the sea, and to derive its hard living therefrom. It was difficult to think of any living at all for the place shown, which was stuck down in a hollow of the mountains, and was named Arrafergus. An uncoloured track was shown between Pollaporra and Arrafergus; the rough road of which I had heard so much, and along which my father's corpse had passed a few years before. One could see the little cross marking the kirk and kirkyard where he lay. It was placed almost halfway between the two names, which seemed oddest of all. For much of the year, no congregation could assemble from either house or village. A footpath was shown between Pollaporra and the sea loch, but one could hardly believe in more than a technical right of way, perhaps initiated by smugglers and rebels.

I had commented upon all this to Jesperson before we left. He had said, 'I expect it was an effect of the clearances.'

'Or of the massacres,' I had replied, not wishing to become involved in politics with Jesperson, even conversationally.

The roads were already becoming pretty objectionable, but Jesperson saw it all as progress, and we took it in turns to drive. On the third morning, we were advancing up the long road, yellow on the map, from the dead centre of Scotland to little Arrafergus. By English standards, it should not have been shown in yellow. Even Jesperson could hardly achieve more than a third of his normal speed. We had seen no other human being for a very long time, and even animals were absent, exactly as I had expected. Why was Arrafergus placed where it was, and how could it survive? Long ago the soaking mist had compelled us to put up the hood of the roadster. I admit that it was April.

In the early afternoon, the road came to an end. We were in a deep cleft of the rock-strewn hills, and it would have been impossible for it to go further. There was a burn roaring, rather than gurgling, over the dark stones. There was no community, no place, not even a road sign saying where we were or prohibiting further progress, not a shieling, not a crow. I speculated about what the funeral cortège could have done next.

'Do you want to get out and look for the foundations?' enquired Jesperson. 'There's probably the odd stone to be found. The landlords razed everything, but I'm told there are usually traces.'

'Not for the moment,' I said. 'Where do you suppose is the track to Pollaporra?'

'Up there,' said Jesperson immediately, and pointed over my head.

How had I missed it? Despite the drizzle, I could now see it quite plainly. Nor must I, or anyone, exaggerate. The track was exceedingly steep and far from well metalled, but, apart from the angle of incline, hardly worse to look at than the yellow road. Obviously, it must be difficult to keep the maps up to date, and in certain areas hardly worth while at present prices.

'Are we game?' I asked Jesperson. 'It's not your car, and I don't want to press.'

'We've got to spend the night somewhere,' said Jesperson, who had not even stopped the engine.

After that, all went surprisingly well. Cars were tougher and more flexible in those days. We ascended the mountain without once stopping, and there were no further major gradients until we came within sight of Pollaporra itself. I had feared that the track would die out altogether or become a desert of wiry weeds such as spring up vengefully on modern roads, if for a moment neglected.

The little kirk was wrapped in rain which was now much heavier. There were a few early flowers amidst and around the crumbling kirkyard walls. By June there would be more.

Jesperson drew up and this time stopped the engine reverently.

'It's all yours,' he said, glancing at me sideways.

I stepped out. The huge new monument dominated the scene.

I scrambled across the fallen stones.

My father's full name was there, and his dates of birth and death. And then, in much smaller lettering, A JUST MAN A BRAVE MAN AND A GOOD. That was it, the commemorated was no one's beloved husband or beloved father; nor were any of his honours specified; nor was confident hope expressed for him, or, by implication, for anyone, he having been so admirable.

Around were memorials, large and small, to others among my unknown ancestors and collaterals; all far gone in chipping, flaking, and greening, or all that I studied. Among us we seemed to cram the entire consecrated area. Perhaps the residue from other families had no mementoes. I was aware of the worms and maggots massed beneath my feet; crawling over one another, as in a natural history exhibit. At any moment, the crepe rubber soles of my shoes might crack and rot. Moreover, did the Church of Scotland ritually consecrate any place? I did not know. I turned round and realized that in the distance I could see Pollaporra also.

The house, though no more than a grey stone, slate-roofed rectangle, neither high nor particularly long, dominated the scene from then on, probably because it was the only work of man visible, apart from the bad road. Also it seemed to stand much higher than I had expected.

Jesperson wisely refused to set his father's car at the final ascent. We went up on foot. From the ridge we could make out the sea loch, green and phantasmal in the driving drizzle.

Cuddy was living in the house now; virtually pensioned off by the Trustees, and retained as caretaker: also as housekeeper, should the need arise, as it now did, almost certainly for the first time.

'Cuddy,' I cried out in my best English university style, and with hand outstretched, as we entered. It was desirable to seem entirely confident.

'Brodick,' she replied, not familiar perhaps, but independent.

'This is Mr Jesperson.'

'It's too late for the shooting and too early for the fishing,' said Cuddy. I think those were her words. I never quite remember the seasons.

'Mr Leith has come to take possession,' said Perry Jesperson.

'It's his for his life,' said Cuddy, as if indicating the duration of evening playtime.

'How *are* things?' I asked in my English university way. I was trying to ignore the chill, inner and outer, which the place cast.

'Wind and watertight as far as this house is concerned. You can inspect it at once. You'll not find one slate misplaced. For the rest you must ask Mr Mason.'

'I shall do so tomorrow,' I replied. 'You must set me on the way to him.'

'It is a straight road,' said Cuddy. 'You'll not go wrong.'

Of course it was not a road at all, but a scramble over rocks and stones all three miles; slow, slippery, and tiring. I could see why Mason spent little of his time visiting. None the less, the way was perfectly straight to the sea; though only from the top could one discern that. Jesperson had volunteered to look for some sport. Cuddy had been discouraging, but the house was as crammed with gear as the kirkyard with ancestral bones.

Mason lived in a small, single-storeyed house almost exactly at the end of the path, and at the edge of the sea. The local letter-box was in his grey wall, with a single collection at 6:30 A.M. each day, apart from Saturdays, Sundays, and Public Holidays. There were a few other small houses, too small for the map but apparently occupied, and even a shop, with brooms in the window. The shop was now closed, and there was no indication of opening hours. A reasonably good, though narrow, road traversed the place, and in both directions disappeared along the edge of the loch. It ran between the path from Pollaporra and Mason's house. There was no detectable traffic, but there was a metal bus-stop sign, and a time-table in a frame. I looked at it. If Jesperson's father's car were to break up, as seemed quite likely, we should need alternative transport. I saw that the bus appeared at 7:00 A.M. on the first Wednesday in each month between April and September. We had missed the April bus. I persisted and saw that the bus returned as early as 4:30 P.M. on the same day, and then went on to Tullochar at the head of the loch. Despite the length of the inlet, the waves were striking the narrow, stony beach sharply and rapidly. A few small broken boats were lying about, and some meshes of sodden net, with shapeless cork floats. There was even a smell of dead crustaceans.

I realized that all these modest investigations were being observed by Mason himself. He had opened the faded brown door of his house and was standing there.

'Brodick Leith,' he said, in the Scottish manner.

'Mr Mason,' I replied. 'I am very glad to meet you. I have heard about you all my life.'

'Ay,' said Mason, 'you would have. Come indoors. We'll have a drop together and then I'll show you the books. I keep them to the day and hour. There's not as much to do as once there was.'

'That was in my father's time?'

'In the Judge's time. Mr Justice Leith. Sir Roderic Leith, if you prefer. A strong man and a mysterious.'

'I agree with what you say.'

'Come inside,' said Mason. 'Come inside. I live as an unmarried man.'

Mason opened a new bottle, and before I left, we had made our way through all of it, and had started on the remains of the previous one. Though I drank appreciably less than half, it was still, I think, more spirit than I had drunk on any previous occasion. The books were kept in lucid and impersonal handwriting, almost as good as my father's, and were flawless, in so far as I could understand them; my career in banking having not yet begun. Mason left me to go through them with the bottle at my elbow, while he went into the next room to cook us steaks, with his own hands. I could see for myself that the amounts brought out as surplus or profit at the end of each account were not large. I had never supposed they would be, but the costs and responsibilities of land ownership were brought home to me, none the less. Until then, I had been a baby in the matter, as in many others. Most people are babies until they confront property ownership.

'I know you attended my father's funeral, Mr Mason,' I said. 'How was it? Tell me about it.' The steak was proving to be the least prepared that I had ever attempted to munch. No doubt the cooking arrangements were very simple. I had not been invited to inspect them.

'Ay,' said Mason, 'and the funeral was the least of it.' He took a heavier swig than before and stopped chewing altogether, while he thought.

'How many were there?' I had always been curious about that.

'Just me, and Cuddy MacFerrier, and the Shepstones.'

The Shepstones were relatives. I had of course never set eyes upon even one of them. I had never seen a likeness. Millais had never painted a single Shepstone, and if one or more of them had appeared upon a criminal charge, my father would hardly have been the Judge.

'How many Shepstones?' I asked, still essaying to devour.

'Just the three of them,' replied Mason, as if half-entranced. I am making little attempt to reproduce the Scottishness of his speech, or of anyone else's. I am far from being Sir Walter or George Douglas.

'That is all there are?'

'Just the three. That's all,' said Mason. 'Drink up, man.'

'A minister was there, of course?'

'Ay, the minister turned out for it. The son was sick, or so he said.'

'I am the son,' I said, smiling. 'And I *was* sick. I promise you that.'

'No need to promise anything,' said Mason, still motionless. 'Drink up, I tell you.'

'And no one else at all?' I persisted.

'Maybe the old carlin,' said Mason. 'Maybe her.'

For me that was a very particular Scottish word. I had in fact sprung half to my feet, as Mason spoke it.

'Dinna fash yoursel'. She's gone awa' for the noo,' said Mason.

He began once more to eat.

'I saw her once myself,' I said, sitting right down again. 'I saw her when my darling mother died.'

'Ay, you would,' said Mason. 'Especially if maybe you were about the house at the time. Who let her in?'

'I don't know,' I replied. 'Perhaps she doesn't have to be let in?'

'Och, she does that,' said Mason. 'She always has to be let in.'

'It was at the grave that you saw her?'

'No, not there, though it is my fancy that she was present. I saw her through that window as she came up from the sea.'

I know that Mason pointed, and I know that I did not find it the moment to look.

'Through the glass panes or out on the wee rocks you can view the spot,' said Mason. 'It's always the same.' Now he was looking at nothing and chewing vigorously.

'I saw no face,' I said.

'If you'd seen that, you wouldn't be here now,' said Mason. He was calm, as far as I could see.

'How often have you seen her yourself?'

'Four or five times in all. At the different deaths.'

'Including at my mother's death?'

'Yes, then too,' said Mason, still gazing upon the sawn-up sections of meat. 'At the family deaths she is seen, and at the deaths of those, whoever they be, that enter the family.'

I thought of my brother whom I had never known. I wasn't even aware that there had been any other family deaths during Mason's likely lifetime.

'She belongs to those called Leith, by one right or another,' said Mason, 'and to no one at all else.'

As he spoke, and having regard to the way he had put it, I felt that I saw why so apparently alert a man seemed to have such difficulty in remembering that I was presumably a Leith myself. I took his consideration kindly.

'I didn't see anyone when the Judge died,' I remarked.

'Perhaps in a dream,' said Mason. 'I believe you were sick at the time.'

That was not quite right of course, but it was true that I had by no means been in the house.

We dropped the subject, and turned once more to feu duties, rents, and discriminatory taxes; even to the recent changes in the character of the tides and in the behaviour of the gannets.

I have no idea how I scrambled back to dismal Pollaporra, and in twilight first, soon in darkness. Perhaps the liquor aided instead of impeded, as liquor so often in practice does, despite the doctors and proctors.

III

After the war, Jack Oliver was there to welcome me back to the office off Cornhill. He was now a colonel. His uncle had been killed in what was known as an incident, when the whole family house had been destroyed, including the Devises and De Wints. The business was now substantially his.

I found myself advanced very considerably from the position I had occupied in 1939. From this it is not to be supposed, as so many like to suppose, that no particular aptitude is required for success in merchant banking. On the contrary, very precise qualities both of mind and of temperament are needed. About myself, the conclusion I soon reached was that I was as truly a Scottish businessman as my ancestors in the kirkyard, whether I liked it or not, as O'Neill says. I should have been foolish had I *not* liked it. I might have preferred to be a weaver of dreams, but perhaps my mother had died too soon for that to be possible. I must add, however, that the business was by no means the same as when I had entered it before the war. No business was the same. The staff was smaller, the atmosphere tenser. The gains were illusory, the prospects shadowy. One worked much less hard, but one believed in nothing. There was little to work for, less to believe in.

It was in the office, though, that I met Shulie. She seemed very lost. I was attracted by her at once.

'Are you looking for someone?' I asked.

'I have just seen Mr Oliver.' She had a lovely voice and a charming accent. I knew that Jack was seeking a new secretary. His present one had failed to report for weeks, or to answer her supposed home telephone number.

'I hope that all went well.'

Shulie shook her head and smiled a little.

'I'm sorry about that.'

'Mr Oliver had chosen a girl who went in just before me. It always happens.'

'I'm sure you'll have better luck soon.'

She shook her head a second time. 'I am not English.'

'That has advantages as well as disadvantages,' I replied firmly.

It struck me that she might be a refugee, with behind her a terrible story. She was small, slender, and dark though not as dark as my mother. I could not decide whether or not she looked particularly Jewish. I daresay it is always a rather foolish question.

'No advantages when you are in England,' she said. 'Can you please tell me how to get out of this place?'

'I'll come with you,' I said. 'It's difficult to explain.'

That was perfectly true. It matters that it was true, because while we were winding through the corridors, and I was holding swing doors, I was successful in persuading Shulie to have lunch with me. Time was gained for me also by the fact that Shulie had a slight limp, which slowed her down quite perceptibly. I am sure she was weary, too, and I even believe that she was seriously underfed, whatever the exact reason. I perceived Shulie as a waif from the start; though also from the start I saw that it was far from the whole truth about her. I never learned the whole truth about her. Perhaps one never does learn, but Shulie refused, in so many words, to speak about it.

It was February, and outside I could have done with my overcoat. Jack Oliver still went everywhere in a British warm. He had several of them. There was snow on the ground and on the ledges. We had been under snow for weeks. Though do I imagine the snow? I do not imagine the cold. Shulie, when the blast struck her, drew into herself, as girls do. She was certainly not dressed for it; but few girls then were. The girlish image was still paramount.

I myself actually caught a cold that day, as I often did. I was laid up for a time in my small flat off Orchard Street, and with no one in any position to look after me very much. Later, Shulie explained to me that one need never catch cold. All that is necessary is a firm resolution against it: faith in oneself, I suppose.

On most days, Jack and I, together or apart, went either to quite costly places or to certain pubs. That was the way of life approved, expected, even enforced; and, within the limits of the time, rewarded. I, however, had kept my options more open than that. I took Shulie to a nearby tea shop, though a somewhat superior tea shop. We were early, but it was filling fast. Still, we had a table to ourselves for a time.

'What's your name?'

'Shulie.'

Her lips were like dark rose petals, as one imagines them, or sometimes dreams of them.

I have mentioned how lamentably sure I am that I failed to make Celia happy; nor any other girl. During the war, I had lived, off and on, with a woman married to another officer, who was never there when I was. I shall not relate how for me it all began. There was a case for, and a case against, but it had been another relationship inconducive to the ultimate happiness of either party.

When I realized that I was not merely attracted by Shulie, but deeply in love with her, and dependent for any future I might have upon marrying her, I applied myself to avoiding past errors. Possibly in past circumstances, they had not really been errors; but now they might be the difference between life and death. I decided that, apart from my mother, I had never previously and properly loved anyone; and that with no one else but my mother had I been sufficiently honest to give things a chance. When the time came, I acted at once.

Within half an hour of Shulie tentatively accepting my proposal of marriage, I related to her what Mason had told me, and what I had myself seen. I said that I was a haunted man. I even said that she could reverse her tentative decision, if she thought fit.

'So the woman has to be let in?' said Shulie.

'That's what Mason told me.'

'A woman who is married does not let any other woman in, except when her husband is not there.'

'But suppose you were ill?'

'Then you would be at home looking after me. It would not be a time when you would let in another woman.'

It was obvious that she was not taking the matter seriously. I had been honest, but I was still anxious.

'Have you ever heard a story like it before?'

'Yes,' said Shulie. 'But it is the message that matters more than the messenger.'

After we married, Shulie simply moved into my small flat. At first we intended, or certainly I intended, almost immediately to start looking for somewhere much larger. We, or certainly I, had a family in mind. With Shulie, I wanted that very much, even though I was a haunted man, whose rights were doubtful.

But it was amazing how well we seemed to go on living exactly where we were. Shulie had few possessions to bring in, and even when they were increased, we still seemed to have plenty of room. It struck me that Shulie's slight infirmity might contribute to her lack of interest in that normal ambition of any woman: a larger home. Certainly, the trouble seemed at times to fatigue her, even though the manifestations were very inconspicuous. For example, Jack Oliver, at a much later date, denied that he had ever noticed anything at all. The firm had provided me with a nice car and parking was then easier than it is now. Shulie had to do little walking of the kind that really exhausts a woman; pushing through crowds, and round shops at busy hours.

As a matter of fact, Shulie seldom left the flat, unless in my company. Shulie was writing a book. She ordered almost all goods on the telephone, and proved to be skilful and firm. She surprised me continually in matters like that. Marriage had already changed her considerably. She was plumper, as well as more confident. She accompanied me to the Festival Hall, and to picnics in Kew Gardens. The picnics were made elegant and exciting by her presence, and by her choice of what we ate and drank, and by the way she looked at the flowers, and by the way people and flowers looked at her. Otherwise, she wrote, or mused upon what she was about to write. She reclined in different sets of silk pyjamas on a bright-blue daybed I'd bought for her, and rested her square, stiff-covered exercise book upon her updrawn knees. She refused to read to me what she had written, or to let me read it for myself. 'You will know one day,' she said.

I must admit that I had to do a certain amount of explaining to Jack Oliver. He would naturally have preferred me to marry a woman who kept open house and was equally good with all men alike. Fortunately, business in Britain does not yet depend so much upon those things as does business in America. I was able to tell Jack that setting a wife to attract business to her husband was always a chancy transaction for the husband. For better or for worse, Jack, having lately battled his way through a very complex divorce, accepted my view. The divorce had ended in a most unpleasant situation for Jack financially, as well as in some public ridicule. He was in no position even to hint that I had married a girl whom he had rejected for a job. His own wife had been the daughter of a baronet who was also a vice-admiral and a former Member of Parliament. Her name was Clarissa. Her mother, the admiral's wife, was an MFH.

After my own mother's death, I should never have thought possible the happiness that Shulie released in me. There was much that remained unspoken to the end, but that may have been advantageous. Perhaps it is always so. Perhaps only madmen need to know everything and thus to destroy everything. When I lay in Shulie's arms, or simply regarded her as she wrote her secret book, I wished to know nothing more, because more would diminish. This state of being used to be known as connubial bliss. Few, I believe, experience it. It is certainly not a matter of deserts.

Shulie, however, proved to be incapable of conception. Possibly it was a consequence of earlier sufferings and endurances. Elaborate treatments might have been tried, but Shulie shrank from them, and understandably.

She accepted the situation very quietly. She did not seem to cease loving me. We continued to dwell in the flat off Orchard Street.

I asked Shulie when her book would be finished. She replied that the more she wrote, the more there was to be written. Whenever I approached her, she closed the exercise book and lifted herself up to kiss me. If I persisted at all, she did more than kiss me.

I wanted nothing else in life than to be with Shulie, and alone with her. Everything we did in the outside world was incorporated into our love. I was happy once more, and now I was happy all the time, even in the office near Cornhill. I bought a bicycle to make the journey, but the City men laughed, and nicknamed me, and ragged me, so that Jack Oliver and the others suggested that I give it up. Jack bought the bicycle himself, to use at his place in the country, where, not necessarily on the bicycle, he was courting the divorced daughter of the local High Sheriff, a girl far beyond his present means. She was even a member of a ladies' polo team, though the youngest. When one is happy oneself, everyone seems happy.

Our flat was on the top floor in a small block. The block had been built in more spacious days than the present, and there were two lifts. They were in parallel shafts. Above the waistline, the lifts had windows on three sides; the gate being on the fourth. They were large lifts, each *Licensed to carry 12 people*; far more than commonly accumulated at any one time. The users worked the lifts themselves, though, when I had first taken the flat, the lifts in Selfridges round the corner had still been worked by the famous pretty girls in breeches, among whom an annual competition was held. The two lifts in the flats were brightly lit and always very clean. Shulie loved going up and down in them; much as she loved real traffic blocks, with boys ranging along the stationary cars selling ice cream and evening newspapers. None the less, I do not think she used the lifts very much when I was not there. Travelling in them was, in fact, one tiny facet of our love. When Shulie was alone, I believe she commonly used the stairs, despite her trouble. The stairs were well lit and well swept also. Marauders were seldom met.

Tenants used sometimes to wave to their neighbours through the glass, as the two lifts swept past one another, one upwards, one downwards. It was important to prevent this becoming a mere tiresome obligation. One morning I was alone in the descending lift. I was on my way to work: Bond Street Underground station to Bank Underground station. There had been a wonderful early morning with Shulie, and I was full of joy; thinking about nothing but that. The other lift swept upwards past me. In it were four people who lived in the flats, three women and one man; all known to me by sight, though no more than that. As a fifth, there was the woman whom I had seen when my mother died.

Despite the speed with which the lifts had passed, I was sure it was she. The back was turned to me, but her sparse hair, her dirty plaid, her stature, and somehow her stance, were for ever unmistakable. I remember thinking immediately that the others in the lift must all be seeing the woman's face.

Melted ice flowed through me from the top of my head to the soles of my feet. There was a device for stopping the lift: *To be used only in Emergency.* And of course I wanted to reverse the lift also. I was so cold and so shaky that I succeeded merely in jamming the lift, and neatly between floors, like a joke in *Puck* or *Rainbow*, or a play by Sartre.

I hammered and raved, but most of the tenants had either gone to work or were making preparations for coffee mornings. The other lift did not pass again. As many as ten minutes tore by before anyone took notice of me, and then it was only because our neighbour, Mrs Delmer, wanted to descend from the top, and needed the lift she always used, being, as she had several times told us, frightened of the other one. The caretaker emerged slowly from his cubicle and shouted to me that there was nothing he could do. He would have to send for the lift company's maintenance men. He was not supposed to be on duty at that hour anyway, he said. We all knew that. Mrs Delmer made a detour as she clambered down the staircase, in order to tap on the glass roof of my lift and give me a piece of her mind, though in refined phrases. In the end, I simply sank upon the floor and tried to close myself to all thought or feeling, though with no success.

I must acknowledge that the maintenance men came far sooner than one could have expected. They dropped from above, and crawled from below, even emerging from a trap in the lift floor, full of cheerful conversation, both particular and general. The lift was brought slowly down to the gate on the floor immediately below. For some reason, that gate would not open, even to the maintenance men; and we had to sink, slowly still, to the ground floor. The first thing I saw there was a liquid trail in from the street up to the gate of the other lift. Not being his hour, the caretaker had still to mop it up, even though it reeked of seabed mortality.

Shulie and I lived on the eighth floor. I ran all the way up. The horrible trail crossed our landing from the lift gate to under our front door.

I do not know how long I had been holding the key in my hand. As one does at such times, I fumbled and fumbled at the lock. When the door was open, I saw that the trail wound through the tiny hall or lobby and entered the living room. When the woman came to my mother, there had been a faint trail only, but at that time I had not learned from Mason about the woman coming from the sea. Fuller knowledge was yielding new evidence.

I did not find Shulie harmed, or ill, or dead. She was not there at all.

Everything was done, but I never saw her again.

IV

The trail of water soon dried out, leaving no mark of any kind, despite the rankness.

The four people whom I had seen in the lift, and who lived in the flats, denied that they had ever seen a fifth. I neither believed nor disbelieved.

Shulie's book was infinitely upsetting. It was hardly fiction at all, as I had supposed it to be, but a personal diary, in the closest detail, of everything we had done together, of everything we had been, of everything she had felt. It was at once comprehensive and chaste. At one time, I even thought of seeking a publisher for it, but was deterred, in an illogical way, by the uncertainty about what had happened to Shulie. I was aware that it had been perfectly possible for her to leave the building by the staircase, while I had been caged between floors in the lift. The staircase went down a shaft of its own.

The book contained nothing of what had happened to Shulie before she met me.

Shulie's last words were, 'So joyful! Am I dreaming, or even dead? It seems that there is no external way of deciding either thing.' Presumably, she had then been interrupted. Doubtless, she had then risen to open the door.

I had been married to Shulie for three years and forty-one days.

I wrote to the Trustees suggesting that they put Pollaporra on the market, but their law agent replied that it was outside their powers. All I had done was upset both Cuddy and Mason.

I sold the lease of the flat off Orchard Street, and bought the lease of another one, off Gloucester Place.

I settled down to living with no one and for no one. I took every opportunity of travelling for the bank, no matter where, not only abroad, but even to Peterhead, Bolton, or Camborne. Previously, I had not wished or cared to leave Shulie for a single night.

I pursued new delights, such as they were, and as they came along. I joined a bridge club, a chess club, a mahjong society, and a mixed fencing group. Later, I joined a very avant-garde dance club, and went there occasionally.

I was introduced by one of the people in my firm to a very High Anglican church in his own neighbourhood, and went there quite often. Sometimes I read one of the lessons. I was one of the few who could still do that in Latin.

Another partner was interested in masonics, but I thought that would be inconsistent. I did join a livery company: it is expected in the City.

I was pressed to go in for regular massage, but resisted that too.

I was making more paper money than I would ever have thought possible. Paper money? Not even that. Phantom wealth, almost entirely: taxes took virtually the whole of it. I did not even employ a housekeeper. I did not wish for the attentions of any woman who was not Shulie. All the same, I wrote to Celia, who replied at once, making clear, among very many other things, that she was still unmarried. She had time to write so long and so prompt a letter. She had hope enough to think it worth while.

It is amazing how full a life a man can lead without for one moment being alive at all, except sometimes when sleeping. As Clifford Bax says, life is best treated as simply a game. Soon enough one will be bowled middle stump, be put out of action in the scrum, or ruled offside and sent off. As Bax also says, it is necessary to have an alternative. But who really has?

None the less, blood will out, and I married again. Sometime before, Shulie's death had been 'presumed'. Mercifully, it was the Trustees who attended to that.

I married Clarissa. I am married to her now.

The Court had bestowed upon Clarissa a goodly slice of Jack's property and prospects, and Jack was recognized by all as having made a complete fool of himself, not only in the area of cash; but Clarissa never really left at all. Even though Jack was now deeply entangled with Suzanne, herself a young divorcée, Clarissa was always one of Jack's house party, eager to hear everything, ready to advise, perhaps even to comfort, though I myself never came upon her doing that. She might now be sleeping in the room that had once been set aside for the visits of her sister, Naomi, but of course she knew the whole house far more intimately than Jack did, or than any normal male knows any house. She continued being invaluable to Jack; especially when he was giving so much of his time to Suzanne. One could not know Jack at all well, let alone as well as I knew him, without continuing to encounter Clarissa all the time.

The word for Clarissa might be deft—the first word, that is. She can manage a man or a woman, a slow child or a slow pensioner, as effortlessly as she can manage everything in a house, at a party, in a shop, on a ship. She has the small but right touch for every single situation—the perfect touch. Most of all, she has the small and perfect touch for every situation, huge or tiny, in her own life. Few indeed have *that* gift. No doubt Clarissa owes much to her versatile papa. On one occasion also, I witnessed Clarissa's mother looking after a difficult meet. It was something to note and remember.

Clarissa has that true beauty which is not so much in the features and body, but around them: nothing less than a mystical emanation. When I made my proposal to Clarissa, I naturally thought very devoutly of Shulie.

Shulie's beauty was of the order one longs from the first to embrace, to be absorbed by. Of course, my mother's dark beauty had been like that also. Clarissa one hardly wished or dared to touch, lest the vision fade. A man who felt otherwise than that about Clarissa would be a man who could not see the vision at all. I imagine that state of things will bear closely upon what happens to Clarissa. There is little that is mystical about Clarissa's detectable behaviour, though there must be *some* relationship between her soul and the way she looks. It is a question that arises so often when women as beautiful as Clarissa materialize in one's rose garden. I myself have never seen another woman as beautiful absolutely as Clarissa, or certainly never spoken to one.

Clarissa has eyes so deep as to make one wonder about the whole idea of depth, and what it means. She has a voice almost as lovely as her face. She has a slow and languorous walk: beautiful too, but related, I fear, to an incident during her early teens, when she broke both legs in the hunting field. Sometimes it leads to trouble when Clarissa is driving a car. Not often. Clarissa prefers to wear trousers, though she looks perfectly normal in even a short skirt, indeed divinely beautiful, as always.

I fear that too much of my life with Clarissa has been given to quarrelling. No one is to blame, of course.

There was a certain stress even at the proposal scene, which took place on a Saturday afternoon in Jack's house, when the others were out shooting duck. Pollaporra and its legend have always discouraged me from field sports, and all the struggling about had discouraged Clarissa, who sat before the fire, looking gnomic.

But she said yes at once, and nodded, and smiled.

Devoted still, whether wisely or foolishly, to honesty, I told her what Mason had told me, and what I had myself seen on two occasions, and that I was a haunted man.

Clarissa looked very hostile. 'I don't believe in things like that,' she said sharply.

'I thought I ought to tell you.'

'Why? Did you want to upset me?'

'Of course not. I love you. I don't want you to accept me on false pretences.'

'It's got nothing to do with my accepting you. I just don't want to know about such things. They don't exist.'

'But they do, Clarissa. They are part of me.'

From one point of view, obviously I should not have persisted. I had long recognized that many people would have said that I was obsessed. But the whole business seemed to me the explanation of my being. Clarissa must not take me to be merely a banker, a youngish widower, a friend of her first husband's, a faint simulacrum of the admiral.

Clarissa actually picked up a book of sweepstake tickets and threw it at me as I sat on the rug at her feet.

'There,' she said.

It was a quite thick and heavy book, but I was not exactly injured by it, though it had come unexpectedly, and had grazed my eye.

Clarissa then leaned forward and gave me a slow and searching kiss. It was the first time we had kissed so seriously.

'There,' she said again.

She then picked the sweepstake tickets off the floor and threw them in the fire. They were less than fully burnt ten minutes later, when Clarissa and I were more intimately involved, and looking at our watches to decide when the others were likely to return.

The honeymoon, at Clarissa's petition, was in North Africa, now riddled with politics, which I did not care for. For centuries, there has been very little in North Africa for an outsider to see, and the conformity demanded by an alien society seemed not the best background for learning to know another person. Perhaps we should have tried Egypt, but Clarissa specifically demanded something more rugged. With Shulie there had been no honeymoon.

Before marrying me, Clarissa had been dividing her life between her flat and Jack's country house. Her spacious flat, very near my childhood home, was in its own way as beautiful as she was, and emitted a like glow. It would have been absurd for me not to move into it. The settlement from Jack had contributed significantly to all around me, but by now I was able to keep up, or nearly so. Money is like sex. The more that everyone around is talking of little else, the less it really accounts for, let alone assists.

Not that sex has ever been other than a problem with Clarissa. I have good reason to believe that others have found the same, though Jack never gave me one word of warning. In any case, his Suzanne is another of the same kind, if I am any judge; though less beautiful, and, I should say, less kind also. Men chase the same women again and again; or rather the same illusion; or rather the same lost part of themselves.

Within myself, I had of course returned to the hope of children. Some will say that I was a fool not to have had that matter out with Clarissa before marrying her, and no doubt a number of related matters also. They speak without knowing Clarissa. No advance terms can be set. None at all. I doubt whether it is possible with any woman whom one finds really desirable. Nor can the proposal scene be converted into a businesslike discussion of future policy and prospects. That is not the atmosphere, and few would marry if it were.

With Shulie, the whole thing had been love. With Clarissa, it was power; and she was so accustomed to the power being hers that she could no longer bother to exercise it, except indirectly. This was and is true even though Clarissa is exceedingly good-hearted in many other ways. I had myself experienced something of the kind in reverse with poor Celia, though obviously in a much lesser degree.

Clarissa has long been impervious to argument or importunity or persuasion of any kind. She is perfectly equipped with counterpoise and equipoise. She makes discussion seem absurd. Almost always it is. Before long, I was asking myself whether Clarissa's strange and radiant beauty was compatible with desire, either on her part or on mine.

There was also the small matter of Clarissa's black maid, Aline, who has played her little part in the immediate situation. On my visits to the flat before our marriage, I had become very much aware of Aline, miniature and slender, always in tight sweater and pale trousers. Clarissa had told me that Aline could do everything in the place that required to be done; but in my hearing Aline spoke little for herself. I was told that often she drove Clarissa's beautiful foreign car, a present from Jack less than a year before the divorce. I was also told, as a matter of interest, that Jack had never met Aline. I therefore never spoke of her to him. I was telling him much less now, in any case. I certainly did not tell him what I had not previously told myself: that when I was away for the firm, which continued to be frequently, Aline took my place in Clarissa's vast and swanlike double bed. I discovered this in a thoroughly low way, which I do not propose to relate. Clarissa simply remarked to me that, as I knew, she could never sleep well if alone in the room. I abstained from rejoining that what Clarissa really wanted was a nanny; one of those special nannies who, like dolls, are always there to be dominated by their charges. It would have been one possible rejoinder.

Nannies were on my mind. It had been just then that the Trustees wrote to me about Cuddy. They told me that Cuddy had 'intimated a wish' to leave her employment at Pollaporra. She wanted to join her younger sister, who, I was aware, had a business on the main road, weaving and plaiting for the tourists, not far from Dingwall. I could well believe that the business had become more prosperous than when I had heard about it as a child. It was a business of the sort that at the moment did. The Trustees went on to imply that it was my task, and not theirs, to find a successor to Cuddy. They reminded me that I was under an obligation to maintain a property in which I had merely a life interest.

It was a very hot day. Clarissa always brought the sun. She had been reading the letter over my shoulder. I was aware of her special nimbus encircling my head and torso when she did this. Moreover, she was wearing nothing but her nightdress.

'Let's go and have a look,' she said.

'Are you sure you want to?' I asked, remembering her response to my story.

'Of course I'm sure. I'll transform the place, now I've got it to myself.'

'That'll be the day,' I said, smiling up at her.

'You won't know it when I've finished with it. Then we can sell it.'

'We can't,' I said. 'Remember it's not mine to sell.'

'You must get advice. Jack might be able to help.'

'You don't know what Pollaporra's like. Everything is bound to be totally run down.'

'With your Cuddy in charge all these years, and with nothing else to do with herself? At least, you say not.'

I had seen on my previous visit that this argument might be sound, as far as it went.

'You can't possibly take on all the work.'

'We'll have Aline with us. I had intended that.'

By now, I had seen for myself also that Aline was indeed most competent and industrious. It would have been impossible to argue further: Clarissa was my wife and had a right both to accompany me and to take someone with her to help with the chores. If I were to predecease her, she would have a life interest in the property. Moreover, Clarissa alone could manage very well for us when she applied herself. I had learned that too. There were no sensible, practical objections whatever.

'Aline will be a help with the driving as well,' added Clarissa.

There again, I had seen for myself how excellent a driver little Aline could be. She belongs to just the sort of quiet person who in practice drives most effectively on the roads of today.

'So write at once and say we're arriving,' said Clarissa.

'I'm not sure there's anyone to write to,' I replied. 'That's the point.'

I had, of course, a set of keys. For whatever reason, I did not incline to giving Mason advance notice of my second coming, and in such altered circumstances.

'I'm not sure how Aline will get on with the Highlanders,' I remarked. There are, of course, all those stories in Scotland about the intrusion of huge black men, and sometimes, I fancy, of black females. They figure in folklore everywhere.

'She'll wind each of them three times round each of her fingers,' replied Clarissa. 'But you told me there *were* no Highlanders at Pollaporra.'

Clarissa, when triumphing, looks like Juno, or Diana, or even Minerva.

Aline entered to the tinkling of a little bell. It is a pretty little bell, which I bought for Clarissa in Sfax; her earlier little bell having dropped its clapper.

When Aline entered in her quiet way, Clarissa kissed her, as she does every morning upon first sighting Aline.

'We're all three going into the wilderness together,' said Clarissa. 'Probably on Friday.'

Friday was the day after tomorrow. I really could not leave the business for possibly a week at such short notice. There was some tension because of that, but it could not be helped.

When we did reach Pollaporra, the weather was hotter than ever, though there had been several thunderstorms in London. Aline was in her element. Clarissa had stocked up the large car with food in immense quantity. When we passed through an outlying area of Glasgow, she distributed two pounds of sweets to children playing in the roads of a council estate. The sweets were melting in their papers as she threw them. The tiny fingers locked together.

When we reached the small kirkyard, Clarissa, who was driving us along the rough road from Arrafergus, categorically refused to stop.

'We're here to drive the bogies out,' she said, 'not to let them in.'

Clarissa also refused to leave the car at the bottom of the final slope, as Perry Jesperson had done. My friend Jesperson was now a Labour MP like his father, and already a Joint Parliamentary Secretary, and much else, vaguely lucrative and responsible. Clarissa took the car up the very steep incline as if it had been a lift at the seaside.

She stood looking at and beyond the low grey house. 'Is that the sea?' she asked, pointing.

'It's the sea loch,' I replied. 'A long inlet, like a fjord.'

'It's a lovely place,' said Clarissa.

I was surprised, but, I suppose, pleased.

'I thought we might cut the house up into lodges for the shooting and fishing,' said Clarissa. 'But now I don't want to.'

'The Trustees would never have agreed,' I pointed out. 'They have no power to agree.'

'Doesn't matter. I want to come here often. Let's take a photograph.'

So, before we started to unpack the car, Clarissa took one of Aline and me; and, at her suggestion, I took one of Aline and her. Aline did not rise to the shoulders of either of us.

Within the house, the slight clamminess of my previous visit had been replaced by a curiously tense airlessness. I had used my key to admit us, but I had not been certain as to whether or not Cuddy was already gone, and Clarissa and I went from room to room shouting for her, Clarissa more loudly than I. Aline remained among the waders and antlers of the entrance hall, far from home, and thinking her own thoughts. There was no reply anywhere. I went to the door of what I knew to be Cuddy's own room, and quietly tapped. When there was no reply there either, I gently tried the handle. I thought the door might be locked, but it was not. Inside was a small unoccupied bedroom. The fittings were very spare. There were a number of small framed statements on the walls, such as *I bow before Thee*, and *Naught but Surrender*, and *Who knows All* without a mark of interrogation. Clarissa was still calling from room to room. I did not care to call back but went after her on half-tiptoe.

I thought we could conclude we were alone. Cuddy must have departed some time ago.

Dust was settling everywhere, even in that remote spot. The sunlight made it look like encroaching fur. Clarissa seemed undeterred and undaunted.

'It's a lost world and I'm queen,' she said.

It is true that old grey waders, and wicker fish baskets with many of the withies broken, and expensive guns for stalking lined up in racks, are unequalled for suggesting loss, past, present, and to come. Even the pictures were all of death and yesterday—stags exaggeratedly virile before the crack shot; feathers abnormally bright before the battue; men and ancestors in bonnets before, behind, and around the ornamentally piled carcases, with the lion of Scotland flag stuck in the summit. When we reached the hall, I noticed that Aline was shuddering in the sunlight. I myself had never been in the house before without Cuddy. In practice, she had been responsible for everything that happened there. Now I was responsible—and for as long as I remained alive.

'We'll paint everything white and we'll put in a swimming pool,' cried Clarissa joyously.'Aline can have the room in the tower.'

'I didn't know there was a tower,' I said.

'*Almost* a tower,' said Clarissa.

'Is there anything in the room?' I asked.

'Only those things on heads. They're all over the walls and floor.'

At that, Aline actually gave a little cry. Perhaps she was thinking of things on walls and floors in Africa.

'It's all right,' said Clarissa, going over to her. 'We'll throw them all away. I promise. I never ask you to do anything I don't do myself, or wouldn't do.'

But, whatever might be wrong, Aline was uncomforted. 'Look!' she cried, and pointed out through one of the hall windows, all of them obstructed by stuffed birds in glass domes, huge and dusty.

'What have you seen this time?' asked Clarissa, as if speaking to a loved though exhausting child.

At that moment, it came to me that Clarissa regularly treated Aline as my mother had treated me.

Aline's hand fell slowly to her side, and her head began to droop.

'It's only the car,' said Clarissa. '*Our* car. You've been driving it yourself.'

I had stepped swiftly but quietly behind the two of them. I admit that I too could see nothing but the car, and, of course, the whole of Scotland.

I seldom spoke directly to Aline, but now was the moment.

'What was it?' I asked, as sympathetically as I could manage. 'What did you see?'

But Aline had begun to weep, as by now I had observed that she often did. She wept without noise or any special movement. The tears just flowed like thawing snow; as they do in nature, though less often on 'Change.

'It was nothing,' said Clarissa. 'Aline often sees nothing, don't you, Aline?' She produced her own handkerchief, and began to dry Aline's face, and to hug her tightly.

The handkerchief was from an enormous casket of objects given us as a wedding present by Clarissa's grandmother (on the mother's side), who was an invalid, living in Dominica. Clarissa's grandfather had been shot dead years before by thieves he had interrupted.

'Now,' said Clarissa after a few moments of tender reassurance. 'Smile, please. That's better. We're going to be happy here, one and all. Remember. Happy.'

I suppose I was reasonably eager, but I found it difficult to see how she was going to manage it. It was not, as I must in justice to her make clear, that normally I was unhappy with Clarissa. She was too beautiful and original for that to be the word at any time. The immediate trouble was just Pollaporra itself: the most burdensome and most futile of houses, so futile as to be sinister, even apart from its associations, where I was concerned. I could not imagine any effective brightening; not even by means of maquillage and disguise: a pool, a discothèque, a sauna, a black-jack suite. To me Pollaporra was a millstone I could never throw away. I could not believe that modern tenants would ever stop there for long, or in the end show us a profit. For all the keep nets and carcase sleighs in every room, I doubted whether the accessible sport was good enough to be marketed at all in contemporary terms. Nor had I started out with Clarissa in order that we should settle down in the place ourselves. When I can get away from work, I want somewhere recuperative. About Pollaporra, I asked the question all married couples ask when detached from duties and tasks: what should we do all day? There was nothing.

'I have never felt so free and blithe,' said Clarissa later that evening, exaggerating characteristically but charmingly. She was playing the major part in preparing a quite elaborate dinner for us out of tins and packets. In the flat, Aline had normally eaten in her own pretty sitting room, but here she would be eating with us. Clarissa would be tying a lace napkin round her neck, and heaping her plate with first choices, and handing her date after date on a spike. Employees are supposed to be happier when treated in that way, though few people think it is true, and few employees.

'We'll flatten the roof and have li-los,' said Clarissa, while Aline munched with both eyes on her plate, and I confined myself to wary nibblings round the fringe of Rognons Turbigo, canned but reinvigorated. The plates at Pollaporra depicted famous Scots, such as Sawney Bean and Robert Knox, who employed Burke and Hare, the body-snatchers. Mr Justice Leith, who despised the criminal law, had never been above such likenesses, as we know; nor had he been the only sporting jurist in the family, very far from it.

'I think to do that we'd have to rebuild the house,' I remarked.

'Do try not to make difficulties the whole time. Let yourself go, Brodick.'

It is seldom a good idea, according to my experience, and especially not in Scotland, but of course I could see what Clarissa meant. There was no reason why we should not make of the trip as much of a holiday as was possible. It would be a perfectly sensible thing to do. If Clarissa was capable of fun at Pollaporra, I was the last person with a right to stand in her way.

'We might build a gazebo,' I said, though I could feel my heart sinking as I spoke.

Aline, with her mouth full of prunes (that day), turned her head towards me. She did not know what a gazebo was.

'A sort of summerhouse,' explained Clarissa. 'With cushions and views. It would be lovely. So many things to look at.'

I had never known Clarissa so simple-minded before; in the nicest sense, of course. I realized that this might be a Clarissa more real than the other one. I might have to consider where I myself stood about that. On the other hand, Pollaporra, instead of bringing out at long last the real woman, might be acting upon her by contraries, and have engaged the perversity in her, and to no ultimately constructive end. I had certainly heard of that too, and in my time seen it in action among friends.

'I don't want to look,' said Aline, expelling prune stones into spoons.

'You will by tomorrow. You'll feel quite different. We're going to drive all the banshees far, far away.'

I am sure that Aline did not know what a banshee was either, but Clarissa's general meaning was clear, and the word has an African, self-speaking sound in itself, when one comes to think about it. Words for things like that are frightening in themselves the world over.

Only Clarissa, who believed in nothing she could not see or imagine, was utterly undisturbed. I am sure that must have played its part in the row we had in our room that night.

There were small single rooms, of course, several of them. There were also low dormitories for body servants and sporting auxiliaries. All the rooms for two people had Scottish double beds. Clarissa and I had to labour away in silence making such a bed with sheets she had brought with us. Blankets we should have had to find in drawers and to take on trust, but on such a night they were unnecessary. Aline, when not with Clarissa, always slept in a striped bag, which that night must have been far too hot. Everything, everywhere, was far too hot. That contributed too, as it always does. Look at Latin America!

I admit that throughout the evening I had failed to respond very affirmatively to Clarissa's sequence of suggestions for livening up the property and also (she claimed) increasing its market value; which, indeed, cannot, as things were and are, be high. I could see for myself how I was leading her first into despondency, then into irritation. I can see that only too well now. I was dismayed by what was happening, but there was so little I could conscientiously offer in the way of encouragement. All I wished to do with Pollaporra was patch up some arrangement to meet my minimum obligations as a life tenant, and then, if possible, never set eyes upon the place again. One reason why I was cast down was the difficulty of achieving even a programme as basic as that. I daresay that Clarissa's wild ideas would actually be simpler to accomplish, and conceivably cheaper also in the end. But there is something more than reason that casts me down at Pollaporra. Shall I say that the house brings into consciousness the conflict between my heraditament and my identity? Scotland herself is a land I do well to avoid. Many of us have large areas of danger which others find merely delightful.

There was no open row until Clarissa and I went upstairs. One reason was that after doing the washing-up, Aline had come into the sitting room, without a word, to join us. I was not surprised that she had no wish to be alone; nor that she proved reluctant to play a game named Contango, of which Clarissa was very fond, and which went back to her days with Jack, even though Jack had always won, sometimes while glancing through business papers simultaneously, as I had observed for myself. Both Clarissa and

Aline were wearing tartan trousers, though not the same tartan. I had always been told by Cuddy that there was no Leith tartan. I have never sought further to know whether or not that is true.

As soon as we were in bed, Clarissa lay on her front, impressing the pillow with moisture from her brow, and quietly set about me; ranging far beyond the possibilities and deficiencies of Pollaporra. Any man—any modern man—would have some idea of what was said. Do the details matter? I offered no argument. At Pollaporra, I spoke as little as I could. What can argument achieve anywhere? It might have been a moment for me to establish at least temporary dominance by one means or another, but Pollaporra prevented, even if I am the man to do it at any time. I tried to remember Shulie, but of course the circumstances left her entirely unreal to me, together with everything else.

And, in the morning, things were no better. I do not know how much either of us had managed to sleep. For better or worse, we had fallen silent in the heat long ago. In the end, I heard the seabirds screaming and yelling at the dawn.

Clarissa put on a few garments while I lay silent on the bed and then told me that as there was nothing she could do in the house, she was departing at once.

'I should leave Aline behind, but I need her.'

'I quite understand,' I said. 'I advised you against coming in the first place. I shall go over to see Mason and try to arrange with him for a caretaker. It won't take more than a day or two.'

'You'll first need to change the place completely. You are weak and pigheaded.'

'They sometimes see things differently in Scotland. I shall come down as soon as I can.' I might have to hire a car to some station, because I did not think Mason owned one, or anyone else in his small community. That was a trifle; comparatively.

'No hurry. I shall use the time deciding what to do for the best.' She was combing her mass of hair, lovely as Ceres' sheaf. The comb, given her by the Aga Khan, was made of ebony. The air smelled of hot salt.

I suppose I should have begged her pardon for Pollaporra and myself, and gone back to London with her, or to anywhere else. I did not really think of it. Pollaporra had to be settled, if at all possible. I might never be back there.

In a few moments, Clarissa and I were together in the hall, the one high room, and I saw Aline silently standing by the outer door, as if she had stood all night; and the door was slightly open. Aline was in different trousers, and so was Clarissa.

'I can't be bothered to pack up the food. You're welcome to all of it.'

'Don't go without breakfast,' I said. 'The lumpy roads will make you sick.'

'Breakfast would make me sick,' said Clarissa.

Clarissa carried very few clothes about. All she had with her was in the aircraft holdall she clutched. I do not know about Aline. She must have had something. I cannot remember.

'I don't know when we'll meet again,' said Clarissa.

'In two or three days,' I said. 'Four at the most.' Since I had decided to remain, I had to seem calm.

'I may go and stay with Naomi. I want to think things out.'

She was wearing the lightest of blouses, little more than a mist. She was exquisite beyond description. Suddenly, I noticed that tears were again streaming silently down Aline's face.

'Or I may go somewhere else,' said Clarissa, and walked out, with her slight but distinctive wobble.

Instead of immediately following her, as she always did, Aline actually took two steps in my direction. She looked up at me, like a rococo cherub. Since I could not kiss Clarissa, I lightly kissed Aline's wet lips, and she kissed me.

I turned my back in order not to see the car actually depart, though nothing could prevent my hearing it. What had the row been really about? I could surmise and guess, but I did not know. I much doubted whether Clarissa knew. One could only be certain that she would explain herself, as it were to a third party, in a totally different way from me. We might just as well belong to different zoological species, as in the Ray Bradbury story. The row was probably a matter only of Clarissa being a woman and I a man. Most of all, rows between the sexes have no more precise origin; and, indirectly, many other rows also.

I think I stood for some time with my back to the open door and my face to the picture of an old gillie in a tam, with dead animals almost to his knees. It had been given us by the Shepstones. It was named *Coronach* in Ruskinian letters, grimly misapplied. Ultimately, I turned and through the open door saw what Aline may have seen. The auld carlin was advancing across the drive with a view to entering.

Drive, I have to call it. It was a large area of discoloured nothingness upon which cars stood, and before them horses, but little grew, despite the lack of weeding. Needless to say, the woman was not approaching straightforwardly. Previously, I had seen her only when she had been confined to the limits of a staircase, albeit a wide one, a landing, and, later, a lift. If now she had been coming straight at me, I might have had a split second to see her face. I realized that, quite clearly, upon the instant.

I bounded forward. I slammed the door. The big key was difficult to turn in the big lock, so I shot the four rusty bolts first. Absurdly, there was a 'chain' also and, after I had coped with the stiff lock, I 'put it on'.

Then I tore round the house shooting other bolts; making sure that all other locks were secure; shutting every possible window and aperture, on that already very hot early morning.

It is amazing how much food Clarissa laid in. She was, or is, always open-handed. I am sure that I have made that clear. Nor of course does one need so much food—or at least want so much—in this intense heat. Nor as yet has the well run dry. Cuddy refused to show me the well, saying the key was lost. I have still not seen either thing.

There is little else to do but write this clear explanation of everything that has happened to me since the misfortune of birth. He that has fared better, and without deceiving himself, let him utter his jackass cry.

Not that I have surrendered. There lies the point. Pollaporra is not on the telephone, nor ever could be, pending the 'withering away of the State'; but before long someone may take note that I am not there. The marines may descend from choppers yet. Clarissa may well have second thoughts. Women commonly do, when left to themselves. She loves Pollaporra and may well devise a means of wrestling my life interest away from me, and welcome. I don't know where Aline would enter into that hypothesis. Possibly I made a mistake in not writing to Mason that I was coming. But I doubt whether in such personal matters his time-scale is shorter than months.

Off and on, I see the woman at one window or another; though not peeking through, which, as will have been gathered, is far from her policy. At least twice, however, it has been at a window upstairs; on both occasions when I was about to undress for some reason, not necessarily slumber, of which I have little. At these times, her slimy-sleek head, always faceless, will tip-tap sharply against the thick glazing bars. The indelicacy, as Jack might put it (I wonder how Cuddy would put it?), set me upon a course of hard thinking.

So long as I keep myself barred up, she can achieve nothing. Mason seemed quite certain of that, and I accept it. But what does the woman aim to do to me? When she appeared to me before, my poor mother soon passed away. When she appeared to me a second time, my dear, dear Shulie vanished from my life. It is not to be taken for granted that either of these precise fates is intended for me. I am not even ill or infirm. There may be a certain room for manoeuvre, though I can foresee no details.

More often, I see the woman at corners of what used to be the lawn and garden, though never in my time. It lies at the back of the house, and far below lies the loch. Sometimes too, the creature perches on the ornaments and broken walls, like a sprite. Such levitations are said to be not uncommon in the remoter parts of Scotland. Once I thought I glimpsed her high up in a bush, like dirty rags in a gale. Not that so far there has been any gale, or even any wind. The total silent stillness is one of the worst things. If I die of heat and deoxygenation, it will be one solution.

Yes, it is a battle with strong and unknown forces that I have on my hands. 'But what can ail all of them to bury the old carlin in the night time?' as Sir Walter ventures to enquire; in *The Antiquary*, if I remember rightly.

Ireland

1896

THE DEATH SPANCEL

Katharine Tynan

Katharine Tynan-Hinkson (1859–1931) lived to write and she wrote to live. For fifty-three years she produced over 100 novels, countless volumes of poetry, five volumes of autobiography and hundreds of short stories. It was said that at her peak she could easily write a 100,000-word novel in a month using only a quill. She spent her formative years living at 'Whitehall', a low thatched farmhouse in Clondalkin, and during her childhood her eyesight nearly failed due to a case of measles that turned into ulcers around her eyes. She would subsequently call herself 'purblind' and would have trouble with her vision for the rest of her life.

She began writing her own poetry at the age of seventeen and met with immediate success. After her debut in a Dublin newspaper her sonnets began to appear in the *London Spectator* and her first real paying poetry was published by *The London Graphic*. Her poetry was also published in *The Irish Monthly* magazine and it was during this time that she met Rosa Mulholland, Oscar Wilde and W. B. Yeats. In the same year she met Yeats, her first book of poems, *Louise de la Vallière and Other Poems* was published by Kegan Paul, Trench and Company (1885). The book was met with critical acclaim and so began her extraordinary career, with her short story writing seeming to begin two years after her marriage to Henry Albert Hinkson, around the years of 1895–6 (her debut novel appeared in 1894). Several short stories appeared in periodicals such as *The Wave* (where 'The Death Spancel' was first published) and these were soon followed by her debut collection *An Isle in the Water*. She moved to London where she stayed for the next eighteen years and became the breadwinner for the family, which had grown to accommodate three children (Toby, Patrick and Pamela—Pamela would become a celebrated and important author in her own right). In 1911 they moved back to Ireland—Tynan's husband's death in 1919 would see Katharine and her children in financial peril and it was her writing, plus the sale of letters written to her by Yeats for £100, that kept them afloat. This would also see the increased output in her work; Katharine wrote at a furious pace, selling story after story, writing reviews and articles that were heavily syndicated throughout Irish and British newspapers. 'The Death Spancel' is her strangest short story and remains to this day a feverish piece of fiction based loosely on the real-life 18th century experiences of Sibella Cottle, the mistress of Sir Henry (Harry) Lynch-Blosse.

High up among the dusty rafters of Aughagree Chapel dangles a thin shrivelled thing, towards which the people look shudderingly when the sermon is of the terrors of the Judgment and the everlasting fire. The woman from whose dead body that was taken chose the death of the soul in return for a life with the man whom she loved with an unholy passion. Every man, woman, and child in that chapel amid grey miles of rock and sea-drift, has heard over and over of the unrepentant deathbed of Mauryeen Holion. They whisper on winter nights of how Father Hugh fought with the demons for her soul, how the sweat poured from his forehead, and he lay on his face in an agony of tears, beseeching that the sinner whom he had admitted into the fold of Christ should yet be saved. But of her love and her sin she had no repentance, and the servants in Rossatorc Castle said that as the priest lay exhausted from his vain supplications, and the rattle was in Dark Mauryeen's throat, there were cries of mocking laughter in the air above the castle, and a strange screaming and flapping of great wings, like to, but incomparably greater than, the screaming and flapping of the eagle over Slieve League. That devil's charm up there in the rafters of Aughagree is the death-spancel by which Dark Mauryeen bound Sir Robert Molyneux to her love. It is of such power that no man born of woman can resist it, save by the power of the Cross, and 'twas little Robert Molyneux of Rossatorc recked of the sweet Christ who perished that men should live—against whose Cross the demons of earth and the demons of air, the malevolent spirits that lurk in water and wind, and all witches and evil doctors, are powerless. But the thought of the death-spancel must have come straight from the King of Fiends himself, for who else would harden the human heart to desecrate a new grave, and to cut from the helpless dead the strip of skin unbroken from head to heel which is the death-spancel? Very terrible is the passion of love when it takes full possession of a human heart, and no surer weapon to the hand of Satan when he would make a soul his own. And there is the visible sign of a lost soul, and it had nearly been of two, hanging harmlessly in the rafters of the holy place. A strange thing to see where the lamp of the sanctuary burns, and the sea-wind sighs sweetly through the door ever open for the continual worshippers.

Sir Robert Molyneux was a devil-may-care, sporting squire, with the sins of his class to his account. He drank, and gambled, and rioted, and oppressed his people that they might supply his pleasures; nor was that all, for he had sent the daughter of honest people in shame and sorrow over the sea. People muttered when they heard he was to marry Lord Dunlough's daughter, that she would be taking another woman's place; but it was said yet again that it would be well for his tenants when he was married, for the lady was so kind and charitable, so gentle and pure, that her name was loved for many a mile. She had never heard the shameful story of that forlorn girl sailing away and away in the sea-mist, with her unborn child, to perish miserably, body and soul, in the streets of New York. She had the strange love of a pure woman for a wild liver; and she thought fondly when she caressed his fine, jolly, handsome face that soon his soul as well as his dear body would be in her keeping: and what safe keeping it would be.

Sir Robert had ever a free way with women of a class below his own, and he did not find it easy to relinquish it. When he was with the Lady Eva he felt that under those innocent, loving eyes a man could have no desire for a lesser thing than her love; but when he rode away, the first pretty girl he met on the road he held in chat that ended with a kiss. He was always for kissing a pretty face, and found the habit hard to break, though there were times when he stamped and swore great oaths to himself that he would again kiss no woman's lips but his wife's—for the man had the germ of good in him.

It was a fortnight to his wedding day, and he had had a hard day's hunting. From early morning to dewy eve they had been at it, for the fox was an old one and had led the dogs many a dance before this. He turned homeward with a friend, splashed and weary, but happy and with the appetite of a hunter. Well for him if he had never set foot in that house. As he came down the stairs fresh and shining from his bath, he caught sight of a girl's dark handsome face on the staircase. She was one of the servants, and she stood aside to let him pass, but that was never Robert Molyneux's way with a woman. He flung his arm round her waist in a way so many poor girls had found irresistible. For a minute or two he looked in her dark splendid eyes; but then as he bent lightly to kiss her, she tore herself from him with a cry and ran away into the darkness.

He slept heavily that night, the dead sleep of a man who has hunted all day and has drunk deep in the evening. In the morning he awoke sick and sorry, a strange mood for Robert Molyneux; but from midnight to dawn he had lain with the death-spancel about his knees. In the blackness of his mind he had a great longing for the sweet woman, his love for whom awakened all that was good in him. His horse had fallen lame, but after breakfast he asked his host to order out a carriage that he might go to her. Once with her he thought all would be well. Yet as he stood on the doorstep he had a strange reluctance to go.

It was a drear, grey, miserable day, with sleet pattering against the carriage windows. Robert Molyneux sat with his head bent almost to his knees, and his hands clenched. What face was it rose against his mind, continually blotting out the fair and sweet face of his love? It was the dark, handsome face of the woman he had met on the stairs last night. Some sudden passion for her rose as strong as hell-fire in his breast. There were many long miles between him and Eva, and his desire for the dark woman raged stronger and ever stronger in him. It was as if ropes were around his heart dragging it backward. He fell on his knees in the carriage, and sobbed. If he had known how to pray he would have prayed, for he was torn in two between the desire of his heart for the dark woman, and the longing of his soul for the fair woman. Again and again he started up to call the coachman to turn back; again and again he flung himself in the bottom of the carriage, and hid his face and struggled with the curse that had come upon him. And every mile brought him nearer to Eva and safety.

The coachman drove on in the teeth of the sleet and wondered what Sir Robert would give him at the drive's end. A half-sovereign would not be too much for so open-handed a gentleman, and one so near his wedding; and the coachman, already feeling his hand close upon it, turned a brave face to the sleet and tried not to think of the warm fire in the harness-room from which they had called him to drive Sir Robert.

Half the distance was gone when he heard a voice from the carriage window calling him. He turned round. 'Back! Back!' said the voice. 'Drive like hell! I will give you a sovereign if you do it under an hour.' The coachman was amazed, but a sovereign is better than a half-sovereign. He turned his bewildered horses for home.

Robert Molyneux's struggle was over. Eva's face was gone now altogether. He only felt a mad joy in yielding, and a wild desire for the minutes to pass till he had traversed that grey road back. The coachman drove hard and his horses were flecked with foam, but from the windows Robert Molyneux kept continually urging him, offering him greater and greater rewards for his doing the journey with all speed.

Half way up the cypress avenue to his friend's house a woman with a shawl about her head glided from the shadow and signalled to the darkly flushed face at the carriage window. Robert Molyneux shouted to the man to stop. He sprang from the carriage and lifted the woman in. Then he flung the coachman a handful of gold and silver. 'To Rossatorc,' he said, and the man turned round and once more whipped up his tired horses. The woman laughed as Robert Molyneux caught her in his arms. It was the fierce laughter of the lost. 'I came to meet you,' she said, 'because I knew you must come.'

From that day, when Robert Molyneux led the woman over the threshold of his house, he was seen no more in the usual places of his fellow-men. He refused to see any one who came. His wedding-day passed by. Lord Dunlough had ridden furiously to have an explanation with the fellow and to horsewhip him when that was done, but he found the great door of Rossatorc closed in his face. Every one knew Robert Molyneux was living in shame with Mauryeen Holion. Lady Eva grew pale and paler, and drooped and withered in sorrow and shame, and presently her father took her away, and their house was left to servants. Burly neighbouring squires rode up and knocked with their riding-whips at Rossatorc door to remonstrate with Robert Molyneux, for his father's sake or for his own, but met no answer. All the servants were gone except a furtive-eyed French valet and a woman he called his wife, and these were troubled with no notions of respectability. After a time people gave up trying to interfere. The place got a bad name. The gardens were neglected and the house was half in ruins. No one ever saw Mauryeen Holion's face except it might be at a high window of the castle, when some belated huntsman taking a short-cut across the park would catch a glimpse of a wild face framed in black hair at an upper window, the flare of the winter sunset lighting it up, it might be, as with a radiance from hell. Sir Robert drank, they said, and rack-rented his people far worse than in the old days. He had put his business in the hands of a disreputable attorney from a neighbouring town, and if the rent was not paid to the day the roof was torn off the cabin, and the people flung out into the ditch to rot.

So the years went, and folk ever looked for a judgment of God on the pair. And when many years were over, there came to Father Hugh, wringing her hands, the wife of the Frenchman, with word that the two were dying, and she dared not let them die in their sins.

But Mauryeen Holion, Dark Mauryeen, as they called her, would not to her last breath yield up the death-spancel which she had knotted round her waist, and which held Robert Molyneux's love to her. When the wicked breath was out of her body they cut it away, and it lay twisted on the ground like a dead snake. Then on Robert Molyneux, dying in a distant chamber, came a strange peace. All the years of sin seemed blotted out, and he was full of a simple repentance such as he had felt long ago when kneeling by the gown of the good woman whom he had loved. So Father Hugh absolved him before he died, and went hither and thither through the great empty rooms shaking his holy water, and reading from his Latin book.

And lest any in that place, where they have fiery southern blood in their veins, should so wickedly use philtres or charms, he hung the death-spancel in Aughagree Chapel for a terrible reminder.

1930

THE SEEKER OF SOULS

Rosalie Muspratt (as Jasper John)

Rosalie Helen Muspratt (1906–1976) was born in Freshfields, Lancashire and authored two volumes of supernatural tales, *Sinister Stories* (1930) and *Tales of Terror* (1931), under the pseudonym Jasper John. The daughter of Horace Muspratt and the niece of Sir James Reynolds and Sir Max Muspratt, she supposedly grew up in several haunted houses. Muspratt was a member of the 'Upper Girl Club' (which became the 'Modern Girl Club')—a society which encouraged its members to serve a useful purpose in their lives. Members included the daughter of the then Bishop of Liverpool and the Hon. Sarah Bowes-Lyon. One of their greatest achievements was a now lost thriller where a chapter was written by each member. Her short stories appeared in the *Supernatural Omnibus*; and her sisters Alicia and Olivia were respected artists and singers. During the war she became a nurse whose expertise was in hospital dressings and then making hospital slippers. Her short story, 'The Seeker of Souls' is the story of an English invasion of an Irish castle and the haunted room that the castle fights back with.

It was in a deathly silence that we awaited the coming of the hour that would release the evil thing. I heard someone cough, and it echoed through the house. The clock ticked away the minutes with a grim satisfaction, and my neighbour breathed in a noisy fashion. But for once I was grateful for both sounds; they were something ordinary and commonplace, belonging to everyday life. The moonlight streamed in at the window, making little pools of silver here and there on the walls and floor.

A clattering whirl of machinery, and the clock in the tower commenced to strike the hour. Every stroke of the chimes reverberated through the house. Dead silence for a moment after the last note had quivered away. Then a door banged and there was the sound of shuffling footsteps out in the passage; a strange cry, half animal, half human, but of something enraged. For three nights it had aroused even the deepest sleepers from their slumbers.

The thing, whatever it was, started coming down the passage, banging at the doors as it did so. What was it—man or beast? We only knew that it was horribly evil and paralysed the bravest of us with fear. Inside was darkness save where the moonlight pierced it, and outside, beyond the door, the unknown, the feared. Not for life itself would I have dared to open the barrier which stood between us.

I looked at John. He had sat up in bed. A shaft of moonlight struck him, and I saw his eyes were fixed and staring; he shook like an aspen.

'My God, man, what is it?' His voice was strained and seemed torn from him in the horror of the moment.

But I had no explanation to offer, nor much taste for conversation, so remained silent.

After a time the thing outside grew tired of wandering and returned to its room. A wave of relief swept over us; we felt that since the hour had struck we had been very near to something from hell, something fiendish and very powerful.

Next morning, as usual, we gathered round the breakfast table, and the host looked round at the black-rimmed eyes. I remember everything: the silver vase on the table, filled with red roses, the shining tea-cups and the tense atmosphere.

Three nights of terror were telling on us all. Philip, as host, found our silence jarred on his nerves. Suddenly and irritably he broke out:

'Anyhow, that thing does no harm knocking on the doors, and I must beg you all to keep it from the servants. The other wing will be inhabitable in a few days, and then we will move over there. In the meantime, if anyone is afraid, he is welcome to go. I don't want to keep anyone against his will.'

We were all sorry for him, and somehow it seemed like rats leaving a sinking ship to desert now, though afterwards we wished we had possessed the courage. If anyone had spoken we others would have joined with him, but no one wished to be the first.

It was bad luck for Philip. The place had taken his fancy; a fine, rambling old castle with good fishing and shooting, it was just what he wanted. The view was superb, for it stood high in the hills.

When he had taken it Philip had heard whisperings of ghosts and strange doings; but what Englishman could believe those things? Owing to pressing circumstances of the impoverished family who owned it, the purchase money had been paid in advance.

When the castle was up for sale only one wing was ready for occupation, and none of the servants' quarters. However, we were none of us averse to roughing it with daily helps when it was a question of first-class fishing. So, when Philip had offered the invitation, it had been eagerly accepted.

At last breakfast drew to a close, and Philip made a sign to me to follow him. He took me into the shrubbery and, sitting down on a stump, took out his pipe.

'No one is likely to bother us here,' he said. 'Now, Peter, I want you, as my greatest friend, to help me to get to the bottom of this. We are going to explore the haunted room in daylight while the others are busy with their letters.'

'I am your man,' I answered, with a laugh.

'Well, let's get to work then. I have the key of the side door.'

He got up and started fumbling about until he found a door hidden away amongst the ivy. The hinges were rusty and gave a heavy groan as we pushed it open. I followed Philip up a steep staircase until we came on to the passage, just by the haunted room. He took a big key from his pocket, and the lock turned without a sound.

'Better to keep it shut,' he said. Then, without the slightest misgiving, we stepped inside.

It was a beautiful room, with costly things, but what struck me was that everything was twisting; the legs of the furniture were carved like snakes. Then my eyes wandered to the tapestry. The same design there: serpents wrought in gold, with gleaming red and green eyes, worked on a black ground, with here and there the face of a grinning devil.

It was a beautiful, dreadful room; that was the puzzling part. There was a strong smell of damp fungus and bad, rotting things, though the sun streamed in at the window and there was no sign of mildew. It was uncanny and fascinating, the way everything twisted and writhed. There was not a breath of wind, but the bed hangings moved in a sinuous fashion, like the coils of a snake.

The actual furniture consisted of a four-poster bed, a writing-table, a few chairs and a huge cupboard. The windows were stained glass with a border of leaded panes.

It came to me suddenly, as I stood gazing, that, terror of terrors, MY SOUL WAS BEING STOLEN AWAY; the spirit of the room was tearing it from me. I knew that I must fight as I had never fought before. The devils were trying to get it from me. The knowledge of what it meant gave me strength; in my imagination I saw the whole army of Dante's inferno arrayed against me.

In silent horror I struggled to get out of that room. I had seen the war through; but that was fighting against flesh and blood; this against spirits. Then the awful thing that happened was that one half of me wanted to stay frantically. I fought against it. I suppose that the evil in my nature joined with the evil in that room to betray me to the devils.

My feet seemed as if they had leaden weights attached, my tongue was powerless, and I felt like a helpless child in the grip of a giant. But I hoped that strength would be given me to resist, and I dared not yield to despair.

How long the agony endured I do not know, for it seemed as if the power of that room would draw me to itself as a straw in a whirlpool; but in the end I won through. It was a wonderful moment when I was out in the passage again.

Then I saw through the open door that Philip was still in the room, and experiencing the same horror. His face was white and so set that it was more like a death mask than that of a human being. I tried to call, to help him, but all power was taken from me; I was helpless. So I stood there in mortal fear, gazing and gazing. Then he was out in the passage and the door of the unholy room banged to.

The tension released, we sank down in utter exhaustion. I heard Philip's heavy breathing coupled with my own for a few minutes; then he made a sound between a sob and a groan, and I found the tears coursing down my face.

Fortunately no one came that way. It was fully lunch-time before we had recovered ourselves. There was a thick white streak in Philip's hair which had not been there before. We told them at lunch that we had been down the river together, and had to go through a good amount of chaff about returning empty-handed.

That afternoon a party had been planned, and we had to go. I expect that it was best for us, though we found it very difficult to listen to the idle chatter round us. I had a talk with Philip about moving before that night, but the only accommodation was cottages, and we lacked the courage to give the word to pack. It would only be a few days more until the other wing was ready.

After all, banging on the doors was nothing to what we had been through. As usual, the thing came that night, knocking at the doors; after it had gone I fell into a deep sleep.

Next morning, when I awoke, there was a great noise; everyone seemed to be talking outside in the passage, and someone was crying hysterically. Above all I heard Philip's calm, deep voice restoring order. A few moments afterwards he came to my room, and I saw that beneath his outward calm he was very worried.

He told me that the milkman, making his early rounds, had been attracted by somebody lying under a yew tree. It was a young boy with his throat cut. There was a blood-stained razor in his clenched hand; it looked like a clear case of suicide.

I hastily donned some clothes, while Philip sent the women away with a few stern words about behaving in a foolish manner. All of us men went with Philip to see the body. It was that of a boy of about eighteen. He must have been a handsome lad, for his features were curiously classical and looked, under the hand of death, as if they were chiselled in marble. A long strand of hair fell across his face, and on his throat was a horrible mass of gashes and cuts, evidently wrought by an inexperienced hand.

Only—such a boy! What could have impelled him to this deed? Had he, too, been enmeshed in the evil of the place? Here came to me the desolation, human and spiritual, which I know no words to describe. The wind moved the branches of the tree and a shower of drops fell, as if even Nature wept at such a tragedy.

It is only a confused memory now of what was done and said. I felt that I could have joined the women in their hysterical sobs, but there was Philip to be thought of. They told me afterwards that I kept my head and gave out orders like a robot, with an unmoved face.

The police, such as they were, took most of the responsibility. The old man in charge did not appear unduly surprised; indeed, he took it quite as a matter of course. He walked up to the house with Philip and I, and sat down in the study for a talk. Mechanically, Philip handed him a cigar, and, amid the heavy fumes of smoke, I remember hearing his voice in a rich Irish brogue.

'Well, sir,' he said, warming to his task, 'you don't know this place. There is something here which attracts them to come and die here. There have been some from the house too. 'Tis an evil placed, and cursed so that none can live here, though 'tis a fine place. But I suppose that you did not know, sir. Anyhow, if I were you, sir, I would leave and go away.' He finished with rather an air of triumph at having proved his point to a couple of prosaic Englishmen.

As for Philip, he had sat staring out of the window all this time. Now he roused himself and gave the sergeant a handsome tip for his trouble, and begged him to say as little as possible.

When he had gone we stood at the window and watched the men preparing to take the corpse away. At last the little dark-clad procession passed out of view. Philip turned to me and said: 'Ever heard of an exhortist? I have sent for one to see if he can expel the evil spirit from this place. The car left early this morning; he should be here this evening.'

Our new guest arrived in time for the evening meal. He was short and jovial and kept us all amused by his chatter, but he never made any mention of spirits or ghosts. He seemed to know most of the details when Philip tried to tell him. He warned us that the thing would make more noise that night, but he promised that no harm should come to us.

All was quiet as usual until the hour struck. Then the thing came out and raged up and down. When it came to the door of the exhortist it rattled at the handle and screamed with rage. At last it wearied of its wanderings and returned to the room. The exhortist told us that he had passed the night in prayer.

Next morning, after breakfast, the ceremony of expelling the evil spirit took place. We all waited outside in the passage while the exhortist went alone into the room, having enjoined us not to come in, whatever happened.

In a loud, clear voice he began the prayers, holding a book and a lighted candle in his hands. First thing the candle went out; then his face began to distort itself in various grimaces. When the prayer was finished candle and book fell to the ground. He appeared to be fighting for breath, and cried out that he was being throttled.

We tried to move, but were transfixed. There were strange moanings, cries and groans; then he was thrown with violence into the passage and the door banged to.

The spell being broken, we bent anxiously over the victim, but he had gone into a dead faint and there were red marks on his throat. We carried him to his room and laid him on the bed. When he recovered consciousness it was very evident that he had been face to face with something very dreadful even for a man used to evil and sinister things.

We were debating to send for a doctor, but he overheard, and forbade us. He said these things were among the incomprehensible and beyond the sphere of man. He spoke to Philip alone, and told him that the place was evil and it was better to go, for there was a terrible power hidden in that room. When Philip came out he told us all to pack, as he had decided to leave next day.

We were all so occupied that it was only when we heard the powerful engines of a car coming up the drive that we remembered Guy Dennis was expected. He was very popular, with his good nature and cheery ways. He asked if we were not glad to see him, and why we all looked like a pack of ghosts. Then Philip started to explain in a mild way what had happened. Guy burst into fits of laughter. So Philip lost his temper and told him the bare truth, and we all bore witness to it. Guy saw that we were really serious about it.

'Dreadfully sorry,' he said, 'to be such an unbelieving sinner.' And he laughed again.

There was something very cheering to have him there laughing at our fears, with his six-foot-four of common sense.

'I suggest a drink all round now, and request that I may sleep in your haunted room,' he said.

The first part of the request was granted, but Philip was very firm in his 'No' to the other.

I must confess that, under Guy's influence, I almost thought that the whole thing was only overwrought imagination, but a sense of fear and depression soon returned. That evening passed fairly quickly. We all got into bed with a feeling of relief that it was to be our last night in that place!

I fell almost immediately into a heavy sleep, and I dreamt that I was in a prison cell and that all around me were people being tortured. They brought in a huge man, bound, and commenced to put out his eyes. His screams were dreadful to hear. Then I woke to find myself in bed, but the cry still rang in my ears. I leapt out of bed, for it was coming from the passage. I stumbled out with a candle, and found the others there before me.

It was with a great shock that I saw Guy Dennis rolling about in the passage, alternately laughing and crying; for he was raving mad. I heard a voice say he had tried to sleep in that room just so as to be able to laugh at us in the morning, and this was what had happened!

We all stood there watching Guy laughing and showing his teeth. Then suddenly his mood changed and he rushed at us in a rage. There was a grim fight; candles fell to the ground and were trodden out, but in the end we overpowered him and bound him with sheets. Most of us were bleeding, for Guy had used teeth and nails against us.

The struggle had exhausted him. He went off into a faint, while the foam dried on his lips. We threw water on him and rubbed his temples. He opened his eyes with a groan and started moving his lips, but he was inaudible at first; then he started talking as if in a dream.

'I sorry—wanted to sleep there... light, such a queer light. No, it was a pillar of whitish matter, near, very near. There was something green in the middle... damp and wet. It came out... I can see it! It is all eyes... no, all hands... no, all face, all claws! It has hundreds of eyes. I must look at it! They are dreadful eyes; they scorch... no, they freeze me, but I must look. Now it has only half a face; but the eyes!... It laughs at me and gibbers. It is thrusting me out. I want to go back. The door is shut and the master calls me. Master, I cannot get back; it is not my fault.' He tried to rise and fell back, quieter.

For a short time he slept, but about two o'clock he woke again and started moaning and praying.

'Take me away, take me away, for Heaven's sake take me away! Have pity, have pity!' He tossed to and fro in his agony and fear. 'It is calling me; I must go back!' he moaned.

We were a weird group round the figure on the bed, all dressed in oddments of clothes.

The exhortist said that we must get him away at once, out of the house; that the power of evil was very prevalent that night.

Six of us carried Guy between us. He had gone into a trance again, so it was not difficult. Down the dark passage and the great oak staircase we went, men up against the great unknown, and very fearful.

Philip had locked and barred the door with care that night. We were obliged to put our burden down to struggle with the fastenings; as our hands were trembling, it took some time. At last the great door swung open on its hinges.

We stepped out into the warm darkness, and the procession continued down the drive, our way lit by a storm lantern. Long, dark shadows stole across the path, and every dark bush seemed to contain some lurking terror. Then, with a soft whirl of wings, an owl flew across our path.

When we reached the gates they were as welcome for us flying from evil in the dark night, as those of Paradise. The gamekeeper's cottage was quite near, Philip said; so we walked on in silence.

The little cabin was all in darkness, but it did not take very long to rouse the good man and his wife. The Irish are very quick to understand and they did not ask an undue number of questions until we were ready to tell them. Nor were they incredulous at our story.

The good woman made a bed for Guy and we laid him on it. Poor Guy, he never recovered from that night; we were obliged to leave him in an asylum in Dublin. From time to time he would break out in violent fits when the memory of what he had seen broke upon him. I often go and see him.

The next day Philip and I went back to shut up the house. It looked very pleasant in the sunlight, that haunt of evil. We did as little as possible; it was too full of awful memories to linger. At the lodge gates we looked back for the last time. The sun was blazing down and the gardens were bright with colour; then the gate shut behind us on the dreadful secret evil which reigned there.

1942

THE GREEN GRAVE AND THE BLACK GRAVE

Mary Lavin

Mary Josephine Lavin (1912–1996) was born in Massachusetts as the only child of an Irish immigrant couple. When she was nine years old the family returned to Ireland and she would spend much of her life in County Meath, the setting for many of her stories. Her first published story, 'Miss Holland' (1939), appeared in *The Dublin Magazine* and the following collection of short stories, *Tales from Bective Bridge* (1942), was awarded the James Tait Black Memorial Prize. Her stories regularly appeared in magazines including *New Yorker* and *Atlantic Monthly* and mainly focused on Irish rural life and Catholic faith. She is notable for many of her stories around widowhood which drew upon her own experiences after her first husband died less than a decade into their marriage. Following her death in 1996 she became the first Irish female writer to have a public space, Mary Lavin Place, named after her. Her granddaughter is the broadcaster and novelist Kathleen McMahon. 'The Green Grave and the Black Grave' is a truly stunning work of fiction and was described by V. S. Pritchett as 'a tale of the Gaelic, but far more moving and richer in meaning than, say, Synge's *Riders to the Sea* and to have a subtler tragic force'.

I

IT was a body, all right. It was hard to see in the dark, and the scale-back sea was heaving up between them and the place where they saw the thing floating. But it was a body, all right.

'I knew it was a shout I heard,' said the taller of the two tall men in the black boat, that was out fishing for mackerel. He was Tadg Mor and he was the father of the less tall man, that was blacker in the hair than him and broader in the chest than him, but was called Tadg Beag because he was son to him. Mor means big and Beag means small, but Mor can be given to mean greater and Beag can be given to mean lesser than the greater.

'I knew it was a shout I heard,' said Tadg Mor.

'I knew it was a boat I saw and I dragging in the second net,' said Tadg Beag.

'I said the sound I heard was a kittwake, crying in the dark.'

'And I said the boat I saw was a black wave blown up on the wind.'

'It was a shout, all right.'

'It was a boat, all right.'

'It was a body, all right.'

'But where is the black boat?' said Tadg Beag.

'It must be that the black boat capsized,' said Tadg Mor, 'and went down into the green sea.'

'Whose boat was it, would you venture for to say?' said Tadg Beag, pulling stroke for stroke at the sea.

'I'd venture for to say it was the boat of Eamon Og Murnan,' said Tadg Mor, pulling with his oar at the spittle-painted sea.

The tall men rowed against the sharp up-pointing waves of the scaly, scurvy sea. They rowed to the clumsy thing that tossed on the tips of the deft green waves.

'Eamon Og Murnan,' said Tadg Mor, lifting clear his silver-dripping oar.

'Eamon Og Murnan,' said Tadg Beag, lifting his clear, dripping, silver oar.

It was a hard drag, dragging him over the arching sides of the boat. His clothes logged him down to the water, and the jutting waves jostled him back against the boat. His yellow hair slipped from their fingers like floss, and the fibres of his island-spun clothes broke free from their grip. But they got him up over the edge of the boat, at the end of a black hour that was only lit by the whiteness of the breaking wave. They laid him down on the boards of the floor on their haul of glittering mackerel and they spread the nets out over him. But the scales of the fish glittered up through the net, and so too the eyes of Eamon Og Murnan glittered up through the nets. And the live glitter of those dead eyes put a strain on Tadg Mor and he turned the body over on its face among the fish, and when they had looked a time at the black corpse with yellow hair set in the silver and opal casket of fishes, they put the ends of the oars in the oarlocks and turned the oar blades out again into the scurvy waves and turned their boat back to the land.

'How did you know it was Eamon Og Murnan, and we forty pointed waves away from him at the time of your naming his name?' said Tadg Beag to Tadg Mor.

'Whenever it is a thing that a man is pulled under by the sea,' said Tadg Mor, 'think around in your mind until you think out which man of all the men it might be that would be the man most missed, and that man, that you think out in your mind, will be the man that will be netted up on the shingle.'

'This is a man that will be missed mightily,' said Tadg Beag.

'He is a man that will be mightily bemoaned,' said Tadg Mor.

'He is a man that will never be replaced.'

'He is a man that will be prayed for bitterly and mightily.'

'And food will be set out for him every night in a bowl,' said Tadg Beag.

'The Brightest and the Bravest!' said Tadg Mor. 'Those are the words will be read over him—"The Brightest and the Bravest."'

The boat rose up on the points of the waves and clove down again between the points, and the oars of Tadg Mor and the oars of Tadg Beag split the points of many waves.

'How is it the green sea always greeds after the brightest and the bravest?' Tadg Beag asked Tadg Mor.

'And for the only sons?' asked Tadg Mor.

'And the men with one-year wives?'

'The one-year wife that's getting this corpse tonight,' said Tadg Mor, pointing down with his eyes, 'will have a black sorrow this night.'

'And every night after this night,' said Tadg Beag, because he was a young man and knew about such things.

'It's a great thing that he was not dragged down to the green grave, and that is a thing will lighten the nights of the one-year wife,' said Tadg Mor.

'It isn't many are saved out of the green grave,' said Tadg Beag.

'Kirnan Mor wasn't got,' said Tadg Mor.

'And Murnan Beag wasn't got.'

'Lorcan Mor wasn't got.'

'Tirnan Beag wasn't got.'

'It was three weeks and the best part of a night before the Frenchman with the leather coat was got, and five boats out looking for him.'

'It was seven weeks before Lorcan Mac Kinealy was got, and his eye sockets emptied by the gulls and the gannies.'

'And by the waves. The waves are great people to lick out your eyeballs!' said Tadg Mor.

'It was a good thing, this man to be got,' said Tadg Beag, 'and his eyes bright in his head.'

'Like he was looking up at the sky!'

'Like he was thinking to smile next thing he'd do.'

'He was a great man to smile, this man,' said Tadg Mor. 'He was ever and always smiling.'

'He was a great man to laugh, too,' said Tadg Beag. 'He was ever and always laughing.'

'Times he was laughing and times he was not laughing,' said Tadg Mor.

'Times all men stop from laughing,' said Tadg Beag.

'Times I saw this man and he not laughing. Times I saw him and he putting out in the black boat looking back at the inland woman where she'd be standing on the shore and her hair weaving the wind, and there wouldn't be any laugh on his face those times.'

'An island man should take an island wife,' said Tadg Beag.

'An inland woman should take an inland man.'

'The inland woman that took this man had a dreadful dread on her of the sea and the boats that put out in it.'

'I saw this woman from the inlands standing on the shore, times, from his putting out with the hard dry boat to his coming back with the shivering silver-belly boat.'

'He got it hard to go from her every night.'

'He got it harder than iron to go from her if there was a streak of storm gold in the sky at time of putting out.'

'An island man should not be held down to a woman from the silent inlands.'

'It was love talk and love looks that held down this man,' said Tadg Mor.

'The island women give love words and love looks too,' said Tadg Beag.

'But not the love words and the love looks of this woman,' said Tadg Mor.

'Times I saw her wetting her feet in the waves and wetting her fingers in the waves, and you'd see she was kind of lovering the waves so they'd bring him back to her.'

'Times he told me himself she had a dreadful dread of the green grave. "There dies as many men in the inlands as in the islands," I said. "Tell her that," I said. "I tell her that," said he. "'But they get the black-grave burial,' she says. 'They get the black-grave burial in clay that's blessed by two priests, and they get the speeding of the green sods thrown down by the kinsmen,' she says. "Tell her there's no worms in the green grave," I said to him. "I did," said he. "What did she say to that?" said I. "She said, 'The bone waits for the bone,'" said he. "What does she mean by that?" said I. "She gave another saying as her meaning to that saying," said he. "She said, 'There's no trouble in death when two go down together into the one black grave. Clay binds closer than love,' she said. 'But the green grave binds nothing,' she said. 'The green grave scatters,' she said. 'The green grave is for sons,' she said, 'and for brothers,' she said, 'but the black grave is for lovers,' she said, 'and for husbands in the faithful clay under the jealous sods."'

'She must be a great woman to make sayings,' said Tadg Beag.

'She made great sayings for that man every hour of the day, and she stitching the nets for him on the step while he'd be salting fish or blading oars.'

'She'll be glad us to have saved him from the salt green grave.'

'It's a great wonder but he was dragged down before he was got.'

'She is the kind of woman that always has great wonders happening round her,' said Tadg Mor. 'If she is a woman from the inlands itself, she has a great power in herself. She has a great power over the sea. Times and she on the cliff shore and her hair weaving the wind, like I told you, I'd point my eyes through the wind across at where Eamon Og would be in the waves back of me and there wouldn't be as much as one white tongue of spite rising out of the waves around his boat, and my black boat would be splattered over every board of it with white sea spittle.'

'I heard tell of women like that. She took the fury out of the sea and burnt it out to white salt in her own heart.'

II

The talk about the inland woman who fought the seas in her heart was slow talk and heavy talk, and slow and heavy talk was fit talk as the scurvy waves crawled over one another, scale by scale, and brought the bitter boat back to the shore.

Sometimes a spiteful tongue of foam forked up in the dark by the side of the boat and reached for the netted corpse on the boards. When this happened Tadg Beag picked up the loose end of the raggy net and lashed out with it at the sea.

'Get down, you scaly-belly serpent,' he said, 'and let the corpse dry out in his dead-clothes.'

'Take heed to your words, Tadg Beag,' Tadg Mor would say. 'We have the point to round yet. Take heed to your words!'

'Here's a man took heed to his words and that didn't save him,' said Tadg Beag. 'Here was a man was always singing back song for song to the singing sea, and look at him now lying there.'

They looked at him lying on his face under the brown web of the nets in his casket of fish scales, silver and opal. And as they looked another lick of the forked and venomous tongue of the sea came up the side of the boat and strained in towards the body. Tadg Beag beat at it with the raggy net.

'Keep your strength for the loud knocking you'll have to give on the wooden door,' said Tadg Mor. And Tadg Beag understood that he was the one would walk up the shingle and bring the death news to the one-year wife, who was so strange among the island women with her hair weaving the wind at evening and her white feet wetted in the sea by day.

'Is it not a thing that she'll be, likely, out on the shore?' he said in a bright hope, pointing his eyes to where the white edge of the shore wash shone by its own light in the dark.

'Is there a storm tonight?' said Tadg Mor. 'Is there a high wind tonight? Is there a rain spate? Is there any sign of danger on the sea?'

'No,' said Tadg Beag, 'there are none of those things that you mention.'

'I will tell you the reason you ask that question,' said Tadg Mor. 'You ask that question because that question is the answer that you'd like to get.'

'It's a hard thing to bring news to a one-year wife, and she one that has a dreadful dread of the sea,' said Tadg Beag.

'It's good news you're bringing to the one-year wife when you bring news that her man is got safe to go down like any inlander into a black grave blessed and tramped down with the feet of his kinsmen on the sod.'

'It's a queer thing, him to be caught by the sea on a fine night with no wind blowing,' said Tadg Beag.

'On a fine night the women lie down to sleep, and if any woman has a power over the sea with her white feet in the water and her black hair on the wind and a bright fire in her heart, the sea can only wait until that woman's spirit is out of her body, likely back home in the inlands, and then the sea serpent gives a slow turn over on his scales, one that you wouldn't heed to, yourself, maybe and you standing up with no hold on the oars, and before there's time for more than the first shout out of you the boat is logging down to the depths of the water. And all the time the woman that would have saved you, with her willing and wishing for you, is in the deep bed of the dark sleep, having no knowledge of the thing that has happened until she hears the loud-handed knocking of the neighbour on the door outside.'

Tadg Beag knocked with his knuckles on the sideboards of the boat.

'Louder than that,' said Tadg Mor.

Tadg Beag knocked another louder knock on the boat sides.

'Have you no more knowledge than that of how to knock at a door in the fastness of the night, and the people inside the house buried in sleep and the corpse down on the shore getting covered with sand and the fish scales drying into him so tight that the fingernails of the washing women will be broken and split peeling them off him? Have you no more knowledge than that of how to knock with your knucklebones?'

Tadg Mor gave a loud knocking against the wet seat of the boat.

'That is the knock of a man that you might say knows how to knock at a door, daytime or night-time,' he said, and he knocked again.

And he knocked again, louder, if it could be that any knock he gave could be louder than the first knock. Tadg Beag listened and then he spoke, not looking at Tadg Mor, but looking at the oar he was rolling in the water.

'Two people knocking would make a loud knocking entirely, I would think,' he said.

'One has to stay with the dead,' said Tadg Mor.

Tadg Beag drew a long stroke on the oar and he drew a long breath out of his lungs and he took a long look at the nearing shore.

'What will I say,' he said, 'when she comes to my knocking?'

'When she comes to the knocking, step back a bit from the door, so's she'll see the wet shining on you, and so's she'll smell the salt water off you, and say in a loud voice that the sea is queer and rough this night.'

'She'll be down with her to the shore, if that's what I say, without waiting to hear more.'

'Say, then,' said Tadg Mor, pulling in the oar to slow the boat a bit, 'say that there's news come in that a boat went down off beyond the point.'

'If I say that, she'll be down with her to the shore without waiting to hear more, and her hair flying and her white feet freezing on the shingle.'

'If that is so,' said Tadg Mor, 'then you'll have to stand back bold from the door and call out loudly in the night: "The Brightest and the Bravest!"'

'What will she say to that?'

'She'll say, "God bless them."'

'And what will I say to that?'

'You'll say, "God rest them."'

'And what will she say to that?'

'She'll say, "Is it in the black grave or the green grave?"'

'And what will I say to that?'

'You say, "God rest Eamon Og Murnan in the black grave in the holy ground, blessed by the priest and sodded by the people."'

'And what will she say to that?'

'She'll say, likely, "Bring him in to me, Tadg Beag!"'

'And what will I say to that?'

'Whatever you say after that, let it be loud and making echoes under the rafters, so she won't hear the sound of the corpse dragging up on the shingle, and when he's lifted up on to the scoured table, let whatever you say be loud then too, so's she won't be listening for the sound of the water drabbling down off his clothes on the floor!'

III

There was only the noise of the oars, then, till a shoaly sounding stole in between the oar strokes. It was the shoaly sounding of the irritable pebbles that were dragged back and forth on the shore by the tides.

They beached in a little while, and they stepped out among the sprawling waves and dragged the boat after them till it cleft its depth in the damp shingle.

'See that you give a loud knocking, Tadg Beag,' said Tadg Mor, and Tadg Beag set his head against the darkness and his feet were heard for a good time grinding down the shifting shingle as he made for the house of the one-year wife. The house was set in a sea field, and his feet did not sound down to the shore once he got to the dune grass of the sea field. But in another little while there was a loud sound of a fist knocking hard upon wood, stroke after stroke of a strong hand coming down on hard wood.

Tadg Mor, waiting with the body in the boat, recalled to himself all the times he went knocking on the island doors bringing news to the women of the death of their men, but island women were brought up in bitterness and they got life as well as death from the sea. They keened for their own, and it would be hard to know by their keening whether it was for their own men or the men of their neighbours they were keening. Island wives were the daughters of island widows. The sea gave food. The sea gave death. Life or death, it was all one thing in the end. The sea never lost its scabs. The sea was there before the coming of man. Island women knew that knowledge, but what knowledge had a woman from the inlands of the sea and its place in the world since the beginning of time? No knowledge. An inland woman had no knowledge to guide her when the loud knocking came on her door in the night.

Tadg Mor listened to the loud, hard knocking of his son Tadg Beag on the door of the one-year wife of Eamon Og Murnan that was lying in the silver casket of fishes on the floor of the boat, cleft fast in the shingle sand. The night was cold, the fish scales glittered even though it was dark. They glittered in the whiteness made by the breaking wave on the shore. The sound of the sea was sadder than the back of the head of the yellow-haired corpse, but still Tadg Mor was gladder to be down on the shore than up in the dune grass knocking at the one-night widow's door.

The knocking sound of Tadg Beag's knuckles on the wooden door was a human sound and it sounded good in the ears of Tadg Mor for a time, but, like all sounds that continue too long, it sounded soon to be as weird and inhuman as the washing sound of the waves tiding in on the shingle. Tadg Mor put up his rounded palms to his mouth and shouted out to Tadg Beag to come back to the boat. Tadg Beag came back running the shingle, and the air was grained with sounds of sliding gravel.

'There's no one in the house where you were knocking,' said Tadg Mor.

'I knocked louder on the door than you knocked on the boat boards,' said Tadg Beag.

'I heard how you knocked,' said Tadg Mor; 'you knocked well. But let you knock better when you go to the neighbour's house to find out where the one-night widow is from her own home this night.'

'If I got no answer at one door, is it likely I'll get an answer at another door?' said Tadg Beag. 'It was you yourself I heard to say one time that the man that knows how a thing is to be done is the man should do that thing when that thing is to be done.'

'How is a man to get the knowledge of how to do a thing if that man doesn't do that thing when that thing is to be done?' said Tadg Mor.

Tadg Beag got into the boat again, and they sat there in the dark. After four or maybe five waves had broken by their side, Tadg Beag lifted the net and felt the clothes of Eamon Og.

'The clothes is drying into him,' he said.

'If I was to go up with you to the house of Sean-bhean O Suillebheain, who would there be to watch the dead?' said Tadg Mor, and then Tadg Beag knew that Tadg Mor was going with him and he had no need to put great heed on the answer he gave to him.

'Let the sea watch him,' he said, putting a leg out over the boat after the wave went back with its fistful of little complaining pebbles.

'We must take him out of the boat first,' said Tadg Mor. 'Take hold of him there by the feet,' he said as he rolled back the net, putting it over the oar with each roll so it would not ravel and knot.

They lifted Eamon Og Murnan out of the boat, and the mackerel slipped about their feet into the place where he had left his shape. They dragged him up a boat length from the sprawling waves and they faced his feet to the shore, but when they saw that that left his head lower than his feet, because the shingle shelved greatly at that point, they faced him about again towards the scurvy waves that were clashing their sharp, pointy scales together and sending up spits of white spray in the air. The dead man glittered with the silver and verdigris scales of the mackerel that were clinging to his clothing over every part.

IV

Tadg Mor went up the sliding shingle in front of Tadg Beag, and Tadg Beag put his feet in the shelves that were made in the shingle by Tadg Mor, because the length of the step they took was the same length. The sea sounded in their ears as they went through the shingle, but by the time the first coarse dune grass scratched at their clothing the only sound that each could hear was the sound of the other's breathing.

The first cottage that rose out blacker than the night in their path was the cottage where Tadg Beag made the empty knocking. Tadg Mor stopped in front of the door as if he might be thinking of trying his hand at knocking, but he thought better of it and went on after Tadg Beag to the house that was next to that house, and that was the house of Sean-bhean O Suillebheain, one to know anything that eye or ear could know about those that lived within three right miles of her.

Tadg Mor hit the door of Sean-bhean O Suillebheain's house with a knock of his knuckles, and although it was a less loud knock than the echo of the knock that came down to the shore when Tadg Beag struck the first knock on the door of the wife of Eamon Og, there was a foot to the floor before he could raise his knuckle off the wood for another knock. A candle lit up and a shadow fell across the window-pane and a face came whitening at the door gap.

'You came to the wrong house this dark night,' said Sean-bhean O Suillebheain. 'The sea took all the men was ever in this house twelve years ago and two months and seventeen days.'

'It may be that we have no corpse for this house, but we came to the right house for all that,' said Tadg Mor. 'We came to this house for knowledge of the house across two sea fields from this house where we got no answer to our knocking with our knuckles,' said Tadg Mor.

'And I knocked with a stone up out of the ground, as well,' said Tadg Beag, coming closer.

The woman with the candle flame blowing drew back into the dark.

'Is it for the inland woman, the one-year's wife, you're bringing the corpse you have below in the boat this night?' she said.

'It is, God help us,' said Tadg Mor.

'It is, God help us,' said Tadg Beag.

'The Brightest and the Bravest,' said Tadg Mor.

'Is it a thing that you got no answer to your knocking?' said the old woman, bending out again with the blowing candle flame.

'No answer,' said Tadg Beag, 'and sturdy knocking.'

'Knocking to be heard above the sound of the sea,' said Tadg Mor.

'They sleep deep, the people from the inland?' said Tadg Beag, asking a question.

'The people of the inland sleep deep in the cottage in the middle of the field,' said Sean-bhean O Suillebheain, 'but when they're rooted up and set down by the sea their spirit never passes out of hearing of the step on the shingle. It's a queer thing entirely that you got no answer to your knocking.'

'We got no answer to our knocking,' said Tadg Mor and Tadg Beag, bringing their words together like two oars striking the one wave, one on this side of the boat and one on that.

'When the inland woman puts her face down on the feather pillow,' said Sean-bhean O Suillebheain, 'that pillow is but as the sea shells children put against their ears, that pillow has the sad crying voices of the sea.'

'Is it that you think she is from home this night?' said Tadg Mor.

'It must be a thing that she is,' said the old woman.

'Is it back to her people in the inlands she'll be gone?' said Tadg Beag, who had more than the curiosity of the night in him.

'Step into the kitchen,' said the old woman, 'while I ask Inghean Og if she saw Bean Eamuin Og go from her house this night.'

While she went into the room that was in from the kitchen, Tadg Beag put a foot inside the kitchen door, but Tadg Mor stayed looking down to the shore.

'If it is a thing the inland woman is from home entirely, where will we put Eamon Og, that we have below in the boat with his face and no sheet on it, and his eyes and no lids drawn down tight over them, and the fish scales sticking to him faster than they stuck to the mackerels when they swam beyond the nets, blue and silver and green?'

'Listen to Inghean Og,' said Tadg Beag, and he stepped a bit further into the kitchen of Sean-bhean O Suillebheain.

'Inghean Og,' came the voice of the old, old woman, 'is it a thing that the inland woman from two fields over went from her house this night?'

'It is a true thing that she went,' said Inghean Og, and Tadg Beag spoke to Tadg Mor and said, 'Inghean Og talks soft in the day, but she talks as soft as the sea in summer when she talks in the night in the dark.'

'Listen to what she says,' said Tadg Mor, coming in a step after Tadg Beag.

'Is it that she went to her people in the inlands?' said Sean-bhean O Suillebheain, who never left the island.

'The wife of Eamon Og never stirred a foot to her people in the inlands since the first day she came to the islands, in her blue dress with the beads,' said the voice of Inghean Og.

'Where did she go, then,' said the old woman, 'if it is a thing that she didn't go to her people in the inlands?'

'Where else but where she said she'd go?' said the voice of Inghean Og. 'Out in the boat with her one-year husband.'

There was sound of aged springs writhing in the room where Inghean Og slept, back behind the kitchen, and her voice was clearer and stronger, as if she were sitting up in the bed looking out at the black sea and the white points rising in it by the light of their own brightness.

'She said the sea would never drag Eamon Og down to the cold green grave and leave her to lie lonely in the black grave on the shore, in the black clay that held tight, under the weighty sods. She said a man and woman should lie in the one grave forever. She said a night never passed without her heart being burnt out to a cold white salt. She said that this night, and every night after, she'd go out with Eamon in the black boat over the scabby back of the sea. She said if ever he got the green grave, she'd get the green grave too, with her arms clinging to him closer than the weeds of the sea, binding them down together. She said that the island women never fought the sea. She said that the sea wanted taming and besting. She said the island women had no knowledge of love. She said there was a curse on the black clay for women that lay alone in it while their men floated in the caves of the sea. She said that the black clay was all right for inland women. She said that the black clay was all right for sisters and mothers. She said the black clay was all right for girls that died at seven years. But the green grave is the grave for wives, she said, and she went out in the black boat this night and she's going out every night after,' said Inghean Og.

'Tell her there will be no night after,' said Tadg Mor.

'Let her sleep till day,' said Tadg Beag. 'Time enough to tell her in the day,' and he strained his eyes behind the flutter-flame candle as the old woman came out from Inghean Og's room.

'You heard what she said,' said the old woman.

'It's a bad thing he was got,' said Tadg Beag.

'That's a thing was never said on this island before this night,' said Tadg Mor.

'There was a fire on every point of the cliff shore,' said the old woman, 'to light home the men who were dragging for Kirnan Mor.'

'And he never was got,' said Tadg Mor.

'There was a shroud spun for Tirnan Beag between the time of the putting out of the island boats to look for him and their coming back with the empty news in the green daylight,' said the old woman.

'Tirnan Beag was never got.'

'Kirnan Mor was never got.'

'Lorcan Mor was never got.'

'Murnan Beag was never got.'

'My four sons were never got,' said the old woman.

'The father of Inghean Og was never got,' said Tadg Beag, and he was looking at the shut door of the room where Inghean Og was lying in the dark; the candle shadows were running their hands over that door.

'The father of Inghean Og was never got,' said Tadg Beag again, forgetting what he was saying.

'Of all the men that had yellow coffins standing up on their ends by the gable, and all the men that had brown shrouds hanging up on the wall with the iron nail eating out its way through the yarn, it had to be the one man that should have never been got that was got,' said Tadg Beag, opening the top half of the door and letting in the deeper sound of the tide.

'That is the way,' said Tadg Mor.

'That is ever and always the way,' said the old woman.

'The sea is stronger than any man,' said Tadg Mor.

'The sea is stronger than any woman,' said Tadg Beag.

'The sea is stronger than women from the inland fields,' said Tadg Mor.

'The sea is stronger than *talk* of love,' said Tadg Beag, when he was out in the dark. It was too dark, after the candlelight, to see where the window was of Inghean Og's room, but he was looking where it might be while he buttoned over his jacket.

V

Tadg Mor and Tadg Beag went back to the shore over the sliding shingle, keeping their feet well on the shelving gravel, as they went towards the sprawling waves. The waves were up to the place where the sea-break was made that spring in the graywacke wall. The boat was floating free out of the cleft in the shingle.

The body of Eamon Og, that had glittered with fish scales of opal and silver and verdigris, was gone from the shore. They knew it was gone from the black land that was cut crisscross with grave cuts by the black spade and the shovel. They knew it was gone and would never be got.

'Kirnan Mor wasn't got.'

'Murnan Beag wasn't got.'

'Lorcan Mor wasn't got.'

'Tirnan Beag wasn't got.'

'The four sons of the Sean-bhean O Suillebheain were never got.'

'The father of Inghean Og wasn't got.'

The men of the island were caught down in the sea by the tight weeds of the sea. They were held in the tendrils of the sea anemone and the pricks of the sallow thorn, by the green sea grasses and the green sea reeds and the winding stems of the green sea daffodils. But Eamon Og Murnan would be held fast in the white sea arms of his one-year wife, who came from the inlands where women have no knowledge of the sea and have only a knowledge of love.

Brittany

1893

THE OTHER SIDE: A BRETON LEGEND

Count Eric Stanislaus Stenbock

Count Eric Stanislaus Stenbock (1860–1895) was the son of Lucy Sophia Stenbock, the daughter of a German cotton importer, and Erich Friedrick Diedrich Magnus Stenbock, a member of Swedish and Russian aristocracy. Information about his early life is meagre but he was by accounts a sickly child. He lived in England for most of his life and attended Balliol College in Oxford, but he only attended four terms, and never completed his studies. He had a reputation for being eccentric and had a life-sized doll, which he referred to as 'The Little Count', accompany him wherever he went. He informed people that the doll was his son and if the doll was absent he would frequently ask about its health. In 1881 he published his first book, *Love, Sleep and Dreams,* a collection of melancholic poems. This was followed by a lengthier collection, *Myrtle, Rue and Cypress* (1883), and a final volume of verse, *The Shadow of Death* (1894). He struggled with alcoholism and opium addiction during his short life and these issues contributed to him dying of cirrhosis of the liver in 1895, the year after his collection of short stories, *Studies of Death* (1894), appeared in print. 'The Other Side', which first appeared in the Oxford-based journal *The Spirit Lamp,* tells the story of Gabriel, a boy who crosses a brook and meets a pack of were-things on the other side…

A la joyouse Messe noire.

'NOT that I like it, but one does feel so much better after it—oh, thank you, Mère Yvonne, yes just a little drop more.' So the old crones fell to drinking their hot brandy and water (although of course they only took it medicinally, as a remedy for their rheumatics), all seated round the big fire and Mère Pinquèle continued her story.

'Oh, yes, then when they get to the top of the hill, there is an altar with six candles quite black and a sort of something in between, that nobody sees quite clearly, and the old black ram with the man's face and long horns begins to say Mass in a sort of gibberish nobody understands, and two black strange things like monkeys glide about with the book and the cruets—and there's music too, such music. There are things the top half like black cats, and the bottom part like men only their legs are all covered with close black hair, and they play on the bagpipes, and when they come to the elevation, then—' Amid the old crones there was lying on the hearth-rug, before the fire, a boy, whose large lovely eyes dilated and whose limbs quivered in the very ecstasy of terror.

'Is that all true, Mère Pinquèle?' he said.

'Oh, quite true, and not only that, the best part is yet to come; for they take a child and—.' Here Mère Pinquèle showed her fang-like teeth.

'Oh! Mère Pinquèle, are you a witch too?'

'Silence, Gabriel,' said Mère Yvonne, 'how can you say anything so wicked? Why, bless me, the boy ought to have been in bed ages ago.'

Just then all shuddered, and all made the sign of the cross except Mère Pinquèle, for they heard that most dreadful of dreadful sounds—the howl of a wolf, which begins with three sharp barks and then lifts itself up in a long protracted wail of commingled cruelty and despair, and at last subsides into a whispered growl fraught with eternal malice.

There was a forest and a village and a brook, the village was on one side of the brook, none had dared to cross to the other side. Where the village was, all was green and glad and fertile and fruitful; on the other side the trees never put forth green leaves, and a dark shadow hung over it even at noon-day, and in the night-time one could hear the wolves howling—the were-wolves and the wolf-men and the men-wolves, and those very wicked men who for nine days in every year are turned into wolves; but on the green side no wolf was ever seen, and only one little running brook like a silver streak flowed between.

It was spring now and the old crones sat no longer by the fire but before their cottages sunning themselves, and everyone felt so happy that they ceased to tell stories of the 'other side.' But Gabriel wandered by the brook as he was wont to wander, drawn thither by some strange attraction mingled with intense horror.

His schoolfellows did not like Gabriel; all laughed and jeered at him, because he was less cruel and more gentle of nature than the rest, and even as a rare and beautiful bird escaped from a cage is hacked to death by the common sparrows, so was Gabriel among his fellows. Everyone wondered how Mère Yvonne, that buxom and worthy matron, could have produced a son like this, with strange dreamy eyes, who was as they said 'pas comme les autres gamins.' His only friends were the Abbé Félicien whose Mass he served each morning, and one little girl called Carmeille, who loved him, no one could make out why.

The sun had already set, Gabriel still wandered by the brook, filled with vague terror and irresistible fascination. The sun set and the moon rose, the full moon, very large and very clear, and the moonlight flooded the forest both this side and 'the other side,' and just on the 'other side' of the brook, hanging over, Gabriel saw a large deep blue flower, whose strange intoxicating perfume reached him and fascinated him even where he stood.

'If I could only make one step across,' he thought, 'nothing could harm me if I only plucked that one flower, and nobody would know I had been over at all,' for the villagers looked with hatred and suspicion on anyone who was said to have crossed to the 'other side,' so summing up courage he leapt lightly to the other side of the brook. Then the moon breaking from a cloud shone with unusual brilliance, and he saw, stretching before him, long reaches of the same strange blue flowers each one lovelier than the last, till, not being able to make up his mind which one flower to take or whether to take several, he went on and on, and the moon shone very brightly, and a strange unseen bird, somewhat like a nightingale, but louder and lovelier, sang, and his heart was filled with longing for he knew not what, and the moon shone and the nightingale sang. But on a sudden a black cloud covered the moon entirely, and all was black, utter darkness, and through the darkness he heard wolves howling and shrieking in the hideous ardour of the chase, and there passed before him a horrible procession of wolves (black wolves with red fiery eyes), and with them men that had the heads of wolves and wolves that had the heads of men, and above them flew owls (black owls with red fiery eyes), and bats and long serpentine black things, and last of all seated on an enormous black ram with hideous human face the wolf-keeper on whose face was eternal shadow; but they continued their horrid chase and passed him by, and when they had passed the moon shone out more beautiful than ever, and the strange nightingale sang again, and the strange intense blue flowers were in long reaches in front to the right and to the left. But one thing was there which had not been before, among the deep blue flowers walked one with long gleaming golden hair, and she turned once round and her eyes were of the same colour as the strange blue flowers, and she walked on and Gabriel could not choose but follow. But when a cloud passed over the moon he saw no beautiful woman but a wolf, so in utter terror he turned and fled, plucking one of the strange blue flowers on the way, and leapt again over the brook and ran home.

When he got home Gabriel could not resist showing his treasure to his mother, though he knew she would not appreciate it; but when she saw the strange blue flower, Mère Yvonne turned pale and said, 'Why child, where hast thou been? sure it is the witch flower'; and so saying she snatched it from him and cast it into the corner, and immediately all its beauty and strange fragrance faded from it and it looked charred as though it had been burnt.

So Gabriel sat down silently and rather sulkily, and having eaten no supper went up to bed, but he did not sleep but waited and waited till all was quiet within the house. Then he crept downstairs in his long white night-shirt and bare feet on the square cold stones and picked hurriedly up the charred and faded flower and put it in his warm bosom next his heart, and immediately the flower bloomed again lovelier than ever, and he fell into a deep sleep, but through his sleep he seemed to hear a soft low voice singing underneath his window in a strange language (in which the subtle sounds melted into one another), but he could distinguish no word except his own name.

When he went forth in the morning to serve Mass, he still kept the flower with him next his heart. Now when the priest began Mass and said 'Intriobo ad altare Dei,' then said Gabriel 'Qui nequiquam laetificavit juventutem meam.' And the Abbé Félicien turned round on hearing this strange response, and he saw the boy's face deadly pale, his eyes fixed and his limbs rigid, and as the priest looked on him Gabriel fell fainting to the floor, so the sacristan had to carry him home and seek another acolyte for the Abbé Félicien.

Now when the Abbé Félicien came to see after him, Gabriel felt strangely reluctant to say anything about the blue flower and for the first time he deceived the priest.

In the afternoon as sunset drew nigh he felt better and Carmeille came to see him and begged him to go out with her into the fresh air. So they went out hand in hand, the dark haired, gazelle-eyed boy, and the fair wavy haired girl, and something, he knew not what, led his steps (half knowingly and yet not so, for he could not but walk thither) to the brook, and they sat down together on the bank.

Gabriel thought at least he might tell his secret to Carmeille, so he took out the flower from his bosom and said, 'Look here, Carmeille, hast thou seen ever so lovely a flower as this?' but Carmeille turned pale and faint and said, 'Oh, Gabriel what is this flower? I but touched it, and I felt something strange come over me. No, no, I don't like its perfume, no, there's something not quite right about it, oh, dear Gabriel, do let me throw it away,' and before he had time to answer, she cast it from her, and again all its beauty and fragrance went from it and it looked charred as though it had been burnt. But suddenly where the flower had been thrown on this side of the brook, there appeared a wolf, which stood and looked at the children.

Carmeille said, 'What shall we do,' and clung to Gabriel, but the wolf looked at them very steadfastly and Gabriel recognized in the eyes of the wolf the strange deep intense blue eyes of the wolf-woman he had seen on the 'other side,' so he said, 'Stay here, dear Carmeille, see she is looking gently at us and will not hurt us.'

'But it is a wolf,' said Carmeille, and quivered all over with fear, but again Gabriel said languidly, 'She will not hurt us.' Then Carmeille seized Gabriel's hand in an agony of terror and dragged him along with her till they reached the village, where she gave the alarm and all the lads of the village gathered together. They had never seen a wolf on this side of the brook, so they excited themselves greatly and arranged a grand wolf hunt for the morrow, but Gabriel sat silently apart and said no word.

That night Gabriel could not sleep at all nor could he bring himself to say his prayers; but he sat in his little room by the window with his shirt open at the throat and the strange blue flower at his heart and again this night he heard a voice singing beneath his window in the same soft, subtle, liquid language as before—

Ma zála liràl va jé
Cwamûlo zhajéla je
Cárma urádi el javé
Járma, symai,—carmé—
Zhála javály thra je
al vú al vlaûle va azré
Safralje vairálje va já?
Cárma serâja
Lâja lâja
Luzhà!'

and as he looked he could see the silvern shadows slide on the limmering light of golden hair, and the strange eyes gleaming dark blue through the night and it seemed to him that he could not but follow; so he walked half clad and bare foot as he was with eyes fixed as in a dream silently down the stairs and out into the night.

And ever and again she turned to look on him with her strange blue eyes full of tenderness and passion and sadness beyond the sadness of things human—and as he foreknew his steps led him to the brink of the brook. Then she, taking his hand, familiarly said, 'Won't you help me over Gabriel?'

Then it seemed to him as though he had known her all his life—so he went with her to the 'other side' but he saw no one by him; and looking again beside him there were *two wolves*. In a frenzy of terror, he (who had never thought to kill any living thing before) seized a log of wood lying by and smote one of the wolves on the head.

Immediately he saw the wolf-woman again at his side with blood streaming from her forehead, staining her wonderful golden hair, and with eyes looking at him with infinite reproach, she said—'Who did this?'

Then she whispered a few words to the other wolf, which leapt over the brook and made its way towards the village, and turning again towards him she said, 'Oh Gabriel, how could you strike me, who would have loved you so long and so well.' Then it seemed to him again as though he had known her all his life but he felt dazed and said nothing—but she gathered a dark green strangely shaped leaf and holding it to her forehead, she said—'Gabriel, kiss the place all will be well again.' So he kissed as she has bidden him and he felt the salt taste of blood in his mouth and then he knew no more.

Again he saw the wolf-keeper with his horrible troupe around him, but this time not engaged in the chase but sitting in strange conclave in a circle and the black owls sat in the trees and the black bats hung downwards from the branches. Gabriel stood alone in the middle with a hundred wicked eyes fixed on him. They seemed to deliberate about what should be done with him, speaking in that same strange tongue which he had heard in the songs beneath his window. Suddenly he felt a hand pressing in his and saw the mysterious wolf-woman by his side. Then began what seemed a kind of incantation where human or half human creatures seemed to howl, and beasts to speak with human speech but in the unknown tongue. Then the wolf-keeper whose face was ever veiled in shadow spake some words in a voice that seemed to come from afar off, but all he could distinguish was his own name Gabriel and her name Lilith. Then he felt arms enlacing him.—

Gabriel awoke—in his own room—so it was a dream after all—but what a dreadful dream. Yes, but was it his own room? Of course there was his coat hanging over the chair—yes but—the Crucifix—where was the Crucifix and the benetier and the consecrated palm branch and the antique image of Our Lady perpetuae salutis, with the little ever-burning lamp before it, before which he placed every day the flowers he had gathered, yet had not dared to place the blue flower.—

Every morning he lifted his still dream-laden eyes to it and said Ave Maria and made the sign of the cross, which bringeth peace to the soul—but how horrible, how maddening, it was not there, not at all. No surely he could not be awake, at least not *quite* awake, he would make the benedictive sign and he would be freed from this fearful illusion—yes but the sign, he would make the sign—oh, but what was the sign? Had he forgotten? or was his arm paralysed? No he could move. Then he had forgotten—and the prayer—he must remember that. A—vae—nunc—mortis—fructus. No surely it did not run thus—but something like it surely—yes, he was awake he could move at any rate—he would reassure himself—he would get up—he would see the grey old church with the exquisitely pointed gables bathed in the light of dawn, and presently the deep solemn bell would toll and he would run down and don his red cassock and lace-worked cotta and light the tall candles on the altar and wait reverently to vest the good and gracious Abbé Félicien, kissing each vestment as he lifted it with reverent hands.

But surely this was not the light of dawn it was liker sunset! He leapt from his small white bed, and a vague terror came over him, he trembled and had to hold on to the chair before he reached the window. No, the solemn spires of the grey church were not to be seen—he was in the depths of the forest; but in a part he had never seen before—but surely he had explored every part, it must be the 'other side.' To terror succeeded a languor and lassitude not without charm—passivity, acquiescence indulgence—he felt, as it were, the strong caress of another will flowing over him like water and clothing him with invisible hands in an impalpable garment; so he dressed himself almost mechanically and walked downstairs, the same stairs it seemed to him down which it was his wont to run and spring. The broad square stones seemed singularly beautiful and iridescent with many strange colours—how was it he had never noticed this before—but he was gradually losing the power of wondering—he entered the room below—the wonted coffee and bread-rolls were on the table.

'Why Gabriel, how late you are today.' The voice was very sweet but the intonation strange—and there, sat Lilith, the mysterious wolf-woman, her glittering gold hair tied loose in a loose knot and an embroidery whereon she was tracing strange serpentine patterns, lay over the lap of her maize coloured garment—and she looked at Gabriel steadfastly with her wonderful dark blue eyes and said, 'Why, Gabriel, you are late today,' and Gabriel answered, 'I was tired yesterday, give me some coffee.'

A dream within a dream—yes, he had known her all his life, and they dwelt together; had they not always done so? And she would take him through the glades of the forest and gather for him flowers, such as he had never seen before, and tell him stories in her strange, low deep voice, which seemed ever to be accompanied by the faint vibration of strings, looking at him fixedly the while with her marvellous blue eyes.

Little by little the flame of vitality which burned within him seemed to grow fainter and fainter, and his lithe lissom limbs waxed languorous and luxurious—yet was he ever filled with a languid content and a will not his own perpetually overshadowed him.

One day in their wanderings he saw a strange dark blue flower like unto the eyes of Lilith, and a sudden half remembrance flashed through his mind.

'What is this blue flower?' he said, and Lilith shuddered and said nothing; but as they went a little further there was a brook—*the* brook he thought, and felt his fetters falling off him, and he prepared to spring over the brook; but Lilith seized him by the arm and held him back with all her strength, and trembling all over she said, 'Promise me Gabriel that you will not cross over.' But he said, 'Tell me what is this blue flower, and why you will not tell me?' And she said, 'Look Gabriel at the brook.' And he looked and saw that though it was just like the brook of separation it was not the same, the waters did not flow.

As Gabriel looked steadfastly into the still waters it seemed to him as though he saw voices—some impression of the Vespers for the Dead. 'Hei mihi quia incolatus sum,' and again 'De profundis clamavi ad te'—oh, that veil, that overshadowing veil! Why could he not hear properly and see, and why did he only remember as one looking through a threefold semitransparent curtain. Yes they were praying for him—but who were they? He heard again the voice of Lilith in whispered anguish, 'Come away!'

Then he said, this time in monotone, 'What is this blue flower, and what is its use?'

And the low thrilling voice answered, 'It is called "lûli uzhûri," two drops pressed upon the face of the sleeper and he will *sleep*.'

He was as a child in her hand and suffered himself to be led from thence, nevertheless he plucked listlessly one of the blue flowers, holding it downwards in his hand. What did she mean? Would the sleeper wake? Would the blue flower leave any stain? Could that stain be wiped off?

But as he lay asleep at early dawn he heard voices from afar off praying for him—the Abbé Félicien, Carmeille, his mother too, then some familiar words struck his ear: 'Libera mea porta inferi.' Mass was being said for the repose of his soul, he knew this. No, he could not stay, he would leap over the brook, he knew the way—he had forgotten that the brook did not flow. Ah, but Lilith would know—what should he do? The blue flower—there it lay close by his bedside—he understood now; so he crept very silently to where Lilith lay asleep, her long hair glittering gold, shining like a glory round about her. He pressed two drops on her forehead, she sighed once, and a shade of praeternatural anguish passed over her beautiful face. He fled—terror, remorse, and hope tearing his soul and making fleet his feet. He came to the brook—he did not see that the water did not flow—of course it was the brook of separation; one bound, he should be with things human again. He leapt over and—

A change had come over him—what was it? He could not tell —did he walk on all fours? Yes surely. He looked into the brook, whose still waters were fixed as a mirror, and there, horror, he beheld himself; or was it himself? His head and face, yes; but his body transformed to that of a wolf. Even as he looked he heard a sound of hideous mocking laughter behind him. He turned round—there, in a gleam of red lurid light, he saw one whose body was human, but whose head was that of a wolf, with eyes of infinite malice; and, while this hideous being laughed with a loud human laugh, he, essaying to speak, could only utter the prolonged howl of a wolf.

But we will transfer our thoughts from the alien things on the 'other side' to the simple human village where Gabriel used to dwell. Mère Yvonne was not much surprised when Gabriel did not turn up to breakfast—he often did not, so absent minded was he; this time she said, 'I suppose he has gone with the others to the wolf hunt.' Not that Gabriel was given to hunting, but, as she sagely said, 'there was no knowing what he might do next.' The boys said, 'Of course that muff Gabriel is skulking and hiding himself, he's afraid to join the wolf hunt; why, he wouldn't even kill a cat,' for their one notion of excellence was slaughter—so the greater the game the greater the glory. They were chiefly now confined to cats and sparrows, but they all hoped in after time to become generals of armies.

Yet these children had been taught all their life through with the gentle words of Christ—but alas, nearly all the seed falls by the wayside, where it could not bear flower or fruit; how little these know the suffering and bitter anguish or realize the full meaning of the words to those, of whom it is written 'Some fell among thorns.'

The wolf hunt was so far a success that they did actually see a wolf, but not a success, as they did not kill it before it leapt over the brook to the 'other side,' where, of course, they were afraid to pursue it. No emotion is more inrooted and intense in the minds of common people than hatred and fear of anything 'strange.'

Days passed by, but Gabriel was nowhere seen—and Mère Yvonne began to see clearly at last how deeply she loved her only son, who was so unlike her that she had thought herself an object of pity to other mothers—the goose and the swan's egg. People searched and pretended to search, they even went to the length of dragging the ponds, which the boys thought very amusing, as it enabled them to kill a great number of water rats, and Carmeille sat in a corner and cried all day long. Mère Pinquèle also sat in a corner and chuckled and said that she had always said Gabriel would come to no good. The Abbé Félicien looked pale and anxious, but said very little, save to God and those that dwelt with God.

At last, as Gabriel was not there, they supposed he must be nowhere—that is *dead.* (Their knowledge of other localities being so limited, that it did not even occur to them to suppose he might be living elsewhere than in the village.) So it was agreed that an empty catafalque should be put up in the church with tall candles round it, and Mère Yvonne said all the prayers that were in her prayer book, beginning at the beginning and ending at the end, regardless of their appropriateness—not even omitting the instructions of the rubrics. And Carmeille sat in the corner of the little side chapel and cried, and cried. And the Abbé Félicien caused the boys to sing the Vespers for the Dead (this did not amuse them so much as dragging the pond), and on the following morning, in the silence of early dawn, said the Dirge and the Requiem—*and this Gabriel heard.*

Then the Abbé Félicien received a message to bring the Holy Viaticum to one sick. So they set forth in solemn procession with great torches, and their way lay along the brook of separation.

Essaying to speak he could only utter the prolonged howl of a wolf—the most fearful of all beastial sounds. He howled and howled again—perhaps Lilith would hear him! Perhaps she could rescue him? Then he remembered the blue flower—the beginning and end of all his woe. His cries aroused all the denizens of the forest—the wolves, the wolf-men, and the men-wolves. He fled before them in an agony of terror—behind him, seated on the black ram with human face, was the wolf-keeper, whose face was veiled in eternal shadow. Only once he turned to look behind—for among the shrieks and howls of beastial chase he heard one thrilling voice moan with pain. And there among them he beheld Lilith, her body too was that of a wolf, almost hidden in the masses of her glittering golden hair, on her forehead was a stain of blue, like in colour to her mysterious eyes, now veiled with tears she could not shed.

The way of the Most Holy Viaticum lay along the brook of separation. They heard the fearful howlings afar off, the torch bearers turned pale and trembled—but the Abbé Félicien, holding aloft the Ciborium, said 'They cannot harm us.'

Suddenly the whole horrid chase came in sight. Gabriel sprang over the brook, the Abbé Félicien held the most Blessed Sacrament before him, and his shape was restored to him and he fell down prostrate in adoration. But the Abbé Félicien still held aloft the Sacres Ciborium, and the people fell on their knees in the agony of fear, but the face of the priest seemed to shine with divine effulgence. Then the wolf-keeper held up in his hands the shape of something horrible and inconceivable—a monstrance to the Sacrament of Hell, and three times he raised it, in mockery of the blessed rite of Benediction. And on the third time streams of fire went forth from his fingers, and all the 'other side' of the forest took fire, and great darkness was over all.

All who were there and saw and heard it have kept the impress thereof for the rest of their lives—nor till in their death hour was the remembrance thereof absent from their minds. Shrieks, horrible beyond conception, were heard till nightfall—then the rain rained.

The 'other side' is harmless now—charred ashes only; but none dares to cross but Gabriel alone—for once a year for nine days a strange madness comes over him.

1916

KERFOL

Edith Wharton

Edith Wharton (1862–1937) was an American novelist whose best-known works are *The Age of Innocence* and *The House of Mirth*. Edith (born Edith Newbold Jones) was born into extreme wealth, with the phrase 'keeping up with the Joneses' attributed to her family name. Her early work was published anonymously or under pseudonyms, her family looked down on writing as a worthwhile endeavour. As well as writing her novels (*The Age of Innocence* winning the Pulitzer Prize, Edith being the first woman to do so), she wrote over eighty short stories. This tale, written in 1916, is unique amongst Wharton's other ghost stories as there are no human ghosts, only those of dogs. In a diary entry from 1924 she wrote:

> I am secretly afraid of animals—of all animals except dogs, and even of some dogs. I think it is because of the Usness in their eyes, with the underlying Not-Usness which belies it, and is so tragic a reminder of the lost age when we human beings branched off and left them; left them to eternal inarticulateness and slavery. Why? their eyes seem to ask us.

She loved dogs all of her life, with many of them buried in a pet cemetery at her home, and was a charter member of the New York Society for the Prevention of Cruelty to Animals. When her last dog Linky died, Wharton passed away four months after. 'Kerfol' features mass dog strangulation, and I did not choose to reprint this story lightly, but it has the right and only ending.

I

'You ought to buy it,' said my host; 'it's just the place for a solitary-minded devil like you. And it would be rather worth while to own the most romantic house in Brittany. The present people are dead broke, and it's going for a song—you ought to buy it.'

It was not with the least idea of living up to the character my friend Lanrivain ascribed to me (as a matter of fact, under my unsociable exterior I have always had secret yearnings for domesticity) that I took his hint one autumn afternoon and went to Kerfol. My friend was motoring over to Quimper on business: he dropped me on the way, at a cross-road on a heath, and said: 'First turn to the right and second to the left. Then straight ahead till you see an avenue. If you meet any peasants, don't ask your way. They don't understand French, and they would pretend they did and mix you up. I'll be back for you here by sunset—and don't forget the tombs in the chapel.'

I followed Lanrivain's directions with the hesitation occasioned by the usual difficulty of remembering whether he had said the first turn to the right and second to the left, or the contrary. If I had met a peasant I should certainly have asked, and probably been sent astray; but I had the desert landscape to myself, and so stumbled on the right turn and walked across the heath till I came to an avenue. It was so unlike any other avenue I have ever seen that I instantly knew it must be *the* avenue. The grey-trunked trees sprang up straight to a great height and then interwove their pale-grey branches in a long tunnel through which the autumn light fell faintly. I know most trees by name, but I haven't to this day been able to decide what those trees were. They had the tall curve of elms, the tenuity of poplars, the ashen colour of olives under a rainy sky; and they stretched ahead of me for half a mile or more without a break in their arch. If ever I saw an avenue that unmistakably led to something, it was the avenue at Kerfol. My heart beat a little as I began to walk down it.

Presently the trees ended and I came to a fortified gate in a long wall. Between me and the wall was an open space of grass, with other grey avenues radiating from it. Behind the wall were tall slate roofs mossed with silver, a chapel belfry, the top of a keep. A moat filled with wild shrubs and brambles surrounded the place; the drawbridge had been replaced by a stone arch, and the portcullis by an iron gate. I stood for a long time on the hither side of the moat, gazing about me, and letting the influence of the place sink in. I said to myself: 'If I wait long enough, the guardian will turn up and show me the tombs—' and I rather hoped he wouldn't turn up too soon.

I sat down on a stone and lit a cigarette. As soon as I had done it, it struck me as a puerile and portentous thing to do, with that great blind house looking down at me, and all the empty avenues converging on me. It may have been the depth of the silence that made me so conscious of my gesture. The squeak of my match sounded as loud as the scraping of a brake, and I almost fancied I heard it fall when I tossed it onto the grass. But there was more than that: a sense of irrelevance, of littleness, of futile bravado, in sitting there puffing my cigarette-smoke into the face of such a past.

I knew nothing of the history of Kerfol—I was new to Brittany, and Lanrivain had never mentioned the name to me till the day before—but one couldn't as much as glance at that pile without feeling in it a long accumulation of history. What kind of history I was not prepared to guess: perhaps only that sheer weight of many associated lives and deaths which gives a majesty to all old houses. But the aspect of Kerfol suggested something more—a perspective of stern and cruel memories stretching away, like its own grey avenues, into a blur of darkness.

Certainly no house had ever more completely and finally broken with the present. As it stood there, lifting its proud roofs and gables to the sky, it might have been its own funeral monument. 'Tombs in the chapel? The whole place is a tomb!' I reflected. I hoped more and more that the guardian would not come. The details of the place, however striking, would seem trivial compared with its collective impressiveness; and I wanted only to sit there and be penetrated by the weight of its silence.

'It's the very place for you!' Lanrivain had said; and I was overcome by the almost blasphemous frivolity of suggesting to any living being that Kerfol was the place for him. 'Is it possible that any one could *not* see—?' I wondered. I did not finish the thought: what I meant was undefinable. I stood up and wandered toward the gate. I was beginning to want to know more; not to *see* more—I was by now so sure it was not a question of seeing—but to feel more: feel all the place had to communicate. 'But to get in one will have to rout out the keeper,' I thought reluctantly, and hesitated. Finally I crossed the bridge and tried the iron gate. It yielded, and I walked through the tunnel formed by the thickness of the *chemin de ronde*. At the farther end, a wooden barricade had been laid across the entrance, and beyond it was a court enclosed in noble architecture. The main building faced me; and I now saw that one half was a mere ruined front, with gaping windows through which the wild growths of the moat and the trees of the park were visible. The rest of the house was still in its robust beauty. One end abutted on the round tower, the other on the small traceried chapel, and in an angle of the building stood a graceful well-head crowned with mossy urns. A few roses grew against the walls, and on an upper window-sill I remember noticing a pot of fuchsias.

My sense of the pressure of the invisible began to yield to my architectural interest. The building was so fine that I felt a desire to explore it for its own sake. I looked about the court, wondering in which corner the guardian lodged. Then I pushed open the barrier and went in. As I did so, a dog barred my way. He was such a remarkably beautiful little dog that for a moment he made me forget the splendid place he was defending. I was not sure of his breed at the time, but have since learned that it was Chinese, and that he was of a rare variety called the 'Sleeve-dog.' He was very small and golden brown, with large brown eyes and a ruffled throat: he looked like a large tawny chrysanthemum. I said to myself: 'These little beasts always snap and scream, and somebody will be out in a minute.'

The little animal stood before me, forbidding, almost menacing: there was anger in his large brown eyes. But he made no sound, he came no nearer.

Instead, as I advanced, he gradually fell back, and I noticed that another dog, a vague rough brindled thing, had limped up on a lame leg. 'There'll be a hubbub now,' I thought; for at the same moment a third dog, a long-haired white mongrel, slipped out of a doorway and joined the others. All three stood looking at me with grave eyes; but not a sound came from them. As I advanced they continued to fall back on muffled paws, still watching me. 'At a given point, they'll all charge at my ankles: it's one of the jokes that dogs who live together put up on one,' I thought. I was not alarmed, for they were neither large nor formidable. But they let me wander about the court as I pleased, following me at a little distance—always the same distance—and always keeping their eyes on me. Presently I looked across at the ruined façade, and saw that in one of its empty window-frames another dog stood: a white pointer with one brown ear. He was an old grave dog, much more experienced than the others; and he seemed to be observing me with a deeper intentness.

'I'll hear from *him*,' I said to myself; but he stood in the window-frame, against the trees of the park, and continued to watch me without moving. I stared back at him for a time, to see if the sense that he was being watched would not rouse him. Half the width of the court lay between us, and we gazed at each other silently across it. But he did not stir, and at last I turned away. Behind me I found the rest of the pack, with a newcomer added: a small black greyhound with pale agate-coloured eyes. He was shivering a little, and his expression was more timid than that of the others. I noticed that he kept a little behind them. And still there was not a sound.

I stood there for fully five minutes, the circle about me—waiting, as they seemed to be waiting. At last I went up to the little golden-brown dog and stooped to pat him. As I did so, I heard myself give a nervous laugh. The little dog did not start, or growl, or take his eyes from me—he simply slipped back about a yard, and then paused and continued to look at me. 'Oh, hang it!' I exclaimed, and walked across the court toward the well.

As I advanced, the dogs separated and slid away into different corners of the court. I examined the urns on the well, tried a locked door or two, and looked up and down the dumb façade; then I faced about toward the chapel.

When I turned I perceived that all the dogs had disappeared except the old pointer, who still watched me from the window. It was rather a relief to be rid of that cloud of witnesses; and I began to look about me for a way to the back of the house. 'Perhaps there'll be somebody in the garden,' I thought. I found a way across the moat, scrambled over a wall smothered in brambles, and got into the garden. A few lean hydrangeas and geraniums pined in the flower-beds, and the ancient house looked down on them indifferently. Its garden side was plainer and severer than the other: the long granite front, with its few windows and steep roof, looked like a fortress-prison. I walked around the farther wing, went up some disjointed steps, and entered the deep twilight of a narrow and incredibly old box-walk. The walk was just wide enough for one person to slip through, and its branches met overhead. It was like the ghost of a box-walk, its lustrous green all turning to the shadowy greyness of the avenues. I walked on and on, the branches hitting me in the face and springing back with a dry rattle; and at length I came out on the grassy top of the *chemin de ronde*. I walked along it to the gate-tower, looking down into the court, which was just below me. Not a human being was in sight; and neither were the dogs. I found a flight of steps in the thickness of the wall and went down them; and when I emerged again into the court, there stood the circle of dogs, the golden-brown one a little ahead of the others, the black greyhound shivering in the rear.

'Oh, hang it—you uncomfortable beasts, you!' I exclaimed, my voice startling me with a sudden echo. The dogs stood motionless, watching me. I knew by this time that they would not try to prevent my approaching the house, and the knowledge left me free to examine them. I had a feeling that they must be horribly cowed to be so silent and inert. Yet they did not look hungry or ill-treated. Their coats were smooth and they were not thin, except the shivering greyhound. It was more as if they had lived a long time with people who never spoke to them or looked at them: as though the silence of the place had gradually benumbed their busy inquisitive natures. And this strange passivity, this almost human lassitude, seemed to me sadder than the misery of starved and beaten animals. I should have liked to rouse them for a minute, to coax them into a game or a scamper; but the longer I looked into their fixed and weary eyes the more preposterous the idea became. With the windows of that house looking down on us, how could I have imagined such a thing? The dogs knew better: *they* knew what the house would tolerate and what it would not. I even fancied that they knew what was passing through my mind, and pitied me for my frivolity. But even that feeling probably reached them through a thick fog of listlessness. I had an idea that their distance from me was as nothing to my remoteness from them. The impression they produced was that of having in common one memory so deep and dark that nothing that had happened since was worth either a growl or a wag.

'I say,' I broke out abruptly, addressing myself to the dumb circle, 'do you know what you look like, the whole lot of you? You look as if you'd seen a ghost—that's how you look! I wonder if there *is* a ghost here, and nobody but you left for it to appear to?' The dogs continued to gaze at me without moving...

It was dark when I saw Lanrivain's motor lamps at the cross-roads—and I wasn't exactly sorry to see them. I had the sense of having escaped from the loneliest place in the whole world, and of not liking loneliness—to that degree—as much as I had imagined I should. My friend had brought his solicitor back from Quimper for the night, and seated beside a fat and affable stranger I felt no inclination to talk of Kerfol...

But that evening, when Lanrivain and the solicitor were closeted in the study, Madame de Lanrivain began to question me in the drawing-room.

'Well—are you going to buy Kerfol?' she asked, tilting up her gay chin from her embroidery.

'I haven't decided yet. The fact is, I couldn't get into the house,' I said, as if I had simply postponed my decision, and meant to go back for another look.

'You couldn't get in? Why, what happened? The family are mad to sell the place, and the old guardian has orders—'

'Very likely. But the old guardian wasn't there.'

'What a pity! He must have gone to market. But his daughter—?'

'There was nobody about. At least I saw no one.'

'How extraordinary! Literally nobody?'

'Nobody but a lot of dogs—a whole pack of them—who seemed to have the place to themselves.'

Madame de Lanrivain let the embroidery slip to her knee and folded her hands on it. For several minutes she looked at me thoughtfully.

'A pack of dogs—you *saw* them?'

'Saw them? I saw nothing else!'

'How many?' She dropped her voice a little. 'I've always wondered—'

I looked at her with surprise: I had supposed the place to be familiar to her. 'Have you never been to Kerfol?' I asked.

'Oh, yes: often. But never on that day.'

'What day?'

'I'd quite forgotten—and so had Hervé, I'm sure. If we'd remembered, we never should have sent you today—but then, after all, one doesn't half believe that sort of thing, does one?'

'What sort of thing?' I asked, involuntarily sinking my voice to the level of hers. Inwardly I was thinking: 'I *knew* there was something...'

Madame de Lanrivain cleared her throat and produced a reassuring smile. 'Didn't Hervé tell you the story of Kerfol? An ancestor of his was mixed up in it. You know every Breton house has its ghost-story; and some of them are rather unpleasant.'

'Yes—but those dogs?'

'Well, those dogs are the ghosts of Kerfol. At least, the peasants say there's one day in the year when a lot of dogs appear there; and that day the keeper and his daughter go off to Morlaix and get drunk. The women in Brittany drink dreadfully.' She stooped to match a silk; then she lifted her charming inquisitive Parisian face. 'Did you *really* see a lot of dogs? There isn't one at Kerfol,' she said.

II

Lanrivain, the next day, hunted out a shabby calf volume from the back of an upper shelf of his library.

'Yes—here it is. What does it call itself? *A History of the Assizes of the Duchy of Brittany. Quimper,* 1702. The book was written about a hundred years later than the Kerfol affair; but I believe the account is transcribed pretty literally from the judicial records. Anyhow, it's queer reading. And there's a Hervé de Lanrivain mixed up in it—not exactly *my* style, as you'll see. But then he's only a collateral. Here, take the book up to bed with you. I don't exactly remember the details; but after you've read it I'll bet anything you'll leave your light burning all night!'

I left my light burning all night, as he had predicted; but it was chiefly because, till near dawn, I was absorbed in my reading. The account of the trial of Anne de Cornault, wife of the lord of Kerfol, was long and closely printed. It was, as my friend had said, probably an almost literal transcription of what took place in the court-room; and the trial lasted nearly a month. Besides, the type of the book was very bad...

At first I thought of translating the old record. But it is full of wearisome repetitions, and the main lines of the story are forever straying off into side issues. So I have tried to disentangle it, and give it here in a simpler form. At times, however, I have reverted to the text because no other words could have conveyed so exactly the sense of what I felt at Kerfol; and nowhere have I added anything of my own.

III

It was in the year 16—that Yves de Cornault, lord of the domain of Kerfol, went to the *pardon* of Locronan to perform his religious duties. He was a rich and powerful noble, then in his sixty-second year, but hale and sturdy, a great horseman and hunter and a pious man. So all his neighbours attested. In appearance he was short and broad, with a swarthy face, legs slightly bowed from the saddle, a hanging nose and broad hands with black hairs on them. He had married young and lost his wife and son soon after, and since then had lived alone at Kerfol. Twice a year he went to Morlaix, where he had a handsome house by the river, and spent a week or ten days there;

and occasionally he rode to Rennes on business. Witnesses were found to declare that during these absences he led a life different from the one he was known to lead at Kerfol, where he busied himself with his estate, attended mass daily, and found his only amusement in hunting the wild boar and water-fowl. But these rumours are not particularly relevant, and it is certain that among people of his own class in the neighbourhood he passed for a stern and even austere man, observant of his religious obligations, and keeping strictly to himself. There was no talk of any familiarity with the women on his estate, though at that time the nobility were very free with their peasants. Some people said he had never looked at a woman since his wife's death; but such things are hard to prove, and the evidence on this point was not worth much.

Well, in his sixty-second year, Yves de Cornault went to the *pardon* at Locronan, and saw there a young lady of Douarnenez, who had ridden over pillion behind her father to do her duty to the saint. Her name was Anne de Barrigan, and she came of good old Breton stock, but much less great and powerful than that of Yves de Cornault; and her father had squandered his fortune at cards, and lived almost like a peasant in his little granite manor on the moors... I have said I would add nothing of my own to this bald statement of a strange case; but I must interrupt myself here to describe the young lady who rode up to the lych-gate of Locronan at the very moment when the Baron de Cornault was also dismounting there. I take my description from a faded drawing in red crayon, sober and truthful enough to be by a late pupil of the Clouets, which hangs in Lanrivain's study, and is said to be a portrait of Anne de Barrigan. It is unsigned and has no mark of identity but the initials A. B., and the date 16—, the year after her marriage. It represents a young woman with a small oval face, almost pointed, yet wide enough for a full mouth with a tender depression at the corners. The nose is small, and the eyebrows are set rather high, far apart, and as lightly pencilled as the eyebrows in a Chinese painting. The forehead is high and serious, and the hair, which one feels to be fine and thick and fair, is drawn off it and lies close like a cap. The eyes are neither large nor small, hazel probably, with a look at once shy and steady. A pair of beautiful long hands are crossed below the lady's breast...

The chaplain of Kerfol, and other witnesses, averred that when the Baron came back from Locronan he jumped from his horse, ordered another to be instantly saddled, called to a young page to come with him, and rode away that same evening to the south. His steward followed the next morning with coffers laden on a pair of pack mules. The following week Yves de Cornault rode back to Kerfol, sent for his vassals and tenants, and told them he was to be married at All Saints to Anne de Barrigan of Douarnenez. And on All Saints' Day the marriage took place.

As to the next few years, the evidence on both sides seems to show that they passed happily for the couple. No one was found to say that Yves de Cornault had been unkind to his wife, and it was plain to all that he was content with his bargain. Indeed, it was admitted by the chaplain and other witnesses for the prosecution that the young lady had a softening influence on her husband, and that he became less exacting with his tenants, less harsh to peasants and dependants, and less subject to the fits of gloomy silence which had darkened his widowhood. As to his wife, the only grievance her champions could call up in her behalf was that Kerfol was a lonely place, and that when her husband was away on business at Rennes or Morlaix—whither she was never taken—she was not allowed so much as to walk in the park unaccompanied. But no one asserted that she was unhappy, though one servant-woman said she had surprised her crying, and had heard her say that she was a woman accursed to have no child, and nothing in life to call her own. But that was a natural enough feeling in a wife attached to her husband; and certainly it must have been a great grief to Yves de Cornault that she bore no son. Yet he never made her feel her childlessness as a reproach—she admits this in her evidence—but seemed to try to make her forget it by showering gifts and favours on her. Rich though he was, he had never been open-handed; but nothing was too fine for his wife, in the way of silks or gems or linen, or whatever else she fancied. Every wandering merchant was welcome at Kerfol, and when the master was called away he never came back without bringing his wife a handsome present—something curious and particular—from Morlaix or Rennes or Quimper. One of the waiting-women gave, in cross-examination, an interesting list of one year's gifts, which I copy. From Morlaix, a carved ivory junk, with Chinamen at the oars, that a strange sailor had brought back as a votive offering for Notre Dame de la Clarté, above Ploumanac'h; from Quimper, an embroidered gown, worked by the nuns of the Assumption; from Rennes, a silver rose that opened and showed an amber Virgin with a crown of garnets; from Morlaix, again, a length of Damascus velvet shot with gold, bought of a Jew from Syria; and for Michaelmas that same year, from Rennes, a necklet or bracelet of round stones—emeralds and pearls and rubies—strung like beads on a fine gold chain. This was the present that pleased the lady best, the woman said. Later on, as it happened, it was produced at the trial, and appears to have struck the Judges and the public as a curious and valuable jewel.

The very same winter, the Baron absented himself again, this time as far as Bordeaux, and on his return he brought his wife something even odder and prettier than the bracelet. It was a winter evening when he rode up to Kerfol and, walking into the hall, found her sitting by the hearth, her chin on her hand, looking into the fire. He carried a velvet box in his hand and, setting it down, lifted the lid and let out a little golden-brown dog.

Anne de Cornault exclaimed with pleasure as the little creature bounded toward her. 'Oh, it looks like a bird or a butterfly!' she cried as she picked it up; and the dog put its paws on her shoulders and looked at her with eyes 'like a Christian's.' After that she would never have it out of her sight, and petted and talked to it as if it had been a child—as indeed it was the nearest thing to a child she was to know. Yves de Cornault was much pleased with his purchase. The dog had been brought to him by a sailor from an East India merchantman, and the sailor had bought it of a pilgrim in a bazaar at Jaffa, who had stolen it from a nobleman's wife in China: a perfectly permissible thing to do, since the pilgrim was a Christian and the nobleman a heathen doomed to hell-fire. Yves de Cornault had paid a long price for the dog, for they were beginning to be in demand at the French court, and the sailor knew he had got hold of a good thing; but Anne's pleasure was so great that, to see her laugh and play with the little animal, her husband would doubtless have given twice the sum.

*

So far, all the evidence is at one, and the narrative plain sailing; but now the steering becomes difficult. I will try to keep as nearly as possible to Anne's own statements; though toward the end, poor thing...

Well, to go back. The very year after the little brown dog was brought to Kerfol, Yves de Cornault, one winter night, was found dead at the head of a narrow flight of stairs leading down from his wife's rooms to a door opening on the court. It was his wife who found him and gave the alarm, so distracted, poor wretch, with fear and horror—for his blood was all over her—that at first the roused household could not make out what she was saying, and thought she had suddenly gone mad. But there, sure enough, at the top of the stairs lay her husband, stone dead, and head foremost, the blood from his wounds dripping down to the steps below him. He had been dreadfully scratched and gashed about the face and throat, as if with curious pointed weapons; and one of his legs had a deep tear in it which had cut an artery, and probably caused his death. But how did he come there, and who had murdered him?

His wife declared that she had been asleep in her bed, and hearing his cry had rushed out to find him lying on the stairs; but this was immediately questioned. In the first place, it was proved that from her room she could not have heard the struggle on the stairs, owing to the thickness of the walls and the length of the intervening passage; then it was evident that she had not been in bed and asleep, since she was dressed when she roused the house, and her bed had not been slept in. Moreover, the door at the bottom of the stairs was ajar, and it was noticed by the chaplain (an observant man) that the dress she wore was stained with blood about the knees, and that there were traces of small blood-stained hands low down on the staircase walls, so that it was conjectured that she had really been at the postern-door when her husband fell and, feeling her way up to him in the darkness on her hands and knees, had been stained by his blood dripping down on her. Of course it was argued on the other side that the blood-marks on her dress might have been caused by her kneeling down by her husband when she rushed out of her room; but there was the open door below, and the fact that the finger-marks in the staircase all pointed upward.

The accused held to her statement for the first two days, in spite of its improbability; but on the third day word was brought to her that Hervé de Lanrivain, a young nobleman of the neighbourhood, had been arrested for complicity in the crime. Two or three witnesses thereupon came forward to say that it was known throughout the country that Lanrivain had formerly been on good terms with the lady of Cornault; but that he had been absent from Brittany for over a year, and people had ceased to associate their names. The witnesses who made this statement were not of a very reputable sort. One was an old herb-gatherer suspected of witchcraft, another a drunken clerk from a neighbouring parish, the third a half-witted shepherd who could be made to say anything; and it was clear that the prosecution was not satisfied with its case, and would have liked to find more definite proof of Lanrivain's complicity than the statement of the herb-gatherer, who swore to having seen him climbing the wall of the park on the night of the murder. One way of patching out incomplete proofs in those days was to put some sort of pressure, moral or physical, on the accused person. It is not clear what pressure was put on Anne de Cornault; but on the third day, when she was brought in court, she 'appeared weak and wandering,' and after being encouraged to collect herself and speak the truth, on her honour and the wounds of her Blessed Redeemer, she confessed that she had in fact gone down the stairs to speak with Hervé de Lanrivain (who denied everything), and had been surprised there by the sound of her husband's fall. That was better; and the prosecution rubbed its hands with satisfaction. The satisfaction increased when various dependants living at Kerfol were induced to say—with apparent sincerity—that during the year or two preceding his death their master had once more grown uncertain and irascible, and subject to the fits of brooding silence which his household had learned to dread before his second marriage. This seemed to show that things had not been going well at Kerfol; though no one could be found to say that there had been any signs of open disagreement between husband and wife.

Anne de Cornault, when questioned as to her reason for going down at night to open the door to Hervé de Lanrivain, made an answer which must have sent a smile around the court. She said it was because she was lonely and wanted to talk with the young man. Was this the only reason? she was asked; and replied: 'Yes, by the Cross over your Lordships' heads.' 'But why at midnight?' the court asked. 'Because I could see him in no other way.' I can see the exchange of glances across the ermine collars under the Crucifix.

Anne de Cornault, further questioned, said that her married life had been extremely lonely: 'desolate' was the word she used. It was true that her husband seldom spoke harshly to her; but there were days when he did not speak at all. It was true that he had never struck or threatened her; but he kept her like a prisoner at Kerfol, and when he rode away to Morlaix or Quimper or Rennes he set so close a watch on her that she could not pick a flower in the garden without having a waiting-woman at her heels. 'I am no Queen, to need such honours,' she once said to him; and he had answered that a man who has a treasure does not leave the key in the lock when he goes out. 'Then take me with you,' she urged; but to this he said that towns were pernicious places, and young wives better off at their own firesides.

'But what did you want to say to Hervé de Lanrivain?' the court asked; and she answered: 'To ask him to take me away.'

'Ah—you confess that you went down to him with adulterous thoughts?'

'No.'

'Then why did you want him to take you away?'

'Because I was afraid for my life.'

'Of whom were you afraid?'

'Of my husband.'

'Why were you afraid of your husband?'

'Because he had strangled my little dog.'

Another smile must have passed around the court-room: in days when any nobleman had a right to hang his peasants—and most of them exercised it—pinching a pet animal's wind-pipe was nothing to make a fuss about.

At this point one of the Judges, who appears to have had a certain sympathy for the accused, suggested that she should be allowed to explain herself in her own way; and she thereupon made the following statement.

The first years of her marriage had been lonely; but her husband had not been unkind to her. If she had had a child she would not have been unhappy; but the days were long, and it rained too much.

It was true that her husband, whenever he went away and left her, brought her a handsome present on his return; but this did not make up for the loneliness. At least nothing had, till he brought her the little brown dog from the East: after that she was much less unhappy. Her husband seemed pleased that she was so fond of the dog; he gave her leave to put her jewelled bracelet around its neck, and to keep it always with her.

One day she had fallen asleep in her room, with the dog at her feet, as his habit was. Her feet were bare and resting on his back. Suddenly she was waked by her husband: he stood beside her, smiling not unkindly.

'You look like my great-grandmother, Juliane de Cornault, lying in the chapel with her feet on a little dog,' he said.

The analogy sent a chill through her, but she laughed and answered: 'Well, when I am dead you must put me beside her, carved in marble, with my dog at my feet.'

'Oho—we'll wait and see,' he said, laughing also, but with his black brows close together. 'The dog is the emblem of fidelity.'

'And do you doubt my right to lie with mine at my feet?'

'When I'm in doubt I find out,' he answered. 'I am an old man,' he added, 'and people say I make you lead a lonely life. But I swear you shall have your monument if you earn it.'

'And I swear to be faithful,' she returned, 'if only for the sake of having my little dog at my feet.'

Not long afterward he went on business to the Quimper Assizes; and while he was away his aunt, the widow of a great nobleman of the duchy, came to spend a night at Kerfol on her way to the *pardon* of Ste. Barbe. She was a woman of piety and consequence, and much respected by Yves de Cornault, and when she proposed to Anne to go with her to Ste. Barbe no one could object, and even the chaplain declared himself in favour of the pilgrimage. So Anne set out for Ste. Barbe, and there for the first time she talked with Hervé de Lanrivain. He had come once or twice to Kerfol with his father, but she had never before exchanged a dozen words with him. They did not talk for more than five minutes now: it was under the chestnuts, as the procession was coming out of the chapel. He said: 'I pity you,' and she was surprised, for she had not supposed that any one thought her an object of pity. He added: 'Call for me when you need me,' and she smiled a little, but was glad afterward, and thought often of the meeting.

She confessed to having seen him three times afterward: not more. How or where she would not say—one had the impression that she feared to implicate some one. Their meetings had been rare and brief; and at the last he had told her that he was starting the next day for a foreign country, on a mission which was not without peril and might keep him for many months absent. He asked her for a remembrance, and she had none to give him but the collar about the little dog's neck. She was sorry afterward that she had given it, but he was so unhappy at going that she had not had the courage to refuse.

Her husband was away at the time. When he returned a few days later he picked up the animal to pet it, and noticed that its collar was missing. His wife told him that the dog had lost it in the undergrowth of the park, and that she and her maids had hunted a whole day for it. It was true, she explained to the court, that she had made the maids search for the necklet—they all believed the dog had lost it in the park...

Her husband made no comment, and that evening at supper he was in his usual mood, between good and bad: you could never tell which. He talked a good deal, describing what he had seen and done at Rennes; but now and then he stopped and looked hard at her, and when she went to bed she found her little dog strangled on her pillow. The little thing was dead, but still warm; she stooped to lift it, and her distress turned to horror when she discovered that it had been strangled by twisting twice round its throat the necklet she had given to Lanrivain.

The next morning at dawn she buried the dog in the garden, and hid the necklet in her breast. She said nothing to her husband, then or later, and he said nothing to her; but that day he had a peasant hanged for stealing a faggot in the park, and the next day he nearly beat to death a young horse he was breaking.

Winter set in, and the short days passed, and the long nights, one by one; and she heard nothing of Hervé de Lanrivain. It might be that her husband had killed him; or merely that he had been robbed of the necklet. Day after day by the hearth among the spinning maids, night after night alone on her bed, she wondered and trembled. Sometimes at table her husband looked across at her and smiled; and then she felt sure that Lanrivain was dead. She dared not try to get news of him, for she was sure her husband would find out if she did: she had an idea that he could find out anything. Even when a witch-woman who was a noted seer, and could show you the whole world in her crystal, came to the castle for a night's shelter, and the maids flocked to her, Anne held back.

The winter was long and black and rainy. One day, in Yves de Cornault's absence, some gypsies came to Kerfol with a troop of performing dogs. Anne bought the smallest and cleverest, a white dog with a feathery coat and one blue and one brown eye. It seemed to have been ill-treated by the gypsies, and clung to her plaintively when she took it from them. That evening her husband came back, and when she went to bed she found the dog strangled on her pillow.

After that she said to herself that she would never have another dog; but one bitter cold evening a poor lean greyhound was found whining at the castle-gate, and she took him in and forbade the maids to speak of him to her husband. She hid him in a room that no one went to, smuggled food to him from her own plate, made him a warm bed to lie on and petted him like a child.

Yves de Cornault came home, and the next day she found the greyhound strangled on her pillow. She wept in secret, but said nothing, and resolved that even if she met a dog dying of hunger she would never bring him into the castle; but one day she found a young sheepdog, a brindled puppy with good blue eyes, lying with a broken leg in the snow of the park. Yves de Cornault was at Rennes, and she brought the dog in, warmed and fed it, tied up its leg and hid it in the castle till her husband's return. The day before, she gave it to a peasant woman who lived a long way off, and paid her handsomely to care for it and say nothing; but that night she heard a whining and scratching at her door, and when she opened it the lame puppy, drenched and shivering, jumped up on her with little sobbing barks. She hid him in her bed, and the next morning was about to have him taken back to the peasant woman when she heard her husband ride into the court. She shut the dog in a chest, and went down to receive him. An hour or two later, when she returned to her room, the puppy lay strangled on her pillow…

After that she dared not make a pet of any other dog; and her loneliness became almost unendurable. Sometimes, when she crossed the court of the castle, and thought no one was looking, she stopped to pat the old pointer at the gate. But one day as she was caressing him her husband came out of the chapel; and the next day the old dog was gone…

This curious narrative was not told in one sitting of the court, or received without impatience and incredulous comment. It was plain that the Judges were surprised by its puerility, and that it did not help the accused in the eyes of the public. It was an odd tale, certainly; but what did it prove? That Yves de Cornault disliked dogs, and that his wife, to gratify her own fancy, persistently ignored this dislike. As for pleading this trivial disagreement as an excuse for her relations—whatever their nature—with her supposed accomplice, the argument was so absurd that her own lawyer manifestly regretted having let her make use of it, and tried several times to cut short her story. But she went on to the end, with a kind of hypnotized insistence, as though the scenes she evoked were so real to her that she had forgotten where she was and imagined herself to be re-living them.

At length the Judge who had previously shown a certain kindness to her said (leaning forward a little, one may suppose, from his row of dozing colleagues): 'Then you would have us believe that you murdered your husband because he would not let you keep a pet dog?'

'I did not murder my husband.'

'Who did, then? Hervé de Lanrivain?'

'No.'

'Who then? Can you tell us?'

'Yes, I can tell you. The dogs—' At that point she was carried out of the court in a swoon.

*

It was evident that her lawyer tried to get her to abandon this line of defence. Possibly her explanation, whatever it was, had seemed convincing when she poured it out to him in the heat of their first private colloquy; but now that it was exposed to the cold daylight of judicial scrutiny, and the banter of the town, he was thoroughly ashamed of it, and would have sacrificed her without a scruple to save his professional reputation. But the obstinate Judge—who perhaps, after all, was more inquisitive than kindly—evidently wanted to hear the story out, and she was ordered, the next day, to continue her deposition.

She said that after the disappearance of the old watchdog nothing particular happened for a month or two. Her husband was much as usual: she did not remember any special incident. But one evening a pedlar woman came to the castle and was selling trinkets to the maids. She had no heart for trinkets, but she stood looking on while the women made their choice. And then, she did not know how, but the pedlar coaxed her into buying for herself a pear-shaped pomander with a strong scent in it—she had once seen something of the kind on a gypsy woman. She had no desire for the pomander, and did not know why she had bought it. The pedlar said that whoever wore it had the power to read the future; but she did not really believe that, or care much either. However, she bought the thing and took it up to her room, where she sat turning it about in her hand. Then the strange scent attracted her and she began to wonder what kind of spice was in the box. She opened it and found a grey bean rolled in a strip of paper; and on the paper she saw a sign she knew, and a message from Hervé de Lanrivain, saying that he was at home again and would be at the door in the court that night after the moon had set…

She burned the paper and sat down to think. It was nightfall, and her husband was at home… She had no way of warning Lanrivain, and there was nothing to do but to wait…

At this point I fancy the drowsy court-room beginning to wake up. Even to the oldest hand on the bench there must have been a certain relish in picturing the feelings of a woman on receiving such a message at nightfall from a man living twenty miles away, to whom she had no means of sending a warning…

She was not a clever woman, I imagine; and as the first result of her cogitation she appears to have made the mistake of being, that evening, too kind to her husband. She could not ply him with wine, according to the traditional expedient, for though he drank heavily at times he had a strong head; and when he drank beyond its strength it was because he chose to, and not because a woman coaxed him. Not his wife, at any rate—she was an old story by now. As I read the case, I fancy there was no feeling for her left in him but the hatred occasioned by his supposed dishonour.

At any rate, she tried to call up her old graces; but early in the evening he complained of pains and fever, and left the hall to go up to the closet where he sometimes slept. His servant carried him a cup of hot wine, and brought back word that he was sleeping and not to be disturbed; and an hour later, when Anne lifted the tapestry and listened at his door, she heard his loud regular breathing. She thought it might be a feint, and stayed a long time barefooted in the passage, her ear to the crack; but the breathing went on too steadily and naturally to be other than that of a man in a sound sleep. She crept back to her room reassured, and stood in the window watching the moon set through the trees of the park. The sky was misty and starless, and after the moon went down the night was black as pitch. She knew the time had come, and stole along the passage, past her husband's door—where she stopped again to listen to his breathing—to the top of the stairs. There she paused a moment, and assured herself that no one was following her; then she began to go down the stairs in the darkness. They were so steep and winding that she had to go very slowly, for fear of stumbling. Her one thought was to get the door unbolted, tell Lanrivain to make his escape, and hasten back to her room. She had tried the bolt earlier in the evening, and managed to put a little grease on it; but nevertheless, when she drew it, it gave a squeak… not loud, but it made her heart stop; and the next minute, overhead, she heard a noise…

'What noise?' the prosecution interposed.

'My husband's voice calling out my name and cursing me.'

'What did you hear after that?'

'A terrible scream and a fall.'

'Where was Hervé de Lanrivain at this time?'

'He was standing outside in the court. I just made him out in the darkness. I told him for God's sake to go, and then I pushed the door shut.'

'What did you do next?'

'I stood at the foot of the stairs and listened.'

'What did you hear?'

'I heard dogs snarling and panting.' (Visible discouragement of the bench, boredom of the public, and exasperation of the lawyer for the defence. Dogs again—! But the inquisitive Judge insisted.)

'What dogs?'

She bent her head and spoke so low that she had to be told to repeat her answer: 'I don't know.'

'How do you mean—you don't know?'

'I don't know what dogs...'

The Judge again intervened: 'Try to tell us exactly what happened. How long did you remain at the foot of the stairs?'

'Only a few minutes.'

'And what was going on meanwhile overhead?'

'The dogs kept on snarling and panting. Once or twice he cried out. I think he moaned once. Then he was quiet.'

'Then what happened?'

'Then I heard a sound like the noise of a pack when the wolf is thrown to them—gulping and lapping.'

(There was a groan of disgust and repulsion through the court, and another attempted intervention by the distracted lawyer. But the inquisitive Judge was still inquisitive.)

'And all the while you did not go up?'

'Yes—I went up then—to drive them off.'

'The dogs?'

'Yes.'

'Well—?'

'When I got there it was quite dark. I found my husband's flint and steel and struck a spark. I saw him lying there. He was dead.'

'And the dogs?'

'The dogs were gone.'

'Gone—where to?'

'I don't know. There was no way out—and there were no dogs at Kerfol.'

She straightened herself to her full height, threw her arms above her head, and fell down on the stone floor with a long scream. There was a moment of confusion in the court-room. Some one on the bench was heard to say: 'This is clearly a case for the ecclesiastical authorities'—and the prisoner's lawyer doubtless jumped at the suggestion.

After this, the trial loses itself in a maze of cross-questioning and squabbling. Every witness who was called corroborated Anne de Cornault's statement that there were no dogs at Kerfol: had been none for several months. The master of the house had taken a dislike to dogs, there was no denying it. But, on the other hand, at the inquest, there had been long and bitter discussions as to the nature of the dead man's wounds. One of the surgeons called in had spoken of marks that looked like bites. The suggestion of witchcraft was revived, and the opposing lawyers hurled tomes of necromancy at each other.

At last Anne de Cornault was brought back into court—at the instance of the same Judge—and asked if she knew where the dogs she spoke of could have come from. On the body of her Redeemer she swore that she did not. Then the Judge put his final question: 'If the dogs you think you heard had been known to you, do you think you would have recognized them by their barking?'

'Yes.'

'Did you recognize them?'

'Yes.'

'What dogs do you take them to have been?'

'My dead dogs,' she said in a whisper... She was taken out of court, not to reappear there again. There was some kind of ecclesiastical investigation, and the end of the business was that the Judges disagreed with each other, and with the ecclesiastical committee, and that Anne de Cornault was finally handed over to the keeping of her husband's family, who shut her up in the keep of Kerfol, where she is said to have died many years later, a harmless mad-woman.

So ends her story. As for that of Hervé de Lanrivain, I had only to apply to his collateral descendant for its subsequent details. The evidence against the young man being insufficient, and his family influence in the duchy considerable, he was set free, and left soon afterward for Paris. He was probably in no mood for a worldly life, and he appears to have come almost immediately under the influence of the famous M. Arnauld d'Andilly and the gentlemen of Port Royal. A year or two later he was received into their Order, and without achieving any particular distinction he followed its good and evil fortunes till his death some twenty years later. Lanrivain showed me a portrait of him by a pupil of Philippe de Champaigne: sad eyes, an impulsive mouth and a narrow brow. Poor Hervé de Lanrivain: it was a grey ending. Yet as I looked at his stiff and sallow effigy, in the dark dress of the Jansenists, I almost found myself envying his fate. After all, in the course of his life two great things had happened to him: he had loved romantically, and he must have talked with Pascal...

1929

CELUI-LÀ

Eleanor Scott

Eleanor Scott (1892–1965), the daughter of barrister and novelist John Kirkwood Leys, was born Helen Magdalen Leys in Middlesex. She trained as a teacher and eventually became a principal of an Oxford teacher training college. Her first published work, 'The Room' (1923), appeared in *The Cornhill Magazine* and was credited to H. M. Leys. Her novel *War Among Ladies* (1928) was the first to feature her chosen pen name. Her most notable collection is *Randalls Round* (1929) which contains creepy short stories all inspired by her dreams. Her final novel, *Puss in the Corner* (1934), followed the pattern of being reviewed favourably but never attaining popular success. Some sources indicate that she wrote mystery novels under the name Peter Redcliffe Shore. 'Celui-Là' is in the tradition of M. R. James; Maddox goes to an isolated village to have a break from his studies and meets a weird figure on the beach but then finds an image of the same figure under the plaster in the rotting remains of an old church.

'I DON'T for a moment expect you to take my advice,' said Dr. Foster, looking shrewdly at his patient, 'but I'll give it all the same. It's this. Pack a bag with a few things and go off tomorrow to some tiny seaside or mountain place, preferably out of England, so that you won't meet a soul you know. Live there absolutely quietly for three or four weeks, taking a reasonable amount of exercise, and then write and tell me that you're all right again.'

'Easier said than done,' growled Maddox. 'There aren't any quiet places left that I know of, and if there were there wouldn't be any digs to be had at no notice.'

Foster considered.

'I know the very thing,' he cried suddenly. 'There's a little place on the Breton coast—fishing village, very small and scattered, with a long stretch of beach, heath and moor inland, quiet as can be. I happen to know the curé there quite fairly well, and he's an extremely decent, homely little chap. Vétier his name is. He'd take you in. I'll write to him tonight.'

After that, Maddox couldn't in decency hold out. Old Foster had been very good, really, over the whole thing; besides, it was nearly as much bother to fight him as it was to go. In less than a week Maddox was on his way to Kerouac.

Foster saw him off with relief. He knew Maddox well, and knew that he was suffering from years of overwork and worry; he understood how very repugnant effort of any kind was to him—or thought he did; but in reality no one can quite understand the state of exasperation or depression that illness can produce in someone else. Yet as the absurd little train that Maddox took at Lamballe puffed serenely along between tiny rough orchards, the overwrought passenger began to feel soothed; and then, as the line turned north and west, and the cool wind came in from across the dim stretches of moorland, he grew content and almost serene.

Dusk had fallen when he got out at the shed that marked the station of Kerouac. The curé, a short, plump man, in soutane and broad-brimmed hat, met him with the kind, almost effusive, greeting that Breton peasants give to a guest, and conducted the stumbling steps of his visitor to a rough country lane falling steeply downhill between two high, dark banks that smelt of gorse and heather and damp earth. Maddox could just see the level line of sea lying before him, framed by the steep banks of moor on either hand. Above a few pale stars glimmered in the dim sky. It was very peaceful.

Maddox fell into the simple life of the Kerouac presbytery at once. The curé was, as Foster had said, a very homely, friendly little man, always serene and nearly always busy, for he had a large and scattered flock and took a very real interest in the affairs of each member of it. Also, Maddox gathered, money was none too plentiful, for the curé did all the work of the church himself, even down to the trimming of the grass and shrubs that surrounded the little wind-swept building.

The country also appealed very strongly to the visitor. It was at once desolate and friendly, rough and peaceful. He particularly liked the long reaches of the shore, where the tangle of heath and whin gave place to tufts of coarse, whitish grass and then to a belt of shingle and the long level stretches of smooth sand. He liked to walk there when evening had fallen, the moorland on his left rising black to the grey sky, the sea, smooth and calm, stretching out infinitely on his right, a shining ripple lifting here and there. Oddly enough, M. le Curé did not seem to approve of these evening rambles; but that, Maddox told himself, was common among peasants of all races; and he idly wondered whether this were due to a natural liking for the fireside after a day in the open, or whether there were in it some ancient fear of the spirits and demons that country people used to fear in the dim time *entre le chien et le loup*. Anyhow, he wasn't going to give up his evening strolls for a superstition of someone else's!

It was near the end of October, but very calm weather for the time of year; and one evening the air was so mild and the faint shine of the stars so lovely that Maddox extended his walk beyond its usual limits. He had always had the beach to himself at that time of the evening; and he felt a natural, if quite unjustifiable, annoyance when he first noticed that there was someone else on the shore.

The figure was perhaps fifty yards away. At first he thought it was a peasant woman, for it had some sort of hood drawn over the head, and the arms, which it was waving or wringing, were covered by long, hanging sleeves. Then, as he drew nearer, he saw that it was far too tall for a woman, and jumped to the conclusion that it must be a monk or wandering friar of quite exceptional height.

The light was very dim, for the new moon had set, and the stars showed a faint diffused light among thin drifts of cloud; but even so Maddox could not help noticing that the person before him was behaving very oddly. It—he could not determine the sex—moved at an incredible speed up and down a short stretch of beach, waving its draped arms; then suddenly, to his horror, it broke out into a hideous cry, like the howl of a dog. There was something in that cry that turned Maddox cold. Again it rose, and again—an eerie, wailing, hooting sound, dying away over the empty moor. And then the creature dropped on its knees and began scratching at the sand with its hands. A memory, forgotten until now, flashed into Maddox's mind—a memory of that rather horrible story in Hans Andersen about Anne Lisbeth and the drowned child...

The thin cloud obscured the faint light for a moment. When Maddox looked again the figure was still crouching on the shore, scrabbling with its fingers in the loose sand; and this time it gave Maddox the impression of something else—a horrible impression of an enormous toad. He hesitated, and then swallowing down his reluctance with an effort, walked towards the crouching, shrouded figure.

As he approached it suddenly sprang upright, and with a curious, gliding movement, impossible to describe, sped away inland at an incredible speed, its gown flapping as it went. Again Maddox heard the longdrawn mournful howl.

Maddox stood gazing through the thickening dusk.

'Of course it's impossible to tell in this light,' he muttered to himself, 'but it certainly did look extraordinarily tall—and what an odd look it had of being *flat*. It looked like a scarecrow, with no thickness...'

He wondered at his own relief that the creature had gone. He told himself that it was because he loathed any abnormality, and there could be no doubt that the person he had seen, whether it were woman or monk, was crazed, if not quite insane.

He walked to the place where it had crouched. Yes, there was the patch of disturbed sand, rough among the surrounding smoothness. It occurred to him to look for the footprints made by the flying figure to see if they bore out his impression of abnormal height; but either the light was too bad for him to find them, or the creature had leapt straight on to the belt of shingle. At any rate, there were no footmarks visible.

Maddox knelt beside the patch of disturbed sand and half idly, half in interest, began himself to sift it through his fingers. He felt something hard and smooth—a stone perhaps? He took it up.

It was not a stone, anyhow, though the loose, damp sand clung to it so that he could not clearly distinguish what it was. He got to his feet, clearing it with his handkerchief; and then he saw that it was a box or case, three or four inches long, covered with some kind of rude carving. It fell open of itself as he turned it about, and he saw that inside was a wrapping of something like, yet unlike, leather; inside again was something that crackled like paper.

He looked round to see whether the figure that had either buried or sought this object—he was not sure which it had done—was returning; but he could see nothing but the bushes of gorse and heath black and stunted against the grey sky. There was no sound but the sigh of the night wind and the gentle lap of the incoming tide. His curiosity proved too strong for him, and he slipped the case into his pocket as he turned homewards.

Supper—a simple meal of soup and cheese and cider—was awaiting him when he got in, and he had no time to do more than change his shoes and wash his hands; but after supper, sitting on one side of the wide hearth while the curé smoked placidly on the other, Maddox felt the little box in his pocket, and began to tell his host of his queer adventure.

The curé's lack of enthusiasm rather damped him. No, he knew of no woman in the whole of his wide parish who would behave as Maddox described. There was no monastery in the neighbourhood, and if there were it would not be permitted to the brethren to act like that. He seemed mildly incredulous, in fact, until Maddox, quite nettled, took out the little case and slapped it down on the table.

It was a more uncommon object than he had at first supposed. It was, to begin with, extremely heavy and hard—as heavy as lead, but of a far harder metal. The chasing was queer; the figures reminded Maddox of runes; and remembering the prehistoric remains in Brittany, a thrill ran through him. He was no antiquarian, but it occurred to him that this find of his might be an extremely interesting one.

He opened the case. As he had thought, there was a scrap of some leathery substance within, carefully rolled round a piece of parchment. That couldn't be prehistoric, of course; but Maddox was still interested. He smoothed it out and began stumblingly to read out the crabbed words. The language was Latin of a sort, and he was so occupied in endeavouring to make out the individual words that he made no attempt to construe their meaning until Father Vétier stopped him with a horrified cry and even tried to snatch the document out of his hand.

Maddox looked up, exceedingly startled. The little priest was quite pale, and looked as horrified as if he had been asked to listen to the most shocking blasphemy.

'Why, *mon père*, what's wrong?' asked Maddox, astonished.

'You should not read things like that,' panted the little curé. 'It is wrong to have that paper. It is a great sin.'

'Why? What does it mean? I wasn't translating.'

A little colour crept back to the priest's cheeks, but he still looked greatly disturbed.

'It was an invocation,' he whispered, glancing over his shoulder. 'It is a terrible paper, that. It calls up—*that one*.'

Maddox's eyes grew bright and eager.

'Not really? Is it, honestly?' He opened out the sheet again.

The priest sprang to his feet.

'No, Monsieur, I must beg you! No! You have not understood—'

He looked so agitated that Maddox felt compunction. After all, the little chap had been very decent to him, and if he took it like that—! But he couldn't help thinking that it was a pity to let these ignorant peasants have jobs as parish priests. Really, there was enough superstition in their church as it was without drafting old forgotten country charms and incantations into it. A little annoyed, he put the paper back into its case and dropped the whole thing into his pocket. He knew quite well that if the curé got his hands on it he would have no scruples whatever about destroying the whole thing.

That evening did not pass as pleasantly as usual. Maddox felt irritated by the crass ignorance of his companion, and Father Vétier was quite unlike his customary placid self. He seemed nervous, timid even; and Maddox noticed that when the presbytery cat sprang on to the back of her master's chair and rubbed her head silently against his ear the curé almost sprang out of his seat as he hurriedly crossed himself. The time dragged until Maddox could propose retiring to bed; and long after he had been in his room he could hear Father Vétier (for the inner walls of the presbytery were mere lath and plaster) whispering prayers and clicking the beads of his rosary.

When morning came Maddox felt rather ashamed of himself for having alarmed the little priest, as he undoubtedly had done. His compunction increased when he saw Father Vétier as he came in from his early Mass, for the little man looked quite pale and downcast. Maddox mentally cursed himself. He felt like a man who has distressed a child, and he cast about for some small way of making amends. Halfway through déjeuner he had an idea.

'Father,' he said, 'you are making alterations in your church here, are you not?'

The little man brightened visibly. This, Maddox knew, was his pet hobby.

'But yes, Monsieur,' he replied quite eagerly. 'For some time now I have been at work, now that at last I have enough. Monseigneur has given me his blessing. It is, you see, that there is beside our church here the fragment of an old building—oh, but old! One says that perhaps it also was a church or a shrine once, but what do I know?—but it is very well built, very strong, and I conceived the idea that one might join it to the church. Figure to yourself, Monsieur, I should then have a double aisle! It will be magnificent. I shall paint it, naturally, to make all look as it should. The church is already painted of a blue of the most heavenly, for the Holy Virgin, with lilies in white—I had hoped for lilies of gold, but gold paint, it is incredible, the cost!—and the new chapel I will have in crimson for the Sacred Heart, with hearts of yellow as a border. It will be gay, isn't it?'

Maddox shuddered inwardly.

'Very gay,' he agreed gloomily. There was something that appealed to him very much in the shabby whitewashed little church. He felt pained at the very thought of Father Vétier's blue and crimson and yellow. But the little curé noticed nothing.

'Already I have begun the present church,' he babbled, 'and, monsieur, you should see it! It is truly celestial, that colour. Now I shall begin to prepare the old building, so that, as soon as the walls are built to join it to the present church, I can decorate. They will not take long, those little walls, not long at all, and then I shall paint...'

He seemed lost in a vision of rapture. Maddox was both amused and touched. Good little chap, it had been a shame to annoy him over that silly incantation business. He felt a renewed impulse to please the friendly little man.

'Can I help you at all, Father?' he asked. 'Could I scrape the walls for you or anything like that? I won't offer to paint; I'm not expert enough.'

The priest positively beamed. He was a genial soul who loved company, even at his work; but even more he loved putting on thick layers of bright colours according to his long-planned design. To have a companion who did not wish to paint was more than he had ever hoped for. He accepted with delight.

After breakfast, Maddox was taken to see the proposed addition to the church. It stood on the north side of the little church (which, of course, ran east and west), and, as far as Maddox could see, consisted mainly of a piece of masonry running parallel with the wall of the church. Fragments of walls, now crumbled, almost joined it to the east and west ends of the north wall of the church; it might almost have been, at one time, a part of the little church.

It certainly, as Father Vétier had said, would not take much alteration to connect it to the church as a north aisle. Maddox set to work to chip the plaster facing from the old wall with a good will.

In the afternoon the curé announced that he had to pay a visit to a sick man some miles away. He accepted with great gratitude his visitor's proposal that he should continue the preparations for the painting of the new aisle. With such efficient help, he said, he would have the addition to the church ready for the great feast of St Michael, patron saint both of the village and the church. Maddox was delighted to see how completely his plan had worked in restoring the little man's placid good-humour.

Shortly after two, Maddox went into the churchyard and resumed his labours. He chipped away industriously, and was just beginning to find the work pall when he made a discovery that set him chipping again eagerly at the coat of plaster which later hands had daubed thickly on the original wall. There were undoubtedly mural paintings on the portion he had begun to uncover. Soon he had laid bare quite a large stretch, and could see that the decoration formed a band, six or seven feet deep, about two feet from the ground, nearly the whole length of the wall.

The light was fading, and the colours were dim, but Maddox could see enough to interest him extremely. The paintings seemed to represent a stretch of the seashore, and though the landscape was treated conventionally he thought it looked like part of the beach near Kerouac. There were figures in the painting, too; and these aroused his excitement, for one at least was familiar. It was a tall shape, hooded, with hanging draperies—the figure he had seen the night before on the beach. Perhaps it was due to the archaic treatment of the picture that this figure gave him the same impression of flatness. The other figure—if it was a figure—was even stranger. It crouched on the ground before the hooded shape, and to Maddox it suggested some rather disgusting animal—a toad or a thick, squat fish. The odd thing was that, although it squatted before the tall figure, it gave the impression of domination.

Maddox felt quite thrilled. He peered closely at the painting, endeavouring to make out clearly what it represented; but the short October afternoon was drawing in fast, and, beyond his first impression, he could gather very little. He noticed that there was one unexpected feature in the otherwise half-familiar landscape—a hillock or pile of large stones or rocks, on one side of which he could just make out words or fragments of words. '*Qui peuct venir*' he read in one place, and, lower down, '*Celuy qui ecoustera et qui viendra... sacri... mmes pendus...*'

There was also some vague object, a pile of seaweed, Maddox thought, lying heaped below the hillock.

Little though he knew either of art or of archaeology, Maddox was keenly interested by this discovery. He felt sure that this queer painting must represent some local legend or superstition. And it was very odd that he should have seen, or thought he had seen, that figure on the beach *before* he had discovered the mural painting. There could be no doubt that he had seen it; that it was no mere fancy of his tired mind there was the box and the incantation, or whatever it was, in his pocket to prove. And that gave him an idea. It would be extremely interesting if he should find that the old French words on the mural painting and the Latin words on the parchment in any way corresponded. He took the little metal case from his pocket and opened it.

'*Clamabo et exaudiet me.*' 'I will call and he will hear.' That might be any prayer. Sounds rather like a psalm. '*Quoniam iste qui venire potest*'—ah! '*qui peuct venir*'!—what's this? *sacrificium hominum*—Heavens! *What's that?*'

Far off across the heath he heard a faint cry—the distant howling of the thing he had seen on the beach...

He listened intently. He could hear nothing more.

'Some dog howling,' he said to himself. 'I'm getting jumpy. Where was I?'

He turned back to the manuscript; but even during the few moments of distraction the light had faded, and he had to strain his eyes to see anything of the words.

'"*E paludinis ubi est habitaculum tuum ego te convoco*",' he read slowly aloud, spelling out the worn writing. 'I don't think there's anything in the painting to correspond with that. How odd it is! "From the marshes where thy dwelling is I call thee." Why from the *marshes*, I wonder? "*E paludinis ubi est habitaculum tuum ego te convoco—*".'

He broke off abruptly. Again there came that dreadful howl—and it certainly was not the howl of a dog. It was quite close...

Maddox did not stop to consider. He leapt up, ran through the yard into the presbytery, and locked the door behind him. He went to the front door and locked that too; and he bolted every window in the tiny house. Then, and not till then, did he pause to wonder at his own precipitate flight. He was trembling violently, his breath coming in painful gasps. He told himself that he had acted like a hysterical old maid—like a schoolgirl. And yet he could not bring himself to open a window. He went into the little sitting-room and made up the fire to an unwonted size; then he tried to take an interest in Father Vétier's library of devotional books until the little curé himself should return. He was nervous and uneasy; it seemed to him that he could hear some creature (he told himself that it must be a large dog, or perhaps a goat) snuffling about the walls and under the door... He was inexpressibly relieved when at last he heard the short, decided step of the curé coming up the path to the house.

Maddox was restless that night. He had short, heavy snatches of sleep in which he was haunted by dreams of pursuit by that flat, hooded being; and once he woke with a strangled cry and a cold shudder of disgust from a dream that, in his flight, he had stumbled and fallen face downwards on something soft and cold which moved beneath him—a mass of toads... He lay awake for a long time after that dream; but he eventually slipped into a drowsy state, half waking and half sleeping, in which he had an uncomfortable impression that he was not alone in the room—that something was breathing close beside him, moving about in a fumbling, stealthy way. And his nerves were so overwrought that he simply had not the courage to put out a hand and feel for the matches lest his fingers should close on—something else. He did not try to imagine what.

Towards dawn he fell into an uneasy doze, and awoke with a start. Some sound had awakened him—a melancholy howling cry rang in his ears; but whether it had actually sounded or whether it was part of his memories and evil dreams he could not tell.

He looked ill and worn at breakfast, and gave his bad night as an excuse for failing to continue his work on the old wall. He spent a wretched, moping day; he could settle to nothing indoors.

At last, tempted by the mellow October sun, he decided to go for a brisk, short walk. He would return before dusk—he was quite firm about that—and he would avoid the lonely reaches of the shore.

The afternoon was delicious. The rich scent of the gorse and heather, warm in the sun, and the cool touch from the sea that just freshened the breeze, soothed and calmed Maddox wonderfully. He had almost forgotten his terrors of the night before—at least, he was able to push them into a back corner of his mind. He turned homewards contentedly—even in his new calm he was not going to be out after sundown—when his eyes happened to fall on the white road where the declining sun threw his shadow, long and thin, before him. As he saw that shadow, his heart gave a sudden heavy *thud*; for a second shadow walked beside his own.

He spun round. No mortal creature was in sight. The road stretched empty behind him, and on either hand the moorland spread its breast to the wide sky. He ran to the presbytery like a hunted thing.

That evening Father Vétier ventured to speak to him.

'Monsieur,' he said, rather timidly, 'I do not wish to intrude myself into your affairs. That understands itself. But I have promised my very good friend M. Foster that I will take care of you. You are not a Catholic, I know; but—will you wear this?'

As he spoke he took from his own neck a thin silver chain to which was attached a little medal, black with age, and held it out to his guest.

'Thank you, father,' said Maddox simply, slipping the chain about his neck.

'Ah! That is well,' said the little curé with satisfaction. 'And now, monsieur, I venture to ask you—will you let me change your room? I have one, not as good as yours, I admit it, but which has in it a small opening into the church. You will perhaps repose yourself better there. You will permit?'

'With the greatest pleasure,' said Maddox fervently. 'You are very kind to me, father.'

The little man patted his hand.

'It is that I like you very much, monsieur,' he said naively. 'And—I am not altogether a fool. We of Brittany see much that we do not look at, and hear much to which we do not listen.'

'Father,' said Maddox awkwardly, 'I want to ask you something. When I began to read out that paper—you remember?—' (The curé nodded uneasily)—'you said that it was an invocation—that it summoned *celui-là*. Did you mean—the devil?'

'No, my son. I—I cannot tell you. It has no name with us of Kerouac. We say, simply, *celui-là*. You will not, if you please, speak of it again. It is not good to speak of it.'

'No, I can imagine it isn't,' said Maddox; and the conversation dropped.

Maddox certainly slept better that night. In the morning he told himself that this might be for more than one reason. The bed might be more comfortable (but he knew it was not that); *or* he might have overtired himself the day before; or the little curé's offerings might somehow have given him a kind of impression of safety and protection without really having the least power to guard him. His feeling of security increased when the priest announced:

'Tomorrow we have another guest, monsieur. M. Foster has done me the honour to accept my invitation for a visit.'

'Foster? Really? Excellent,' cried Maddox. He felt that the doctor stood for science and civilization and sanity and all the comfortable reassuring things of life that were so utterly lacking in the desolate wildness of Kerouac.

Sure enough, Foster came next day, and was just as stolid and ugly and completely reassuring as Maddox had hoped he would be and half feared he would not. He seemed to be ignoring his friend's physical condition at first; but on the day after his arrival he got to business.

'Maddox, I don't know how you expect to get fit again,' he said. 'You came here for the air as much as anything. I said you were to take moderate exercise. Yet here you stick, moping about this poky little house.' (Needless to say, Father Vétier was not present when this conversation took place.) 'What's wrong with the place, eh? I'd have said it was excellent walking country.'

Maddox flushed a little.

'It's a bit boring, walking alone,' he said evasively, well aware that 'boring' was not the right word.

'Perhaps… Yes. But you can get out a bit more now I'm here to come along. You might take me out this afternoon; the cure's going off to some kind of conference.'

Maddox wondered uneasily how much Foster knew. Had he come by chance, off his own bat? Or had Father Vétier been worried about his first guest and sent for him? If that were so, what exactly had the priest said? He thought he'd soon get that out of Foster.

They walked along the beach, farther than Maddox had yet been. He had avoided the shore of late, and he had not felt up to going so far when he first came to Kerouac; yet, though he knew he had never been on that particular reach of shore, the place seemed familiar. It is, of course, a common thing to feel that one knows a place which one is now seeing for the first time; but the impression was so extremely vivid that Maddox couldn't help remarking on it to his companion.

'Rot, my dear man,' said Foster bluntly. 'You haven't been in Brittany before, and you say you've never been as far as this. It's not such uncommon country, you know; it's like lots of other places.'

'I know,' said Maddox; but he was not satisfied.

He was poor company for the rest of the walk, and was very silent on the way home. No amount of chaff from Foster could rouse him, and at last the doctor abandoned the effort. The men reached the presbytery in silence.

The next day was close, threatening rain, though the downpour held off from hour to hour. Neither of the two Englishmen felt inclined to walk under that lowering sky. Father Vétier had a second urgent summons from his sick parishioner at Cap Morel, and set off, wrapped in a curious garment of tarpaulin, soon after the second déjeuner. He remarked that he might take the occasion of being so near to Prénoeuf to pay some visits there, and that he probably would not be in until nightfall.

'If monsieur should feel disposed,' he said rather shyly to Maddox before he left, 'M. Foster might be interested to see the alterations I propose for the church. He has taste, M. Foster. It might amuse him…'

He was so clearly keen to display his decorations, and yet a little afraid of appearing vain if he showed them himself, that Maddox smiled.

'I'm sure he'd like to see them,' he said gently.

Yet, though he could have given no possible reason for it, he felt strongly disinclined to go near that half-ruined wall with its stretch of painting only half displayed. He knew it was absurd. He had worked there till he was tired; he had been startled by the howling of a dog. That was all. No doubt, when he came to look at it again, he would find that the fresco was the merest clumsy daub, and that his own overwrought nerves, together with the uncanny light of the gloaming and the beastly dog, had exaggerated it into something sinister and horrible. He declared to himself that if he had the courage to go and look again, he would simply laugh at himself and his terrors. But at the back of his mind he knew that he would never have gone alone; and it was a mixture of bravado and a kind of hope that Foster's horse-sense would lay his terror for him that finally induced him to propose a visit to the place.

Foster was interested, mildly, by what Maddox told him of the painting on the ruined wall. He went out first to the rough little churchyard; Maddox, half reluctantly, went to fetch down the little case he had picked up on the beach in order that Foster might with his own eyes compare the two inscriptions; and when he did go out to join his friend he could hardly bring himself to go over to the wall he had worked on. It took quite an effort to force his feet over to it.

The decoration was not quite as he had remembered it. The figures were so indistinct and faint that they were hardly visible. In fact, Maddox could well believe that a stranger would not recognize the daub as representing figures at all. His relief at this discovery was quite absurd. He felt as if an immense and crushing weight had been lifted from his spirit; and, his first anxiety over, he bent to examine the rest of the painting more attentively. That was nearly exactly as he remembered it—the pile of stones with the half-illegible words; the tumbled huddle of seaweed or rags lying before it; the long reach of shore—ah! that was it!

'Foster! Come and look here,' he said.

'Where?' asked the doctor, strolling over.

'Look—this fresco or whatever it is. I said that bit of shore we saw yesterday was familiar. This is where I saw it.'

'Mmmm. Might be... All very much alike, though, this part of the beach. I don't see anything to get worked up about.'

'Oh! If you're going to take that line!' cried Maddox, exasperated. 'You doctors are all alike—"Keep calm"—"Don't get excited"—"Nothing to worry about"!...'

He broke off, gulping with sheer rage.

'My dear Maddox!' said Foster, startled by his silent friend's outburst. 'I'm awfully sorry. I wasn't trying to snub you in the least. I simply thought—' He too broke off. Then he decided to risk another annoyance. 'What have you got on your mind?' he asked, rather urgently. 'Tell me, Maddox, there's a good chap. What is it?'

He paused hopefully; but Maddox had dried up. He could not explain. He knew that his solid, comfortable friend would never, *could* never understand that his terror was not imaginary; he could not bear to watch him soothing down his friend, to see the thought 'hysteria' in his mind... Yet it would be a relief to tell...

'Look at this,' he said at last. He took from his pocket the case he had found on the beach. 'What do you make of that paper?' he asked.

Foster moved out of the shadow of the wall so that the pale watery sunlight, struggling through the clouds, fell on the parchment. Maddox, a little relieved by the serious way he took it, turned back to examine the painting again. It was certainly very odd that the figures, which he remembered so clearly and which had seemed so very distinct, should now appear so dim that he doubted their reality. They seemed even fainter now than they had when he had looked at them a few minutes ago. And that heap flung beneath the hillock—what did that represent? He began to wonder whether that, too, were a figure—a drowned man, perhaps. He bent closer, and, as he stooped, he was aware that some one beside him was looking over his shoulder, almost leaning on him.

'Odd, Foster, isn't it?' he said. 'What do you make of that huddled thing under the stones?'

There was no answer, and Maddox turned. Then he sprang to his feet with a shuddering cry that died in his throat. The thing so close to him was not his friend. It was the hooded creature of the beach...

Foster found the parchment so interesting that he was anxious to see it more clearly. He peered at it closely for a minute, and then decided to go into the presbytery for a light. He had some difficulty with the old-fashioned oil lamp; but when he finally got it burning he thought that the document fully repaid his trouble. He became so absorbed that it was not for some minutes that he realized that it was growing very dark and that Maddox had not yet come in. He felt quite disproportionately anxious as he hurried out to the tiny overgrown churchyard.

He was startled into something very like panic when he found no one there. Without reason, he knew that there was something horribly wrong, and, blindly obeying the same instinct, he rushed out of the tiny enclosure and ran at his top speed down to the beach. He knew that he would find whatever there was to find on that lonely reach that was pictured on the old wall.

There was a faint glimmer of daylight still—enough to confuse the light until Foster, half distraught with a nameless fear, could hardly tell substance from shadow. But once he thought he saw ahead of him two figures—one a man's, and the other a tall wavering shape almost indistinguishable in the gloom.

The sand dragged at his feet till they felt like lead. He struggled on, his breath coming in gasps that tore his lungs. Then, at last, the sand gave way to coarse grass and then to a stretch of salt marshland, where the mud oozed up over his shoes and water came lapping about his ankles. Open pools lay here and there, and he saw, as he struggled and tore his feet from the viscous slime, horrible creatures like toads or thick, squat fish, moving heavily in the watery ooze.

The light had almost gone as he reached the line of beach he knew: and for one terrible moment he thought he was too late. There was the pile of stones; beneath them lay a huddled black mass. Something—was it a shadow?—wavered, tall and vague, above the heap, and before it squatted a shape that turned Foster cold—something thick, lumpish, like an enormous toad...

He screamed as he dragged his feet from the loathsome mud that clooped and gulped under him—screamed aloud for help...

Then suddenly he heard a voice—a human voice.

'*In nomine Dei Omnipotenti...*' it cried.

Foster made one stupendous effort, and fell forward on his knees. The blood sang in his ears, but through the hammering of his pulses he heard a sound like the howling of a dog dying away in the distance.

'It was by the providence of the good God that I was there,' said Father Vétier afterwards. 'I do not often come by the shore—we of Kerouac, monsieur, we do not like the shore after it is dusk. But it was late, and the road by the shore is quicker. Indeed I think the good saints led me... But if my fear had been stronger so that I had not gone that way—and it was very strong, monsieur—I do not think that your friend would be living now.'

'Nor do I,' said Foster soberly. 'My God, Father, it—it was nearly over. *Sacrificium hominum,* that beastly paper said... I—I saw the loathsome thing waiting... he was lying in front of that hellish altar or whatever it was... *Why,* Father? Why did it have that power over him?'

'I think it was that he read the—the invocation—aloud,' said the curé slowly. 'He called it, do you see, monsieur—he said the words. What he saw at first is—is often seen. We are used to it, we of Kerouac. We call it *Celui-là*. But it is, I believe, only a servant of—that other...'

'Well,' said Foster soberly, 'you're a brave man, Padre. I wouldn't spend an hour here if I could help it. As soon as poor Maddox can travel I'm going home with him. As to living here alone—!'

'And you are right to go,' said Father Vétier, gravely. 'But for me—no, monsieur. It is my post, do you see. And one prays, monsieur—one prays always.'

Isle of Man

1899

OUTWITTING THE DEVIL

Bill Billy

Bill Billy—with a name like Bill's, it has been impossible to find any trace of him and is likely to be a pseudonym. His work appeared in one of the earliest folklore anthologies from the Isle of Man, *Manx Tales* (S. K. Broadbent & Company, *c.*1899). His stories from *Manx Tales* include 'Riding the Devil', 'A Night with the Fairies', 'The Fairies' Victim' and the final story in the book, 'Outwitting the Devil', which this *Celtic Weird* reprints for the first time in 123 years. Told in original Manx dialect, can the Devil really take the form of a horse?

I GOT the yarn I'm goin' to tell yer from an' oul' man tha' used to live down at the North. He said they wor' pirreagh hard up for a lil chapal to meet togathar in ov a Sunday for worship. Lots ov the farmers livin' roun' wor' middlin' well off, an' they wor' thinkin' it was time they hed a battar place till a barn, an' where they might be comfible an' dacent. So they called a meetin' one everin', an' it was settled to build a lil chapal.

Now, the Northside people hev got the name ov bein' middlin' free with their money. Bur I believe in me hart the Southside ones are jus' as kind-harted with a birra mate or the lek ov that, if they've gor it to spare. Enyway, big Johnny Teare gave them the groun', an' they got lave tor all the stones they cud draw erruf the quarry. Joughin the mason got the job of doin' the buildin' an' the English praacher from town was to pur a lil sight on them sometimes, an' see that they wor' doin' all right.

Everybody was agreein' nice, an' the buildin' was goin' on bravely; an' the people wor' sayin' thar it wudn' be long, if the wather kep' fine, till they'd hev the roof on. Theer hed been nice dryin' for a while, an' then the weather bruk again, an' wan night theer was a ter'ble storm, an' nex' mornin' the walls ov the chapal wor' laval with the groun'. The poor masons wor' gettin blamed (jus' lek they are yit) for their maul work, an' they wor' excusin' themselves, sayin' the walls wor' on'y green, an' cudn' be expected to stand.

Well, after a bir ov a houl' on, they agreed to pay the masons, so they made another start. After clearin' away the rubbidge, they began again, an' all went well till they wor' ready to set scaffold. Nex' mornin' when they cum to work, behoul' ye! the walls wor' down again, an' scatter'd that theer warn' one stone lef' stannin' atop ov another. All the mortar tubs an' the mason's tools wor' all scatter'd an' buried under the rubbidge.

Joughin was awful mad, an' began to jaw the men. They all said it warn' their fault, but that theer was some 'butcheragh' [witchcraft] on the place, an' they warn' goin to work on the job eny more.

So another meetin' was held by the people tha' was buildin' the chapal, an' they all agreed that they wudn' be bet, but they wud pay for the work tha' was done, and let the masons begin again.

The men warn' very willin' at fust to start again, bur at las' Joughin got them bissuaded, an' they started. Ye see, the winter was comin' on, an' the days wor' gettin' short, so they wor' anxious to ger it roofed while the weather was dry.

Everything seemed to be goin' on all right at las'. They hed been workin' ar it for several weeks, an' theer was no sign ov the walls givin' a bit, so everybody was thinkin' that the wuss was over, an' that they wudn' be bothared again.

The English praacher hed been out ar a farmhouse that night, seein' a man tha' was sick and not expected to ger over it. He was anxious to ger home, so as he knew the road, he started in the dark, expectin' to ger in the town by daylight. As he went pass the lil chapal on his way, he tuk a notion to hev a walk roun' it an' see how it was shapin'. As he cum closer, he hard the soun' of dull heavy blows strikin' agin the wall.

He thought it queer tha' enybody wud be about at that time, for it was too arly for the masons to be at work. He warn' a coward, bur he began to get narvous, an' then he thought to himself, 'Why should I be afraid and run away, even if is the devil himself? Wasn' that the very rason he was a praacher, to fight the devil an' try an' save poor souls from him.' So up the lane he went, an' roun' to the other side of the chapal, an' he saw a quare sight.

An' oul' scraggy grey horse was backed up agin the walls, an' kickin' at them with his hind feet. At fust the praacher was inclined to laff, bur he soon saw it wasn' a laffin' matter, for the blows wor' beginnin' to make the walls tremble, so he went up to the horse to drive it away.

As he cum close, the horse noticed him an' stopped kickin', but before he could run away the praacher gripped him by the nose with both hands, an' said in a quiet voice, 'Thou are in my power now, an' as a horse thou will hev to labour for the cause thou has tried to hinder and destroy.'

The brute knew very well wha' he was sayin', for his eyes wor' flashin' lek fire with wickedness, an' the 'coughty' [wicked] baste foamed at the mouth an' struggled to ger away, bur it warn' eny use.

The divil hed tuk the shape ov a horse, an' the praacher gripped him lek a horse, an' held on to him, an' hed the mastery ov him, so at las', after a struggle, the brute hed to give in.

By this time the day hed bruk, and it was jus' beginnin' to get light. As the east began to get rosy with the risin' sun, the sleepin' craturs begun to stir themselves. Fust the cocks begun to crow a harty good mornin', an' then the sounds ov the cattle movin' in the farm yards, and the voices of the farmers an' their man-sarvants, as they put their heds out to pur a sight on the weather, bruk on the quiet mornin' air.

The horse cudn' stan' the daylight an' the sounds of livin' craturs, so he begun to get restless again, an' it tuk all the strength an' pluck ov the preacher to houl' him.

It warn' long till he hard the soun' ov voices comin', an' soon the masons wor' at the place. They tuk ter'ble wonder to see the preacher there before them, howlin' on to an oul' horse.

Howavar he didn' give them time to stan' lookin' ar' him, but shouted to them to ger him a bit of a thow an' make a haltar, so thar he cud houl' the horse aisier, for his hands wor' beginnin' to get cramped and stiff. When the haltar was pur on him, he tied him to a gate post, an' begun to consider what to do with him.

The masons seemed lek as if they wanted the skeet, but as the praacher didn' make a shape to tell them, they didn't lek to ask, so they started work.

One of the men ses to Joughin, 'We'll soon be stuck for stones, for Harry Bill's horse is lame, an' can't draw today.'

Then a notion tuk houl' ov the praacher to make the divil help to build the very place he was bent on destroyin', so he ses, 'This is a strong horse, though rather unruly an' difficult to manage, an' if the owner of the sick horse is willin' to lend his cart, I'll drive this horse an' fetch you stones from the quarry.'

One of the masons went to show him where Harry Bill lived, an' to ask for the loan of the cart. Ov coorse. Harry Bill was quite willin', poor man, so they cum back an' got the oul' horse, an' harnessed him in the cart, an' away to the quarry with tham.

'Deed, an' they hed a job gettin' the horse in the cart, bur at long las', after a deal of 'sthaaga' [bother], they managed it. Ov coorse the quarrymen wor' surprised to see the praacher from town so soon in the mornin', an' especially to see him drivin' Harry Bill's cart. They sed, 'We'll hev to load light, for that baste won't be able to drag the cart up the road empty, let alone a good load.' But the praacher made them pur a good load on, an' all the time he stood by the horse's head, houlin' him.

When the cart was full, the men sed, 'The trace horse will be here in a few minutes to give yer a pull up the quarry road, for is alwis takin' two good horses to pull the loaded cart up the lane to the high road.'

'Navar mind,' ses the praacher, 'This horse is as strong as eny two in the parish.'

So he give him a lick with the whip, an' away he went lek smook, thinkin nothin' ov it. When they gor up to the high road, the horse tried to bolt, an' it tuk the praacher all his time to houl' him in, so he lashed him with the whip, an' ripped at the lines, an' made the brute feel thar he was his master; so at las' the horse give in, an' went on pretty quate.

When they cum in sight ov the buildin', the horse tuk the sterriks again, an' the drivar hed to give him a good latherin' before he went on. At las', thor, he got the load kicked, an' started for another; an' the nex' time the oul' horse seemed more aisier, an' gradually he becum quiet enough, an' at las' went for his load without eny mustha.

It was gettin' on towards dinner time, an' the praacher hedn' a birra mate since the day before, so he was gettin' hungry. He sent word to Harry Bill to cum an' drive the cart in the everin'.

When Harry cum, the praacher toul him that this was a rather queer horse in some ways, bur he would manage all right if he was firm with him. He said, 'I'm goin' for me dinner an' a short sleep, so I may be a while away; but on no account lave the horse's hed, or let go the lines till I cum back.'

'But the crathur'll want somethin' to ate, for all,' ses Harry Bill.

'No,' ses the praacher, 'Nawthin' till I cum back, an', if he gets botharsome, use the whip.'

'Well, well,' ses Harry Bill to the masons when the praacher hed gone. 'This is the queeras horse I avar seen. He don't want a "scaveen" [morsel] to ate all day, an' yit he's as strong as eny two horses in the parish, an' yer can lather him all yer want. I'd lek to buy him; I wondar if he'd sell him chape.'

At las' Harry started for the quarry, walkin' by the horse's hed. The oul' horse went fuss rate, an' they gor a good load an' cum back an' kicked it.

One of the masons called to Harry, 'Well, how is thee self an' the horse gerrin' on?'

'Aw, bravely, bravely,' ses Harry Bill. 'I don't see nawthin' abour 'im to make such a mustha about. He's strong uncomman, for all he's so "maganagh" [awkward] lookin' bur I mus' be goin' for anothar load, I suppose,' an' he led the horse away.

Now, Harry Bill was a kind-harted man, an' he thought it wasn' justice to load the poor baste so hevy, for he thought it mus' be gettin' tired. When they wor' passin' the water trough at the public house, the horse showed signs he was gettin' dry. Harry druv pass, howavar, for he was thinkin' ov what the praacher hed ordered him.

At las', thor, as the everin' went on, Harry begun to get dry himself an' when they wor' passin' the pub nex' time, he lef' the horse outside in the road, an' went in for a glass ov ale. As soon as he gor inside, he set down to drink his ale, an' got tawkin' with some other fallas that wor' in, an' forgot all about the horse an' cart.

After a quile, he thought on himself and jumped up, sayin', 'I mus' give the horse a drink an' be goin'.' When he cum to the door, theer was the cartload o' stones in the middle o' the road, but the horse was gone. He climbed up on the hedge an' looked all roun' the fields, but theer wasn' no horse to be seen, so he lef' the cart in the road, an' started for the buildin', expectin' he wud get in throuble for his neglect.

He met the praacher waitin' for him, an' towl him the truth, an' how he hed los' the horse, an' finished up by sayin', 'The divil mus' ha' been in the brute enyway.'

'Navar mind,' ses the praacher, 'You hev guessed the truth; bur I think we hev given the rascal more than he bargained for, an' I don't think we shall be bothared with him hereafter.'

1899

THE BLACK DOG OF COLBY GLEN

Billy Pheric

Billy Pheric is a pseudonym. The name 'Billy Pheric' comes from *Yn Lioar Manninagh: the Journal of the Isle of Man Natural History and Antiquarian Society, 1889*. Noted by Miss A. M. Crellin; she describes a Manx folk tale of a musician named Billy Pheric who was crossing the mountains from Druidale when he heard fairies singing by a thorn tree next to the river. The song that they were singing was called 'Bollan Bane' ('white wort', a specific ingredient in the fight against the Evil Eye and witchcraft). He wanted to learn the tune but each time he did, he forgot it, and had to go back to the river. It wasn't until the third visit that he remembered it. 'The Black Dog of Colby Glen', written in traditional Manx dialect, is reproduced here for the first time since 1899.

WHEN a boy nothing gave me more pleasure than to visit old Tom Juan Dick and hear him relate some of his stories of the Bugganes. Tom was a typical Manxman of his period; was a good-humoured, honest-hearted creature, and was considered by his neighbours to be 'the best man for a good turn' in Ballakilpheric—that being the village in which he lived. It was therefore a pleasure to visit 'Ould Tom' at his little thatch cottage, where he lived all alone in single blessedness—except for the company of his old faithful dog 'Rover.'

It was one cold winter's night, the wind howling and whistling down the chimney of Tom's cottage, that I sat on a low stool before the bright and cheerful-looking turf fire, listening with all eagerness as he told eloquently and positively the following story.

'Bugganes is nor as common now as they weer when I was a young falla' (he began); an a good job it is too mavee, for the young fellas now can thravel afther the gels without anything molestin' them. Bur it was very different when I was young. I can well remember, Billy bogh, one nite that Jemmy Dick gor agate wantin' me to go over with him to Ballayelse to purra site on the gels. At fuss I wasn' very willin' to go. I was naver much ov a hand at that job. Bur he kep' coaxin' me so much thar at las' I agreed to go. It wasn' long tel we weer makin' thracks through the 'Big Fiel's' by Colby Mill. Well, man, we got to the road, an' we went along right enough tel we got to the glen. Jemmy was plannin how we wud get to talk to the gels without owl Ballayelse knowin'. He was a terbil madman, was the Ballayelse, when fallas came about the house at nights after the gels. All ov a sudden, lek, there was a big black dog ran pas' us. There was sumthing mortal queer lookin' about him. We were a bit scarr'd, as the sayin' is. Thinkin we wud see no more ov him, we soon gor over it. We gor agate yarnin' about the gels an' other things tell we got to the glen gate. But, bless thee sowl, man, we heerd an' seen sumthin' there that made the hair stan' on our heads. Down in the glen we heerd a noise louder than the heaviest thunder. The black dog stood afore us with his eyes shinin' lek fire. Jemmy shouted an' gripped houl o' me. Afore we had time to move the dog went lek a shadder, lavin us breathless an' frekened urrov our wits. However, we gor a bit o' courage, an' started on our journey once more. Once pas' the glen we were all right. When we gor to Kitty Tommy Hal's we thought it was time for a sup o' jough—for Kitty kep' a tavern. But Kitty was gone to bed, it bein' then close on midnight. Howaver, we managed to ger her roused up, an' it wasn' long afore we had a couple o' pints lowered, an' with fresh courage set off for Ballayelse.

But luck was agin us that night, for we hed to go from there jus' as fas' as we came.

Jemmy had climbed up to the gels' bedroom winder an' was tappin' his fingers on the pane when a dog inside commenced growlin' terbil. Thinkin' thar it was the big dog we had seen afore, Jemmy let go his grips an' fell down among a lor o' milk cans.

This wakened Ould Ballayelse, an' afore we had time to think, he had his head out through a winder, an' was threatenin' to shoot us if we wudn' make ourselves sceerce.

Now, Ould Ballayelse was no fella to play with, as the sayin' is, an' we knew that the bes' for us to do was to ger away as soon as our legs cud carry us, though we thought terble hard of goin' without seein' the gels, an' mavee missin' a good supper. That wus nor all, if we went afore daylight we were mighty ap' to come foul ov the Black Dog in Colby Glen.

But go we mus' for by this time Ould Ballayelse, half dressed, had opened the door, an' was jawin' out o' massey, an' declarin' that he wud give the rapscallions lead. We ran for our lives. Afore we had time to look back we were once more rattlin' at Kitty Tommy Hal's door. Kitty was terble slow to ger up this time, but we war detarmined to have another peint afore facin' the glen, an' we kep' weltin at the door til Kitty—for feer ov it geddin' broke—gor up an' ler us in. We had another sud o' jough, an' then, feelin' a bit plucky lek, made a start for home.

It was a brave sorrov a nite, the sky was clear an' starry, but no moonlight. Jemmy thought it was light enough to cross the river by the plank at the top o' the glen, near Ballachrink, an', by goin' that way, give the 'slip' to the Bugganes.

But in this we weer mistaken. We gor over the river, an' into the field. All at once it gor as dark as if we weer in a mine hole. We knew we cudn' make our way, so we stud there houlin' on each other, an' tremblin' with fear and cowl for very near half-an-hour. Sumthin' toul us we had batthar pray. Neither ov us cud do much at that job. Howaver, Jemmy managed to say a few 'good words,' an' the nex' thing we knew was the darkness all gone. We cud see it, lek a cloud, goin' down the glen, til it went out o' sight. Then we heard growlin' an' yelpin' that was fit enough to waken everybody in the parish.

That was the las' we seen or heerd ov the Black Dog. It wasn' long til we were home an' thryan to gerra few hours' sleep.

When Tom had finished his story I found that it was late. Although I had only about a few minutes' walk in order to get home, I longed to be there without going. However, I said 'Evoi' to Ould Tom, and started. I did not dare to look around, for fear of seeing the 'Black Dog of Colby Glen.'

1949

THE TARROO-USHTEY

Nigel Kneale

Nigel Kneale (1922–2006) was born in Barrow-in-Furness but spent much of his early life on the Isle of Man where his father was the editor of a daily newspaper. After initially training to become a lawyer on the island Kneale, known as Tom to his family and friends, enrolled at RADA with ambitions to become an actor. At the same time he was writing short stories and these would form the basis of his first book, *Tomato Cain* (1949), which would go on to win the Somerset Maugham Award in 1950. Following this Kneale gave up acting to write full time and in 1951 he became one of the first staff writers at the BBC. It was here that he would form a partnership with the producer Rudolph Cartier which resulted in ground-breaking television drama milestones such as *The Quatermass Experiment* (1953), *Nineteen Eighty-Four* (1954) and *Quatermass and the Pit* (1957). He broke into cinema production with adaptations of the John Osbourne plays *Look Back In Anger* (1958) and *The Entertainer* (1960). He continued to work for the BBC up until the early 1970s when he left the corporation to work with ITV on such projects as the horror anthology series *Beasts* (1976) and a final *Quatermass* series in 1979. In 1954 Kneale married Judith Kerr, author of *The Tiger Who Came To Tea* (1968), and the couple had two children; Matthew who is also an author and Tacy who is a respected artist. 'The Tarroo-Ushtey' taps into villagers' ancient superstitious beliefs—but what's really in the loch?

IN far-off days before the preachers and the schoolmasters came, the island held a great many creatures besides people and beasts. The place swarmed with monsters.

A man would think twice before answering his cottage door on a windy night, in dread of a visit from his own ghost. The high mountain roads rang in the darkness with the thunderous tiffs of the bugganes, which had unspeakable shapes and heads bigger than houses; while a walk along the seashore after the sun had set was to invite the misty appearance of a tarroo-ushtey, in the likeness of a monstrous bull, ready to rush the beholder into the sea and devour him. At harvest-time the hairy troll-man, the phynod-deree, might come springing out of his elder-tree to assist in the reaping, to the farmer's dismay; for the best-intentioned of the beings were no more helpful than interfering neighbours, and likely to finish the day pulling the thatch off the house or trying to teach the hens to swim. What with the little people, the fairies themselves, so numerous that they were under everybody's feet, turning milk sour and jamming locks and putting the fire out; and with witches waiting at every other bend in the road with their evil eye ready to paralyse the horses, ordinary people led a difficult life. It was necessary to carry charm-herbs, or beads, and to remember warding-off rhymes that had been taught in early childhood.

As the generations went by and people took to speaking English on polite occasions, the old creatures grew scarcer. By the time that travellers from the packet boats had spread the story about a girl named Victoria being the new queen of the English, their influence was slipping; at night people put out milk for the fairies more from habit than fear, half-guessing it would be drunk by the cat; if they heard a midnight clamour from the henhouse, they reached for a musket, not a bunch of hawthorn. But back hair could still rise on a dark mountain road.

From the gradual loss of the old knowledge, came dependence on the wise men and women.

Charlsie Quilliam was one of these.

He was the fattest man on the island, said those who had travelled all over it and could speak with authority.

He carried his enormous body with special care, like a man with a brim-full jug; but he still stuck in doors and caused chairs to collapse; and people meeting him on a narrow path had to climb the hedge to let him pass. The right of way was always Charlsie's.

His fatness, coupled with a huge black beard, left little shape to his face, but his eyes were quick. Above them, like a heathery ledge, ran a single, unbroken line of eyebrow, which denoted second sight.

Whatever question was asked, he would be able to answer it. Even if he said nothing, the expression in his eyes showed that he knew, but considered the questioner would be better in ignorance. It was Charlsie who had had a vision of the potato blight crossing to Ireland in a black cloud, but he kept the frightening secret to himself until long afterwards, when the subsequent famine was common talk and nobody could be alarmed by what he had seen.

Old secret customs; birth-charms and death-charms, and rites for other dark days; Charlsie's big head held them all. Folk in trouble might set out for the minister's house, think better of it, and go to find Charlsie where he sat on a hump of earth outside his cottage, his thick fingers busy with scraps of coloured wool and feathers.

Ever since he became too fat for other work, his secret knowledge had supported him; and gifts of food from grateful clients kept his weight creeping up.

Many a winter night he would be at the centre of a fireside gathering. Charlsie's guttural, hoarse voice could hold a packed cottage in frightened suspense for hours as it laid horror upon horror. Personal experience of dealing with witches was his chief subject. Most of his stories had little point, which made them all the more uncanny and likely. People went home in groups after an evening with Charlsie.

Apart from the witches, he had only one open enemy.

This was a Scottish peddler named McRae. The man had lost a leg in the Crimea, and called himself a Calvinist. He sneered at the old beliefs and tried to tell his own war experiences instead; but people were chary of listening, in case Charlsie got to know. They bought Duncan McRae's buttons and shut the door quickly.

The little Scot hated it. At hardly a single house in the fat man's territory could he get himself invited inside for a free meal; even the news he brought from the towns was received with suspicion, when at all, as if he had made it up on the road. He would have cut the district out altogether, except that he sold more elastic there than anywhere else.

One hot afternoon in the late summer, the peddler sweated up the hill towards the village.

A dense sea-fog had smothered the sun, the air was close, and his pack wearied him. Time after time he had to rest his wooden leg.

Duncan McRae had news. A tit-bit he had picked up before he left town particularly pleased him, and had gone down well in two villages already. For once it was an item that people would be able to put to the proof themselves later on.

A new machine was to be tested on the English side of the channel, less than thirty miles away. It was said to be able to warn ships in fog.

McRae hastened. He had heard that when the new 'fog horn,' as they called it, was tested, people on the island might be able to hear it blowing faintly. Today's weather seemed very suitable for such an experiment, but even if nothing happened, surely this story at least had enough interest to call for hospitality.

At the top of the hill he leaned on a hedge to ease his leg. The air was heavy, and the quietness a relief after the clumping of his iron-tipped stump in the grit.

He held his breath, listening.

Far away there was a moan. He pulled himself up the hedge and faced towards the fog-blanketed sea.

The sound came again, faint and eerie; a growl so low-pitched that it could hardly be heard at all. It could only be one thing.

Excitedly, McRae slid down the hedge and straightened his pack. Within ten minutes, bursting with news, he had reached the first outlying cottage door. He rattled the latch and pushed it open.

'Hallo, there!' he called. 'D'ye hear the new invention yonder?'

There was silence; no one at home.

He hurried out, and on to the next fuchsia-hedged cabin. 'Hallo, missis! D'ye hear the wonders that's going on across the water—?'

No one to be seen.

McRae frowned. He was at the top end of the village now, looking down the winding street as it sloped towards the sea. There was nobody moving in it, and no sound. Even the blacksmith's forge was silent.

The peddler shouted, 'Where is everybody? Is there no' a single body up the day?'

His voice went quietly away into the mist.

Charlsie Quilliam had been in his cottage when they came for him. He was threading a dried caul on a neckband as a cure against shipwreck, working indoors because the damp grieved his chest.

People came clustering round his door, muttering.

'Come in or go out!' called Charlsie. He pricked his thumb. 'Devil take it! This caul is like the hide of a crocodile!'

They saw that he did not hear what they heard; he suffered at times from deafness. At last old Juan Corjeag persuaded him to come outside.

Charlsie was surprised to see nearly all the village assembled at his door.

'Just listen, Charlsie!' said old Juan.

The frightened faces seemed to be expecting something from him. 'Well, what is it at all?' he said after a moment.

'Oh—listen, do!'

Then Charlsie heard it. A sound that might have been made by a coughing cow far away on a calm night.

'Some beast that wants lookin' to,' he decided. 'Is that all? Whatever's got into everybody?'

Old Juan's face was too horrified to express anything. He pointed.

'Them sounds is from out at sea!' he said. There was a shocked murmur from the villagers at the speaking of the words.

Charlsie made no move. His little eyes sharpened.

'Tell us what it is, Charlsie! What've we got to do? Oh, an' it's far worse down by the water! The twist of the land smothers it here!'

Without a word Charlsie Quilliam turned back into his cottage; the crowd were alarmed by his stillness When he reappeared, he had his big blackthorn walking-stick in one hand; in the other was a bunch of dried leaves.

'I'm goin' down there for a sight,' he said. 'Anybody that wants to, can come.'

He set ponderously off.

For a little space they hesitated, whispering among themselves. Old Juan licked his lips and went after Charlsie. When he looked round, a few dozen paces down the shore path, he saw the rest following behind him in a body on the sandy track.

Charlsie stopped for breath. Old Juan caught him up.

'Ye're right. It's clearer down here.'

Old Juan spoke slowly. 'Charlsie, I'm hopin' it won't put bad luck on me, but I was the first that heard it.' He swallowed, remembering. 'Down in the tide, diggin' for lug-worms.'

'Ah?' said Charlsie. He grunted. 'Let's get nearer.'

As they came over the low brow of the foreshore, where the yellow sandy grass ended and the pebbles began, the sound hit them. It travelled straight in along the surface of the water; still very far away, but plainer to the ear; so unnatural that it shocked everybody afresh. It ended with a throaty gulp.

Charlsie made his way slowly across the stones, picking his way with the stick among the puddles. They all followed in silence towards the water's edge.

There he stood, leaning and listening.

Again and again and again the distant cry came from the fog, and they shivered. Old Juan made to speak, but Charlsie silenced him.

'Yes,' said Charlsie, turning back casually, 'it's a tarroo-ushtey.'

A woman screamed and had a hand clapped across her mouth. People drew back hastily from the creamy water's edge.

'What'll happen?' whispered old Juan.

Charlsie's single brow bent in a frown. 'Queer thing for it to come out in the daylight,' he said. 'It goes to prove such creatures is no fancy.'

He turned to the crowd and addressed them.

'Now listen, all! It's a tarroo-ushtey out yonder. Hush, now, hush! It's in trouble over somethin'—maybe lost an' callin' out to another one.'

'Aye, its mate, likely!' said Juan.

Charlsie ignored him. 'For all that they're not of this world, they can get lost in thick fog like any other creature. It's a terrible long way off at present; so the best thing to do is be quiet and go home, and do nothin' to draw it this way.

'An' I'll tell ye what he's like. They look like a tremendous big black bull, but their feet is webbed. An' in th' ould days they've had many a person eaten. So nobody must come down here tonight, for fear of the fog clearin' and it seein' him. There's no tellin' what it might do if it got up in the village.'

He showed the bunch of herbs in his left hand. 'Now everybody go home quiet, an' I'll see about layin' a charm on the water. Keep all the childher indoors!'

He sat on a low rock near the tide as they went.

Peering back at him, they saw him wave the leaves back and forth in his hand. He seemed to be chanting something. In the sight of old Juan, the last to cross the sandy bluff, he finished by tossing the bunch into the sea and turning abruptly away.

Charlsie laboured up the track without a look behind. The lowing sounds still continued. He felt satisfied with what he had done, but was checking the rites over in his mind to make sure. Ahead, the last stragglers reached the safety of the village.

But when he came to the houses, Charlsie found people still talking in small groups.

'Look here, I told ye to get the childher out of sight!' he said. 'An' it'd be just as well if everybody kept themselves—'

A commotion was going on farther up the street.

'What the devil is it now?' Charlsie shouted; he felt privileged to make a noise.

Old Juan hobbled towards him. 'It's that Scotch peddler!' he said. 'He's got some nonsense tale! Oh, ye'd better give him a word, Charlsie—he'll be puttin' foolishness in their heads!'

Charlsie scowled.

He came ponderously to where Duncan McRae sat on a wooden bench outside a cottage. People parted before him, but he felt that there was a questioning quality in their respect.

'What's goin' on here?' he said.

The little Scot grinned up, hands tucked comfortably behind his head.

'Och, I've been sitting here wondering if ye'd all fled awa' into a far country. I was thinking ye had a nice day for it,' he said.

'What are ye bletherin' about?'

'Have ye got a strait-jacket on yon sea monster?' The peddler chuckled. 'Look him in the eye, man. That's what they say; look him in the eye and put salt on his tail. I've a new brand of table salt in ma pack—would ye care to try some?' He began to laugh loudly.

Charlsie's face was purple. 'Is the feller crazy or what? Shut up, will ye!' He seized the little man by the hair and shook him violently. 'Stop laughin'! Haven't I ordered quiet!'

The peddler squealed as he tried to escape; his wooden leg skidded, and he thrashed about.

The staring villagers broke into explanation.

'He's got a tale that the noises is from a machine, Charlsie!'

'A warnin' of fog, for the ships!'

'That's what he said.'

There was dead silence, apart from the spluttering breath of the dazed peddler. Charlsie slowly released him.

They were all tense, watching Charlsie's face. It showed no expression; he might have been thinking, or working something out, or studying his victim, or listening. 'Juan,' he said at last, pointedly.

'Yes, Charlsie?'

'Can ye still hear it?'

They all waited, listening. The noise at sea had stopped.

'No, Charlsie. No! It's gone!'

It was Charlsie's moment. He glowered down at the wretched peddler, and took a chance.

'It's gone because I stopped it,' he said. 'I put a charm on the water to send it away. Now tell me somethin', me little Scotchman! Could I ha' done that if it was only some kind of a steam-engine across the water?'

He felt the awe all round him.

'Ye poor ignorant cuss, ye're not worth mindin'! I pity ye!' said Charlsie kindly.

'Och, look here! You go down to the town, and they'll tell ye there—'

Charlsie gave a laugh. It began deep inside him, where there was plenty of room, and rose in a throaty bellow.

'In the town! Oh—oh, my!' Charlsie was overcome. 'Ye'd better stick to sellin' buttons, master! He heard it in the town! An' he believed it! In the town!—where they're washin' themselves from mornin' to night, an' where they have to give each other little bits of cardboard to know who they are, an' get special knives out for t' eat a fish! There was a feller in the town thought he was Napoleon of the French! Oh, yes, the town! That's where they know everythin'! I'm sure!'

There was a howl of laughter.

It was a complete victory. The peddler protested and raged against their laughter, but he could do nothing to stop it; only Charlsie could do that, by a finger to his lips and a warning nod at the sea.

Charlsie watched McRae go stumping away in a fury without selling anything. His face was dark and thoughtful.

'Juan,' he said, loudly enough for others to hear, and with great conviction, 'this has given me an idea! Ye know, the sound of a tarroo-ushtey's voice would be a good thing t' imitate, as a warnin' to the ships; it needs a frightenin' sort of a noise. I've a mind to suggest that to th' English government! In fact I will; I'll send the letter now. An' describe how it can be done.'

He went indoors, where he felt weak now that the crisis was over; praying for the silence to continue, but ready to make another journey to the beach with a bunch of herbs. His luck held.

The foghorn did not sound again that day, or again for more than a week.

When at last it did, Charlsie reassured the village and bade them observe the sound: they would find, he said, that it was copied from the cry of the tarroo-ushtey, according to a simple invention of his own. They listened, and it was so.

He was often to be seen after that, sitting outside his home on foggy days, listening to the far-off hooting with a critical expression. When he went indoors, they said it was to write to the English government again, advising them.

Charlsie's fame as an inventor spread. He was rumoured to be working on a device for closing gates automatically, and another to condense water from clouds. Even strangers came to the village to have their ailments or troubles charmed away, or to undergo his new massage treatment.

But Duncan McRae did not sell another inch of elastic in the whole district.

Wales

1802

THE KNIGHT OF THE BLOOD-RED PLUME

Ann of Swansea

Ann of Swansea (Ann Julia Hatton née Kemble) (1764–1838) was born into a family of strolling players and actors, though Ann was prevented from working in performing arts by a physical disability. By the age of nineteen she had married an actor called Curtis but the union ended in disaster when it was discovered that he was a bigamist. Left in financial ruin, Ann survived by working as a 'model' in a brothel. In 1792 she married William Hatton and she accompanied him to America where her libretto *Tammany: The Indian Chief* premiered on Broadway in 1794. The couple returned to England and settled in Wales where they ran a bath-house lodgings until William's demise in 1806. From 1809 she established herself as a poet and author, publishing fourteen gothic-flavoured novels which she wrote between 1810 and 1831 mainly for Minerva Press, and including the far-out *Cesario Rosalba: or the Oath of Vengeance* (1819) under the pseudonym of 'Anne of Swansea'. 'The Knight of the Blood-Red Plume' is one of those stories that rewards with each and every reading of it. And we all love a good tale when someone's head is turned by a wrong-un, and things can only go downhill from there.

'—STAY, pilgrim; whither wendst thou?'

'—Cold is the north wind that plays around the mountains—heart-chilling the snow that's wafted across the moor—still bleaker blows the blast, cutting, keen, and freezing, as the grey mist of evening falls upon the vales;—frozen is the path that winds through yon forest; upon the leafless trees hangs the winters' hoary frost—and cheerless the bosom of him doom'd to wander along the lone path in such a night as this.'

'—Turn thee, pilgrim! and bend thy step to Rhuddlan's ruined walls, where thou mayst, undisturbed, waste the gloomy night, and take the morning to enjoy the road.'

'—Pious hermit! knowst thou not, from dusky eve until return of morn, that tortured spirits in yon castle rove? E'en now, the blood runs chill in my veins, while I do think on what I've seen. Such groans have met my ears—such sights my eyes—and screams and riotous laughs mingled with the winds that whistled through the broken arches of the courts—e'en now, the sweat of terror dews my brow, and languid beats my heart.'

'—Say, didst thou penetrate the hall?'

'—I did; and, on the hearth, some dried leaves to warm my shivering frame. I spread my wallet's fare upon the ground—with joyful heart, began to merry make—but angry spirits broke upon my glee, and fearful noises hailed my livid cheek. Instantly I dropped upon my trembling knee, and told my beads; but the screams increased—a ray of flame shot through the room, and before me stood a warrior in complete armour clad—his casque was down, and above his brow there waved a blood-red plume. No word he spake, but looked upon me with earnestness; his eye was as the sloe, black—as the basilisk's fascinating—his cheek was wan and deathlike. I would have fled, but my feet seemed chained to the ground, and my heart feared to beat against my bosom. At this moment I heard a female voice, that loudly sounded in the hall.—"I come, Erilda," cried the red-plumed knight; and instantly vanished. Again were the screams repeated; and showers of blood fell upon the marble flooring on which I stood.—My veins were filled with icicles from my heart; but, rendered desperate by fear, in the midst of the most horrible howlings, I flew; and the expiring embers of my fire casting a faint light, guided me along the courts through which I darted with the rapidity of lightning. Venerable hermit, again I dare not trust myself in Rhuddlan's walls. I have opposed my bosom to the Saxon's sword, and never trembled; I have braved dangers for my country, and was never known to tremble;—but I dare not face the spirits of the angry Clwyd.'

The hermit smiled.

'—Thou seest yon rock, which, threatening, hangs above the river—which, rippling along, now laves against its broken sides. In the bosom of that rock, I dwell. Peace is its inmate. My cell is humble, but hospitable; and in its lap the weary pilgrim has often found repose. Rest thou with me this night to share it, friend, and eke my frugal meal.'

'—Holy father with joy I follow you; hunger and fatigue sore oppress me; and my wearied limbs almost refuse their wonted office.'

The venerable hermit conducted the wearied pilgrim to his cell, which was clean—his meal was wholesome. The pilgrim ate of the frugal repast; and a crystal water, springing from the rock, was the beverage on which the man of piety regaled. This was proffered in a rudely carved wooden bowl to his guest, who drank, and felt relieved. He now drew his stool near the hearth, on which the faggot blazed; and the hermit, to beguile the moments, and remove the fear which occupied his companion's breast, thus related of the Knight of the Blood-red Plume and the fair Erilda.

High on the walls of Rhuddlan waved the black flag of death—loud the bell of the neighbouring priory tolled the solemn knell, which every vale re-echoed round, and the sad response floated to the ear through every passing gale.—The monks, in solemn voice, sung a mass for the everlasting repose of the deceased—a thousand tapers illumined the chapel—and bounteously was the dole distributed to the surrounding poor. The evening blast was keen—the grey mist circled the mountain's craggy brow—and thin flakes of snow beat in the traveller's face, while cold and shivering airs wafted his cloak aside. Sir Rhyswick the Hardy heard, as he advanced, the echo of the distant bell; and spurring his mettled steed, with heart harbouring many fears, pursued his course fleetly through the forest.

'Use speed, Sir Knight!' cried a voice in his ear. 'Egberta dies!'

Rhyswick turned pale.

'Egberta's bosom's cold;' continued the voice, 'and vain will be your sighs.'

The Knight in dismay checked his horse, and inclined his head to whence he thought the sound proceeded; but nothing met his eye; all was vacant before him, and only the quivering bough, fanned by the breeze, was heard. Rather alarmed, he set spurs to the sides of his steed—still the snow was drifted in his face. Night was now ushered to the heavens, and it was with difficulty he could maintain the path that branched through the forest. The web-winged bat brushed by his ear in her circular flight; and the ominous screech-owl, straining her throat, proclaimed the dissolution of the deceased.

Sir Rhyswick heaved a sigh; a melancholy thought stole across his brain, and, arriving at the banks of the Clwyd, he beheld, with trembling, the many tapers in the priory of Rhuddlan, and heard more distinctly the solemn bell.

'Egberta is no more,' cried the voice that had before accosted him; 'Egberta is in Heaven.'

The Knight turned round; but, beholding no one, and agonized by the prediction, again he roused his steed, and flew, pale and breathless to the castle. He blew the loud horn suspended at the gate of Twr Silod, the strong tower which stands upon the banks of the river: and the loud blast echoing in the courts, aroused the ominous bird that had alighted on its battlements, who, flapping her heavy wings, resumed her flight, uttering a wild, discordant scream. The portal was opened to receive him; and Sir Rhyswick entered through a long range of vassals, habited in mournful weeds.

'Is the prediction true, then?' he exclaimed: and, rushing to the apartment of Egberta, found her cold and breathless. The colour that once adorned her cheek was faded—her eyes were shrouded—and her lips became more pale, from which the last breath had so lately issued. A serene smile mantled her countenance—her locks were carefully bound in rose-bands—her corpse was prepared for the earth—and two monks sat on each side of her, offering up their holy prayers for her repose. Sir Rhyswick, overcome by this unexpected sight, with a groan, fainted upon the couch. Some servants that had attended him from the hall, conveyed him in a state of insensibility to his chamber; and, the next day, the virtuous Egberta was deposited in the chapel of the castle. Maidens strewed the path with flowers, along which their sainted lady was borne; and some monks from the neighbouring priory sung a solemn dirge over her—bare-headed and with their arms crossed upon their bosoms. The fair Erilda with her own hands decked the person of her mother with flowers; and those flowers were moist with a daughter's tears. A requiem, chaunted by the monks, and in which the maiden joined, closed the ceremony; and Erilda, with oppressed heart, returned to the castle.

Sir Rhyswick, whose grief would not permit him to attend the funeral rites, pressed the affectionate girl to his bosom; and they sought mutual consolation in each other.

Rhyswick the Hardy was the friend and favourite of his prince; he had fought in all the wars of his country, since the first moment he could hurl the spear—victory had always attended his arms; but now, his beard was silvered with age—peace was restored to the land, and he had hoped, at Rhuddlan, in the bosom of his Egberta, to pass away his few remaining years. Bliddyn ap Cynvyn had united in himself by conquest, the sovereignty of Gwynedd, or North Wales, with Powys: and thus had terminated a war that had long threatened destruction to either nation. With pleasure did Wales observe her implacable enemy, the English, struggling to overcome a foreign foe—bloody were the battles fought with William of Normandy, surnamed the Bastard; and, with secret satisfaction, did Bliddyn ap Cynvyn, a silent spectator, see either army reduced and weakened in the sanguinary contest. Sir Rhyswick had by his beloved Egberta, (from whose fond arms the war had often torn him, and who, in his last absence, being attacked by a sudden and violent illness, in a few days expired), one only daughter. To Erilda he now looked forward for future happiness. She was beautiful as the morn—roseate health sat upon her smiling cheek—meekness and charity in her lustre-beaming eye—her teeth were as so many snowdrops, regularly even—her breath, like the dewed rose-bud, of glowing fragrance—a dimple revelled playfully near her mouth—and the rich ringlets of her yellow hair floated carelessly on her fine curved shoulders. Upon her snowy breasts she wore a ruby cross, suspended by a gold chain—and down her taper limbs the dazzling folds of her white garments flowed. Erilda was not more beautiful in person than in mind; for, as lovely a bosom as ever nature formed, encased a heart enrich with every virtue. She was the subject of universal admiration; all tongues were lavish in her praise, and many suitors came to ask her hand: but, though extremely sensitive, no one, as yet, claimed an interest in her heart: the warm shaft of love had not pierced her glowing veins; and gay and affable to all—reserved to few—she preserved that freedom which the lover cannot retain. The loss of her mother imparted a melancholy to her cheek, that rendered her far more lovely. Sir Rhyswick indulged in grief, and the castle was one scene of mourning. On the brow of the rock, that o'erlooks the angry Clwyd, which rolls beneath, the poorer vassals and dependants of Rhuddlan, every evening came to receive the bounty of their young mistress. It was these excavations in the rock that echoed the soft plaintive notes of her melodious harp.—On this rock she sung, and the spirits of the murmuring river were charmed, as they lay in their oozy bed, with the soft pleasing strains—the billows ceased to roll in admiration, and Zephyrus drew back his head, in mute attention to the rapturous lay.

Once, when the return of twilight was announced in the heavens, by the rich crimson streaks and blushing gold that occupied the vast expanse of sky, and Erilda accompanied with her voice the trembling harp, a warrior Knight, mounted on a barbed steed, in sable armour clad, with a Blood-red Plume waving on his brow, approached the spot from whence the sound proceeded. Erilda, on hearing the advance of horses' feet, turned hastily around; and, with modest courtesy, welcomed the Knight, who had thus obtruded on her privacy. There was something in his gait and appearance that struck her with awe; and the unknown, dismounting from his steed, occupied a seat beside her. Again she struck upon the trembling chords, with fearful hand. The stranger sighed, as he gazed upon her; and, when her eye met his, she withdrew it, blushing, on the ground. The shade of night approached, and misty fogs obscured the starry sky.

'Sir Knight,' she cried, with a courteous smile, while an unusual palpitation thrilled through her heart, of admiration mingled with fear, 'Rhuddlan's hospitable walls are ready to receive you; and no warrior passes her warlike towers, without partaking and acknowledging the munificence of Rhyswick the Hardy.'

'Fair lady!' replied the unknown, 'the hospitality of the gallant chieftain, so famed, is not unknown to me; but I must onward on my journey, nor taste the bounty which all admire.'

'Sir Knight! this is not courteous.'

'Lady, adieu! it must not be: I live in hopes that we shall meet again.'

Saying this, he pressed her hand to his lips, and mounting his steed, flew with the rapidity of the winds along the shadowed plain that stood before her. His horse, so fleet, seemed to skim along the ground: and in an instant he was borne from her sight.

Erilda was astonished; there was a wildness in the jet black eye of the unknown, that, while it fascinated, alarmed her—a beautiful colour tinged his cheek; but not of that nature to which she was accustomed. His locks were black and sleek—his figure was noble and commanding—his voice, though harmony itself, still conveyed a hollow sound that was not pleasing. In short, his whole appearance, while it charmed to admiration, filled her with a kind of tremor; and she returned to the palace of Rhuddlan, charmed, and at the same time awed, with the martial appearance of the stranger.

'What majesty in his countenance!' exclaimed she to herself.—'What nobleness in his demeanour! And, ah! what melancholy seems to occupy his soul, that dims the sparkling lustre of his jet black eye, and clouds those animating features, otherwise beaming with cheerfulness. Surely such dejection is not natural in him? No, no; some hidden secret preys upon his heart; perhaps love, which, as I have heard bards relate, feeds upon the roseate hue of health—gives languor to the eye—paleness to the cheek—and despoils the heart of its manhood—that reduces firmness to trepidity—and poisons the noble mind with weaknesses that are engendered by timidity.'

Erilda sighed.—Sir Rhyswick met her as she was seeking her chamber; the good old man bore the resemblance of his grief upon his fretted cheek; but he endeavoured to be cheerful; and, with an assumed smile, he conducted her to the supper-hall.

Erilda vainly attempted to be gay, but variety of thought occupied her brain; the soul-inspiring song of the family bard charmed not her ear, who, at the board, when the gay goblet circulated at the tables, raised high his tuneful voice to the sublimest pitch, in commemoration of deeds of other days, and sung of triumph, and of glorious war.

Erilda, whose heart was affected by another subject, was not moved with the sweet sounds of the trembling harp, nor participated that emotion which the song of patriotism inspired in the breasts of the auditors. Had the theme been love, the air been plaintive as the ring dove's tender tale, Erilda's soul had wasted in the strain, and owned the power of music, when in melody with her feelings. Affectionately imprinting a kiss upon the bearded cheek of Sir Rhyswick, attended by her page, she bade adieu to the knight; and, retiring to her couch, attempted to lull those wild and troubled thoughts that agitated and oppressed her; but the blood-plumed knight, in her slumbers, stood before her: his graceful form—his pensive, melancholy countenance, she pictured to herself: and sighs of regret, when she awoke, and found the unreal image vanished, stole from her heaving breast.

With the first dawn of morning, Erilda arose, and flew to the monastery of Rhuddlan, to offer up her daily prayers. The holy father confessor gave her absolution, on a declaration of her errors; and again she sought the much-loved spot, where she had met the unknown. She looked towards the path he had taken the preceding evening, he no longer occupied it; and, seating herself upon the rock, she played an air, soft and melodious as the strains of Philomel; but, dissatisfied with her execution, she turned the instrument aside; her voice, she conceived, wanted its usual sweetness—the harp was out of tune—and her fingers, lingering upon the strings, damped the swelling note.

Erilda sighed, and sighed so deep, that the echo, from the excavated rocks, returned them to her ear.—At length the tear glistened in her eye.

'Why, why am I thus concerned for a wandering unknown, whom chance, perhaps, conducted to this spot for a first, and only time? Who, ere now, is leagues distant from my sighs, and who does not entertain one thought of me? Away, hope, thou delusive image, from my bosom—I never shall behold him more—my heart must harbour no such sighs.'

Saying this, with the firmness of resolution, she turned her step towards the castle. Sir Rhyswick was preparing for the chase; the hounds and hawks were abroad—all was noise and confusion—and Erilda consented to make one of the throng. Buckling on her breast the mantle of green, and slinging across her shoulder the bow and arrow quiver, mounted on a cream-backed palfrey, she joined them.

The adjacent forest echoed back the huntsmen's loud horns, and the affrightened deer pricked up their ears to the well-known blast. The yell of the dogs sounded in the deep glens—the loud halloo succeeded—and nimbly o'er the bogs and marshes bounded the fleet object of their sport. It was noon when Sir Rhyswick ordered his vassals to strike their tents upon the plain; and, after refreshing them with a rich repast, again they repaired to renew the chase; the ripe mead, in a golden goblet, was presented to the fair Erilda, who, in the midst of her damsels, looked like the goddess of the wood—and Sir Rhyswick drank from the hirlas horn the soul-reviving cwrw. Soon again was the panting deer pursued up craggy cliffs—through streams and valleys—over the heath—across the moor—and through the mazy forest. Erilda startled a speckled doe from the bosom of a dark glen; and drawing her arrow to the head, in the silver bow, pierced her in the breast. Though wounded the animal made good her flight, and darted away like lightning.

The heroic huntress fleetly pursued; while the horns and hounds echoed from another part of the plain. Long did the doe maintain her speed, and kept in sight, with the arrow in her breast, until the pale-faced moon appeared, emerging from a cloud, and silvering the glassy lake. At length, the wounded animal dropped, and instantly expired.

Erilda dismounted her steed; and now, she first discovered herself to be absent from her train, and at an hour when angry demons ride upon the air and mutter mischief. Cold winds wafted her brown hair aside; and fast descended the grey mist of evening. In vain Erilda listened to catch the halloo of the huntsmen. No longer the horn sounded in the vale—all was drear and silent, save the hollow murmuring of the wind, forcing its passage, sighing through the trees. Almost fainting with fear, she leaned upon her bow: she endeavoured to blow the horn that was suspended at her breast, but it fell from her grasp, and the bow shrunk from her hand. At length, summoning more fortitude, she remounted her steed; and not knowing what road to take, gave her horse the reins, trusting herself to the protection of her household spirit.—Away flew the impatient steed through the forest—over hill and dale: the turf trembled beneath his hoofs, and the white foam frothed at his extended nostrils. On a sudden, the bell of a neighbouring monastery sounded in the gale, and blazing torches were seen waving through different parts of a wood that lay before her. 'Hilli, oh ho!' cried the huntress, with hope animating her bosom; 'Hilli, oh ho!' but her voice returned responsive to her ear, and the flaming brands disappeared. Still she pursued the path, and fleetly flew the cream-backed palfrey on which she rode—now again the huntsman's horn was heard winding at a great distance, and now the approaching clank of horses' hoofs convinced her that the attendants of the chieftain, her father, were in pursuit of her. Erilda, checking her steed, awaited their coming up with her; but those in pursuit took a different route; and the sounds dying away, as the attendants receded, all was again hushed. At length, weary of suspense, she proceeded; and, turning the angle of a jutting rock that bulged in the fertile Clwyd, she observed a horseman slowly parading its banks. Pensive was his face—his right hand rested on a battleaxe—his left held the reins of a nut-brown courser—his soul seemed occupied by melancholy—his brain to be distracted by tormenting thoughts.—Erilda advanced towards him, and fixing her blue eyes upon his cheek, to her astonishment recognized the stranger Knight of the Blood-red Plume. His vizor was up, and melancholy tinged his whole countenance—a sigh, half suppressed, trembled on his lips—despondency seemed to depress his heart, that shed a transitory gloom over every feature, and preyed upon that energy of mind, which his interesting eye betrayed as certainly possessing. Erilda, unable to curb her impetuous steed, who reared upon his hind legs, and snorted in rage, called to the Knight, who, wrapped in thought, observed her not.

'Good stranger,' cried the daughter of haughty Rhuddlan's chieftain, 'I throw myself under your protection; conduct the strayed Erilda to Rhuddlan's hall, and the blessings of a distracted parent shall be yours.'

'Divine daughter of the first of chieftains,' replied the Knight, eagerly grasping his horse's reins; 'I am subject to your commands—my life shall be to your service.'

Erilda, smiling, gave him her hand, which he pressed respectfully to his lips: and, proceeding, the lofty turrets of Rhuddlan appeared in view. The pale moon, shedding her rays on its dark battlements, reflected them to the Clwyd, which in soft billows rippled beneath the mount on which it stood. Numberless torches were seen glaring in the hands of the disconsolate attendants of the chieftain, who, in the agony of grief, dispersed them round the country in search of her. All was bustle; and, no sooner did she appear among them, than loud shouts rent the air, and they flew to bear the welcome tidings to Sir Rhyswick. The stranger Knight conducted her across the courts; and the fond father, impatient to clasp her to his arms, hastened towards her. Erilda fell upon his bosom; and the tear of joy dropped from the old man's beard upon her shoulder. The Knight, in his turn, received the caresses of the venerable chieftain, who, boundless in his joy, would have lavished on him empires, had he had them to command.

'Tell me, Sir Knight,' cried Rhyswick, 'to whom am I indebted for the restoration of Erilda to my aged arms? Let me fall upon my knees at his feet, and bless him.'

'Hospitable chieftain, my name is Wertwrold, a forlorn and suffering wanderer; the world contains no home to shelter me—no friend to welcome me; but, though sorrows oppress my heart, I am ever ready to give joy to others,—Erilda is once more yours,' he added with a sigh, and bowing his head, was about to depart.

'Nay, stranger, this night you must share that joy which you have imparted to our breast, and make Rhuddlan your residence.'

'Your pardon,' cried the Knight, 'my envious fortune denies that I should taste of pleasure—I must away, ere the stars fade on the horizon.'

'Wertwrold,' returned Erilda, 'the maid whom you have protected entreats your stay—upon her knee entreats it: do not dispirit our festivity by your departure. Come, let me conduct you to marble-hall.'

The Knight, overpowered by their entreaties, at length yielded; and Erilda taking him by the hand, introduced him to the festive board, where sat the harpers, tuning their strings, awaiting the approach of the chieftain and his guests. Wertwrold appeared struck with the dazzling splendour of the hall that had regaled princes: rich crimson tapestry hung down the walls in festoons fringed with gold, between pillars of the fairest marble, disposed at equal distances, supporting cornices of polished silver; the carved ceiling displayed emblematical devices of war and of the chase; in one part, Diana was painted with her bow; in another, Caractacus engaging the Romans.

Erilda conducted the Knight to a cedar stool, covered with crimson, and edged with gold, at the table, on which were profusely scattered carved goblets, sumptuously embossed, and flowing with ripe mead. The harpers, during the repast, raised their voices in praise of the ancestors of Rhyswick, and regularly traced his descent, in bardic song; describing each great feat his fathers had performed. And now, the midnight bell sounding, dissipated their mirth—the bards were dismissed—and Wertwrold was led to a couch by one of the attendants, after saluting the fair hand of Erilda, which she offered to him, in token of her favour. The morning dawned unusually splendid—the early dew sparkled on the grass blade—and the effulgent sun rising, tinted the horizon with his gay beams—gentle was the air that played around the mountains—sweet and odoriferous was the scented gale—the river Clwyd timidly flowing, fearful lest it should interrupt the calmness that prevailed, was scarcely seen to move—and Erilda, whose troubled thoughts the preceding evening had denied her rest, hastened to the delightful rock where she first beheld the stranger, Wertwrold; there to indulge in sighs, and those thoughts that, while they pained, pleased. The solitary spot afforded her an opportunity to indulge in the melancholy of her mind; here she could sit and gaze with pensive eye upon the calm waters, as they laved against the shore, and involve her brain in a chaos of bewildering reflection, unobserved by anyone. Erilda never knew till now what it was to love—never knew till now what sighs the absence of him or her we love creates—and now she felt the pains, was unable to sustain them. The Red-plumed Knight was master of her heart and of her fate; violent was the passion that raged in her bosom, threatening to consume her by a slow lingering fire; for it appeared impossible the passion could be gratified. Seated upon an arm of the rock that overhangs the Clwyd, tears flowing down her lovely cheeks, agitated by similar thoughts, and overcome by weight of her emotions, weary, not having tasted of repose the preceding night, she sunk into a slumber, her head reclined upon her lily arm.

Wertwrold left the castle to taste of the refreshing air, ere the Baron descended from his chamber, or the loud bell summoned them to breakfast. His feet, as if by instinct, led him to the spot where first Erilda had attracted his notice. How much was he astonished to behold the lovely maiden in a sweet sleep! He stood awhile to observe her, and the tenderest sensation thrilled through his whole soul; her auburn locks played carelessly upon her temples, and her blue eyes were shrouded with long dark lashes; the tint of the carnation was displayed upon her cheek—a perfect ruby colour were her lips—the white rose leaf, through which runs the blue enamelled vein, was not more fair than her forehead, or more sweet than her breath—the soft air that played around her, wafted the thin gauze aside that shadowed her snowy bosom, and revealed beauties, which monarchs, on beholding, would have languished to enjoy.—Wertwrold, transported in the ecstasy of passion, dropped upon his knee, and imprinted a kiss upon her cheek.

Erilda, at this moment, awoke; and the Knight, conscious of the crime he had committed, drew back, abashed and trembling. Erilda was alike confused, and Wertwrold, seizing this opportunity, clasped hold of her hand with fervour, and pressing it between his, exclaimed, 'Lovely Erilda, pardon the presumption which your beauty has inspired—if 'tis a crime to adore you, then am I most criminal; but I bow to my fate—doomed to be unhappy, I willingly resign myself the victim of cruel fortune.'

'Say, Sir Knight,' cried the embarrassed Erilda, lending her hand to raise him from the ground, 'why are you thus persecuted? Repose your sorrows in my bosom; indeed, you will find in me one much interested for you.—Erilda, from her heart pities you.'

'And does Erilda pity me?' he returned, rising, and assuming a seat by her side. 'Oh, welcome, ye sorrows! for, henceforward, mingled with your bitter tears, ye convey a pleasure in the thought, that she whom all the world adores, feels for my sufferings: the scalding tear shall no longer flow without its balm—the arrow of anguish, while it wounds, shall on its poison-tipped point, convey a healing balsam to my soul.'

'But say, Sir Knight—why is your fate involved in mystery? Lend me your confidence—make me mistress of your secret—my bosom shall be its prison-house; and so tenacious will I be in retaining it, that even to myself I will not dare to whisper it.'

'Oh, lady, could I burst the fetters that chain my tongue to secrecy, I should enjoy a luxury in my grief; but, no, it is forbid—you behold in me a houseless wanderer, against whom the vengeance of Heaven is imprecated, doomed, for a term, to be a solitary inhabitant of the earth—with no settled home to shelter me—no friend to console me—no one to whom I can confide my sorrows.'

'Well!' cried Erilda, with impatience.

'Lady, I dare reveal no more—the cause must remain unknown.'

Erilda could scarce conceal her agitation. 'And when,' with a tremulous voice, she added, 'will the term expire, that frees you of your misery?'

'Then—when a virgin shall be found, of noble birth, and honour speckless as the mountain's dazzling snow, whose beauty shall be the theme of courts and palaces—whose virtue shall be the admiration of those, whom, with parent bounty she has fostered—whose hand shall be urged by knights of rank and enterprise—who shall withstand the temptation of wealth and power, equipage and title—who shall sincerely love me for myself alone, and brave all dangers, to arrive at the haven of my arms.'

Erilda turned pale; the colour on her cheek flew, and her whole frame became agitated. At this moment the loud bell of the castle tolled the breakfast hour, and endeavouring to reassume her wonted spirits, 'Come,' she cried gaily, 'we have wasted much time in idle talk.'

Wertwrold lent her his arm, and they proceeded to Rhuddlan. The young Knight at their earnest solicitation, consented to remain at the castle a few days, and various sports were devised to amuse him: nothing was spared to make him forget his griefs. But, in the midst of splendid gaiety, Wertwrold was still himself—melancholy still clouded his brow, and stole the roseate colour of his cheek.

On the second evening, as the last rays of the sun were reflected upon the lakes, and the misty crown of twilight circled the mountain's peak, Erilda, whose bosom was tortured by the love she bore the unhappy Wertwrold, strayed in the garden adjoining the castle. The day had been rather sultry, and, attended by her little foot page, she made towards the fountain, with an intent to bathe. She had already unloosed her hair, when she observed, extended upon the yellow sands, Wertwrold; he was in a sound sleep—and, approaching with tremulous step, she hung over him with an eye brimful of tears.

'Unhappy Knight!' she cried.—'Where shall be found the maid who can assuage the anguish of thy bosom, and restore to its former peace?—Where shall that maid be found, speckless as thou hast described, who will renounce every pretension for thee? Alas! alas I let me not buoy myself up with faint hopes—Wertwrold shall yet be happy, but Erilda will be for ever miserable. Yes, yes, some more happy maid than thou, Erilda, will gain the heart of Wertwrold, and tear the bond asunder that dates his misery.'

Faster flowed her tears—her agony became more acute—and, clasping her hands together, she sunk down by his side—her eyes were pensive, fixed on his, that were shrouded in sleep; and wrapped in ecstasy, she watched every breath that swelled his bosom, and escaped his lips. How beautiful did he appear, as he lay reclined upon the ground—what a dew sparkled on his lips—what a colour revelled upon his cheeks; his jet black hair, on which the water-drop, from bathing, glistened, clustered in silky curls around his head. He had laid aside his armour, and the true shape and mouldings of his manly limbs were visible; his neck and bosom were bare—they were of the most masculine beauty.

'Ah, Erilda!' exclaimed he in his slumbers, 'you alone can liberate my anguished heart—you alone can restore the smile to my fretted cheek—but you do not love me.'

'Hear it, Heavens!' cried the enraptured maid; 'Oh, Wertwrold!' and fainted upon his bosom.

The Knight awoke from the violence of her fall, and he gazed upon her in astonishment.—'Erilda!' he exclaimed, and bathing her temples with cold water, she soon revived; her wild eyes were timidly revealed to the light—and as soon as she discovered herself in the arms of Wertwrold, she gave a faint scream, and broke from his embrace. 'Erilda!' cried the Knight with fervour, 'my fate is in your hands—do with me as you please—you alone can avert my cruel destiny. From this moment, I cease to hope or to despair.'

Erilda was in an agony insupportable—tears choked her utterance, and pressing his hand between her's, she flew to conceal her anguish in another part of the garden. They met at the supper board, but she, feigning indisposition, begged leave to retire; and full early did the Baron and his guests press the downy pillow.

In her chamber Erilda indulged her sighs: Sir Rhyswick had chosen the heir apparent of Wales for her future lord, and she well knew it was in vain to contest his choice. The chieftain loved the happiness of his child, but the love of aggrandizement he cherished in his bosom; and he looked forward with fond delight to the time when Erilda might, with the partner of her pleasures, share the thrones of Gwynedd and Powys. A few days was to see the young Prince at Rhuddlan—preparations were making for his reception—Sir Rhyswick with pleasure beheld the nuptial day advancing—but Erilda viewed its approach with agony. The night was far advanced, ere her troubled thoughts were invaded by sleep, yet still maintaining their empire, they conjured up visions to the closed eyes. Erilda dreamed, that her father, overpowered by his affection for her, and her entreaties, yielded his consent to her union with Wertwrold, and placed her hand in his. Transported with joy, she threw her arms round her lover's neck; at this junction awaking, she found the Knight clasped in her embrace. Recoiling with horror from his arms, and recovering her senses, that were at first bewildered, 'Away,' she cried in a tone of terror: 'perfidious Knight, leave me; your conduct calls for my indignation. Oh, Wertwrold! was it possible for me to imagine you would thus repay the hospitality you have here experienced, by invading, in the midnight hour, the chamber of the defenceless?—Begone,' she added, with a contemptuous frown, 'ere I call my attendants, and expose the serpent who repays the favour of Rhuddlan's lord with abusing his confidence.'

'Yet hear me, Erilda,' returned the Knight, 'ere I am gone for ever; I came but to gaze my last farewell on that lovely countenance that dooms me to everlasting misery: my neighing steed now waits at the castle gate, and I must bid these much loved haunts adieu for ever. Farewell, Erilda—irresistible fate leads me hence—and, oh! sometimes give a thought on him who, added to his agonies, harbours for you a fruitless passion!' Wertwrold paused.

'For ever!' exclaimed Erilda; 'Oh, Wertwrold!'

'Could my absence,' continued the Knight, 'create one pang in your breast, though grateful would the knowledge be to my heart, still it would inflict a wound, Erilda, urging my brain to distraction, when I paused on your unhappiness.—Which ever way I turn, misery attends me—endless sorrow is my bitter portion: that I am indifferent to Erilda creates another pang.'

'Oh, Wertwrold!' cried the maid; and, sinking on his bosom, 'I am yours, and yours alone.'

'Do not my ears deceive me,' cried the enraptured Knight; 'does Erilda really love me—will she renounce the world for me?'

'The world!'

'Yes,' returned Wertwrold, 'and then shall my felicity dawn: Erilda must renounce everything to be mine—to share with me those transports which virtuous love creates.'

'You speak in mystery.'

'Erilda must, with heroic fortitude, overcome every obstacle to our union—must place implicit confidence in my faith—and sacrifice everything for me. The firm mind can stand, unshaken, on the stupendous rock, and smile upon the gulf beneath that threatens to devour—so must the woman who would gain my arms.'

'Wertwrold!'

'Take this ring, Erilda, it is a charmed one: which, when breathed upon, brings me to your presence: use it as you need me, and I fly, in obedience to your command, though at the extremity of the world.'

'Yet stay; you leave me in doubt.'

'Erilda must use her own discretion, I have not power to direct her. Farewell,' he cried; and pressing her to his bosom, instantly retired, leaving her lost in wonder and amazement.

For a time she could scarcely believe her senses—everything appeared as a dream before her eyes—but she possessed the charming ring—and the deluding thought vanished, that told her the preceding scene was the mere fabrication of her imagination.

At breakfast time she met Sir Rhyswick, who was not a little surprised and angered with the abrupt departure of his guest.

Erilda endeavoured to plead his cause—urging that business of the utmost import demanded his immediate attendance, and that to her he apologized.

The generous chieftain was well satisfied with the excuse, although he had hoped Wertwrold, in whose favour he was much interested, should have been present at the solemnization of Erilda's nuptials, which the fourth day was to see performed, according to a message which he had received from the young Prince, who, impatient to call Erilda his bride, thus early appointed the day.

Sir Rhyswick, with joy expressed in his countenance, imparted the news to his daughter, who, falling upon her knees—her cheeks bathed in tears—and grasping his hand, entreated him, as he considered her happiness, to forego his intentions.

'How?' cried the astonished Baron.

'I shall never know happiness with a man whom my heart will not acknowledge for its lord,' returned the afflicted Erilda: 'Oh! as you love my peace of mind, send back the prince—Erilda cannot be the bride of Morven—another object has enchained her heart.'

'How?' exclaimed the indignant Baron; 'Does Erilda reject the heir to the throne of Wales?'

'It would be criminal to my hand, when another possesses my heart. Oh, my father! the happy Morven will find one more worthy of being his bride—one more closely in conjunction with his soul—who will return his fond affection with affection.'

'Erilda,' cried the venerable chieftain with firmness, 'I seek not to know him whom your heart has chosen. If you value my affection, Morven must be your future lord; if not, your father is lost to you for ever.' Thus saying, he retired, leaving the distracted maid overwhelmed with grief.

Sir Rhyswick would not see her the rest of the day: and a messenger in the evening coming to her chamber, bid her prepare on the morrow to receive Morven, who was expected at the castle, attended by a numerous retinue.

Erilda, in an agony of distraction, threw herself upon the couch; her tears more plenteously flowed to her relief, and eased those labouring sighs that swelled her agitated bosom. She, casting her eyes upon the magic ring that encircled her finger; pressed it to her lips, and her warm breath sullying the ruby that sparkled upon it, instantly the Blood-red Knight stood before her.

'I come,' he cried, 'at your command, from the bosom of the vasty deep, to serve the mistress of my heart.'

Wertwrold took a seat by her side—Erilda hung her head upon his shoulder; her cheek was pale with weeping—her eyes languid and heavy.

'Oh, Wertwrold!' she exclaimed, 'this must be our last meeting; the son of Cynvyn claims Erilda's hand, and even now is on the road to Rhuddlan, to lead her to the bridal altar.'

'And will Erilda yield her honour, then, at the sordid entreaties of avarice and pride? Will she prostitute herself, embittering the remainder of her days to gratify another's passion?'

'Wertwrold! you—'

'Oh, lady! the fond affection glowing in my bosom has heaped a world of ruin in my heart—I see the gulf yawning at my feet—I see what tortures are preparing for me, and fly to meet my doom.—It Erilda is who hurls me to destruction—it is Erilda who mocks my sighs, and points me to the spot where angry demons wait to glut them on my blood. But these inflictions

I can brave—for, she I love proves false—she who deceitfully sighed, "I am yours, and yours alone."'

'You amaze and terrify me: what tortures what inflictions are those you dread? Oh, Wertwrold! do not keep me in suspense—tell me who, or what are you.'

'Who I am, lady, must remain a secret—what I am, my warm sighs, my great affliction have revealed—your lover. Oh, Erilda! I am man, with half his fortitude—man, with all his weaknesses: love animates and distracts my bosom; and she whom I wed, must wed me for myself alone.'

'Fond Wertwrold! I question you no more—and oh! how shall I convince you that my heart is yours—doomed as I am to misery and Morven.'

She fixed her languishing eyes upon his countenance—Wertwrold paused.

Erilda's chamber looked into the castle garden; the woodbine and honeysuckle climbed above her window, and a rose-tree entwined itself with the odorous branches of the honeysuckle—some sprigs hung pendant near the sashes of the casement, where the flower blowed and scented the air with its refreshing sweets.

Wertwrold eagerly slipped a spray that boasted a full blown flower and a ripening bud, which he presented to Erilda.

'Look you,' he cried; 'look on these flowers—the beauty of the one withers, while the other ripens. Here we see a rich bloom upon the cheek of youth; what a glowing fragrance does its breath impart! how sweet is the dew that hangs upon the expanding leaf! how rich! how luxuriant! how captivating to the senses! Would it not be cruel to pluck this early bud, ere it hath tasted of that dew which now sparkles on its lip—and, at the moment when it is about to enjoy those sweets which are prepared for early life?—Lady, this new plucked bud, in an hour shall perish—life shall fly its newly created bosom—the hand of man hath deprived it of its succours, and, ere it ceased to charm, it dies, unpitied, unrespected.' Then turning to the other—'This full-blown rose, whose shrivelled leaf betrays a speedy dissolution, having tasted of all the pleasures life affords, and enjoyed them in their full sense, prepares to die. The morning sun, instead of cheering, shall wither its juiceless fibres—the flavour of its breath is fled—and the falling dew animates it not—the airs are cold and freezing that play around it—and plucked, it would not perish sooner than were it left to wither upon the spray.'

'I do not understand you.'

'Lady, if one of these flowers must be torn from the branch of life, which would you sacrifice?'

'The full-blown.'

'Then live, Erilda—live to enjoy the tide of pleasure and of happiness.'

'Wertwrold, your words convey a horrible meaning; my soul shudders at the thought.'

'What thought, Erilda?—I ask you but to live—is the thought mercenary? I ask you but to taste of those pleasures, which he for whom you would sacrifice your happiness and person, cannot enjoy. Sir Rhyswick has nearly numbered his years—and dissolution betrays its approach upon his cheek: his infirm limbs—his shrivelled form—his silvery beard—and aged eye, like the full-blown rose, confirms a speedy termination of his life.'

Erilda fainted upon his bosom—his arms encircled her waist—hers were entwined round his neck: the colour of returning life soon crimsoned her cheek: her lips were pressed to his; the kiss was exchanged that imparted a mutual glow to the heart, and filled it with voluptuous thoughts.

'Erilda is mine, eternally,' cried the Knight.

'I am yours, for ever,' sighed the maid with half fainting voice.

'Tomorrow she will leave Rhuddlan for my arms?'

'Tomorrow, I am yours.'

They parted—each transported with the warmth of passion; and the ensuing eve was to see Erilda preparing her flight from her paternal home.

The next morning, Morven and his numerous retinue were heard upon their march across the mountain: the martial clang of their warlike instruments was heard at a great distance; and some messengers preceding, brought the early news of his approach and presents for the bride. The castle gates were thrown open to receive them—white flags waved upon the walls, that were thronged with armed soldiers, who owned Rhuddlan's powerful lord for their chieftain; and bards and harpers raised high their voices in praise of the fair Erilda.

Morven entered the castle, amidst the acclamations of the generous people, who loudly testified their joy at his approach, and whose loud shouts rent the air. Sir Rhyswick received him with every demonstration of pleasure, and instantly conducted him to the presence of his daughter.

Erilda, habited in robes of virgin white, that flowed adown her taper limbs, in the midst of her maidens, welcomed him with a smile. She looked beautiful—her cheeks were flushed with the ripe tincture of the rose—her blue eyes beamed with expression—her hair was tastefully disposed upon her forehead—and silver beads flowed down her fine-shaped bosom.

Morven saluted her with affability. For a while the young Prince was transfixed with wonder and admiration; her beauty far exceeded, in his estimation, the report that had reached his ear; and he looked with impatience for the moment that was to make her his bride.

The day was spent in merry pastimes; but Erilda was depressed with fears; she trembled at the promise she had made to Wertwrold, and more than once resolved to break it. The evening fast approached, and she grew more and more alarmed; at length the last rays of the declining sun were reflected upon the lake—the tinkling bell of the goat-herds caught her ear—the much dreaded time was arrived—her heart fluttered in her bosom—and wild and unknowing what she did, she sought the harbour where she had promised to meet the unknown.

Wertwrold was already there; with eagerness he clasped her to his bosom—with unallayed passion pressed her lips to his.

'Oh, Erilda!' he sighed, 'do I hold you in my arms, and shall my present bliss be equalled by the future? Come,' he continued, 'let us hasten our departure; a coracle waits us on the Clwyd, to waft us to the opposite shore.'

'Wertwrold!' exclaimed the affrighted maid; 'I dare not—do not tempt me—I must remain—and—be the bride of Morven.'

'Perjured Erilda! false fleeting woman—is this your truth—is this your constancy? Then farewell for ever.'

'Yet stay,' she cried, 'one moment: Oh, Wertwrold! do not leave me a prey to my own thoughts.'

'Will Erilda be mine?'

'Yes, yes.'

'Voluntarily mine?'

'Oh, yes!' exclaimed the maid, unconscious of what she said, observing lights at the further end of the walk, and fearful lest they should discover her with the unknown.

'Erilda will fly her paternal roof for Wertwrold?'

'Yes, yes.'

'Regardless of a father's tears and remonstrances?'

'I am Wertwrold's, and Wertwrold's alone!' she exclaimed, more alarmed by the nearer approach of the lights; 'and no power on earth shall separate me from his arms.'

The Knight of the Blood-red Plume smiled—it was the smile of satisfaction; and he placed in her hand a dagger.

'Use it,' he cried, 'in self-defence alone. Where is Sir Rhyswick?'

At this moment, a number of torches were seen flaming down the walks—Sir Rhyswick was at the head of a party of servants, whose countenances were expressive of fear.

'See!' cried Erilda, 'they bend their steps this way; we shall be discovered.'

'Take this dagger,' returned the Knight, thrusting it into her hand.

'How am I to use it?' exclaimed the maid in terror.

'Sir Rhyswick advances; 'tis him alone we have to fear.—Plunge it in his bosom.'

'In the bosom of my father?' cried she, with horror. 'Wertwrold—Merciful heavens! do not my ears deceive me? Horror! Horror! In the bosom of my father!—Away, monster.'

'Come to my arms, Erilda,' exclaimed the Knight, 'I have proved your virtue, and you are doubly dear to me.' He pressed the trembling maid to his bosom.

At this moment, Sir Rhyswick entered the arbour.

'This way—this way!' cried Wertwrold: and hurrying through a small outlet, that led to the river; footsteps pursued them. Still Erilda held the dagger in her hand, and the pale moonbeams silvering the path, betrayed the shadow of a person in pursuit, wrapped in a long cloak.

'We are betrayed,' cried Wertwrold; 'our pursuer must die.'

'I see the coracle; it is at shore,' said Erilda. And, at this moment, some one seized her white robe behind.

'Plunge your dagger in his heart,' cried Wertwrold.

'Hold your impious hand!' returned a hollow voice.

'Strike!' demanded the Knight.

'Stay, murderess!' uttered the voice.

'Our safety pleads for his death,' rejoined Wertwrold.

The hand of the pursuer now clasped Erilda's shoulder; who, disentangling herself and rendered frantic, turned hastily round, and plunged the dagger in her assailant's breast.

The wounded man dropped upon the ground. 'Cruel Erilda!' escaped his lips, and he instantly expired.

'Hence God-abandoned murderers;' muttered the voice that had before arrested the arm of Erilda. 'Fly to meet thy doom.'

'Hark!' cried the maid; 'heard you nothing?—What voice was that?'

Terror sat on her brow—her lips were pale with fear—her eyes looked wild and fiery.

'I heard nothing but the winds sighing along the strand.'

'Do you hear nothing,' exclaimed she. 'Merciful God! What have I done—"Murderess!"—Oh, let me look on him I have slain.'

She approached the corpse, spite of the entreaties of Wertwrold; and discovered, wrapped in a long cloak, the bleeding body of Sir Rhyswick! A crimson stream flowed from the fresh-made wound—his eyes were filmed and closed in death—his cheek was wan—his mouth wide and distended.

'Oh, God! my father!' exclaimed Erilda,—'Murdered by my hands!' And fell fainting upon his bleeding breast.

Wertwrold endeavoured to recall her to recollection; but, for a long time, vain were his attempts. At length, recovering, 'Leave me,' she cried; 'leave me to die with my murdered father.—Away! Anguish gnaws my breast.—Abandoned by Heaven, leave me to die, and receive the punishment of my guilt.'

'You rave, Erilda!—See, the vassals of the Baron draw near!—Hark now their voices are heard—their torches gleam in the walks; we shall be discovered, Erilda, let me arouse you from this torpor—let us fly, Erilda, and save ourselves from an ignominious death.'

'Away!' cried the distracted maid; 'I am a wretch unfit to live—more unfit to die: yet I will expiate the foul offence by submitting to those tortures that await me—which exceed not the agonies of my own bosom. Oh! my much loved father!' she exclaimed, 'your daughter—your own daughter, is your murderer.'

She fell upon his bosom; and still the Blood-plumed Knight urged her to fly.

'Erilda!' he returned, 'what false notions occupy your breast! Rather by penitence expiate the crime: the foul offence is not to be atoned by death. Heaven in its wrath has doomed your soul to everlasting torments; live then, and, by penitence, seek to appease its vengeance.'

'What mercy can the wretched murderer of her parent hope for?—Leave me, Wertwrold; distraction rages through my brain.—I am lost—for ever lost—God-abandoned—doomed to everlasting torments.'

'Oh, Erilda! think on your spotless fame to be blasted by the scandalizing tongue of futurity—think on the curses each peasant slave will mutter on her who was once her country's boast; the name of Erilda shall be shuddered at by those who judge not of the motive but the act—children shall be rocked to their slumbers with the frightful relation of her guilt, and she shall live for ever in the detestation and abhorrence even of the criminal.—The pilgrim shall hear and tremble at her tale—the monk shall cross himself, and tell his beads, when he passes Rhuddlan's blood-stained towers—all nature shall be shocked with her enormities; and not a pitying sigh shall be heaved to her memory. Come, Erilda, let us fly; penitence shall soon restore peace to your bosom, and your crime shall be forgotten.'

'Oh, no! I will remain and sigh out my last breath on the cold bosom of my father.'

'See, Erilda, the torches advance, Prince Morven is at their head; this way he bends his steps—he has his eye upon us—Distraction!—we are lost.'

'Ah! Morven! comes he hither to witness my shame?' exclaimed the maid; 'I cannot stand the inquiring glance of his penetrating eye.'

'Then hasten to the coracle, Erilda, which now awaits us on the shore.—Haste, Erilda, hear you not their voices?—They approach—they are at our heels.'

At this moment, a number of voices exclaimed, 'This way!'

'Oh, hide me—hide me from them; they come—they come;' cried Erilda. And clasping the hand of Wertwrold, she flew to the strand where the coracle was anchored.

The footsteps approached; and numberless torches lined the strand. Sir Rhyswick was discovered by the vassals of Rhuddlan, wrapped up in his cloak, and bathed in his blood. His heart was cold in his bosom—no signs of life animated his cheek, that was pale and deathlike. His silvery beard was distained and clotted with gore;—the last breath had issued from his mouth.

Morven had the corpse borne to the castle, where it lay in state for three days; when it was deposited in the earth, and five-hundred masses were sung for his eternal repose.

In the meantime, the despairing Erilda having set her foot on board the vessel, was borne over the thin wave with the rapidity of lightning. Torches still lined the stand; and their glaring light was reflected to the opposite shore, breaking through the horrible darkness that clouded the earth.

'Vain is your flight, murderess!' whispered a voice in the breeze.—'Mountains cannot conceal your guilt, or cover you from the wrath of the great avenger.—To the furthermost corner of the world, the retributive sword of justice shall pursue you.'

'Hark!' cried Erilda, clinging to the bosom of her seducer, while horror distorted her countenance. 'Hark; heard you not a voice? Oh, heard you not a voice? Oh, Wertwrold!—hide me—hide me.'

She buried her face in her cloak, while the warrior Knight maintained a contemptuous silence; at length, gazing upon her with satisfaction, he exclaimed:

'And is Erilda mine—do I now press her in my arms—do I now hold her to my heart, beyond the power of man to tear her from me? Why, this, indeed, is triumph—she is mine, voluntarily mine—she has fled her paternal roof for me, an unknown—she has rejected Morven, the heir apparent to the crown of Wales, who came to her with a heart full of love, and proffered the wealth of his country at her feet, to share her smiles, for me an unknown! She has renounced her claim to virtue, embraced infamy for a spotless name, has preferred the blast of scandal to the mild breath of praise, and all this for me, an UNKNOWN!'

A horrible smile, as he concluded, played upon his cheek.—Erilda started from his bosom.

'Wertwrold?' she exclaimed;—'Do you upbraid me?'

'Enamoured beauty, no! To ME, this guilt is pleasure: had you deluged the world in a sea of blood, or brought another chaos on the earth—Wertwrold would have smiled.'

'For Heaven's sake,' cried the almost expiring criminal; 'tell me, who are you?'

'*The Warrior Knight of the Blood-red Plume*: but,' he continued, 'Erilda is beyond the reach of mercy—is inevitably mine—and I will reveal myself in all my glowing colours. I am an agent of the great infernal—my residence is in the bosom of the Clwyd—my occupation is to aggravate the crimes on earth, and be the great instigator of war and rapine: in my bosom spring those seeds of faction, which I scatter in the breasts of princes, urging them to raise the sword against each other's life, and plunge each other's nation in a torrent of destructive war: but this had ceased—Morven's father had restored Wales to prosperity and peace—and I, in the bosom of my native stream, was doomed to sleep and brood new broils, in painful inactivity. While thus my mind was occupied with thought, an incubus approached my oozy bed, and breathed Erilda's fame into my ear: I was aroused with the sweet image my fancy drew; and, on beholding the enchanting object, found her sweeter than my imagination had painted her—and, from that moment, I resolved to make her mine. I heard of her many virtues—of her piety—and what a feeling heart she boasted; this news instructed me what shape to assume; and the Warrior Knight of the Blood-red Plume answered every purpose. Erilda was easily ensnared: she pitied me, because she thought me unfortunate—pity instantly begat love—love the glowing fire of all-consuming passion. I had no power to deceive, but speciously—'

'Monster!' exclaimed the frantic wretch, 'you were all deception.'

'There Erilda wrongs me,' cried the fiend; 'she deceived herself—she thought me what her heart hoped I was—I did not need much art to gain her—she readily entered into all my views—embraced my projects as fast as they were uttered.'

Erilda threw herself upon her knees.

'Nay, prayer is vain,' continued the fiend; 'you are lost to Heaven—you scrupled to commit an immediate murder, yet planned a lingering death for the parent who had nurtured you—you would not stab, but preferred planting daggers in your father's bosom.—Murderess! you bid him who gave you life, live for a time in agony, to reflect on his daughter's infamy.'

Erilda shrunk with horror and affright from the hideous monster, who now resumed his original shape, amidst the yell of demons, who rose from the sandy deep, upon the curling wave, to greet their chief. The eyes of the sanguinary fiend, emitting a sulphureous flame, were fixed upon the pale countenance of the guilty maid, whom he grasped round the waist in malignant triumph. Green scales covered his body; from his mouth and nostrils he breathed the white frothen waters—and various animals, fostered by the liquid element, trailed their pestiferous slime across his carcase. In his right hand he held a trident, which he raised on high to plunge in the bosom of his victim, who, screaming, burst from his embrace, and falling upon her knees, implored of Heaven protection. Loud thunders shook the sky—terrific lightning flashed in her eyes—and the furious winds bursting through the mountains, swelled the agitated river beyond its bounds. The fiend, with malignant yell, pursued Erilda—the trident entered her bosom—and crimson torrents of her virgin blood gushed from the yawning wound—in agony she fell—the demon, twining his hand in her fair locks, hurled her to the deep, and, sated with triumph, vanished with his coracle.

Long time did the white-browed waves bear up Erilda: in her last moments, she beheld the pale spectre of Sir Rhyswick, who advanced upon the rolling waters, that seemed to shrink from his feet, placing his forefinger to the deep wound in his breast. More dreadful were her screams—and billow succeeding billow, bore her near the shore. Struggling for life, she clung to a loose rock to save herself, which yielding to her grasp, came rolling down, and crashed her to pieces.

The hermit paused.—

Since then has Rhuddlan's castle been the seat of anarchy.—Monarchs, indeed, have made it their residence; but, each night, Erilda's screams are heard, and the Warrior of the Blood-red Plume is seen pursuing her through the ruined courts.

Such is the tale of Rhuddlan's ruined towers. Pilgrim, go thy way, stop not within its blasted walls, foul fiends ride upon the misty air, and the demons of the angry Clwyd claim it as their right.

1927

THE GIFT OF TONGUES

Arthur Machen

Arthur Machen (1863–1947), born as Arthur Llewellyn Jones (Machen was his mother's maiden name) into a long line of Anglican clergymen in Gwent, South Wales, was fascinated by the occult from an early age. After his poem *Eleusinia* (1881) was published Machen pursued a career as a journalist in London existing in relative poverty. He preferred an isolated and aloof life-style and would occupy himself with rambling walks around the city before writing in the evening. Following the publication of his novel *The Anatomy of Tobacco* (1884) Machen worked as a magazine editor and translator of French literature. He married the music tutor Amelia Hogg in 1887 and she introduced him to London's Bohemian literary circle including the poet and occultist A. E. White. His first great success came with the novel *The Great God Pan* (1894) which became controversial due to its sexual and horror content. In 1899 Amy died from cancer after a protracted illness and A. E. White became a close friend whilst helping Machen to recover from his grief. White introduced him to the Hermetic Order of the Golden Dawn, a ritual magic group which also included Aleister Crowley and W. B. Yeats amongst the membership. Whilst never closely involved with the group it did enable Machen to start developing his own form of mystical Celtic Christianity. After a short career change as an actor in a repertory theatre company he accepted a job as a full-time journalist on *The Evening News* and returned to literary prominence with his most widely recalled story 'The Bowmen' (1914). The tale gave rise to the legend of The Angels of Mons and to Machen becoming a well-known figure. 'The Gift of Tongues', first published in the December 3rd issue of *T.P.'s and Cassell's Weekly*, 1927, tells the story of a Christmas Day service held at Bryn Sion Chapel and the struggle of the Reverend Thomas Beynon.

MORE than a hundred years ago a simple German maid-of-all-work caused a great sensation. She became subject to seizures of a very singular character, of so singular a character that the family inconvenienced by these attacks were interested and, perhaps a little proud of a servant whose fits were so far removed from the ordinary convulsion. The case was thus. Anna, or Gretchen, or whatever her name might be, would suddenly become oblivious of soup, sausage, and the material world generally. But she neither screamed, nor foamed, nor fell to earth after the common fashion of such seizures. She stood up, and from her mouth rolled sentence after sentence of splendid sound, in a sonorous tongue, filling her hearers with awe and wonder. Not one of her listeners understood a word of Anna's majestic utterances, and it was useless to question her in her uninspired moments, for the girl knew nothing of what had happened.

At length, as it fell out, some scholarly personage was present during one of these extraordinary fits; and he at once declared that the girl was speaking Hebrew, with a pure accent and perfect intonation. And, in a sense, the wonder was now greater than ever. How could the simple Anna speak Hebrew? She had certainly never learnt it. She could barely read and write her native German. Everyone was amazed, and the occult mind of the day began to formulate theories and to speak of possession and familiar spirits. Unfortunately (as I think, for I am a lover of all insoluble mysteries), the problem of the girl's Hebrew speech was solved; solved, that is, to a certain extent.

The tale got abroad, and so it became known that some years before Anna had been servant to an old scholar. The personage was in the habit of declaiming Hebrew as he walked up and down his study and the passages of his house, and the maid had unconsciously stored the chanted words in some cavern of her soul; in that receptacle, I suppose, which we are content to call the subconsciousness. I must confess that the explanation does not strike me as satisfactory in all respects. In the first place, there is the extraordinary tenacity of memory; but I suppose that other instances of this, though rare enough, might be cited. Then, there is the association of this particular storage of the subconsciousness with a species of seizure; I do not know whether any similar instance can be cited.

Still, minor puzzles apart, the great mystery was mysterious no more: Anna spoke Hebrew because she had heard Hebrew and, in her odd fashion, had remembered it.

To the best of my belief, cases that offer some points of similarity are occasionally noted at the present day. Persons ignorant of Chinese deliver messages in that tongue; the speech of Abyssinia is heard from lips incapable, in ordinary moments, of anything but the pleasing idiom of the United States of America, and untaught Cockneys suddenly become fluent in Basque.

But all this, so far as I am concerned, is little more than rumour; I do not know how far these tales have been subjected to strict and systematic examination. But in any case, they do not interest me so much as a very odd business that happened on the Welsh border more than sixty years ago. I was not very old at the time, but I remember my father and mother talking about the affair, just as I remember them talking about the Franco-Prussian War in the August of 1870, and coming to the conclusion that the French seemed to be getting the worst of it. And later, when I was growing up and the mysteries were beginning to exercise their fascination upon me, I was able to confirm my vague recollections and to add to them a good deal of exact information. The odd business to which I am referring was the so-called 'Speaking with Tongues' at Bryn Sion Chapel, Treowen, Monmouthshire, on a Christmas Day of the early Seventies.

Treowen is one of a chain of horrible mining villages that wind in and out of the Monmouthshire and Glamorganshire valleys. Above are the great domed heights, quivering with leaves (like the dear Zacynthus of Ulysses), on their lower slopes, and then mounting by far stretches of deep bracken, glittering in the sunlight, to a golden land of gorse, and at last to wild territory, bare and desolate, that seems to surge upward for ever. But beneath, in the valley, are the black pits and the blacker mounds, and heaps of refuse, vomiting chimneys, mean rows and ranks of grey houses faced with red brick; all as dismal and detestable as the eye can see.

Such a place is Treowen; uglier and blacker now than it was sixty years ago; and all the worse for the contrast of its vileness with those glorious and shining heights above it. Down in the town there are three great chapels of the Methodists and Baptists and Congregationalists; architectural monstrosities all three of them, and a red brick church does not do much to beautify the place. But above all this, on the hillside, there are scattered whitewashed farms, and a little hamlet of white, thatched cottages, remnants all of a pre-industrial age, and here is situated the old meeting house called Bryn Sion, which means, I believe, the Brow of Zion. It must have been built about 1790–1800, and, being a simple, square building, devoid of crazy ornament, is quite inoffensive.

Here came the mountain farmers and cottagers, trudging, some of them, long distances on the wild tracks and paths of the hillside; and here ministered, from 1860 to 1880, the Reverend Thomas Beynon, a bachelor, who lived in the little cottage next to the chapel, where a grove of beech trees was blown into a thin straggle of tossing boughs by the great winds of the mountain.

Now, Christmas Day falling on a Sunday in this year of long ago, the usual service was held at Bryn Sion Chapel, and, the weather being fine, the congregation was a large one—that is, something between forty and fifty people. People met and shook hands and wished each other 'Merry Christmas', and exchanged the news of the week and prices at Newport market, till the elderly, white-bearded minister, in his shining black, went into the chapel. The deacons followed him and took their places in the big pew by the open fireplace, and the little meeting-house was almost full. The minister had a windsor chair, a red hassock, and a pitch pine table in a sort of raised pen at the end of the chapel, and from this place he gave out the opening hymn. Then followed a long portion of Scripture, a second hymn, and the congregation settled themselves to attend to the prayer.

It was at this moment that the service began to vary from the accustomed order. The minister did not kneel down in the usual way; he stood staring at the people, very strangely, as some of them thought. For perhaps a couple of minutes he faced them in dead silence, and here and there people shuffled uneasily in their pews. Then he came down a few paces and stood in front of the table with bowed head, his back to the people. Those nearest to the ministerial pen or rostrum heard a low murmur coming from his lips. They could not make out the words.

Bewilderment fell upon them all, and, as it would seem, a confusion of mind, so that it was difficult afterwards to gather any clear account of what actually happened that Christmas morning at Bryn Sion Chapel. For some while the mass of the congregation heard nothing at all; only the deacons in the Big Seat could make out the swift mutter that issued from their pastor's lips; now a little higher in tone, now sunken so as to be almost inaudible. They strained their ears to discover what he was saying in that low, continued utterance; and they could hear words plainly, but they could not understand. It was not Welsh.

It was neither Welsh—the language of the chapel—nor was it English. They looked at one another, those deacons, old men like their minister most of them; looked at one another with something of strangeness and fear in their eyes. One of them, Evan Tudor, Torymynydd, ventured to rise in his place and to ask the preacher, in a low voice, if he were ill. The Reverend Thomas Beynon took no notice; it was evident that he did not hear the question: swiftly the unknown words passed his lips.

'He is wrestling with the Lord in prayer,' one deacon whispered to another, and the man nodded—and looked frightened.

And it was not only this murmured utterance that bewildered those who heard it; they, and all who were present, were amazed at the pastor's strange movements. He would stand before the middle of the table and bow his head, and go now to the left of the table, now to the right of it, and then back again to the middle. He would bow down his head, and raise it, and look up, as a man said afterwards, as if he saw the heavens opened. Once or twice he turned round and faced the people, with his arms stretched wide open, and a swift word on his lips, and his eyes staring and seeing nothing, nothing that anyone else could see. And then he would turn again. And all the while the people were dumb and stricken with amazement; they hardly dared to look at each other; they hardly dared to ask themselves what could be happening before them. And then, suddenly, the minister began to sing.

It must be said that the Reverend Thomas Beynon was celebrated all through the valley and beyond it for his 'singing religious eloquence', for that singular chant which the Welsh call the hwyl. But his congregation had never heard so noble, so awful a chant as this before. It rang out and soared on high, and fell, to rise again with wonderful modulations; pleading to them and calling them and summoning them; with the old voice of the hwyl, and yet with a new voice that they had never heard before: and all in those sonorous words that they could not understand. They stood up in their wonder, their hearts shaken by the chant; and then the voice died away. It was as still as death in the chapel. One of the deacons could see that the minister's lips still moved; but he could hear no sound at all. Then the minister raised up his hands as if he held something between them; and knelt down, and rising, again lifted his hands. And there came the faint tinkle of a bell from the sheep grazing high up on the mountainside.

The Reverend Thomas Beynon seemed to come to himself out of a dream, as they said. He looked about him nervously, perplexed, noted that his people were gazing at him strangely, and then, with a stammering voice, gave out a hymn and afterwards ended the service. He discussed the whole matter with the deacons and heard what they had to tell him. He knew nothing of it himself and had no explanation to offer. He knew no languages, he declared, save Welsh and English. He said that he did not believe there was evil in what had happened, for he felt that he had been in Heaven before the Throne. There was a great talk about it all, and that queer Christmas service became known as the Speaking with Tongues of Bryn Sion.

Years afterwards, I met a fellow countryman, Edward Williams, in London, and we fell talking, in the manner of exiles, of the land and its stories. Williams was many years older than myself, and he told me of an odd thing that had once happened to him.

'It was years ago,' he said, 'and I had some business—I was a mining engineer in those days—at Treowen, up in the hills. I had to stay over Christmas, which was on a Sunday that year, and talking to some people there about the hwyl, they told me that I ought to go up to Bryn Sion if I wanted to hear it done really well. Well, I went, and it was the queerest service I ever heard of. I don't know much about the Methodists' way of doing things, but before long it struck me that the minister was saying some sort of Mass. I could hear a word or two of the Latin service now and again, and then he sang the Christmas Preface right through: "*Quia per incarnati Verbi mysterium*"—you know.'

Very well; but there is always a loophole by which the reasonable, or comparatively reasonable, may escape. Who is to say that the old preacher had not strayed long before into some Roman Catholic Church at Newport or Cardiff on a Christmas Day, and there heard Mass with exterior horror and interior love?

1962

MERMAID BEACH

Leslie Vardre

Leslie Vardre was the pseudonym of L. P. Davies (1914–1988). Born in Crewe, Cheshire, Leslie Purnell Davies produced many short stories under several other names. His work, which combines both horror and science fiction elements, has been compared to Philip K. Dick due to themes of identity and human consciousness being manipulated. Davies served in the Royal Army Medical Corps during the Second World War and worked in various other roles, such as pharmacist, tobacconist and gift shop owner, to support his writing. His novels *The Artificial Man* (1965) and *Psychogeist* (1966) helped to form the basis of the William Castle film *Project X* (1968), and *The Alien* (1968) was adapted as the film *The Groundstar Conspiracy* (1972). 'Mermaid Beach', first published in *London Mystery Magazine*, December 1962, sees two workmates visit a beach in Wales. They're told not to visit it at night and that men have been found drowned with smiles on their lips.

We came upon the beach purely by chance one Sunday morning when we were motoring south along the Cardigan coast and Brett, whose turn it was to drive, became intrigued by the narrow sand road and impulsively swung the car to follow its tortuous way through the dunes.

We were barely out of sight of the main road when our new way narrowed into little more than a footpath. Brett stopped the car and the morning was filled with the muted and tempting sound of the sea. Following the sound on foot we came upon a broken-down beach hut with paint-stripped wooden walls and a sagging verandah. Despite the bright sunlight it looked uncanny in the way that lonely, desolate houses often do. I remember that I remarked about it, and Brett, made of less imaginative stuff, turned and grinned and passed some comment about highly desirable residences.

The beach was some fifty yards farther on, and we came on it almost unexpectedly, through a deep rift in the grass-covered dunes. Two small headlands were linked by a perfect half-circle of firm, tide-rippled sand on which the low waves broke in steady rhythm. It was the ideal spot for a bathe. Brett was so much taken with it that despite our original intention to carry on to Aberayron he would have it that we spend the rest of the day there. We went back to the car to collect all the essentials of comfort: blankets, towels, transistor radio, picnic-basket and cushions.

The water was warm and had a velvety texture. Although it was late September and the breeze held a promise of winter, the headlands and the dunes seemed to shelter the little beach, giving it a climate all its own.

Dusk was beginning to fall as we made our way back to the car. A few paces ahead Brett said back over his shoulder, 'You'd think a beach like that would be packed. Even at this time of the year.'

'It probably would be if the road to it was marked more clearly,' I suggested as we came abreast of the cabin.

'Somebody else found it once, anyway,' he said, stopping to look at the warped timbers. He mounted the verandah and peered through the one window. 'It looks all right inside,' he added, and set down his load so that he could try the door. It opened at his touch and he ventured inside. I followed him only as far as the threshold of the beach hut.

'In reasonably good shape,' he decided, his voice echoing. Then he came out again. 'You know something, John? It doesn't look like it's been used in ages. We could use it for the odd week-end. I mean, we could come down on a Saturday and stay here right through until Monday morning.'

'It would make a change,' I agreed as we walked on to the car. 'But even though it seems to be derelict it'll be somebody's property.'

But apparently it wasn't. Brett, backing into the main road, stopped when he saw the old man, sack over his back, trudging steadily along. He wound down the window and waited for him to come abreast.

'You live in these parts?' he asked.

'Up by Llanffynnon,' said the old man, 'but a step. And thanking you if it's a lift you're offering, but not far to go.'

Brett nodded backwards to the beach. 'There's an old hut of sorts back there. Would you happen to know if it belongs to anyone?'

The other looked closely into Brett's face, shook his head and said slowly: 'Empty for some time, now; ever since—' Then he stopped and was for going on his way. Brett called after him:

'D'you think anyone would mind if we made use of it?'

And at that the old man stopped and then came back, his face intent.

'You won't be wanting to use that place,' he said.

'It looks all right. I grant you it could do with some paint—'

'That's Mermaid Beach that lies beyond,' said the old man in such a way that it was as if he expected us to realize some significance.

Brett grinned. 'I expected it to have some unpronounceable Welsh name. And what's wrong with Mermaid Beach?'

The old man muttered something in his own tongue and turned to go for the second time. Brett had to grasp at his tattered sleeve while he repeated his question.

'It is a bad place,' said the other reluctantly. 'Drownings there's been. Three of them that I'm knowing of.' He watched our faces.

'A treacherous current?' Brett hazarded.

'Could be, sir; but that wasn't why—'

'Then what?'

'Folks don't generally go bathing at night. An' not when the wind's blowing in from the sea.'

'And it was like that when these three handed in their dinner-pails?' Brett asked lightly.

Now there was resentment at the implied derision.

'They drowned and that's all there is to it. An' all at night. It's only at night when the wind's comin' in from the sea that you can hear her—' And then he stopped, biting his lip as if annoyed with himself for having been nettled into such an explanation.

'Good Lord!' Brett cried in delight. 'A Welsh Lorelei. Is that why it's called Mermaid Beach?'

'The last one was washed up a bit down the coast. I was the one to be finding him. An' the one before, he came in about the same place. I saw him when they took him to Aberayron. The first was picked up by a trawler. They was all smiling.'

And then the old man freed his sleeve and went on his way.

Brett was hugely amused. 'They were all smiling, so they died happy. What a load of rubbish. You get a bay with an under-tow or something, and three men get drowned, and a legend is born. The night and the wind have been added as atmosphere. As if anyone in their right mind would go bathing in the dark when the wind's blowing in from the sea.' He grinned. 'I don't know about you, but it would take more than a female voice to drag me down to the sea if I didn't want to go. How about coming down next Saturday and spending the week-end here?'

Oddly enough I would have given a lot to have been able to produce some reason for not coming. But Brett and I work together and he knew that

I would be free. And he had that faintly supercilious look on his face that would have exploded into open derision if I had refused.

Saturday was a prolongation of the Indian summer, warm and sunny with a nip in the air first thing. Late in starting, we reached the sand road about the middle of the afternoon. It took several journeys to transfer the stuff from the car. We had oil stoves, a hurricane lamp, two camp beds and a supply of canned food in addition to our usual bathing essentials.

The water was calm and warm. As we lay on the sand afterwards Brett said drowsily: 'There's an under-current all right. I felt it. Given the right conditions it could be nasty. That's what happened to those three. Inexperienced bathers. There's a place on the south coast that's just as tricky. To be on the safe side we'd better keep well inshore. And at the first sign of wind we leg it for the beach.'

That night we both slept like logs, walking to a sunrise that promised another day of fine weather. But the breeze had a chill tang after lunch, so we did our basking in the shelter of the dunes.

The clouds must have built up inland, hidden by the headlands. The first we knew of the change was when a cold wind blew sharply, setting the fine sand swirling. And with it came the first spots of rain.

There was a few moments of scurry as we hastily gathered our things together and then set off back, the wind buffeting, along the steep path to the hut.

We had the two stoves, our beds and a good supply of blankets, so we were comparatively comfortable. The comfort was accentuated by the lowering sky seen through the solitary window and the soughing of the wind. Making up his bed, Brett turned and grinned over his shoulder.

'One thing at least,' he said, 'this wind isn't blowing off the sea and so we shan't be troubled with singing mermaids.'

As we ate our tea the sky darkened even more, anticipating nightfall, and a new sound came to the wind. It was such a different sound that I went to the window, seeing now how the grass was being blown away from the direction of the sea. I turned to pass some comment, and Brett was poised, pillow in hand, listening...

'Did you hear something?' he asked.

'The wind. It's changed round.'

He shook his head impatiently. 'No, not the wind. Listen...'

The darkness was coming down now as if a curtain was being dragged across the sky. I listened, aware of the thudding of my pulse. And then, as a gust moaned past the walls, I heard the other sound. A fragment of music, tossed and torn by the wind, seeming to come from far away. It went as suddenly as it had come.

Brett fingered his lip, puzzled. 'I could have sworn...' He shook himself. 'A trick of the wind.'

There was another fierce gust that set the cabin rocking and as it died, so the music was back again, louder now and clearer. A woman's voice singing a snatch of melody that was at the same time strangely alien and yet nostalgically familiar. It rose and fell on the wind so that now it seemed to come from across the sea, now from outside the very door.

I remember staring at the dark square of window. I was frightened.

It came again while I stood there, the words now almost distinguishable.

Brett's face was white. 'It's only the wind,' he said, 'and our imagination. It has to be.'

And then suddenly he dropped the pillow and slapped his knee and burst into laughter, shaking so much that he had to lean against the wall. For the moment I fancied it to be hysteria, and I started towards him. He found his breath as I reached his side.

'That damned mermaid,' he gasped; 'here we are, both scared out of our wits, and d'you know what it is? My radio. We tucked it under one of the dunes and we left it there when the rain drove us in. It's out there now, blaring its head off. We didn't hear it until the wind changed.'

And then relief flooded through me and I joined him in his laughter. But my legs trembled and I had to sit on my bed. Brett started to put on his raincoat.

'You're not going for it?' I asked in surprise.

'You bet your life I am,' he replied. 'It's a new one. It's still all right by the sound of it, but once the rain gets to it it'll be ruined.' Then he fought with the door and was gone, still smiling, out into the darkness and the wind blowing off the sea.

Alone, I laughed again at my fears and set about making up my bed. A mental picture of Brett, head down and struggling against the weather, took me to the corner where we had earlier dumped the things we had brought back from the beach. I could at least have two warm towels ready for his return.

And when I picked up the first towel, the radio tumbled out.

I started instinctively for the door and then stopped with my hand on the latch. The fear had come back again, stronger than before. I couldn't for the life of me have opened that door and stepped out into the darkness beyond.

I spent the long night sitting on my bed, shivering and listening and waiting. But the voice remained silent and Brett never returned. His body was washed up the next day a little way down the coast. I was taken to Aberayron to identify it. An echo of his laughter still clung to his lips. But then those others too had been smiling when they were found.

Cornwall

1947

ALL SOULS' NIGHT

A. L. Rowse

A. L. (Alfred Leslie) Rowse (1903–1997) was a Cornish writer of over 50 books that sold in their millions. A Shakespearean scholar, one of his greatest achievements was identifying the 'Dark Lady of the Sonnets' as Emilia Lanier, mistress of Queen Elizabeth's Lord Chamberlain. He was made a Bard of Gorseth Kernow (a non-political Cornish organization), taking on the bardic name *Lef A Gernow* ('Voice of Cornwall') which reflected his stature in the region. His short stories are as excellent as his academic work, and the following story, 'All Souls' Night' from his 1947 collection *West-Country Stories* is the best tale Rowse ever wrote, detailing the unfortunate journey of a young man invited to an old manor house who... well, let's not spoil it.

THEY were sitting—the Dean and two of his colleagues—in the quiet of a summer evening upon the terrace of that college, that quadrangle which gives you a panorama of the spire of St Mary's, with its gathered pinnacles clustered at the base, the light and classical elegance of Aldrich's spire of All Saints in the background, the bulky Roman magnificence of the Radcliffe Camera in the foreground, and away to the innumerable crockets and finials of the Bodleian Library. It was that hour of summer evening when the late light lit up the clock upon the northern face of St Mary's tower: a rare and disturbing thing to the hearts of those few whose attention was caught by it. Somehow it brought home to them, in an inexpressible way, the feeling of the transcendence of things, the mutability of the temporal order, the immutability of the eternal.

Nine was striking upon all the brazen tongues of the clocks of Oxford. There was the old-lady-stepping-up-stairs chime of New College that began the clamour, followed by the lugubrious descent and ascent of St Mary's, like going down into the tomb. Last of all, the deliberate, suspensive, velvety boom of Tom from Christ Church.

> Midnight has come, and the great Christ Church bell
> And many a lesser bell sound through the room;
> And it is All Souls' Night...

the words ran through the dreamy mind of the young English don, while his attention wandered from the desultory conversation the Dean was having with his senior colleague, the Classic.

The Fellows had had their coffee in the open air, so warm was the evening. And now, replete, at leisure, these three were enjoying the evening air, the Classic his pipe, the Dean his cigar. When the youngest of them next attended, his colleague was asking the Dean:

'By the way, what was it that overtook young Colenso? I remember he was a lad of considerable promise as an undergraduate—great things were expected of him when he was elected to his Fellowship. I never really rightly understood what came of him. I dare say you know, my dear Dean: wasn't he one of your West-Country clientèle?'

This was the regular phrase with which they teased the Dean about the interest he took, the almost fatherly interest, in the long file of young men coming up to the University from the West Country, from scholarship candidates to D.Phil. researchers. Anybody of West-Country connections had a claim upon his attention, if not upon his affections.

'Well, in a manner of speaking, he was,' said the Dean. Then, after a pause, unhurriedly savouring his cigar, turning it round on his lips:

'There was no mystery about it, you know. It is quite clear what happened.' He laid emphasis upon 'what happened', as if there were some mystery *before* what had happened.

'Poor fellow, he's still alive, though in a bad way, I gather.'

(A ghost may come;

—mused the abstracted, ruminating mind of the young English don—

For it is a ghost's right,
His element is so fine
Being sharpened by his death,
To drink from the wine-breath
While our gross palates drink from the whole wine.

But it wasn't the poor fellow of the Dean's acquaintance who was the ghost, he reflected. Perhaps he had seen a ghost? He sat up and began to attend in earnest.)

'No, there was no mystery attached to it,' the Dean was saying. 'But it was certainly a very curious story.

'You see, I knew the lad—or rather the part of Cornwall he comes from—well. His was a sweet nature, a charming disposition; and very level-headed and sensible, too. He was the last person you would have expected to—' He paused to inspect the end of his cigar, to see if it were properly alight.

'Expected to what?' said the eager young Fellow, a little tense.

The Dean took no notice, went on his unhurried way. 'He had got here on his own steam, won a lot of scholarships. He was quite capable of looking after himself. He hadn't much of a family in the background. I believe there was a father, who had gone off to America, or something of the sort, leaving the mother to fend for herself. The lad was brought up largely by his sister, who was much older than he was, ten or fifteen years. She was more of a mother to him.

'Up here young Colenso (Tristram was his name: rather curious, too—I believe it ran in the family), well, he did very well, got his first and was elected to a Research Fellowship almost at once. Perhaps it was rather a rush, a bit too much for him; it may have overtaxed his strength. Better that these things should come slowly—let them ripen in due season,' said the Dean, who had had several set-backs in his early academic career and thought it a good principle for everybody else that things should not come to them too easily.

'But he had to get something, poor lad,' he added kindly. 'And he had a very good subject for research right on his own doorstep, so to speak. You know the old Cornish family, the Lantyans, of Carn Tyan, who were the greatest landowners in Cornwall in the Middle Ages—though they have lost a good deal of their property there since. They were absentees from the county for a long time, from the sixteenth century to the eighteenth. They were Catholics, and during the years of Elizabeth's war with Spain they were not allowed to live in so dangerous an area, so remote from the centre, so near the sea, and with the sympathies of their peasantry all Catholic like their own. It was for them a prohibited area—as for strangers today. How little things change in human affairs!' (The Dean enjoyed a good ripe platitude as it might be a peach or a nectarine.) 'Well, the Lantyans have gone on being

Catholic in an unbroken tradition—and very proud they are of the fact. They say that in their chapel at Carn Tyan there is a lamp that has never been allowed to go out since the Reformation.

'The old Lady Lantyan bore an extraordinary character in those parts. Jane Lucinda: she was the last representative of the Blanchminsters who owned a great deal of land in North Cornwall in the Middle Ages, and also one half, the secular half, of the Scilly Islands. The old lady was a regular termagant, a well-known character all over the West Country. For one thing she had a terrific temper; was immensely family-proud and haughty; a dominating old woman who lived to be ninety and led her household and servants and everybody near her the devil of a life. Particularly, for some odd reason, her chaplains. She seemed to hate them; she certainly persecuted them. Yet it never occurred to her to dispense with them: there always had been a priest in the household, and she simply couldn't conceive of a house without one—for her. It may be that she wanted somebody or something to torment. She had no children. Her husband had died years before, leaving her in control of the money. So she remained on in possession, keeping her heir, an elderly cousin of her husband's, at arm's length. He couldn't have afforded to dispossess her anyway; he was entirely dependent on her for what would, or might, come to him after her death.

'So she lived on at Carn Tyan, tormenting priests her chief pleasure in life, you might say. One after the other they left her, driven to distraction. One poor man, the last of them, a French priest, a cultivated, quiet, melancholy sort of man, who already seemed to have enough on his mind—as if there was a something in the background—was driven over the edge. He became stark raving mad. To begin with, she starved them. It wasn't that she was mean. It was just that she had very odd views about diet. She lived on next to nothing herself, with the aid—it is true—of the very best old cognac, such as she had a good store of in her cellars. You never come across brandy like that nowadays.' The Dean gave a heartfelt sigh.

'The old lady was immensely aristocratic; she couldn't believe but what suited her very well must be good for everybody else. She fed her priests mostly on rice and currants, relieved with brandy at every meal to wash it down. She insisted that to keep your health you had to drink brandy five times a day. Such of them as survived the endless rice and currant puddings became hopeless topers on the brandy. The combination was too much for her last priest. But then he had something else on his mind.

'Not that that much worried the old tartar, Jane Lucinda. Protest after protest at her treatment of her priests had been made by her bishop, the Bishop of Lysistrata. Without the slightest effect. At last a writ of excommunication was made out to be served upon her. Did that defeat her? Not a bit of it. On the threshold of ninety, she called for her carriage and at once drove off to a Carmelite convent the other side of the county, to enter upon a long retreat, leaving instructions that on no account should any correspondence be forwarded. So that the writ never reached her. When the bishop at length learned where she was, she left for the house of a relation in Worcestershire. By the time it reached Worcestershire she was in London. For the bishop it was a regular wild-goose chase, making him look ridiculous in the eyes of the whole Catholic community who knew perfectly well what was going on. I believe the old termagant thoroughly enjoyed the last months of her life. Having outwitted her ecclesiastical superiors, she took to her bed at her town house in London and died still officially at peace with the Church, and fortified with all the accustomed rites.

'At last her cousin, the thirteenth baronet—an elderly man of sixty—entered into possession of the almost derelict estate, a great house in which nothing had been changed since the eighteen-sixties. He was the last of the family. Like many another bachelor who had himself done nothing to keep going the succession, he was interested in his family history. And on coming into possession, he found a muniment room stuffed full of old deeds and documents, letter-books and papers, and wanted some help in going through them. This is where young Tristram Colenso came in. Sir Richard had heard of his expertise in deciphering medieval handwritings, and the idea was that he should write a family history of the Lantyans and Blanchminsters. After all, the least the baronet could do for posterity, since he hadn't produced any issue of his own to continue it—so far as we are aware; at any rate not any legitimate issue,' the Dean added cautiously.

'So young Colenso was invited down for a week-end to take a preliminary look through the papers in the muniment room. It was his first experience of stopping in a great country house—and alas, poor lad, I suppose it will be his last. He was very excited and impressed. All very natural. He had heard of Carn Tyan all his life, but had never so much as set eyes on it.

'The house is in a very remote and un-get-at-able part of Cornwall—the Tamar Valley. Also one of the most lovely, with a singular fascination of its own. You know, my dear Done, how people up here are liable to say, "Of course the coast of Cornwall is very beautiful, but the county has no interior." What nonsense it is!' The Dean, a very patriotic Cornishman, grew quite angry. 'Just the impression of ignorant tourists rushing through the county along the main motor-road to Newquay or St Ives or the Lizard. As a matter of fact, all the river valleys are extremely beautiful country: Helford, the country of the Fal, the Fowey, the Camel, and not least, the Tamar. In spite of Plymouth being at its gate, the Tamar country is the most unspoiled, as it is the least accessible.'

Having made his point, the Dean sent the junior Fellow into the smoking-room to get him a whisky-and-soda, and on his return resumed the story. Meanwhile they watched the last rosy flush of light catching the topmost cupola of the Radcliffe Camera. The Dean's colleague, the Classic, thought of the lovely orange-and-rose flush in the sky of Rome as you look from the Pincio Gardens to the dome of St Peter's in the west across the darkening spaces of the city. Yes, he thought, the Camera is the most Roman thing in Oxford—and as good as anything in Rome. Fortified by his whisky-and-soda, the Dean resumed.

'When Colenso arrived at the station at Launceston after an all-day journey, there was a car to meet him. They drove for miles through the failing light—it was the very beginning of November—until he recognized the long serrated crest of the woods, the nearest he had ever been to the house, upon the next ridge. It was not without a thrill that he passed through the gates, the pillars surmounted by lions upholding shields, the arms of the Lantyans, and into the grand gloom of the park. He just caught sight of the splendid fans of the cedars upon the lawn when they drove up to the front door.

'His first impression was of the magnificence of the great double staircase which swept down its marble arms into the hall. He was shown up to his room by a maid carrying a little hand lamp through the vast and shadowy gloom. At the head of the staircase there were at least eight great mahogany doors in a semicircle. They went through one on the right and along an unfinished corridor, through several large rooms, of which one was a book-room, and down a little curved passage to his own door. It opened into a huge state-bedroom, with great state-bed under a canopy at the farther end. His heart sank a little at the spectacle: it was altogether too grand for him, he thought. He felt that it was a mistake, his coming.

'Opening a note the maid had given him, he found that it was from Sir Richard, regretting that he couldn't be there to receive him. He had had to go urgently into Plymouth that afternoon and hoped to be back in time for dinner at eight. Tristram had plenty of time to look round and dress at leisure. He was evidently expected to occupy this room: there was a wood fire lit for him in the Adam fireplace. It burnt up cheerfully. But the room was far too large to be cheerful in itself. Fancy sleeping in a bedroom that had a couple of columns at each end, thought Tristram; in a state-bed large enough for four. How does one sleep in it? he wondered; does one sleep on the outer edge, or leap boldly into the middle?

'He looked round by the light of the lamp and the candles lighted on the dressing-table. No electricity anywhere. The room gave an impression of the gloomy splendour of a former age, rather than of opulence in this. There were eighteenth-century portraits on the wall, and beautiful things about: silver candlesticks on dressing-table and writing-table, and a smaller one for the hand with snuffers beside the bed. All very well, he thought, but no electric light to turn on, if you should want it in the night.

'With time on his hands he settled down to write the journal-letter that he wrote to his sister when anything special happened to him, such as going away on a visit. Then it was time for him to change. He put on his newly starched shirt and trousers and silk socks, arranged his studs and cuff-links, when he discovered that he had forgotten to bring a dress tie. The kind of accident that happens to us all, when we are young,' said the Dean sympathetically, with a memory of some similar misadventure to himself before he had lost his youthful diffidence.'And what upsets us far worse than many things in themselves more important.

'Tristram was struck with horror. He had specially packed everything himself that morning so that nothing of the kind should happen. Young and inexperienced, he regarded this in the light of a major disaster. It took him a long time to summon up courage to ring the bell. It took an even longer time for the maid to answer his summons from somewhere in the depths of this vast, silent house. She came back with an old-fashioned tie of Sir Richard's, with his compliments.

'As the hour of eight approached he took his lamp and made his way back, not without some doubt and a few wrong turnings, to the head of the magnificent staircase, and downstairs. Going under the arch into the small dining-room he saw a figure in a corner strenuously engaged in drawing a cork. He took him to be the butler. It was in fact Sir Richard, acting as butler himself.

'They shook hands and went into the dining-room together. Tristram was rather set at ease by the unexpected manner of their meeting, was made to feel completely at home by the way Sir Richard chaffed him about the tie—he said it was what he always did himself when *he* was young; the young man ended by being quite conquered by his host's old-fashioned charm of manner. The baronet was very tall and good-looking, with crisp grey hair; in spite of a gouty leg, he would himself get up to fetch Tristram a cigarette or ashtray, or open the door. Sir Richard certainly knew how to render himself agreeable to the young scholar. During dinner there was a good deal of amusement at the expense of the departed dowager and her ways—fantastic stories of which Sir Richard had a whole repertoire. (She had her revenge, in her own way,' commented the Dean.) 'Tristram concluded that if the redoubtable Jane Lucinda were after an Elizabethan pattern, haughty and overbearing, like the famous Bess of Hardwick or Lettice Knollys, her successor the baronet was the perfection of eighteenth-century courtesy, easy and affable.

'The meal was very simple; there was only one maid to wait at table. The baronet did his own butling. Though the silver was beautiful, Tristram couldn't but observe that the carpet was threadbare. Dinner ended with a couple of glasses of port from the bottle that Sir Richard had been caught in the act of decanting. He took it as a joke and made fun of his impoverished estate. None the less it was evident what a pride he had in his ancestry and everything that concerned his family's history. Tristram could hardly keep up with his references to the seventh or tenth Sir Richard or the heiresses who had brought in this or that estate in the distant past, or his way of thinking of English history as episodes in the more continuous and certain story of his family.

'After dinner, taking their light with them, they went out and down through a stone passage to the muniment room. It was a young researcher's paradise. So many cupboards and presses and chests of drawers, boxes and trunks and iron deed-boxes, crammed full of old documents—most of them medieval, it seemed. There were rent-rolls and accounts, copies of inquisitions, terriers and fines, duplicates of wills, letters and letter-books—all in the most agreeable confusion. Many a day's pleasant work for a couple of enthusiastic antiquarians. But the box which most tickled Tristram's intuitive sense as a researcher—his nose for documents: a sort of sixth sense—was locked and the key lost. Nothing would induce it to open. They tried all the keys, but none would fit the lock. It was most provoking, for from the lettering outside Tristram could see that it contained documents relating to the most interesting of Cornish monastic houses. He tried various little keys of his own upon the lock, but only succeeded in breaking them and leaving their heads in the wards.

'It was after eleven when they gave up, and Sir Richard accompanied his guest up the grand staircase to his room. The fire was burning brightly, throwing elongated shadows across the high ceiling. Tristram got into bed, keeping to the edge of it; there was an interminable space unoccupied the other side of him, he thought. He was surprised at the bed's comfort. He put out his light and tried to settle himself to sleep. But there was still the firelight and those long wavering shadows like fingers pointing across the room at him. Whether it was the port, or the excitement of the muniment room, his head was in a whirl. He was just falling asleep, when the thought of Lady

Lantyan's French priest came into his mind. He had gone mad in this house, perhaps in this very room.

'After that, there was no sleep for Tristram. He lay there for a bit, his heart beating audibly beneath the bedclothes of the great bed, listening, straining his ears to catch every sound in the vast silence, an owl hooting outside in the park, the swish-swish—what was it?—of the twigs of a tree against the window-pane. Unable to bear it any longer, unable to sleep, he lit his candle, got out, put on his dressing-gown, and went to the writing-table to take refuge in the comfort of writing to his sister.

'It was the worst thing he could have done, probably; writing only heated his imagination the more, stimulated his nervous sensibility, made him doubly aware of every sound and movement.

'I don't quite know what happened next; one can only piece it together from his account of that night afterwards. He was never very sure of the order in which things happened, even at his best. And, of course—at the worst—' The Dean paused, finished his whisky-and-soda, and went on:

'It seems that he was looking for something to read, something to take back to bed with him. I don't know whether there were any books in the room; he may have gone out through the little passage into the book-room to find something. Or he may have found it in the drawer of that writing-table. Wherever it was, with the unfailing flair of the born researcher—which he undoubtedly had, poor fellow—he put his hand on a little manuscript book that had belonged to the French priest.'

The Dean stopped and lit a cigarette to keep off the gnats which were beginning to pester him, like a cloud of disagreeable memories that one wants to exorcize.

'That little manuscript book, a sort of diary, gave the clue to the secret of the French priest. He had an irremediable sin upon his conscience, which tormented him and turned his life into agony. Apparently he had been in his early years left with the charge of a small child, a boy, whose parents were his near relations. He regarded this charge with distaste, as a burden upon his career (he was poor and ambitious). In his early years he did the minimum he could for this child, had him placed in an orphanage and barely kept touch with his responsibility. Some dozen or fifteen years later he received a message to come to the bedside of his young relation. The lad was now in a seminary.

'The priest found that his uninteresting charge had grown into a youth, intelligent and of great charm—but, alas, far gone in consumption. Touched to the heart at last, but too late, he remained there with him all through that summer and autumn. Until, in fact, the end. The boy died on All Souls' Day, the second of November.

'Every day for the rest of his life when All Souls' Day came round the priest said a requiem for him. When he came to Carn Tyan, as All Souls'-tide approached, he became more and more plunged into profound gloom. An inconsolable misery seemed to possess him, turning him inwards upon himself. During that period he was in the habit of inflicting on himself austerities, which left him in a mingled state of physical exhaustion and mental excitement. It was really the first symptom of his madness. He thought himself responsible for the death of his young charge. This was his retribution.

'As Tristram picked up the threads of this story of suffering and penance, this confession of guilt from a dead man, something of the priest's state of morbid excitement communicated itself to him. He was already in a very susceptible condition: the strangeness of the house, the excitement of the muniments, the listening silences of the great room in which sleep was now impossible.

'The fire had burned down to a last occasional flicker, making more absolute the shadows in all the room, save for the patch of light by the bedside.

'What was that that stirred at the farther end of the room? Tristram listened with every nerve in his body on edge. In the confusion of his senses he could not tell whether it was something that registered itself to the sense of sight or hearing. He sat up, listening, peering between the great bed-posts into the darkness. The sound came more distinctly from that direction: it was something like a low moan. He listened: the strange hoarse sibilance became clearer: it was a pattern, a mutter of words. But the words did not seem to make sense.

'At last Tristram caught quite distinctly the words, "mea culpa, mea culpa, mea maxima culpa", uttered with an inexpressible anguish such as he thought no human voice could attain. Tristram wasn't a Catholic; he had been brought up an Anglican, a rather High Church Anglican. He recognized the Confession of the priest at the beginning of the Canon of the Mass. The Latin words were spoken with an unmistakable French accent.

'With all his senses alive, his nerves on edge, he watched intently: it was as if he saw everything in the room at once, out of the corners of his eyes. Sitting up in bed looking straight before him to the other end of the room, upon which his fears were concentrated, he suddenly saw the great door behind him at *this* end of the room open softly, slowly on its hinges, as if for someone to pass through. He was transfixed there, waiting. Nobody. Nobody passed through. The great door closed as noiselessly, as slowly as it had opened.

'But was there nobody that had passed through? A sense of unutterable grief, of inconsolable suffering, had invaded the room. It was unnerving. Tristram could stand it no longer.

'Hardly knowing what he was doing, he got out of bed and out of the room at the other end to find himself in darkness outside. His brain was working with the unnatural clarity that goes with such an experience; all his apprehensive senses were aroused by what was about him. He realized, quite rationally, with the disjunctive logic of a dream, that the reason for the curve in the passage leading to the great room was that it was here the end of the chapel abutted on to the house; and he found himself looking down from the family pew high up in the gallery at the west end of the building upon the scene that enacted itself below.

'He had no doubt about what was going on down there. There were the shadowy figures, vested, before the altar; upon the altar itself the two candles of the rubric. Fascinated, unable to move from the spot, he heard the immemorial Roman mutter, the introit of the Mass for the Dead:

Requiem aeternam dona eis, Domine, et lux perpetua luceat eis.

It seemed to him that he heard the strange toneless voices articulating the *Dies Irae* from the beginning:

Dies irae, dies illa
Solvet saeclum in favilla,
Teste David cum Sibylla

to the very end:

Judicandus homo reus:
Huic ego parce, Deus.
  Pie Jesu, Domine,
  Dona eis requiem.

His eyes were so fixed upon the figures round the altar, that it was only when the whimper of the *Dies Irae* was over that he noticed in the gloom before the sanctuary that there was a catafalque, with one taper, no more than a rushlight, burning at the head. It was a small coffin, very slender and shapely. Then he knew whose requiem it was that was proceeding down below.

'With that thought there came over him a sense of inextinguishable grief such as had passed through the great room. Only now it seemed to invade him by every crevice open to its penetration, eyes, ears, mouth, throat. Overwhelmed with a grief that was not his, he stumbled back into the room, lit the candles one by one, every one of them, upon writing-table, dressing-table, at the bedside. If there had been a hundred candles, still he would have lit them all to lighten the oppression weighing upon his spirits.

'He sat down before the dressing-table, face plunged in hands. It was when he removed his hands for a moment that he noticed something strange about his appearance. There were creases, there were lines upon his face, at the corners of mouth and nostrils, around the eyes. It seemed to him that the more he looked, the more lined his face became. It was like the face of someone else. But above all it was the eyes that arrested his attention. His eyes were dark; but the eyes that fixed him in the mirror were grey and steely, with that strange fanatic quality you sometimes see in Frenchmen's eyes. As he watched, the whole face began to twitch: it was the face of a madman.

'In the morning when it was daylight, they found him still seated there before the mirror, gibbering.'

1967

SHEPHERD, SHOW ME...

Rosalind Wade

Rosalind Wade OBE (1909–1989) published her first novel, *Children, Be Happy!*, in 1931. This became the centre of several lawsuits as Wade had based some of her characters on identifiable real people who eventually won damages from the publisher. The judge ordered every copy of the book and the original manuscript be destroyed, resulting in the book never being republished. Wade married fellow writer William Kean Seymour and had two sons, one of whom is the thriller author Gerald Seymour of *Harry's Game* (1975) fame. As well as writing under the pen name of Catharine Carr, she also was the editor for *The Contemporary Review* between 1970 and 1989. Wade also served as the president of the Society of Women Writers and Journalists (1965–1989) and taught courses on writing and literature at Moor Park College in Farnham, Surrey. In 1985 she was awarded an Order of the British Empire in recognition of her contribution to literature. A tale of a husband who asks a 'sensitive' woman to liberate his wife from spirit healers, 'Shepherd, Show Me...' was originally published in James Turner's *The Unlikely Ghosts* (1967) and has only been reprinted in *Haunted Cornwall* (1973) and *Ghosts in Country Houses* (1981), the two latter books both edited by Denys Val Baker.

As I approached the house, my curiosity increased. In this uncultivated landscape, punctuated only by derelict mineshafts and an occasional slag-heap, it seemed impossible that any habitation could be concealed. My impression was of the Atlantic Ocean boiling up all around me like a vast cauldron, on the surface of which a couple of distant tramp steamers were no more noticeable than match-heads.

I stopped the car, hoping that no unwieldy farm cart would wish to pass, and studied my directions. Once the car was still the full force of the gale sounded like giant hand-slappings. Even a gull, irresolutely straying inland, barely maintained its poise.

The instructions were meticulously clear... 'Continue after leaving St Huthy for two miles. At the first bend you will see a farmhouse with the shutters painted bright yellow. I should warn you, it's a one in four descent after that, but it leads you straight to Lancevearn...'

Very soon I identified that farmhouse—and why anyone should have chosen such a bilious colour for the woodwork remained a mystery. I skirted it with caution and changed gear, speculating as to what manner of man had written that letter. '...I do indeed hope you will forgive me for being so presumptuous as to trouble you, a complete stranger...' it continued. 'My only excuse is that a very old friend of yours, Miss Queenie Newton, has told me of the wide experience you have in so many spheres, including that unknown quantity, the power of mind over matter. I myself know virtually nothing about "spiritual" treatment and so I am quite unable to cope with my present predicament which, briefly, is that my wife is completely dominated by a couple of faith-healers. And so, seeing that you are spending a few days in the St Huthy neighbourhood...'

I began then to form a mental picture of him as a fussy, precise person, practical enough when describing a route but a crank and, even more deplorable, husband of another crank. This could be a case of *folies à deux*; and it was more than ever puzzling to know what I was expected to do about it.

Almost without warning I came upon a pair of elaborate stone gate-posts set in the high granite wall which enclosed the grounds of Lancevearn. On one side the boundary sliced through a strip of moorland; on the other, a narrow path led directly to the sea. Within, a riot of escallonia. A young gardener was hacking away apathetically at the overgrown plantation. The house appeared to be of medium size and rather squat in appearance; the wonder was that stone and timber has ever been transported to this inaccessible spot.

An agreeable-looking maid opened the front door to me. She was very dark, although her eyes were china blue, suggestive of a lingering element of the Spaniards who, in remote times, had invaded these shores and intermarried with the indigenous Celts. She led the way across a large square hall to the drawing-room. The furniture was strangely heterogeneous and I paused to inspect one of the most striking pieces. At that moment I heard my name spoken and turned to greet my host. With difficulty I concealed my astonishment. For here was no elderly eccentric but an undeniably handsome young man.

'You *are* Mr Stephen Hallam?' I inquired unnecessarily.

He nodded. 'Let me say straight away how terribly grateful I am to you for coming to the aid of a complete stranger. I was feeling quite desperate when I wrote to you, but Queenie assured me you wouldn't mind. I mean, you have so much experience…'

I raised my hand to ward off the unwelcome and undeserved compliment. 'Please, Mr Hallam, may I make this absolutely clear? I am not an authority on faith-healing; nor, indeed, on anything else. It's true I'm interested in a great many subjects, but purely as an observer and, if you like, a commentator.'

'You're far too modest. Why, Queenie was telling me…'

Not for the first time I shook my fist, figuratively speaking, at Queenie. Her interpretation of the obligations of our lifelong friendship was to belittle such modest talents as I possess to my face while recommending them fulsomely in other quarters.

'But how did you happen to discuss me with Queenie in the first place?' I asked. 'I haven't seen much of her since she became Matron at St Benyn's school, although we keep in touch in a vague kind of way.' Frankly, I could not see my garrulous, muddle-minded little friend in this man's orbit.

'We often have tea together in her sanctum; at the school, that is.'

'You're a schoolmaster, then?' I exclaimed.

'Does it astonish you so much? I should have mentioned in my letter that I'm on the staff at St Benyn's.'

'Forgive me,' I begged him, 'I didn't mean...'

'I don't look like a teacher?'

'Well, no...'

'Then what do I look like?'

The question at first sounded a mere provocation until I realized that he was attaching a quite disproportionate importance to my reply. I inspected him covertly. His eyes were amber-coloured; his hair combed back to conceal an unobtrusive wave. And his voice, vibrant though unaffected, was rich with subtle cadences.

'An actor,' I replied impulsively.

'Well, that's exactly what I am—or was!'

The explanation proved simple. He had originally trained at a teacher's college and then gone on the stage, following a totally unexpected invitation from a West End manager who had seen him playing in an amateur production. But despite this promising start he ended up in a provincial repertory company and it was there that he met his wife, Mira. Alas, the strain of the life told on Mira and she suffered a complete breakdown after the loss of an eagerly awaited first child. And so it seemed wise to get right away from the theatre and fortunately he was able to return to his early profession in an ideal post at St Benyn's.

I listened attentively to this story, filling in the gaps, wondering whether the affinity between acting and teaching was sufficient to support his *amour propre*. And then I found myself voicing the inevitable query. What precisely was I expected to do about it?

'You've every right to ask that after listening to my tale of woe so patiently.

Mira was much better by the time we came here but she still wasn't off the sick-list. She injured her leg, you see, when she collapsed during a performance.'

'She's not actually crippled, or lame?'

'No, no. Nothing like that. Her leg just needs massage or "light" treatment. You know the kind of thing.'

'And she isn't getting it?'

'I'm afraid not. A few days after we came here—in January that was—I registered with the local doctor, asking him to call on Mira as soon as possible. For some reason he didn't come at once. I was rather annoyed about it at the time. Anyway, when he did appear at Lancevearn it was too late. By that time the faith-healers had moved in on us and Mira was entirely satisfied with them. In fact, she got furiously angry when I questioned their qualifications. Since then the doctor has looked in several times and been sent away by Mira—rather rudely, I'm afraid. Unfortunately, I was out each time. I should think it must have been about mid-March that he telephoned me at school and put it pretty clearly that there was nothing further he could do.'

'Well,' I suggested, 'is it possible that she really has recovered from the breakdown and wants to establish the fact?'

'I'd like to think that. It did occur to me at first. But no, I believe she really needs quite a bit of help. She still suffers from insomnia. I see a light under her door all night. And there's the leg. I'm sure she's in pain. Anyway, it's bad enough to keep her in bed. She hasn't been downstairs for weeks now.'

'That's terribly frustrating for both of you.'

I found myself considering two kinds of faith-healer: one, a visiting lay preacher conducting a service in the parish church with people queueing up to receive his blessing without noticeable results; and the other, a frowsty spiritualist of the kind a woman of my acquaintance consulted in a fit of emotional despair. Into which category did the present practitioners fall?

His reply was surprising. 'I can't say. I've never seen them. You see, weekends and holidays when I'd be at home, they've never shown up. They don't wish to meet me, obviously.'

'Then why don't you write or telephone them, forbidding them to call here except by appointment with you personally?'

'That would be the obvious thing, of course, if I knew their names and where they come from. But Mira absolutely refuses to tell me. Naturally, I've asked her again and again.'

As though a curtain had been abruptly drawn back I witnessed the extent of his inner turmoil and deprivation. 'You could easily find out,' I answered gently. 'There can't be so many faith-healers in the St Huthy district! But, in any case, is it so important? I expect she will come through, with or without a doctor.'

'Perhaps. But you see, it isn't only a matter of her health. In some strange way, these people have turned her against me. She hates me now. When she speaks to me, which isn't often, she's like a hostile stranger. The summer term starts tomorrow and they'll be back, for sure. That's really why I wrote to you, to ask you to talk to her for me, before it's too late.'

I refused unconditionally. As a stimulus to my creative imagination the complexities of the human predicament might have their uses; yet I shied away from actual participation in them. But he persisted. Just *because* I was a stranger I might break the impasse... And in the end I capitulated, reflecting that I undertook very little of practical service to fellow humans less fortunate than myself.

He fetched a decanter and glasses and together we sat out in the conservatory. His hand trembled as he poured the wine. Tentatively, I sought to distract his attention. What chance had led him to settle in such an out-of-the-way place as Lancevearn?

'Oh, simply seeing an advertisement.'

He had rented the house furnished, for one year, at a surprisingly modest figure. Eventually, the place would be auctioned as part of a much larger estate. Lancevearn was built some seventy-five years earlier by a Cornishman who had spent most of his life in the United States and made a fortune there. Nearly all the furniture had been collected in the United States and shipped to England. Each piece was listed with the price paid and where purchased in a large leather-bound volume reposing on the hall table. We laughed a little at this evidence of Victorian precision.

But soon he was glancing at his watch. 'I have to go into St Huthy to fill up with petrol,' he explained. 'And I may need to have the engine looked at. After you've seen Mira, do you think you could wait for me until I get back? Our maid, Rhoda, would get you anything you wanted. And then, if these people should show up, you could cope with them for me; or, better still, persuade them to wait until I get back.' He assured me that he had already told Mira that a great friend of Queenie's would be calling and she had raised no objection. Presently I heard the engine of his car purring away up the track. For a full minute I waited on in the conservatory, gazing out at the incomparable view.

The surface of the hall floor shone like polished ebony. The carving of the balustrade struck me as unique. But it was the magnificently sited landing window which finally captured my attention. Set within a large recess, the alcove afforded the illusion of being built right out over the sea, with Godrevy, a gleaming platinum strip, just visible on the western horizon. There was some furniture, conveying the effect of a small extra room, a rocking-chair and a most unusual escritoire or 'lady's bureau'.

Of the six doors opening onto the landing all but one were closed. 'Is that my visitor?' a faint voice inquired and I braced myself for the ordeal, for the thought of the invalid, immured from the morning freshness, was repellent rather than pitiful.

I do not quite know what I expected her to look like, although names do conjure people and 'Mira' is the 'variable' star. At any rate, the person who greeted me from the vantage of an enormous four-poster bed was one of the most beautiful women I had ever seen and I thought what a striking pair the Hallams must have made at that Repertory theatre. But that she was genuinely ill I now had no doubt. There were about her mouth the traces of deep suffering. And as she shifted her position she winced involuntarily with pain.

'Come and sit down,' she invited, quickly mastering it. 'Stephen told me you were going to call this morning. You're a great friend of Queenie's, aren't you?'

'We were at school together,' I explained. 'I'm sorry you're ill. How very disappointing for you when you've just moved into this glorious place.'

She acknowledged my sympathy with a polite nod. 'Well, we've been here nearly four months now, you know. It might be disappointing if I didn't know for certain that I can be completely cured. In fact, I *am* cured, although that's rather a negative way of putting it because, actually, there never was anything the matter with me. It's just a matter of time until my own faith is strong enough to banish all these—illusions—of "evil". I have to fight all these wicked whisperings which try to tell me I'm an invalid, but also I have to stand up against—er—people who try to make me believe my body and my mind are still sick.'

She outlined her problem in a common-sense manner which would be hard to combat. She wore a lace-topped nightgown and through it her breasts showed firm and opaque. It was not difficult to imagine the emotional frustration which her husband suffered.

'All that might be so, in a general way,' I agreed cautiously. 'But does it apply to every kind of ailment? Haven't you hurt your leg? I think I noticed when I came in that it was paining you. A thing like that can do with some orthodox medical treatment, surely?' I was uncomfortably aware that I was catechizing her, and until this moment she had not appeared to resent it. But my last comment stung her to anger.

'You mean, by a doctor? I wouldn't have one inside the place. Don't you know that they are mere "purveyors of evil". "Confectioners of disease", someone once called them, and that describes them perfectly!' I saw then that her husband had not exaggerated. She spoke with such concentrated venom that the immediate effect was of an actress rehearsing an unpleasant part.

'Aren't you a bit hard on the profession?' I countered lightly. 'I feel sure your husband would be greatly relieved if you would agree to, say, a routine check-up?'

'Then I must resist him.' Her voice rose to a shout.

I was shocked and shaken: 'But you do have some advice, don't you, Mrs Hallam?' I cut in quickly, determined to keep control of the situation. 'What kind of people are they, these "faith-healers" of yours?'

'Oh. I see he *has* been complaining about them to you. I thought as much.' Her lips tightened into a thin vindictive line. 'Actually, they are two charming, very devout people, who certainly have my interests at heart!'

'I'm sure they have. Do they call regularly? Are they both women, by the way?'

'They come when they can. No, it's a man and a woman. *She* is quite elderly and rather delightfully old-fashioned. *He* is much younger, but not at all "modern" in the way he talks and dresses. I *think* they're married but I've never been quite sure. Anyway, they have a perfect mutual understanding,' she concluded rather wistfully.

'I can see they mean a great deal to you.' I stood up and held out my hand. 'I do hope you'll soon be up and about again.'

'Oh, but I *do* get up, nearly every afternoon. I sit in the window recess.' She spoke quite pleasantly as though unwilling to part on bad terms. Perhaps because of Queenie?

I responded in the same spirit: 'On the landing, you mean? It's lovely there at the moment.'

'Well, I may not trouble today.'

I paused at the alcove, thinking that the reclining chair and the low bureau might have been specially constructed for an invalid. Idly, I rested my hand on the leather-topped desk and as I did so I experienced the strangest sensation. It was as though an overmastering personality took complete control of me. Darkness obscured my vision, while insistent voices reverberated in my head like a distorted radio. Involuntarily I took a step backwards; and stood very still, waiting for the attack to pass. Gradually, the scene lightened and silence reigned. Though still trembling, I began to feel normal again. By the time I reached the hall the odd, frightening indisposition might have happened only in my imagination.

On the table lay the leather-bound inventory Stephen had mentioned. I turned to the relevant entries. 'One lady's correspondence bureau, one reclining chair, Boston, Mass. (1911).' Also, from the same source, an umbrella-stand in the hall. I was quite amazed at the price paid for these three items. At that moment the telephone bell rang and the maid, Rhoda, came hurrying from the kitchen quarters to answer it.

The caller was Mr Hallam. The garage at St Huthy needed to keep the car for a couple of hours. Thus, he must not detain me if I wished to leave.

'In that case,' I said to Rhoda, 'I'll be getting along.' Through the open dining-room door I could see the table laid for one. 'I suppose Mrs Hallam won't be coming down for lunch?' I inquired.

'She has never done so since I've been working here,' Rhoda answered. 'When Mr Hallam is at school I take her up a tray and see she has everything she requires before I go home at two o'clock.'

'That's very helpful. I do hope she'll soon be better. I understand she is being treated by faith-healers,' I remarked with assumed detachment. 'Do they strike you as reliable people?'

Now her china-blue eyes were directed at me with merciless disapproval. If I had anticipated the co-operation of a garrulous Mrs Mop I was doomed to disappointment. 'I really couldn't say,' she replied coldly, 'I've not been here when they called.'

Outside, the sun's rays were quite scorching. I negotiated the track carefully, castigating myself for having handled a delicate situation so clumsily. By the time I reached the cross-roads I was still smarting from the rebuffs I had received. And who was responsible? Why, Queenie, with her inveterate passion for putting in her oar. On impulse, I decided to tell her so without waiting for our pre-arranged meeting three days hence.

Skirting St Huthy, I was soon bowling along a coast road ribboned by the azure sea; the skyline notched by dolmens and barrows. Within this narrow strip of territory was contained the very essence of early Cornish civilization—the witches' wishing stone and the foundations of the oldest Christian church in the Duchy. St Benyn's school, once a vicarage, was situated just beyond the ruins.

Queenie seemed surprised and not too pleased to see me, although she invited me into her sanctum, which was stacked with bed linen and trunks. She switched on the electric kettle and set out a tea-tray while listening to my complaints. 'I thought you'd be only too pleased to help Stephen, the poor lamb,' she protested indignantly. 'Tied down here as he is all day while these wretched people sit closeted with Mira, poisoning her mind against him. Oh, it's too cruel. And his teaching suffers. I've heard some of the staff say so.'

I began to wonder whether she was in love with him, and repeated the basic question, 'But why pick on *me*?'

Her answer really astounded me: 'As you were brought up a Christian Scientist, I thought you'd know about faith-healing, and that kind of thing.'

'But, Queenie, that was *years* ago.'

It was perfectly true that my parents had been close adherents of that faith; but they died when I was ten years old and I was brought up by a humanist. For this reason, I had virtually no contact with any organized religion during the formative years; since when I had given the matter very little thought. Briefly, I reminded Queenie of my guardian's views and of the fact that in general terms I had accepted them. 'So if that's all you had to go on,' I concluded, more amiably, 'please explain to your friend that I don't really want to get involved with his problem.'

'If you say so, boss.' She pushed a brimming cup towards me with scant grace. I could see how seriously annoyed she was that her impulsive suggestion had so badly misfired. I confirmed that I would be expecting her at my hotel to lunch on the Sunday. She acknowledged the invitation with a curt nod and left me to see myself out.

The hotel at which I had elected to pass the week of my enforced solitude was picturesquely situated in a charming woodland glade. Yet my spirit was no longer attuned to the pleasantness. I hurried through dinner and as soon as possible returned to the lounge for coffee. The waiter mentioned that a visitor had arrived to see me. Inwardly I groaned. Queenie!

But the caller was Stephen. 'Mr Hallam,' I began as he came forward to greet me. 'I'm so sorry...'

'No, please don't apologize. How could I expect you to spend a whole day of your holiday hanging around Lancevearn?...' He explained that the work on his car had taken longer than expected. It was past five o'clock before he reached the house, only to discover that 'the worst' had happened. Mira admitted that the faith-healers had been with her for most of the afternoon. 'I protested and accused her of caring more about them than for me. It was most unwise. She flew into a terrible rage and then, suddenly, she went quite calm and cold. She told me that she had decided to leave me and go to live with them if I interfered or criticized them any more. And I could see she meant it.'

'But how could she leave Lancevearn? She isn't well enough?'

'That's what I said. "Taunting" her, was what she called it.'

'You must see them,' I said, 'it's gone too far.'

'Then *you* will have to help me to find them.'

This time I raised no objection for suddenly I felt curiously uneasy and apprehensive about the situation. We went into the bar and carried our drinks over to a corner settee, trying to assess what little information we had to go on.

'There's just one thing I've suddenly remembered,' he exclaimed after a long pause. 'Quite soon after we came here we had a very heavy fall of snow and I nearly skidded getting my car round the farmhouse. Mira seemed surprised when I told her because she said the faith-healers hadn't mentioned having any trouble. She was quite willing to talk to me about them in those days. It suggests they were familiar with the Lancevearn track or they'd have stayed away in such bad weather.'

I agreed. 'Oh, they must be local people. No doubt about that.'

I could only promise to do my best. Soon after midnight a gale blew in from the Atlantic rendering sleep intermittent. My dreams, too, were disturbed. In one of them I was with my parents, walking along a river-path, until suddenly they were drawn from me into a swirling torrent. I awoke, jaded and heavy-eyed, to an enveloping mist through which I could barely identify the golden landscape of the previous afternoon.

After an early breakfast I set off in my car, driving straight into a bank of fog so that soon I was completely lost. Presently, a grey stone building loomed ahead of me. This was a typical Wesleyan chapel. Placards affixed to the gate exhorted the sinner to repent while time was on his side. 'Hell-fire awaits the wicked. Ye shall be saved when ye see Christ.' At that moment the minister rode up on a motor-bicycle and inquired if there was anything he could do.

He was a genial man with an open rugged countenance. I mentioned my interest in the Wesley brothers, and he invited me to step inside. A woman was practising the harmonium; the atmosphere struck agreeably warm and musty. When we had spoken of the eighteenth-century sectarian divisions in

Cornwall I decided to make a tentative inquiry about the faith-healers. And I gave him, briefly, such details as I possessed.

'"Faith-healers?"' He seemed astonished; even resentful. 'No, I've never heard of any practising in these parts. Our mission is to heal the spirit rather than the flesh, by the unquestioning acceptance and acknowledgement of God's will. We would have nothing to do with such people in our ministry.'

I realized that I had drawn a complete blank. The minister had lived in the St Huthy district all his life, yet he could not identify these people, nor any remotely like them.

And that was the uniform reaction I received throughout a long sodden morning, during which I called at churches and chapels, even at the Citizens' Advice Bureau. The nearest I came to a clue was the casual mention in a village post-office of a bone-setter at Tintagel, but it appeared that his remarkable 'cures' were due simply to manipulation and he claimed no more for them. By early afternoon, when the drizzle had become a steady downpour, I admitted defeat. The time by then was three o'clock. I considered whether I should telephone Stephen at St Benyn's from a call-box or wait to ring him from the hotel during the evening, and decided on the latter course.

And then, as disconsolately I drew level with the Lancevearn cross-roads, a new thought struck me. Was not this the very hour at which the faith-healers usually called? While I exhausted myself running hither and thither on this inclement morning, wasting my own time and everybody else's, the prize lay all the while within my grasp. I had only to break in upon them, insist that they remained until Stephen returned, and my unwelcome involvement would be at an end.

The approach to the house was a quagmire. Rain fell with a chattering sound on the leaves of the escallonia. The place looked utterly deserted. An enamelled bin stood in the porch with an order for bread scribbled on a piece of cardboard. Fortunately, the front door was open and I stepped thankfully into the hall, depositing my mackintosh and umbrella on the hat-stand. As I did so I became aware of loud voices; at first a mere jangle of conflicting sound, but presently identifiable as a man's vigorous recital of a prayer, followed by a woman singing a hymn in quavering, falsetto tones.

'Shepherd, show me how to go,
O'er the hillside steep...'

Hastily I withdrew, taking my mackintosh and umbrella with me; ignoring the rain and slanting wind, for I had decided to revise my tactics. It would be far more effective to waylay the faith-healers just as they were leaving, thus obviating any risk of Mira warning them against me. There was a gazebo on the far side of the drive, with windows facing the sea. Into this I retreated to watch the wind playing weird games with the oncoming tide. Far more time than I realized must have slipped away. Had I, while resting comfortably in a wicker-chair piled high with cushions, actually fallen asleep? I never knew; only that, when belatedly I glanced at my watch, the hands pointed to four o'clock.

The rain had almost ceased. As I hesitated for a moment in the porch I was conscious of the gentle ticking of the hall clock and the distant throbbing of a refrigerator. Apart from that, silence enveloped the house like a blanket. I could not bear the possibility that I had missed the moment of departure. I looked into the various rooms, not liking myself for doing so. But there was nothing to see—two guest apartments, a small library, Stephen's bedroom and a second staircase leading to the domestic quarters. Mira's sewing and a book lay on the escritoire in the window recess but she herself was asleep in her bed. From the doorway I stood for a full minute watching the rhythmic rise and fall of her breast.

Somehow they had eluded me. Bitterly I upbraided myself: but then, as I paused before a small window looking on to a kind of enclosed inner yard, the question slid into my mind as insidiously as an asp. When did they leave Lancevearn—and how? For it seemed impossible that a vehicle could have driven out through the main gates while I was in the summer house without attracting my attention.

At that moment I heard a car outside and hurried downstairs to the porch. I could hardly conceal my disappointment when I realized that the sound came from the baker's van. The roundsman was the gardener whom I had seen working among the escallonias on the previous morning.

'Have you just passed a car in the lane?' I inquired breathlessly.

He shook his head. 'Who'd be out on such a day? I wouldn't myself, but people must have their bread.' He explained that he had a puncture just as he passed the St Huthy cross-roads and spent half an hour mending it.

I made a rapid calculation. If the faith-healers had driven up the track while I was in the gazebo they must have passed him.

'Is it possible,' I asked, 'that anyone could leave Lancevearn by some other route? Or even without a car? There's a footpath to St Huthy, isn't there?'

He deposited a couple of loaves in the bread bin and glanced at me pityingly. 'On a day like this? It's every bit of five mile to St Huthy round by the cliff.'

'As much as that? Well, it certainly doesn't seem very likely. But I mustn't keep you,' I added, for he seemed to be waiting, though unwillingly.

'Good day to you, then,' he said, 'I'll be getting along. I've still most of the round to do,' and away he went up the track in a cloud of petrol fumes. I noted that I could see and hear the van until it reached the farmhouse.

When he had gone I concentrated my gaze on what could be seen of the footpath from where I stood. The boundary of the Lancevearn grounds on this side of the estate was little more than a collection of leaning posts. I pushed aside a strand of trailing wire and stepped over it on to the moor. Bushes and thistles pressed around me as I followed the path until it terminated abruptly at a sheer cliff face. Far, far below, I could see white ribbons of foam as the incoming sea licked at the sides of the ravine. On the opposite side of the inlet, at a distance hard to estimate, the path reappeared, meandering towards the skyline, against which a deserted mineshaft provided a distinctive landmark. With the wisps of grey mist clinging to the vegetation and the leaden sky above it was the most desolate place imaginable, untrodden for months, even years by the look of it.

Clearly, the two faith-healers could not possibly have left Lancevearn by this route. The ageing woman, even with the assistance of a much younger man, would never have been able to negotiate it in the time. Somewhere, they would still have been visible from my vantage point above the ravine.

So where were they then, and what in heaven's name was the explanation of their disappearance? For a moment I waited, still scanning the forbidding landscape; and then, almost without realizing it, I answered my own question. They had never been on the cliff-path: nor in the house for that matter, *because they did not really exist.*

I could not possibly have explained by what means I arrived at this extraordinary conclusion. Yet once stated, it was unanswerable. A cold terror seized me then, so that I shivered violently while my body temperature seemed to drop to a degree far below normal.

I ran from the place in a kind of panic frenzy, averting my eyes from the house lest I should glimpse the phantom forms awaiting me there in the porch. I started up the car and covered the distance between Lancevearn and St Huthy with more speed than caution.

From the porter's desk I telephoned St Benyn's, leaving a message for Stephen that I had been unable to locate the two people of whom we had spoken, and that as I would be out the entire evening it would be useless for him to call or ring me at the hotel. In fact, I went straight to bed, fortified by two hot-water bottles and an electric fire. Yet still I shivered convulsively, as though suffering from malaria or ague. Release came only when, half drugged by aspirin, I fell into deep sleep.

As on the previous night, my dreams related to childhood. I was standing on a dark stairway leading from the Christian Science Sunday School which I attended while my parents were at the morning service. I feared they had forgotten me, but when my sense of abandonment and loss became unendurable a porter, with the face of the Lancevearn gardener, appeared to comfort me. 'Silly kid,' he chided me, 'your mum and dad won't be long. Listen, they've just started on the last hymn.'

And so they had. The reverberating swell of several hundred eager voices rose to engulf me like a cool, lapping wave.

> 'Shepherd, show me how to go,
> O'er the hillside steep,
> How to gather, how to sow,
> How to feed thy sheep.'

And I was warmed by a rosy comfort which, alas, was short-lived. For that incident, or something very like it, really happened a few days before the accident in which my parents lost their lives.

The trouble with dreams, as Jonathan Swift once remarked, is that they tend to leave us very much as we were before dreaming! I awoke abruptly some hours after midnight, still shivering. Nevertheless, the words of that hymn remained quite clearly in my mind, although I had not consciously thought of them in all these years. I recited all the stanzas unhesitatingly. By the time the sun rose, on a very chilly dawn, I was beginning to understand.

I dressed before anyone was up, roaming about the hotel garden in the soft bright light of early morning, while I attempted to analyse and assess the situation. That I myself was acutely sensitive to supernatural manifestations I already knew as a result of a very disturbing experience. This concerned a brooch purchased from a small antique-dealer in my home town. Whenever I wore it I was subject to moods of such acute depression and fear of the future that I thought it worth while to investigate the history of that brooch. I learned that it had belonged to a young woman who had committed suicide. This was my first intimation that an inanimate object could be permanently invested with the personality of the individual who had once possessed it—also that certain people, myself in this case, might unwittingly tune in, as though on a kind of one-way radio telephone, to span the limbo which separates the living from the dead.

My doctor, who insisted that he did not for one moment accept the possibility, none the less urged me to get rid of the brooch as quickly as possible and this I did, by throwing it into a pond.

I could not reasonably expect such tidy, conclusive proof in the present situation. All the same, I decided to seek some confirmation of my theory, if that were possible in this out-of-the-way locality.

Immediately after breakfast I drove into the nearest of the coastal towns and there by sheer good fortune discovered in the public library a copy of a book on faith-healers which I remembered reading some thirty years earlier. In it I found reasonable corroboration of my own grotesque conclusions.

I knew then that I must remain no longer in the St Huthy neighbourhood. For I dared not again risk brushing even the garments of the supernatural. I gave notice at the hotel, packed, and wrote a letter to Queenie saying that I had been unexpectedly called away and so was obliged to cancel the invitation to lunch. And early in the afternoon I drove off, feeling infinitely relieved, with the intention of reaching my own home sometime on the following day.

But as I passed the Lancevearn cross-roads a dark cloud of guilt descended on me. I alone suspected the true identity of the Lancevearn 'visitors': yet I had taken no steps to warn Mira either about her own occult sensitivity or of the 'other-world' influences to which she was being subjected. More important still, should I not have told her husband? For whatever principles the two faith-healers might have upheld when living and breathing in the material world, their motives seemed to have become frighteningly distorted while breaking the barrier between this universe and the next.

I could imagine Stephen's astonishment only too easily.

'But of *course* the faith-healers are real people. Certainly, they have a peculiar hold on Mira and I mean to put an end to it. That's why I begged you to help me find them.'

Rather than face a conversation along these lines I was putting distance between Lancevearn and myself. And yet... If I made no attempt to communicate my reading of the situation, surely I would always despise myself? So, torn by one of the strangest conflicts I have ever experienced, I reversed the car and drove back to the Lancevearn turning. The sun was stronger now; cotton-wool clouds floated high above my head. Away towards the sea a kestrel hovered: and I heard lark song on the still air. It would have been difficult to imagine a more tranquil scene, and deeply I regretted leaving it after so short a stay.

I reached the house just after four o'clock. Once again, the place seemed utterly deserted. The front door was slightly ajar, as before. This time a plastic container with an order for the butcher propped up against it stood just inside. Although not unexpected, the silence was uncanny, for there was something final and menacing about it. And yet on the surface, all seemed normal: the dining table set for supper and through the open conservatory window great gusts of clean, billowing sea-air made nonsense of my apprehensions.

I braced myself to ascend the stairs. Gently, I knocked on Mira's door, but there was no answer. 'Please may I come in, Mrs Hallam?' I called out, 'I have something very important to say to you.' But had I? Suddenly, I was no longer sure.

At last I looked into the room, not quite sure what I expected to see. Mira was not there. The bedclothes had been carefully folded back into position and several small toilet items removed from the dressing table. There were no clothes or books lying about and the thought struck me that Stephen must have prevailed upon her to leave Lancevearn for a while and recuperate elsewhere. He would have had no obligation to tell me of any such arrangement after my telephone call to the school and if this was really the case I need have no further feeling of responsibility.

I did not linger in this room, scene of so much suffering and acrimony, for suddenly I felt spent and exhausted after the anticlimax of finding her gone. I almost fainted as I crossed the landing and sank down on the rocking chair, resting my head against the escritoire, until the blood flowed slowly back to my brain. At that moment I saw them, in the diffused grey light which made a startling contrast to the brightness outside, yet distinct in every detail. A slight, elderly woman, plainly though expensively clad in a dark enveloping garment made of some kind of brocade with, at her throat, a diamond brooch in the shape of a cross. She moved with extreme difficulty; yet maintained an air of authority and purpose. The man who supported her wore an old-fashioned jacket and knee-breeches. His manner was solicitous and quietly deferential.

I have often wondered how eventually I found courage to follow them down the stairs, although I felt certain they would be gone before I reached the hall. And I was right; not even a wraith of mist remained; although the conviction was hard to put to the test!

*

In the weeks that followed I sometimes speculated as to where Mira had been that afternoon and whether she was by now fully recovered. Yet soon, with the press of family and other interests, I forgot her. But before that happened I had found time to look up various biographies and reference books in an attempt to clarify my impression of the two figures who had appeared before me on the staircase at Lancevearn. From prints and reproductions I recognized without any hesitation the Founder of my parents' faith, Mary Baker Eddy; by her sparse, carefully waved white hair, the material of her dress and the diamond brooch. There was no picture available of her companion; but sufficient published information for me to identify him as one of the two principle 'disciples' who supported the closing years of her long, tempestuous life. In a photograph of one of the rooms at her last home, Chestnut Hill, Massachusetts, I noted pieces of furniture identical with those on the landing at Lancevearn, and the wonder was that they had ever come into the market, rather than the high price paid for them, which at first surprised me.

Gradually, I came to accept the extraordinary experience as a fact. I had no wish to arrive at a final judgement. Whether ultimately a force for good or the reverse, I realized that the projection had been trapped between cross-currents of time and resurrection at the most autocratic and doctrinaire period of a controversial career. I asked only to forget the Lancevearn episode as quickly as possible.

But this, alas, I was not permitted to do. My contact with Queenie had reverted to a state of suspended animation. I feared she must have been very annoyed at my abrupt departure and it might be that I would never hear from her again. But early in December a Christmas greeting arrived. Much information about her activities was compressed into a small space in almost illegible handwriting. I was relieved that she bore me no ill will: although as I read the postscript on the back of her card, a kind of electric shock seemed to pass through me.

'I don't suppose,' she had written, 'that you ever heard about the tragedy the day you left St Huthy. Mira Hallam was found drowned in the Lancevearn cove. Later on, her suitcase was washed up farther along the coast and the coroner said she must have been trying to leave home while "the balance of her mind was disturbed". It was a terrible shock for Stephen. You see, he blamed himself. The only thing you can say is that in some ways it was a "happy release"...'

The room in which I sat seemed to darken. I crumpled the Christmas card in my hand, dropping it into the heart of the fire...

1983

THE GREEN STEPS

Frank Baker

Frank Baker (1908–1983) moved to St Just, on the tip of Cornwall in 1929, and was the author of the 1936 novel *The Birds*, a tale about millions of our avian friends who descend upon London. They then become quite problematic and start to kill humans. Upon the release of Hitchcock's film *The Birds* in 1963, Frank threatened to sue, but never carried it out. The author of the short story on which the film was based, fellow Cornish resident Daphne Du Maurier (whose cousin Peter Davies published Baker's original work), claimed to have never read Baker's book, and wrote Baker a letter stating: 'I wish for your sake Hitchcock had bought your novel rather than my short story from which to adapt the film'. Baker also wrote the escapist masterpiece that is *Miss Hargreaves* (1940), a tale of two men who invent an 83-year-old woman called Miss Hargreaves to pass the time, only for their creation to come to life. I have selected 'The Green Steps', published in his collection *Stories of the Strange and Sinister* (1983), to showcase how inventive a writer Baker could be; he absolutely brings to life the many strange and ambling paths that can be found on Cornwall's coastline that connect hidden fishing villages together.

THE man who sweeps the narrow twisting streets and alleyways in our village, is he human? Has he a story, has he past and future like other people? Or has he only the present? Is he time, sweeping away our withered illusions?—the drift and dross of our leaflike years, the potato parings, the tattered bits of old newspapers, envelopes, cigarette cartons, paid and unpaid accounts, drawn by his long stiff brush into the shovel and thus to the little cart to be wheeled away by him, as evening comes, to the rubbish dump, the waste land in a stony valley overhung by frowning, glowering woods behind the village.

Whenever I encounter him I think of the finger of fate, of something that awaits us all that we least expect, of a signpost on the moor when we cannot turn back. I think of the sad great songs of Schubert, and the tormented starlike innocence of Hans Andersen, of Don Quixote reborn without the desire to tilt at windmills. And yet he is a kindly man. One sees that at once. His long, lean, spindly figure; his shuffling, mincing gait; his knuckly, fumbling fingers; his thin nose and chin that seem to want to close like a pair of pincers; his opaque, chestnut-coloured eyes; his frostbitten fortitude—all these give an air of detached and consecrated beneficence. That man couldn't hurt a fly, one would say. If a living fly were struggling on a flypaper in the road, and the stiff brush bristled towards it, the Scavenger would make a detour, avoiding the victim, and probably pick up the wounded fly, take it home, feed it, tend it, train it to understand the cruelty in the world and go out again, aware of flypapers and all that comes between flies and their heaven. That is the sort of man he is, you would say. And you guess that he has suffered much, seen much, seen some visions perhaps, knows many secrets, embraced scavenging as the last symbol of man's destiny. Back to dust before his time this man seems to wish to go. Or is he working off a long penance, bowed down by an old crime against humanity?

This is more near to the truth, though not all of it; for this man was once a murderer. I have got his story and I will tell it to you.

I had observed him often and I had good reason to know where he lived, for it was very close to our cottage, up the cliff path, that bends sharply uphill over the harbour and the boatmasts that swing and sway in the gales; a path too narrow for any traffic, with rows of cottages, different sizes, shapes and colours, on one side. From the windows of our living-room which overlooks an area—a waste bit of land where kids keep rabbits in hutches and women dry clothes and men saw wood in the winter—I would often, and still often see, the Scavenger. Above the area there are steps, the Green Steps they are called, worn away dangerously, all uneven, ground by the feet of many generations, the stone crumbling, little weeds growing from the cracks. I'd always had a curious familiar feeling about the Green Steps; they brought back a hint of the past to me, a paragraph of my boyhood, as though I'd been there years ago; and I knew I hadn't. Then, it seemed to me, it was just the name—the Green Steps—that carried some old memory I couldn't place. Anyway, there Robert Starling the Scavenger lived, up the Green Steps; and on moonless nights, however familiar you were with those few steps (there are only about five, or seven; one can never count straight, they seem to change their number every day) you were likely to lose your footing and tumble backward, or forward. Up to a grassy hillside sloped over harbour and sea and village roofs, the steps ascend; to a drying-ground where on Monday mornings pants and shirts and socks and pyjamas and overalls and exuberant nightdresses billow and flutter in the dry east wind; a happy place, where little boys play wild games of Touch and Bang-you're-dead, and little girls nurse dollies and dress up like the Queen of Egypt. (I saw one once; she was swathed with bright-coloured stuffs pinched from an old drawer of Mother's; a kid of about eight, and when I asked her who she thought she was, she said Cleopatra.)

These dangerous steps ascend between cottages built on all levels that overhang courtyards where the fishermen dry nets and make baskets from willows. A very narrow passageway it is; always something of an effort to get up there at night or when the rain gushes down and the wind slashes you round a corner. Every late afternoon when his job was finished, Robert Starling climbed up there and drifted down again in the very early morning to gather up another day's débris. He lived in one of the cottages opening on to the passage, a very old place, with the rain streaming in where slates had clattered off the roof, slates that he himself swept next day into his little cart. It was when I watched him sweeping those slates of his, gathering up his own protection against the elements, that I first spoke to him. There was something grim and yet humorous about his expression, as though he knew just what he was doing. I talked about it having been a terrible wild night, to which he agreed; and I went on to say that he'd have to get into touch with his landlord to do something about the roof. To which he only shrugged his shoulders.

I made some inquiries. It appeared there wasn't a landlord. Starling had taken over the cottage years and years ago from an old man whose wife had died and who didn't want to use it any more. Then the old man had died in the workhouse, the children had emigrated, as Cornishmen do, far away to mines in search of gold; Starling lived on in the cottage, never paying any rent, and nobody bothered him. In our village people talk about you and invent tales about you; but ultimately they leave you alone. You can go to heaven or hell your own way, blow your nose on your sleeve or use the best silver teapot to shave from. Nobody really cares. We live on the sea and the sea blows into the harbour and over the walls in the high spring tides and seeps and sucks its way into the narrow streets. Plundering this sea, fishermen live perilous and precarious lives and nobody believes in that great civilized myth, Security. Everybody's their own destiny, and if Robert Starling chose to live alone for twenty-five years in a two-roomed cottage that was slowly falling down, let him do so. Bob Starling was accepted as part of the village, and no more questions were asked about him.

But I wanted to know more. He tormented me, trudging so primly up the steps every late afternoon, so far away in a world of his own, like a figure in a story book come to life. So I asked our neighbour, Jack Williams, about him.

Jack is a fisherman and there is little he doesn't know about everybody, new or old, in the village. So when I said, 'Jack, tell me something about old Bob Starling,' out came a lot, but not enough, nothing quite hung together.

'Oh, old Starling, he'm as mad as a hare, yet there's nothing that man couldn't do if he chose. I don't know what he hasn't done in days gone by. He's drove the fish lorry into market, he's served in shops, he's done window-cleaning, rat-snaring, wood-chopping, house-painting, coal-heaving. Time was, he used to write signs and letters for they who couldn't read nor write theirselves. Twenty-five years he's lived up Green Steps. He's got a room back there stacked with bits of paper full of fancy poems. Some of them was published, they do say. He had a woman once, pretty maid she were; but that were in his drinking days.'

'Drinking days?'

'Didn't you know old Starling used to be the biggest raging thirst in the town? There was nothing he wouldn't put away as a young man, crazy mad he used to get, shouting and swearing and singing up the steps. They say he'd fall on the paraffin can when nothing else was left. And all the time scribbling on bits of paper that used to flutter out of his pockets and drift about the square. Just words, he used to write. That man had more words in his head than the sea's got fish. And he'd sing like a lark in they days, all the pretty old songs were ABC to him. Bob was a fine chap. But after he gone over cliff and landed up in the Infirmary, that were the end of en. He never drunk another drop and it didn't do him no good either. It lost him his woman, for one thing. What was the maid called, now? Stella, that's the name; and he used to call her his Star, said that was what the word meant. And she were like a star, too; shining, pretty, twinkling face she had, fit to break through any cloud in a man. But away she went and she's never come back. If she's alive and knows about him, I reckon if he were to start in on the drink again, she'd come back to en, she couldn't help it.'

'Did she drink too?'

'Just a bit, to keep Bob company, never much. But she liked en drunk, everybody did like Bob drunk, you couldn't help it. Even when he bashed her about a bit, she still loved en. Then one night, in one of his fits, he rushed up Green Steps—wild, roaring night it was, sea like heaving mountains over quay—he rushed up there like a whirlwind cursing black hell. He were chasing someone, he said. "I'll kill you," he was hollering, "I'll bash your brains out, I'll chuck you over cliff." God knows who he thought he was after. Anyway, over the cliff, up Battery, he went; and how he didn't break himself into little pieces isn't reasonable; but he didn't. I reckon Stella would've been glad, in a sense, if he had. He broke his leg and arm and bruised and cut himself something terrible, and had to be dragged up with ropes by the coastguard and me and other chaps. Took us all night. He'd landed twenty feet down on a bit of jutting-out rock; another inch and he'd have gone a hundred and fifty feet to the bottom and that'd been the finish of Bob Starling. But he were lucky. He spent about six months up to the Infirmary, and when he come back to Stella he were as quiet as Sunday morning. "I killed en," he kept saying. "I finished en off, Stella. He'm gone for ever." Poor maid couldn't make sense of en. No more strong drink for he. No more of they songs and poems. Job after job he takes and comes slinking home with his pay-packet till Stella could scream. Never any fun like the old days. That's why she left en. She was a high-spirited maid and wasn't born to bide with angels.'

'Wait a bit, wait a bit!' I cried. I had been half listening, half following another train of thought in my mind. And now at last I understood the significance (for me) of the Green Steps. Going to a cupboard in my study where I keep piles of old literaries and periodicals, I searched for what I wanted: copies of the *London Alchemist* for 1923–4.

'You say,' I said, 'that he published some of these poems of his?'

'So they did say. There were lots of writing chaps around here in those days, chaps with beards and coloured shirts. And Bob were one of them.'

'Did he ever call himself *Robin* Starling?'

'Not Robin. No. It were always Bob.'

'Ah!' I gave an exclamation of triumph. I had found the poem that had so vaguely yet so significantly lurched back into my mind, lines that I had read years ago as a schoolboy. 'The Green Steps,' it was called. It was about a scavenger who 'feeds on wasted vision'. And it was by Robin Starling.

*

Well, I said to myself, when Jack Williams had gone presently and I pondered over the strange lines of this forgotten old poem of the neo-Georgians—tantalizing as it is to play with the idea that this queer old scavenger is Robin Starling grown old—it just will not do. For Robin Starling, a brief and brilliant voice in the early twenties, had died almost before his evocative lyricism had had time to linger in the ear. By only a few present-day critics would even his name be remembered. And probably not one poem of about a dozen that got published in various literaries of the period would now be recalled by anybody. Except me? Was I the only person who had been moved by 'The Green Steps'? And had lingered over it in my boyhood, feeling that it had a special meaning for me that I only half understood? I had come across no other lines by this poet; he had quite gone out of my mind; and now returned by the strangest coincidence—that he bore almost the same name and wrote about the Green Steps—and a scavenger.

But was this coincidence? I couldn't, of course, let it rest here. Robin Starling was dead, that was pretty certain. For now I recalled a brief obituary notice about him, that I couldn't find in any of my old magazines. But, Jack Williams had said, the Bob Starling of twenty-five years ago had written poems; and he had tumbled over a cliff, apparently under the illusion that he was chasing somebody. *Had it been an illusion?* Had this old scavenger really been chasing somebody up the Green Steps that dark wild night of twenty-five years ago? Had he—?

Innumerable questions. The beginning of an exciting quest. All simplified, you might say, by direct questions to the man himself. Not so. For you could not get beyond that amber-like glint in his eyes, and never any more than a few words would he mutter to you, always courteous, always humble, but about as talkative as a Trappist monk in Holy Week.

I thought about it endlessly. I read and re-read the strange, sad, yet exciting poem. Not a very good poem as we would think now. It made sense and it rhymed; but it said far more under its simple words than a first reading made clear. Was I to believe that this was not the work of the old man himself? A room stacked with manuscripts, Jack Williams had said; and literary high-yap in the twenties, coloured shirts and beards and Bloomsbury gone wild as Bloomsbury does once it goes west.

Two burning questions. How had 'Robin Starling' died? And—had 'Bob Starling' actually been chasing somebody up those steps?

The first question was easily answered. I wrote to a friend of mine, a critic whose pleasure it is to ponder over the oddities of literature—the forgotten ones who find their unlamented way into the Charing Cross Road book troughs. What could he tell me about Robin Starling?

The answer was terrifyingly what I had expected. Starling, after spending the early years of his life wandering about France and England, a sort of Villon with ever a rabble of noisy scoundrels at his heels, and ever a woman to worship him, had written a handful of verse. Like Rimbaud he had become a flame, rapidly to die out, yet kindle other sleeping fires. The last two years of his life, said my friend, he had spent in the West of England. 'You should know all about him' (I quote from his letter), 'since he lived in your village and gathered a rusty-fusty greenery-yallery crew around him. He went the whole hog with drink and had, I believe, one faithful woman who loved him; dead now, probably like him. His death was "correct". Dead drunk, he ran up a steep cliff path and smashed himself to bits two hundred feet below. That was the story put round by a brother of his, anyway; and this brother had the handling of some poems published—only in the literaries—shortly after his death; I believe he wrote one critical article in praise of his work in a thing I now can't trace, an ephemera of the middle twenties. Then the brother seems to have gone silent, and all Starling's rackety set came to nothing. Starling's was a brief, but certain trumpet note that died in the air before anyone heard it properly. You should make it your business to discover all you can about him. For all we know he might have left a mass of work behind him that should see the light. Does the brother still live, I wonder?'

O, my Scavenger, how dear you became to me! How lovingly I studied you from that day, watching your devouring broom over the sea-washed streets in the sleeping morning when sometimes I rose early and walked to the harbour to see what news lay in the east! How keenly I observed the sharp inward curve of your nostrils, your fastidious yet workmanlike hands, your shuffling yet ambassador walk! Like a man with a train of princes behind him, all ghosts, you seemed to me. Bowing in to life the great ones of the earth, and then waiting for them to be flung out by the wind to drift in the streets and come under the drag of your brush. Ushering in and gathering up, day by day you assumed more importance for me. There was a major work in you, I said. A major work for a novelist of supreme imagination and superb craft. Henry James, Flaubert and Dostoevsky linked as one, could not do justice to you.

For some time I made no attempt to gather up the threads of the story. Good stories linger in the air like flower scents of autumn smoke, about the tongue like wine, about the touch like silk; and shift and struggle before the eyes like the ever-changing patterns and colours seen through a child's kaleidoscope. They do not mature in a hurry. Were I to rush forward and breast the tape of truth, should I indeed have won the truth? For truth is the whole tale, and had it yet ended? Had I, perhaps, to wait till the Scavenger died and the contents of that back room could be examined?

Then, one night, something very strange happened and I was suddenly dragged, as it were by the scruff of a too inquisitive neck, right into the heart of the tale. Now it is mine, gone for ever, and as I relate it, so it will cease to be his or mine. It will be anybody's, and anybody can learn what they like from it.

It was a night in January, after days of rain and gales, gales that battered the side of our cottage and made it sway like a ship in a full and roaring sea. A Moby Dick night; and the high spring tides seventeen feet up in the fifteen-foot harbour, the boats all swaying their masts like a wind-thrashed forest of leafless larches. The fishermen had been to the boats in the early evening, before the tide came high, setting their tackle straight, prepared for a bad night. Boards were up in houses down by the quay and in the low, flat parts of the village street. At the Ship Tavern, where we drink what is left to drink these days, I went with some friends and we talked about old times as you do when there are high storms and fine music in the wind; and we drank a good deal, sitting there in the long kitchen till near closing time; when suddenly everybody looked to the door which had swung wildly open.

'God bless my soul,' said an old fisherman, ''tes the first time in nigh thirty years I see Bob Starling come in here.'

I said nothing, but watched him. I was aware that I was drunk, in a sort of guarded drunkenness, prepared for anything, knowing this was the night I would get the story I wanted, and didn't want. He stood in the dark passage between the bar and the kitchen, and he asked, so quietly that it could hardly be heard, for a double whisky. Doubles aren't served now in this almost liquorless corner of England; he had to be content with a single. Drinking it at one nervous quick gulp he asked for another. I watched. He was a most extraordinary figure, in a long dirty leather jacket reaching nearly to his knees, his long thin legs in brown corduroy trousers much too short for him, which showed black woollen socks, full of holes, and made his feet seem huge. Over the leather jacket he had a mackintosh cape; on his head a yellow sou'wester cap tied under the chin, that gave his sharp ruddy face a babylike innocence. I thought he should be sitting in a pram dressed just as he was, sucking a dummy or playing with a rattle.

The second whisky went as quickly as the first. He asked for a third and was refused. He could have beer, he was told. But no, he didn't want beer. Out he went, with no sign of recognition to a soul, giving only a peering, darting look round the kitchen, as though he were looking for somebody; out he went and the door swung to and fro behind him, letting in a shivering snarl and twist from the wind.

Everybody started to chat about him. But suddenly, in my curiously alert condition, driven by the subconscious voice who commands most clearly under the stimulus of alcohol, I leapt up from my seat, snapped good night to my friends, and swung out of the door as though a pistol had shot me forward. Across the square, where the moon plunged from a continent of massed clouds, I could see him. He was going quickly up the cliff path, towards his own cottage, in that forward-leaning pensive walk of his, his great feet most oddly delicate, like a ballet dancer wearing enormous clogs. I got just behind him; then slackened my speed. He was muttering. 'The tide'll bring him back. It's a seventeen-foot tide, like it was then, and it'll throw him back, God help me.'

I nearly ran back to the Ship. I confess I was, for a few seconds, frightened. What had I stumbled upon? Leaning over the wall of the slipway I looked down to the harbour, which seemed to have come adrift in a churning mass of muddy sea. The night was roaring and howling, the wind playing havoc with slates and tiles and anything it could snatch. Dustbin lids clattered along the cobbled alleyways. Waiting there, gathering strength from the gale, I lost sight of old Starling. Had he gone up the Green Steps to his cottage? I didn't know. But suddenly I found my legs again and a new zest for life within me. When huge winds blow, either you must skulk with your face turned to the wall like a cornered rat; or else you must let the wind take you and blow you where it will. With enough liquor inside me, I felt suddenly mad, wild and very young. I had almost forgotten about old Starling. All I wanted to do was to soar up the cliff path like a rocket, charge round the corner, bellow some insult at the windows of a cottage where lived a rigid nonconformist family I disliked (and who disliked me), race recklessly up the dark slippery steps and find my way to the long slopes above the town and the harbour where you can watch the moon or the sun in a great expanse of sky. In short, if you like to put it more simply, I was flaming drunk and didn't care a damn what happened.

And so I went charging up the Green Steps, for the first (and only) time in my life not caring whether I stumbled and fell, only determined to get to the top and fill my lungs with wind.

I didn't get there as quickly as I had intended. Singing and shouting I don't know what, I stumbled halfway up, and nearly fell, reached out a hand to grab at something. My fingers closed round a door-knob. The door tottered open on weak hinges and I burst forward into a room dimly lit by a lamp with an untrimmed wick. I smelt the smoke of many years of oil-lamps. Bits of plaster dribbled down walls black with smoke. I was in old Starling's cottage, hurled into it, it seemed; and there he stood, his back to an inner door, his teeth chattering, the most abject picture of stark terror I had ever encountered.

I stared at him, he at me, and we didn't move for nearly a minute. Then he muttered in his thin cracked voice: 'You've come then. You've come to take your revenge.'

I was stark sober all at once. 'Who do you think I am?' I asked quietly.

'Him. Him I killed. A night like this too, when the wind got me and drove me to do it. You swore you'd come back, that was your last dying cry up the cliff when the—' His words trailed away. (I was to notice how he had a habit of not finishing his sentences.)

'I'm not the man you killed—if you did kill a man. I'm your neighbour down the cliff. You know me. Look at me.'

I went a bit closer, turned up the spluttering lamp, and smiled at him in a forced sort of way. I didn't feel like smiling. I felt oddly angry. I felt it was a pity I wasn't 'him'; I felt he deserved what he so dreaded.

'You're not—you're not him—then why did you come up the steps like that, the way he always did, drunk and blind and mad after his nights down in the—and she, poor girl, having to keep a meal for him, keep him alive somehow, year in and year out, feeding a drunken maniac who had the insolence to think he could live as other people didn't because he could write poetry that—it's the highest tide for years and it was the night I killed him. He always said, his cry rang in my ears—but I've done the right thing, haven't I?'

He spoke in a disconnected, gasping way.

'I'm sure you've done the right thing,' I said, feeling none so sure. 'But look, couldn't you calm down? I'm not here to hurt you any way. I burst in by mistake. I admit I was drunk; but I'm sober as a judge now—'

'Not a judge, no, don't talk about a judge. I escaped. They wouldn't judge me. They wouldn't believe me.'

'Let's sit down and have a talk. I believe—'

'You shouldn't have come in here like that. It was a wicked thing to do, scaring me a night like this when the boats—as they did years ago and him trying to write poetry all the time, a maze of wild words he was, blood and bone and sun and moon raced in his veins, wild as a devil and greedy like a pig.'

He wouldn't move away from the door to the inner room.

'Tell me this,' I said very gently, 'are you talking about Robin Starling?'

'Yes, that's what he called himself and he was to be the great apocalyptic poet of the age, and because of that he could trample on everything and everybody and stamp up the Green Steps back and down without thought for a soul. And Stella pouring out her love to him, always ready to take him back, whatever he did. I loved her too, but I never got her. Never.' He snapped his teeth and snarled on the word.

'Who was Robin Starling? Your brother?'

'Oh, closer than that, much closer. There are relationships, if you can understand, that are not defined in the books, closer than brother to brother, husband to wife, friend to friend, mother to child, much closer, so close that neither of us could breathe decent air. We lived here together, the three of us, him and me and Stella, and listen, what I shall tell you is the whole truth, what they won't believe, which is why I'm left alive to tell it now, because if they'd believed I'd have been hanged for it, justice they call that and—you don't believe me, do you, I can see you don't?'

'I believe every word you say. Please go on. I shan't tell anybody.'

'But I wish you to. I want everyone to know. When a man's committed a great crime the burden's too much to bear if nobody will believe he bears it. Will you tell them, will you tell the whole truth to help me bear it?'

'Yes, if you want me to, yes, I will.' (And this story began to be written from that moment.)

'But what *is* the truth?' I asked. 'You and him, this poet, Robin Starling, who was so close to you that—'

'All lived together and life was hell. For years I never spoke, never warned, only watched what was happening to him, the rot and the disease of his mind while he wasted his wonderful words on to paper at the price of other people's hearts. He wrote in the blood of others. And I watched him, never warning, never speaking. Silent all the time and in the evening—there was plenty to drink in those days, a man could get drunk on a few shillings, and Stella, she would have to sell things of her own, little bits of jewels given to her by her mother; she valued them, and paintings and books, they all had to go to get money for drink while I never said a word. Then I warned him; I said, if this doesn't stop I shall make it stop. He wouldn't listen. Sometimes in the grey morning light when he woke up all bleary and sick and parched in the throat with Stella beside him, then he would listen to me; and he'd agree, he'd say yes, he'd mend his ways, turn another direction, give up poetry and all the cheap tricks he'd turned his rotting mind to.

'In the mornings he'd admit to me that his fine spate of words meant nothing. He juggled words in a hat, like a conjuror; and people believed that what came out had the divine fire, but never had—a jingle, a prolonged nursery rhyme, that was all he was, aping all the raging poets who've ever dishonoured their manhood and left misery behind them. Yes, in the morning he'd see a little sense. But then, as time went on, he saw less and less; and even in the morning he'd drink, drink himself drunk again so that he could pour out more words. In there, behind me, I've got stacks of his writings, foolscap sheets with long lists of words on them and lines of poems he never finished. He never stopped; he was devoured by a fire.

'It wouldn't have mattered if it hadn't been for her. I couldn't stand by and watch her throw herself away; and other women he'd take when he wanted them, and always expect her to take him back as she always did. Then I got jealous, I wanted her for myself, I wanted to give her the things he couldn't give, a decent home and nice things like she longed to have from life. But she would never see me; never believed I had any independent existence... So it went on that way—years.'

There was a long pause. I still did not know what to make of the story. 'What did *you* do?' I mumbled. 'I mean—had you got work of your own?'

'Me? I was a shadow. *I was what was to be.* Didn't I tell you I was close to him, so close that I never left him for a second? I hadn't any work, only to watch him and trip him up; and he knew it all the time and would try to throttle me. Many a time he'd wake screaming, his hands round my throat, trying to shake the life out of me. Then she'd stop him somehow and I'd be safe again. It was him or me—don't you see—always him or me—one of us had to go. Well, he went.'

'Yes. You chased him up the cliff, didn't you—'

'Yes, yes—' He spoke eagerly and came nearer to me. The door behind him blew open suddenly. In the dim light I could see masses of loose sheets of paper on the floor, and many books thrown down in a mass with fallen plaster and laths from the rotten roof. 'You know what happened then?'

'No. I was only told you chased him up the cliff.'

'Oh, more than that, much more. One night he came up the steps more drunk than usual, waking everybody, bellowing like a bull. Then I went mad, all reason left me. If he could sing and scream and bellow, so could I. If he had long black hair to scream in the wind, so had I. If he had nimble legs to leap like Pegasus up the Green Steps to the drying-ground, so had I. It went into me like poison into my blood, like a man suddenly charged with electricity—at the top, beyond the battery, where the cliff falls sheer down, there I got him. He was singing and swaying on the edge of the cliff as though he weren't subject to the rules of ordinary people. There was no thought about it. I had him round the waist in a second and over we both went in each other's arms, locked tight in mid-air. I don't know how it happened, but he wrestled with me in the air, and got free of me, and went hurtling to the bottom and—or did he, did he? That's what I never know. Did he float away like a lost angel? I never saw him. He'd gone and I clutched the cliff face and found a foothold and managed to cling there till they came with ropes to drag me up and—the Infirmary comes back to me now, I can see the ward where I lay, I was badly hurt and Stella came, every week she came to see me and said it would be all right, she'd always stay with me, always. But when I got back, and he'd gone for ever, and it was just the two of us, and I told her what I'd done, she only stared at me and called me Robin and said I'd never change for her, whatever happened. She wouldn't believe me, that I'd killed him. Nobody would listen—'

'I don't understand this. Somebody must have known he'd gone? There must have been an inquest or—'

'Nothing, nothing. Don't you understand the frightfulness of it? They all said *I* was him. You see, we were so close, we were so alike, we exactly resembled one another. All the time the three of us lived here, even Stella never noticed me, never tried to draw me out from my silences. Only when he and I were quite alone could I talk to him and him to me. Then, when I'd killed him and came back, she thought I was him, and nothing—until I started to get work and earn a living which he'd never done; and one day some editor wrote and said he wanted to print some of his poems and I wrote back and said that Robin Starling had fallen over the cliff and was dead and that I was his brother and dealing with his affairs. Then Stella began to behave strangely. She said I was mad, that the fall had affected my brain, and that I ought to have medical treatment and—I worked, so hard I worked, and I saw my life's ambition before me and knew I'd achieve it. But not her; I couldn't win her. She left me and never came back.'

'Your life's ambition? What was that?'

In a corner, by the grate where dead ashes lay with charred paper, was his long stiff broom. Pointing to it, 'That,' he said. 'I knew I'd have to come to it. Each man must fulfil his destiny, you see; that's how it works. It was prophesied for me, by him, and it's come true as I knew it must come true. And now—now, though I dread it, I want him back. I want to hear him sing again as he used to, I want to watch his legs flying up the Green Steps to the hillsides he loved, and I want to follow him. When he comes back, I'll follow him, yes, I'll follow him, in a great wind when the tide's high he'll come back as he said he would and then—' He muttered away into himself and I could no longer hear the words.

The wind gave a sudden charge at the house and papers rustled along the floor in the darkened inner room. I thought of the wild and happy parties that must have taken place here years ago. I saw the old scavenger bending down to pick up a sheet of yellowed paper. 'His,' he muttered. 'His words. All meaningless. All meaningless.'

He handed the paper to me and turned his back. Taking a poker he toyed the ashes with it, then crouched on a chair, holding his long hands out to no spark of warmth. Above him on the wall was a great patch of dampness, furry and mildewed, like a map of some fabulous country. Suddenly I knew that I hadn't a word of consolation to give and I turned back to the door, feeling desperately miserable. I wished I had been 'him', that slain self who so tormented him.

At the door, 'I know he'll come back to you one day,' I said; and felt that it was true.

Then I went outside, closed the door, and walked inch by inch up the slippery steps to the hillside where the pure moon had soared through a gap in the black clouds. The wind was easing off a little. The night was fresh and the salt of the sea strong in my nostrils. I read the lines on the bit of paper he'd given me.

> 'Landlocked in this sandpride of westfallen moonflowers
> I (in my archery) to you before wisdom its windows
> Swings follywards, turn with the splint of the stinging finger.'

It made no sense, but it was strangely contemporary. I could see by the freshness of the ink that it had only recently been written. But the writing was of an old man.

He is still living, still the village scavenger, and never a word have I had with him from that day, and never shall I. I am tormented whenever I see him; and yet there is a strange feeling of certainty within me about him, as though I knew that he would find the way up the steps and follow, as he wished to follow, that once-hated, bitterly-resented truer self of his whom he killed years ago. When I see him I know that because of the great division in him the great union is already achieved. He is a poet who has had to work out fatally in his own nature the disintegration of our times. Like the Poet, the Scavenger is lifted outside the laws of men. One by one his own words go into the dust-cart to be burnt in the waste land behind the village. The smoke of those words rises and drifts over the roofs to the sea. And the lines that he wrote which moved me as a boy prophesy for him the destiny he desires.

Gaelic

c.1861

MACPHIE'S BLACK DOG

Donald Cameron

While I have been unable to find out anything on the teller of the story, Donald Campbell (although I have been able to confirm he was not the 24th chief of Clan Cameron), the person who took the story down and translated it, John Gregorson Campbell (1836–1891), was a Scottish folklorist and Free Church minister in Tiree. Gregorson transcribed the stories as they were told to him with minimal comments, a trait not held by other Christian ministers who often held their parishioners' tales and myths with nothing but contempt. His books included *Clan Traditions and Popular Tales of the Western Highlands and Islands* (1895) and *Superstitions of the Highlands and Islands of Scotland* and *Witchcraft and Second Sight in the West Highlands* that were both published in the years after his death. 'MacPhie's Black Dog' existed in oral tradition long before it was first written down and it is a fascinating story; there are several Highland tales that represent women as deer; and they were also looked upon as fairy cattle. The common form that a fairy woman transformed herself into was more often than not a red deer. There have also been several versions of 'MacPhie's Black Dog'; in one the black dog is represented as killing a mermaid—this version would die away but slowly morph into the ballad 'The Maid of Colonsay' by John Leyden (1775–1811).

MAC-VIC-ALLAN of Arasaig, lord of Moidart, went out hunting in his own forest, when young and unmarried. He saw a royal stag before him, as beautiful an animal as he had ever seen. He put his gun to his eye, and the stag became a woman, the most beautiful he had ever seen at all. He let down the gun from his eye, and it became a royal stag as it was before. Every time he put his gun to his eye the animal became a woman, and every time he let it down to the ground it became a royal stag.

Upon this he put his gun to his eye, and went until he was close to her breast. He then gave a leap, and caught her between his two hands. 'You will not be at all separated from me,' said he; 'I will never marry any but you.' 'Don't do that, Mac-vic-Allan,' said she, 'you have no business with me. I will not suit you. There will never be a day while you have me but you will require to kill a cow for me.' 'You will get that,' said the lord of Moidart, 'though you should require two a day.'

But Mac-vic-Allan's herd began to grow thin; he then wished to send her away, but could not. Upon this, he went to an old man, who lived in the township, and was his counsellor. He said that he would become bankrupt; and that he did not know what plan to take to get rid of her. The old honest man told him that unless MacPhie of Colonsay would send her away, there was no man at all alive who could send her away. That very minute a letter was sent off to MacPhie. MacPhie answered the letter, and came to Arisaig.

'What business is this you have with me,' said MacPhie, 'Mac-vic-Allan?'

Mac-vic-Allan told him how the woman came to him, and that he could not send her away.

'Go you,' said MacPhie, 'and kill a cow for her today as usual, send her dinner to her to the room as usual, and give me my dinner on the other side of the room.'

Mac-vic-Allan did as he was told. She began her dinner, and MacPhie began his own dinner. When MacPhie got his dinner past, he looked across at her: 'What's your news today, Sianach?' said he. 'What's that to you, Brian Brugh?' said she. 'I saw you, Sianach,' said he, 'when you held meetings with the Fingalians, when you went away with Diarmid o Duibhne, and accompanied him from covert to covert.' 'I saw you,' said she, 'Brian Brugh, when you rode on an old black horse, the sweetheart of the slim fairy woman, and ever chasing her from brugh to brugh.' 'Dogs and lads after the wretch,' said MacPhie; 'long have I known her.' Every dog and man in Arasaig were called, and sent after her. She fled away out to the point of Arasaig, and they did not get a second sight of her.

MacPhie then went home to his own Colonsay. He went out one day shooting, and night came upon him before he got home. He saw a light and made straight for it. He saw a number of men sitting within there, and an old grey-headed man along with them, in their midst. The old man spoke and said, 'MacPhie, come forward.' MacPhie went up forward, and what should come in his way but a bitch as beautiful as he had ever seen, and she had young pups. He saw a pup with her, black in colour, that he had never seen a pup so black or so beautiful as it was. 'I shall have this dog,' said MacPhie to the man. 'No,' said the man, 'you will get your choice of the dogs she has, but you will not get that one.' 'I will not take any that she has,' said MacPhie, 'but this one.' 'Since you are resolved to have it,' said the man, 'it will not do for you but the service of one day, and it will do that well for you. Come back on a certain night and you will get it.'

MacPhie reached the place on the night he had promised to come. They gave him the dog, 'And take care of him well,' said the old man, 'he will never do service for you but the one day.'

The black dog began to grow a beautiful whelp, that no one had ever seen a dog so large or so beautiful as it was. When MacPhie went out hunting, he would call the black dog, and the black dog would reach the door, and would then turn back and lie where it was before. The gentlemen who used to come to MacPhie's house would be urging him to kill the black dog, that it was not worth feeding. MacPhie would say to them, to let it alone, that the black dog's day would come yet.

After this, a number of gentlemen came across from Islay to visit MacPhie, and to ask him to go to Jura to hunt. Jura was at that time a desert, without a man dwelling in it, and without a place in the world like it for hunting deer and roe. There was a place there where it was usual for gentlemen who went hunting to stay, which was called the Big Cave. They made ready a boat to cross the sound that day. MacPhie rose to go, with sixteen young gentlemen along with him. Each one of them called the black dog, and he reached the door and returned and lay down where he was before. 'Shoot him,' said the young gentlemen. 'No,' said he, 'the black dog's day has not yet come.' They took their way to the shore, and the wind rose, and they did not get across that day. They made ready next day to go; the black dog was called, and he reached the door, and went back where he was before. 'Kill him,' said the gentlemen, 'and don't be feeding him any longer.' 'I will not kill him,' said MacPhie, 'the black dog's day will come yet.' But they failed to get across that day also, from the violence of the weather, and they returned. 'The dog has fore-knowledge,' said the gentlemen. 'He fore-knows that his own day will come yet,' said MacPhie.

On the third day, the day was beautiful. They took their way to the harbour, and they did not say a syllable to the black dog this day. They launched the boat to go away. One of the gentlemen looked and said the black dog was coming, and that he had never seen such a creature from the fierce look it had on as it was coming. It gave a leap, and was the first creature into the boat. 'The black dog's day is drawing near us,' said MacPhie. They took with them food, and provision, and bedclothes, and went ashore in Jura. They passed that night in the Big Cave; and next day they went out to hunt the deer. Late in the evening they came home; they prepared supper; they had a fine fire in the cave, and light. There was a big hole in the very top of the cave, that would barely allow a man to go through it. When they had taken their supper, the young gentlemen stretched themselves on the beds. MacPhie rose and stood warming the back of his feet to the fire. Each of the young men said that he wished his own sweetheart was along with him there that night, and if she were, he would be well off. 'Well,' said MacPhie, 'I prefer my wife to be in her own house; it is enough for me to be here myself tonight.'

MacPhie gave a look from him, and saw sixteen women coming in at the door of the cave. The light went out; and they had no light but what the fire gave them. The women went over where the gentlemen were in their beds. MacPhie was not seeing a particle on account of the darkness that came over the cave; he was not hearing a sound from the men there. The women stood up, and one of them looked at MacPhie. She stood opposite to him, as though she were going to make an attempt upon him. The black dog rose, and put on such a fierce, bristling look; he made a spring at her; they took to the door, and the black dog after them to the mouth of the cave. When they went away, the black dog returned down and lay at MacPhie's foot. A little afterwards, MacPhie heard a hurried noise above him in the top of the cave, such that he thought the cave would be about his head. He looked above him, and saw a man's hand coming down from the hole, as though it were going to catch him, and take him out through the hole, through the top of the cave. The black dog gave one spring, and caught the hand between the shoulder and the elbow, and lay on it. The play began between the hand and the black dog. Before the black dog let go his hold, he chewed the hand till it fell on the floor. The thing that was on the top of the cave went away, and MacPhie thought the cave would be about his head. Out rushed the black dog after the thing that was outside. This was not time at which MacPhie felt himself most at ease, when the black dog left him. When the day was dawning, what but that the black dog had returned. He lay down beside MacPhie. In a few minutes he was dead.

When daylight came, MacPhie looked, and he had not a single man of those who were with him in the cave. He took with him the hand, and went to the shore to the boat. He went on board; he went home to Colonsay, unaccompanied by dog or man. He took up with him the hand, that men might see what horror he had met with that night he had been in the cave. No man in Isla or Colonsay had ever seen such a hand, or had ever imagined that such could have existed.

Nothing remained but to send a boat to Jura to take home the bodies that were in the cave. That was the end of the black dog's day.

(Written down about twenty years ago from the dictation of Donald Cameron, Ruag, Tiree.)

J. G. C.

MANSE OF TIREE,

1ST JANY, 1883.

1905

THE BUTTERFLY'S WEDDING

Eachann MacPhaidein

I cannot find anything about Eachann (Hector) MacPhaidein apart from the fact that he wrote *Pòsadh An Dealan-dè* ('The Butterfly's Wedding') for *Uirsgeulan Gaidhealach / Highland Legends* (1905). The following story is, in my opinion, astonishing, I don't think I've ever read anything so out there and he distils the very essence of Gaelic folklore and outré imagination into every single word. This is one *weird* tale.

LONG, long before your grandfather's time, when the world was young and the cocks spoke Greek, the butterfly thought that he would marry a wife. She must be fair as the primrose in the glens; stately as the fairy lady of the hills, and good at housewifery as the ant of the feal-dyke.

He told the fly; but she only crooked her nose and laughed. 'I'll walk up and down, I'll walk here and there,' said the butterfly, 'till I find my heart's desire.' 'The prayer of the seven grey goats go with you,' said the fly; 'the meeting of the seven foxes, and the blessing of the seven fairies be with you, till you find your heart's desire; I will take a little wink of sleep in a daisy's breast for a year and a day, and then I will expect to hear news of your wedding.'

So it was. The butterfly bound a circlet of gold on his left foot; he put three shining cowrie shells in the hollow of his thigh; he spread his speckled wings to the soft, warm wind of evening, and he set out. He set his back to the north and his face to the south, and for seven summer weeks he went without resting, over rivers, over fields, over ridges, over bens and glens and seas, till he came to the green isle, where sun does not set and moon rises not, and where never sound was heard but the sound of the sea and the note of the white swan that sits on a green hillock in its very centre. Seven weeks this swan sleeps without waking; but on the seventh Sabbath Day she wakes, and she utters three notes so sweet that the round world listens and the harper of the hills gives three groans of sorrow for envy. The butterfly reached the hill; he flew three times round the swan; he leaned against a grass blade; he put a cowrie under his head and slept. He dreamed that he was in a king's castle, where the house beams were of silk thread; the king's daughters danced on them, each with a tuft of sweet herbs in her bosom. He heard the sweetest music that ever ear heard or heart inspired, music to wake love, and banish fear; music that would wile milk from the yeld cattle. What was this but the song of the awakening swan. The swan raised a silver stalk in her beak, and at once a black cloud came over the face of the sun, and every grass blade on the island began to quiver. This was a flight of seashore birds, answering the note of the swan, and coming with food and drink to entertain the butterfly.

'Drink seven celled cups of honey; eat seven fat baps of bread; then tell the cause of your journey,' said the swan. The butterfly sneezed, and the swan frowned. 'If it please you, the oyster-catcher put snuff in the honey,' said the butterfly. The swan whistled and the oyster-catcher fell cold and dead. The meal ended, and talk began.

Said the butterfly: 'I am the bright son of the sky, and I go from the north lands to the south, seeking my heart's desire. She must be fair as the primrose in the glens; good at housewifery as the ant of the feal-dyke.' The swan said that she would sleep for the seven weeks till she should get the knowledge of the three worlds: the world whose beginning is memory, the world whose mid part is memory, and the world whose end is memory; then she would give him three signs whereby he would find his heart's desire.

So it was. The butterfly passed the time in bathing, and insulting the rainbow for that it had fewer colours than his wings. On the seventh Sabbath Day the swan awoke, and she uttered her cry ere a juggler could perform a feat. The butterfly was there, and he stood on one foot and made obeisance. The swan whistled. Instantly a stonechat came where they were. 'Here,' said the swan, 'you have the bird of sharpest eye and keenest ear in the bird world. He has got lore of the weather from the old man of the moon; knowledge of the earth from the old woman of night (the owl), and skill of the ocean from the maiden of the sea. He comes and none knows whence; he goes, and no man knows whither; he will be to you a guide to your heart's desire. You will fold your wings and sit on the stonechat's back till he lights on a bare grey flag that is before the cottage where lives your heart's desire. Three autumn weeks the stonechat will go in the nostril of the wind, over rivers, over fields, over ridges, over glens and bens and seas, till he comes to the bounds of the Land of Calm. The first Saturday thereafter you shall see five wonders, and then you will know that you are near to the flagstone that lies before the cottage where lives your heart's desire.'

Thus it was. The butterfly folded his glittering wings; he put three shining cowries of the shore in the hollow of his thigh; he sat on the stonechat's back, and that bird flew away. The butterfly's head grew dizzy with the speed of the going. It was as swift as the hunter's arrow; swifter than the spring wind; nimble as the lightning. The stonechat sped eastwards. Three autumn weeks they spent so, without food or drink or weariness; and then they came to a loch of spring water in the midst of a wood. Such peace and quiet were over that loch that the bees that live in the stars could see their shadows in it. The butterfly knew that this was the Land of Calm. They alighted on a creek in the middle of the loch; they drank their fill of dew, and slept.

They awoke on the morning of the first Saturday, and no sooner were they awake than they saw a beetle making for the creek, sailing on a cabbage leaf, and steering with his foot. 'Do you see that?' said the stonechat. 'I see what I never saw before,' said the butterfly, 'one of the five wonders of the Land of Calm.' They went then to the wood, and, at a tree's root, they saw a cat shaving a calf-herd with a woollen thread. 'See you that?' said the stonechat. 'I see what I never saw: one of the five wonders of the Land of Calm,' said the butterfly. They climbed a tree, and they faced eastwards. 'What see you?' said the stonechat. 'I see two suns and two moons dancing a reel, and the stars clapping their hands,' said the butterfly. They descended, and they went on till they came to a green hill. When they came to it, the top rose off the hill, and there were gulls in grey breeches and tartan bonnets, schooling red bees. 'Another of the wonders of the Land of Calm,' said the butterfly. They were coming back to the creek when they saw a little deserted house at a rock's foot. They set an eye to the window, and *there* was a cock plaiting a straw rope with the spurs of one foot and playing a whistle with the other foot. He invited them in; he would play them the *Chickens' Lament* till food was ready. So it was. The cock gave them food and drink, music and conversation, and at the dusk of evening they left.

The stonechat set his face to the east and flew; with the speed of his going he would leave the swift spring wind far behind. In the mouth of lateness, he alighted on a smooth grey flag before a cottage, and the butterfly knew that this was the end of his journey. A fence of trees was round the house, with apples of gold growing on them; dew milk on the head of each small blade of grass. The windows of the cottage were like a mirror, and thrushes sang music on every bush. They went in; and sitting in a room they saw the maiden of golden-yellow locks, a maid mild as night, beautiful as the sun, faithful as the echo of the rocks.

'Welcome to the butterfly,' said the maiden; 'great is your travel, long your journey. I dreamed last night that you would come today.' The golden circlet that was on the butterfly's foot leaped on the maiden's arm; the cowries leaped and settled themselves in her bosom; and the butterfly knew that she was his heart's desire: he stood on one foot and saluted her and kissed her. The stonechat drank his fill of the breath of the skies; he set his back to the east and his face to the west; he left wind and storm-rain behind, and he sped over rivers, over fields, over bens and glens, to the green isle, to tell the swan of the butterfly's journey. The butterfly folded the maiden in his wings, and set his face for the daisy where he had left the fly asleep. The fly awoke; she looked on the maid of golden-yellow locks, and she crooked her nose again at the marvel of her beauty.

A wedding was made on a ragweed's top that lasted for a day and a year; every insect of the plain and every bird of the air was invited. The oyster-catcher got drunk and attacked the gulls; they screamed at the curlews. The peewit got drunk on snuff and assaulted the sea-swallows. The coots piped and the ants danced. When the wedding was over, the butterfly raised his wings, and he and his wife left for the cottage at the bounds of the Land of Calm. And if no lie was told me, they are there still.

1905

THE LOCH AT THE BACK OF THE WORLD

Reverend Lauchlan MacLean Watt

Reverend Lauchlan MacLean Watt (1867–1957) was the minister of Glasgow Cathedral, a poet, author and literary critic. As well as being a correspondent for *The Times, The Scotsman* and *The Manchester Guardian,* he was a chaplain for the Gordon Highlanders. During the Great War he said that his duty was as a 'roving missioner, with my bagpipes for companion' and was given the nickname of 'the Piping Padre'. In 1933 he was made Moderator of the General Assembly of the Church of Scotland. His literary work focused mainly on soldiers and antiquity as well as Celtic folklore. His books include *In the Land of War* (1915) and *While The Candle Burns* (1933). His story 'The Loch at the Back of the World' is a deeply impressive work, full of nature and deep haunting, where you can find Death and Life. It is a beautiful discovery.

THE Loch at the Back of the World is the sweetest place of all my dreaming.

It was far away, in ages long forgot, that the waters under Moruisg and the great hills up the glen said, 'We must rise, and seek the sea. We have heard the song of ocean, and the beating of his sorrow on the sands afar. Come, let us go and hear what he is saying all the long nights and days.'

So they rose, and sought the sunlight, and trickled through the heather, and gurgled down the braes. And wild birds sang above them in their going, and the lithe grasses trembled as they passed, and the irises, all queenly in the marsh, woke from their dreams, and wondering, gazed abroad. And they gathered in a deep, shady hollow under a moss-grown crag, and made a pool where the dun-deer stooped to drink, and fairies peered, and saw their queer, quaint faces reflected under the stars. And then, still on they pressed; and the springs, hid under the hills, heard the chatter of their passing, and leaped from the cool deeps where they slumbered, and joined in the progress seawards. Great rocks and precipices barred the way, but the waters found a door, and washed away the shingle, and deepened the rough channels they had made; and then, with a laugh and a song, sprang on the way of their pilgrimage. And still fresh help came up from under the heather to force a way to the sea. And the fays and elves leered from boulder and from pool as they saw the steady ripples breaking the pride of the rocks. For here and there a wall of adamant would stretch across their path, and, seek as they might, no corner of exit could be found. But ever they sought the higher level, and still the waters rose, and the stream became a pool, and deepened day by day, till it rose to the crest of the crag, and then, with a roar full of a thousand echoes, rushed in white foam like snow into the startled glen.

And at last, when the moon rode low, and swathed in mist, and the sad sea sobbed on the ridge of drenched sand, with a laugh that stirred the seabirds from their sorrow, the child of the hills leapt into the lap of ocean. Great was the news that passed, and many the stories they told, that night and all nights for ever; but the first was the sweetest of all, for it spoke of the heather, and the cool, dewy brows of the hills at the head of the glen, to the old sad sea, bitter with brine, and weary.

And that soft, misty night, with the low moon brooding over it, grew into ages, and still the stream came on—now brawling and battling, now sighing and singing, now full of laughter and peace. And the pools grew deeper and stiller, till the big hills saw their beauty reflected in fulness, with the sky and the stars in their depths. And the fall became a torrent, the hoarse roar of the past, with its passion and battle, deep in its open throat. And the rocks crumbled and widened, till the path of the stream to the sea was a path like the track of a dream—wild with great dark corries and gaunt ravines, and fair with smooth pebbly places, and long lown tracts; and all the way, the purple of the heather, the yellow, gold, and green of the moorland whin.

And one day man came into the solitudes, borne like a wave from the bosom of the sea. And he sat by the shore, and sang strange songs of a land across the water, where men did not die. There was none to tell him the secrets of the glens, and what sweet shadows lay far up where the corries were; nor what the eagle cried to the deer on the crest of Moruisg, but only the broadening stream, with its song of sobbing undertones.

So he listened, and still the stream sang on—not the sad song it sings today, with its sighings over dear dead faces, and the sorrows of the old sheilings, and the memories of the fair women and brave men and children golden-haired, among the grasses where they sleep for ever, in the glens. For sorrow in this world, the stream has learned, gathers in quiet places like the dust. To him, in the beginning, it sang only of beauty, brightness, and the solemn joy of the mountains, in the morning sunshine, or in the hour of gloaming, when the hills sit close together, like kings and queens whose glory is departing, but whose majesty remains.

So, as he sat and listened, his heart sang within him, for he knew nought of sadness.

'Here I will dwell for ever,' so he sang. 'Stream of the mountains, sweet with the dreams of fairies. Ever and ever you shall sing your song to me. Ages are nothing. Only your song is all.' But the stream sighed strangely to his singing, and the salt sea shivered along the sand.

So he came and went; and there was none to ask him of his coming or his going, and he brought no being with him to share the sunlight and the sea.

And the echoes up the glen caught his song, and flung it back to him again with laughter, as though they knew he dreamed. Ah yes, they knew, the old, old solitudes! Their wisdom was a greater thing than he! 'Come to us!' they cried. 'There are places for your tired limbs, when you weary. Deep is the heather, soft the tangled grass when you are tired; and the corries are cool for your sleeping, when the sun rests high on Moruisg, and the breezes die!' He knew not, but they knew. And they drew near each other in the shadows, and they laughed low laughter that had sobbing in it, like the moan of the water in the moss… till the deer in his covert woke in fear, and shook the dew from his fell, and fled like a hunted thing through the darkness. But he knew not the meaning of these, the signs and the voices of sorrow.

'I am coming, O sweet fountains, where the stream has learned its song,' so he sang. 'And for ever through the ages I shall dream through music here.' But they sighed, the ancient solitudes, for they saw and knew what eye of man had never looked upon, nor the heart of man had known. So they made the heather deeper for his coming, and they made the grasses softer for his bed. And the winds drew down near Moruisg of the waters, stirring the stream to music, as a minstrel sweeps his strings. And the ripples bore it all down to him where he sat beside the sea—like bits of broken dreams and broken song. So, while the waves sighed sunwards, great weariness and yearning came across his soul. 'I am tired, O streamlet. I would learn your song, and sleep.' Softly the shadows sent their echoes, 'Sleep!'

So he rose, and sought the heights, seeking the beginnings of the music, yearning for the fountain where the song had birth. 'Then let me slumber. I am weary here!'

He left the sea behind him, till its cry sounded faint and far away, though he turned sometimes and listened to its calling, calling to him up the glen. And in the dark he lay down in the bracken, while the shadows and the stars kept watch. But still he found not the fountainhead of song in that far land. Till at last, full weary, in a corrie upon Moruisg of the waters, he slept. And the air grew still, and saddened into silence; and the sky grew dark, and drew near the world, as though to listen to the breathing of the glens. And no sound broke on the night; no bird stirred in its nest—no deer in the heather. No sob of wind mourned among the pines. Only Silence, like Slumber asleep, fell over all. And the waters from the heart of Moruisg stole softly, without a ripple, through the moss at the dreamer's feet.

It was only God that knew his dreamings, and the sad hills know what God knows, hence their sadness in the gloaming, when the birds have stopped their song. But he slept on, and the night passed, and a breeze stole through the heather, and kissed his brow. And a leveret stood up, and looked upon his face, for it saw that his eyes were veiled. And a deer came to the stream, and gazed on his form, and fled not. And the day stood still, and said, 'Lo, this is death!' But a grey linnet out of the rocks came down, and perched upon his pale hand where it lay across his bosom, and it looked the sun in the face, and sang—sang till the world woke to music,—but the dead man did not wake.

And the hills said to one another, when the shadows sank again across the land, 'He has found Death and Life. For we know, and God knows, all his dreams. And in this land of ours at the Back of the World, he has found the fountainhead of song, the secret of the sea, the message of all the streams.'

So they spread it over the world—gave it to the burns to carry, and they bore it to the sea. And that is why the waves have sadness in them still today, in the Loch at the Back of the World.

And the heather faded, and the grasses drooped, and the leaves dropped from the trees. And the dust out of the world blew into the glens, and covered the dead man where he lay asleeping. And no man knows his grave.

And the ages passed, and brought people with them, and galleys with oars of thunder, and shields like shining gold, and men with war upon their lips. And they, too, passed, and faded; for the waves were sad and bitter, and tasted always of sorrow, and graves grew by the sea. But still the stream sang on; and some who heard it with the ear of knowledge, which the wind and the sun had spoken to, said that it sang of the dreams of him whose dust was in the heather—dreams of broken music, without a thought of dying, and lands across the waters, where death was never known. And that is the secret of the sorrow of the Loch at the Back of the World.